Praise for ".

"The Pilgrims' leaving England, landing in Plymouth and celebrating the first Thanksgiving in America are foundational myths taught every American school child. Amy Martin's fictionalization of these events brings new life to this well-known story. Using meticulous research, Ms. Martin tells the much more interesting, true story of Massachusetts' settlement. Religious dissenters, speculators hoping to earn their fortune and return to England and Native-Americans struggling to recover from a mysterious epidemic competed and cooperated through difficult circumstances that led to the establishment of a second British colony in North America."

-Brien Brown, author of *The Fourth Son* and *Abigail's Tale*

"Faithful to recorded history, *All Will Be Well* reveals the complexity of early European settler's relationships with and attitudes towards the native people of New England. Author Amy Martin masterfully crafts a page-turner that reveals many long-forgotten truths about the early days of colonization at Plimoth Plantation. She unmasks the myth of the pious, united, freedom-seekers and bares the disheveled machinations of a band of people with mixed objectives who laid the foundation of the United States of America. Martin exposes the birth of the "Shining City on the Hill," in all its naked confusion, frustration, and pain as the settlers carve out a world reminiscent of the one they left behind, often at the expense of their aboriginal neighbors. This fascinating narrative is by turns both tender and stark and is a compelling look at colonial history."

-Christine Duffy Zerillo, author of *Still Here*

For Regina

All Will Be Well

A *Mayflower* Novel

Amy C. Martin

Amy C Martin (signature)

BookLocker
Saint Petersburg, Florida

Published by BookLocker.com, Inc., St. Petersburg, Florida.

Printed on acid-free paper.

The characters and events in this book are fictitious. Any similarity to real persons, living or dead, is coincidental and not intended by the author.

BookLocker.com, Inc.
2020

First Edition

Excerpts from *Mourt's Relation* and *Good News from New England* are taken from the Applewood Books editions of these works originally published in 1986 and 1996 respectively.

Excerpts from *Of Plymouth Plantation* are taken from Caleb Johnson's *Of Plymouth Plantation: Along with the Full Text of the Pilgrims' Journals for Their First Year at Plymouth* published 2006 by Xlibris Corporation.

Excerpts from *Revelations of Divine Love* are taken from christianhistoryinstitute.org and from Project Gutenberg.

Library of Congress Cataloging Data
Martin, Amy C.
All Will Be Well by Amy C. Martin
Library of Congress Control Number: 2020908013

Cover Images: Jackson R. Phillips
Cover Design: Todd Engel

For my grandpa, Chet, who never knew he was a Mayflower *descendant.*

Prologue

But Jesus… answered with these words and said: "It was necessary that there should be sin; but all shall be well, and all shall be well, and all manner of thing shall be well."

—Julian, Anchoress at Norwich,
Revelations of Divine Love, written
circa. 1373, published 1670

Tuesday, 1 August 1620

Priscilla Mullins hoisted herself up the ladder onto *Mayflower*'s top deck, heart pounding. She would never understand her mother. How could she sit all day with her mending and her darning, cooking or embroidering, always busy but never *doing* anything? They had been stuck in port for two weeks already, and Priscilla was exhausted from trying to keep still. She pounded her fist on the rail in frustration and slumped forward, wishing she could scream instead of stifling the small noises in her throat. A scream would catch the attention of the sailors, if not the passersby on the dock. She was trying, after all. Her father had proposed the ludicrous notion that they sail to the New World with a congregation of Separatists, and her mother, of course, said nothing against it. They left behind, along with most of their worldly goods, Priscilla's older half-siblings, William and Sarah, with their families back in Dorking. So now, Priscilla was the eldest. Instead of playing with her little brother Joseph, she was tasked with looking after him. She took on more of the household responsibilities, since her father chose to bring a male servant, Robert Carter, but no woman to help them. Well, it was not as though they *needed* help. It was the

1

fact that she did not have enough to do which was so frustrating. There was no shopping to do, no neighbors to visit, no means nor reason to leave the accursed ship where they sat, useless.

She gazed out over the port of Southampton, a view which had not changed since they docked on arrival from London. The town bustled, with sailors and tradesmen shouting and passing by at all hours. Chimneys drifted trails of smoke into the blue summer sky. The air reeked of salt water and fish, but it was better than the scent 'tween decks where the passengers were quartered. It was in Southampton they would join their companion ship *Speedwell*, loaded with the congregation from Leiden. The Separatists lived in Holland for twelve years, her father told her, because their practice of religion was illegal in England. Priscilla wondered what they might be like, having chosen to live first in Holland, and now in the New World, all to be separated from the King's church. A seagull cried overhead, and she gazed up at it, following its looping path through the wind. She wondered what it might be like to fly and no longer be stuck on this vessel like cattle in the market square. Below deck, families were packed together with their belongings on a transport ship designed to carry cargo, not passengers. She grew frustrated again just thinking of it and shook her head with irritation. Doing so, she noticed an unfamiliar young man boarding the ship.

As he climbed the gangway, he walked right into a low-hanging rope. He wore a brown felt capotain hat that added half a foot to his height, and his hat took the blow with the ease of long practice. The man did not seem to notice it at all. Priscilla stood up straighter. She'd been leaning on her forearms such that her rump stuck out across the narrow aisle between the ship's rail and the hatchway leading belowdecks.

But the stranger made no move to pass her by. Instead he turned and rested his small sea chest against the railing, scant inches away from her. He looked out over the view of Southampton.

His face was not one of unusual beauty, nor ugly, scarred, or pockmarked. His nose was long, and his chin the flat edge of a square jaw. His smooth cheeks were red with the prickle of skin unused to a razor's edge. His eyes squinted against the sun, pulling his thick eyebrows down toward his nose. She realized she was staring at him and turned her face away, feeling herself flush with embarrassment. He seemed not to have minded, nor even noticed her. She felt her heart in her chest, thrumming as though she had just run from her father's shop to St. Martin's Church. Her palms sweated, too, in the heat of the summer, although the breeze off Southampton Water kept the ship cool. She buried her hands in her blue skirt, wiping them dry, and stood next to the ordinary man looking out over *Mayflower*'s rail.

Part I: October 1620–April 1621

Chapter One

They put to sea again with a prosperous wind, which continued divers days together, which was some encouragement unto them…

After they had enjoyed fair winds, and weather for a season, they were encountered many times with cross winds, and met with many fierce storms, with which the ship was shroudly shaken.

—William Bradford, *Of Plymouth Plantation*, 1651

Monday, 2 October 1620

"Man overboard! Man overboard!" John Alden shouted into the howling wind. He heaved himself farther up the ladder, pulling his body into the torrent on the top deck. The sailors were already scrambling toward the ship's rail, where one of *Mayflower*'s ropes was pulled taut, dragging underwater.

"Stay down there, landlubber," one sailor shouted at him, rushing past.

"Do you want to go over the side too?" another asked, kicking at him for good measure.

John wobbled, and he descended one rung of the slick wet ladder to keep himself steady. His head and shoulders were above decks, the rest of his body suspended in the hatchway which led below. John squinted against the rain that pounded the deck in sheets. He had seen his friend Howland, who was ill with fever, ascend the ladder just moments before. John rushed after him, but as he reached the top of the ladder, a mighty wave crashed into them, causing the ship to roll like a barrel turned on its side. Howland had been swept from John's field of view.

Rain tore at the canvas overhead and soaked the sailors who rushed about the deck grasping for ropes and shouting words John couldn't understand. The sting of salt water filled his nostrils. He hesitated; he had been told to stay down, and in truth he did not trust his sea legs enough to dash about the sodden deck. Yet he wanted to do something, rather than stand unsure, wobbling on this ladder like a dullard. The sailors gathered near the rail, heaving against a pitch-coated rope. John's cooper's strength could aid in their efforts, surely? But before John steeled himself to finish his ascent, the sailors pulled a sodden body over the rail and dropped him to the deck.

"Get him back 'tween decks, where he belongs," snarled the bosun. "We've enough else to do in this squall without looking after the kine." Howland rolled onto his side, coughing and spluttering. Two of the sailors grabbed him under the arms and heaved him toward the hatchway.

John was still standing on the ladder, his torso poking above decks through the opening. He reached up to steady his friend, as the sailors lowered him through the hole. Howland was a strong man, made lean during the course of their voyage, but at present he could not control his limbs. Getting down the steep ladder proved difficult. The ship rocked, buffeted by the crash of giant waves. As John reached the 'tween deck, he heard the thud of the hatch above closing. He glanced up to see a tarpaulin slide over the top. This was always done at first sign of a storm. *Why had it been delayed so long?* he wondered. At least there would be no more jaunts above decks by *Mayflower*'s unwitting passengers tonight.

A crowd of interested passengers gathered around the base of the ladder, and a few men came forward to help balance Howland's coughing body. As John ducked, Howland's arm banged into his brown felt capotain hat, knocking it off his head. John lifted one of Howland's arms over his shoulder and found the ship's surgeon, Giles Heale, on Howland's other side. Together, the surgeon and John carried Howland over to his pallet, stumbling through the mess of belongings piled on the floor; the darkness of the 'tween deck was seldom broken by lamp or candlelight for fear of fire. The thick stench of vomit and piss pervaded the air. John's exposure to the storm had cleared his nose, and the odors of the 'tween deck struck him afresh. The wetness made matters worse, as the aroma festered in the humidity. The tarpaulin would at least prevent the spill of further rain into the ship, though this would not alleviate the dampness. John had not felt dry since the start of their voyage two months ago.

Master Heale disappeared for a moment and came back with an oil lamp, which illuminated a small circle of light about him. John wondered if the surgeon came down 'tween decks to treat one of the passengers; perhaps that was why the hatchway was open in the midst of a torrent? Heale kept to his quarters above, with the crew, rather than with the passengers, who had been relegated to the cramped cargo deck.

"Fetch blankets," Heale instructed John, who was closest. "This man is freezing."

John faced the crowd, uncertain how to move through them. He was surprised when he saw blankets being passed forward, hand to hand. He seized them as they drew near and dropped to his knees beside the doctor. In the flickering light, John could see Heale's face was unlined, still soft in the cheeks, still filled with concern and worry rather than the wary resignation most doctors wore. Heale did not look much older than John, perhaps two or three and twenty. He furrowed his brows in concentration. John dropped the blankets and retreated; the doctor and his patient were crowded by the growing number of passengers, drawn like moths to a flame. There was so little entertainment on the two-month voyage that the sight of a dying man became the height of interest. The increasing crush made John uncomfortable, and he wanted to seek out his own corner of the ship, to curl up as far from the other passengers as he could, pressed together as they were. However, there were few enough men on *Mayflower* John considered friends that he did not want to leave Howland if there was some way he could help. He found a post against which he could lean, to avoid the feeling of jostling at his back. His height gave him the advantage of sight even over the heads of many other passengers. He watched the ship's surgeon tap on Howland's chest, peer into his eyes, lean close to listen to his breath. Howland still lolled about, unconscious in the delirium of fever.

"Is he dead?" John heard a trembling voice ask. He turned to see the neat white coif of a girl's head at his elbow, a slice of ash blonde hair visible where the coif was slipping. She stood on her tiptoes, trying to peer above the crowd.

"It would be a shame to lose your dear intended over something such as this," replied her companion. John recognized the daughter of the cordwainer, Master Mullins, who carried an enormous store of shoes and boots in the cargo hold. Her voice and smile were teasing, as though it were a laughing matter.

The blonde girl looked horrified. "Oh, Priscilla, you know he is not—but what if he is to die?"

"Then your grand plans for matrimony may be upset, dear Tilley." Miss Mullins' grin irked John. How could she joke over the death of his friend?

"If he were dead, Master Heale would not need to tend him," John interjected.

Both girls looked up, startled. Miss Mullins' expression turned from mischief to shock in an instant. Her face flushed, and she looked away from John.

"Goodman Howland's condition will not improve by virtue of you all standing here," the ship's surgeon chided, waving at the gathered crowd to usher them away. "This is no spectacle. Go back to your own beds."

Grumbling, the crowd dispersed, each man or family retreating to the heap of possessions and the mattresses they called their own, squeezed between other men and families. John cast one last worried glance at his friend before heading to his own straw-stuffed pallet near the rear of the deck. His doublet was sodden from his exposure to the rain, and he would be glad to strip off his wet shirt to replace it with a damp one.

Priscilla pulled Tilley away from Goodman Alden, her face burning with embarrassment. Her heart was jumping along at a pace that frayed Priscilla's nerves, too rapid even for the excitement of Howland's rescue. She had not meant to be overheard; she was just teasing her friend a little. Elizabeth Tilley had been making eyes at Howland since their voyage began. Priscilla did not mean to keep the jest going more than a moment, yet she felt immediate regret when Alden's dark eyes looked down at her. She knew her cheeks had warmed, as they did every time she found herself in his proximity.

"Who was that?" Tilley whispered as they picked their way around heaps of furniture and huddled passengers to a corner of the ship where someone was sleeping in a piece of the shallop. The small boat was stowed 'tween decks with the passengers and their goods, as were the cannons.

"Goodman John Alden, the ship's cooper."

"A cooper just for the ship?" Tilley asked. There was no room for barrel-making aboard *Mayflower*.

"He maintains the casks that hold our provisions. He was hired on at Southampton."

"So, he is not one of the merchant adventurers?"

Priscilla shrugged. "He seems not to speak much to anyone aboard, whether from Holland or amongst the merchant adventurers."

Tilley was a member of the separated church, whose congregation made up about a third of the ship's passengers. Priscilla's father was one of the merchant adventurers, who made up the rest. Tilley spent most of her time with her mother and the other women from her congregation, but she and Priscilla became friends despite their different affiliations, and Tilley's youth. Priscilla made a habit of easy conversation with everyone.

Everyone but Goodman Alden. Priscilla felt the flush creep down her neck, making her hairs stand on end. They had been on the ship together more than two months already, but since their first encounter by the ship's rail she became feeble-minded and mute every time she saw him. It was unpleasant to feel herself strangled, to feel her thoughts go blank and her tongue still at the sight of this common man. She could not fathom why Goodman Alden had such an effect on her, when before today he never even spoke to her. He seemed to prefer solitude, at his work with the cargo, or to talk with other single men. It would not be appropriate for Priscilla, as an unmarried young woman, to approach him without reason. She wondered if asking after Howland's health would be sufficient grounds to invite him to conversation, if she should find a good time to speak with him. If she spoke with him, she hoped these uncomfortable feelings might disappear.

Chapter Two

Now next after this heavenly peace with God and
our own consciences, we are carefully to provide
for peace with all men what in us lieth, especially
with our associates, and for that end watchfulness
must be had, that we neither at all in ourselves do
give, no, nor easily take offense being given by
others.

— *Mourt's Relation*, 1622

Thursday, 5 October 1620

"How do you fare?" John asked Howland with concern a few
days later.

His friend was sitting up on his pallet, grinning with good
humor.

"How can I fare but well, when God has spared me?"
Howland ruffled a hand through his thick blond hair.

John could not sense any jest or bitterness in his words.
"He could have spared you from going over the edge to start,"
John said with a smile.

"Aye, no, Alden, that was the Devil's work to be sure.
That is what Mistress Carver says. It felt so, when I had wits
enough about me to feel at all. I cannot imagine what fevered
delirium led me up there. I remember the sensation of falling
into the water, and when I opened my eyes the hand of God
reached down and lifted me up."

He said it so simply, as though there could be no doubt it
was God's own hand, and not the sailors, that rescued him.
This belief in God's direct intervention was not one which
John could comprehend.

"Mayhap the ship does sail with God," Howland continued. "Elsewise, why would he have chanced to look on me? It could not be my good fortune that left the halyard line dangling in the waves and placed me near enough to grasp it."

Howland took his employ among the Separatists, and this line of thought was influenced by their beliefs. John's smile faded.

"Mayhap," was all he could reply.

The ship had passed through the worst of the storm, though it was still dank 'tween decks. A little light filtered through the hatchway, which stood open this afternoon. It was a rare invitation for the passengers to go up and walk about the deck.

John made his goodbyes to Howland, who was still recovering from his illness, and headed for the ladder. He needed to clear his head of all these Separatist sentiments. How could God reach out himself to one man, without his intermediaries? More than that, how could a man cast aside the King as head of the church in order to pursue direct contact with God? Such was vanity! More than vanity, it was treason. John could not understand it.

He reached for the ladder and hauled himself up the rungs. Perhaps sailors' talk could help rid his mind of this theological quagmire. He got along with the sailors he met while working in the cooperage near the docks at Southampton. Their stories of Virginia were the reason he'd been keen to join *Mayflower*'s voyage. It was his chance to see this New World, the hot, unfamiliar land, and of course the Indians. His chance to do something independent of the master he served as an apprentice. Perhaps John could make his own name as a cooper and would return to England no longer reliant on the goodwill of others. He was added late to the ship's roster, hired by the Virginia Company, who financed the journey and fitted out the ship. He lodged 'tween decks with the passengers, but he was not one of them. Working in the hold, rather than above decks, he wasn't considered crew either. He was not sympathetic to Separatism, as were many of the merchants, so he tended to keep his own counsel. Nevertheless, his conversations with Howland accorded him cheerful company. Howland was an unburdened soul who took things as they came to him.

John meandered over to the ship's rail and leaned against a short stretch of wood that was free of tarred and tangled ropes. He tried to keep out of the way of the rushing sailors, who appeared too busy to stop and talk to him. The sky was cloudless, and the ocean lay as quiet as John had seen it. The two masses of blue met at a never-ending horizon. He drew in a deep breath of the tangy sea air. One grew accustomed to the putrid odor 'tween decks, but now fresh scents chased the smell of it away. There was a peace in this moment. *What might my life have been,* he wondered, *if I'd been sent aboard a ship as a boy, rather than apprenticed to a cooper?* He'd have gained some resistance to the seasickness which plagued him, as well as all the other passengers, for the first several weeks aboard. Some still lay incapacitated, unable to do much but vomit. But in that world, John would not know a curved froe from an adze, which was unimaginable. Nor would he know the delight of having something in front of him which he made with his own hands.

He felt the brush of a sleeve against his arm and turned to see who joined him at the rail. Miss Mullins stood there, placing her petite hands on the balustrade. He took a step back in surprise. Her eyebrows rose and her lips quirked up, giving her an expression of curious delight.

"Good morrow, Goodman Alden," she said.

John was startled, not knowing what to do. Though he had encountered her about the ship, they had not yet been introduced. He had never been approached by a young woman in such a straightforward manner. The circumstances of the ship contributed to a certain lack of propriety, but it did not mean John had any idea what to say.

"I hear Goodman Howland has recovered from his... unexpected swim," Miss Mullins said, inviting conversation.

John nodded.

She looked out over the rail. Loose, dark curls of hair escaped the constraints of her white coif. Her face was round, her cheeks a light wind-stung pink that stood out against her pretty paleness. It was clear she was not a young woman who worked much outdoors. She looked soft, the fullness of her figure accentuated by the bulk of her blue wool skirt.

"Papa says we are sure to reach the New World soon," Miss Mullins said, "though I cannot see how. When I look about and see so much of water and naught else, it feels as though we are the only souls left in the whole of creation."

He could see the thought did not perturb her, as she bounced on her toes. John wondered what this woman might fear. She jested without concern over Howland's death, and she seemed unworried that there was nothing around for miles but their ship.

"Priscilla!" called a man's voice from a few feet down the deck.

They both turned to see who summoned her. Though several passengers milled about, it was the girl's father who looked at them. She waved in his direction with a sparkling smile.

"Would you have leave to come and meet my father?" she asked John.

Leave? he wondered. *Leave from what?* But John could think of no reply, and Master Mullins approached, panting with his efforts to catch his wayward daughter.

"Priscilla—" he started, but she interrupted him.

"Papa, I want to introduce you to Goodman Alden," she said. "He is the ship's cooper."

"How now, Goodman Alden," Mullins made curt acknowledgment.

"I fare well, Master Mullins," Alden replied with a small bow and a touch to the narrow brim of his hat.

Mullins grunted and turned back to his daughter. "Are you not meant to aid your mother with the mending, girl? How is she to tend to Joseph and do the mending all at once?"

"But Papa, we have not been able to come on deck in weeks. I will mind Joseph, if he will come up here. It is far too dark to see to mending down there in any case, and Mama shouldn't strain herself so."

"You know she will not cease for such a sensible suggestion," Mullins replied with a smile. "You must go and fetch your brother, so she will have a modicum of peace."

Miss Mullins made a face and went off toward the ladder.

"She's a lovely girl," her father said with a sigh, "but too free with herself, I'll admit."

John did not know whether this warranted argument or acquiescence. Miss Mullins' lack of propriety seemed to be inherited. He settled on making a noise in his throat and retreating again to the rail, out of the way of the passing pedestrians. Mullins stepped back with him.

"You are not amongst the congregation that sails with us to the New World?"

"No, I came not from Holland," answered John, "but from Southampton."

"What said your family to your taking such a voyage?" Mullins asked.

"I have no family, Master Mullins."

"Had you no shop to tend?"

"No, indeed. I have just completed my apprenticeship. I expect I shall begin working as a journeyman after I return to England," John explained.

"Return?" Mullins asked, surprised. "Do you not intend to settle with us in Virginia?"

John shook his head. "I was hired on as ship's cooper. The crew will want me with her on her voyage back."

Mullins looked him over afresh, though John knew not why this information would alter the stranger's opinion of him.

"And you, Master Mullins? You are not of the separated church?" John asked.

Mullins' face relaxed into a smile. "No, no, we've not been to Holland. I'm a cordwainer by trade and sought the opportunity for my family. We are of the other party—the merchant adventurers, if you will have it so."

As he spoke, Miss Mullins emerged from the hatchway, a small boy climbing up after her. His ascent was impeded by something clenched in his fists which he would not relinquish to grasp the ladder.

"Never thought I'd sail with Brownists," John admitted.

Mullins frowned at him as Miss Mullins and Joseph ran up to join them. "Though we are not of their congregation, Goodman Alden, we are together in this venture," he admonished. "And I do not think the members of the separated church would appreciate your insult."

Ah, John thought. *He's a sympathizer.*

"Priscilla, do take Joseph for a few turns about. I have business to attend with Carter, and your mother needs her rest." With a narrow glance at John, Master Mullins made his way 'tween decks.

"He can't need aught of Carter." Miss Mullins looked after him, perplexed.

John shook his head. He was unwilling to repeat his conversation with her father for fear she would take equal offense on behalf of the congregation.

Joseph was a boy of about eleven, whose breeches were somehow stained at the knee, although they had not left the ship for months. His brown hair flopped about his face, getting in the way of his eyes. He must not have cut it since their departure from England. He sat down in the corner by the forecastle cabin and emptied his fists of the game of knucklebones he carried with him. The knobbly white bones scattered across the deck. He tossed one bone into the air and, while it was aloft, swept up as many of the others as he could in one hand. He tried to catch the airborne bone on its way down, but missed.

"He will not move until he's played his game through a dozen times. Would you care to walk with me instead, Master Alden?" Miss Mullins asked, taking him by the arm and steering him away from the rail.

The deck was not large. It would take but a few strides between the closed-off cabins to cross the whole of it. There were several other passengers ambling about, enjoying the air.

"Who on the ship have you met?" Miss Mullins asked. "Having come on as a cooper, you can't have known many of them before your employ."

He shook his head. "Goodman Howland," he told her, "and Master Hopkins' family, and Captain Standish and his wife." He spotted Captain Standish, who stood with his wife next to the main mast. Standish was difficult to miss, for although he was near a foot shorter than John, his hair was a fiery red and he always carried his cutlass strapped to his side. John was sure he would have worn his helmet and kept a belt of powder and shot as well, were it not for his wife Rose. Their quarters next to John aboard the ship gave him much occasion to speak with them both, as the closeness of the 'tween deck meant they slept about a foot away. Standish was a rough-and-tumble sort, typical of a soldier, but he engaged John in one-sided conversations about military campaigns through history, and he was at least not a Brownist.

Miss Mullins nodded beside John. He hadn't realized before that her head was at his shoulder. Her small stature was well matched with her plump figure. Her vivacious personality was the first overwhelming facet of her character and made her seem much larger than she was. He smiled, despite himself. John had no doubt that Miss Mullins made the acquaintance of each of the hundred souls aboard *Mayflower*. How she came to know them, he had no notion. He was not inclined to mingle with the Separatists and was not much practiced in greeting strangers of any stripe.

As they turned the corner, Miss Mullins dropped John's arm and scampered over to the ship's rail. She leaned so far over the edge, John worried she would topple forward. He reached out to steady her but hesitated, unsure where he ought to place his hands.

"Praise be, praise be, for this is the day the Lord hath made, and we will rejoice and be glad in it," she sang with joy out over the water.

A surge of laughter bubbled up in him. It was a fine day, indeed.

"Alden?" asked Captain Standish, a mere step closing the distance between them. "Do you have any notion what she means by such as this?"

John shrugged, unable to understand the woman himself.

"I mean to be glad of the sun and the sky and the sea, and glad of the ship *Mayflower* and the providence of God which has put us together in her," Miss Mullins answered.

"Take note," Standish replied, "unexpected outbursts can be alarming to men-at-arms and will alarm the Indians we encounter in Virginia."

"I hardly see anyone of whom to be wary in our vicinity, Captain," she answered.

Standish's eyes widened as though he took personal offense.

"It has been too long since any of us had a breath of air unsullied by sea sickness," John said, unsure who he was trying to appease. It took Standish aback, and his gaze flicked between John and Miss Mullins.

"Aye. Though some take more delight in it than others," Standish grumbled, then stepped back to lead his wife away.

Miss Mullins giggled, and John gave her a frown. This did not improve matters; she giggled harder.

"What a terrible man," she said, loud enough that the retreating captain might still have heard her. John looked after his back, but Standish did not turn.

"The captain mayn't be having such a glad day as you," John muttered.

"Do you think not? Whenever I see the captain, he is in such a mood. He seems always threatened by Indians, where I see none." Her restrained smile still lifted the corners of her cheeks in a fashion from which John could not look away.

"He is a good man," John said, wary of how informal their conversation became. "He has been one of the few men to speak with me since I have come aboard."

"That," Miss Mullins said, "is because *you* speak not to anybody." With this, she flounced back to her brother Joseph, leaving John agape.

Joseph was still tucked away in his corner, tossing bones into the air and snatching at the collection remaining on the ship's deck. Priscilla crouched beside him, careful not to let her skirts disturb his game. She felt warmth rising from her gut, and her insides squirmed. She had been so nervous to even muster the courage to speak to Goodman Alden. To then be caught in such a situation! To be reprimanded by the captain in front of him, of all people—and why had she not been able to stop giggling? Had she behaved too frivolously? Her mother often accused her of frivolity. Had she embarrassed herself?

"Joseph, have you not played enough?" she asked, wanting to distract herself from her encounter.

He shook his head, still concentrating on the scattered bones below him.

"Well then, may I at least have a turn? Would it not be more fun to play with me than by yourself?"

"You said you weren't going to play children's games with me anymore." There was a gap in his mouth where he had lost a tooth, and his tongue prodded at the hole.

Priscilla sighed; a pang of regret mixed with her embarrassment.

"Yes, Mama keeps telling me that I am to behave more as a young woman who will, in a matter of years, be wed. But, well, I do not have a husband yet, do I?"

Joseph shook his head, but he still did not look at her. He tossed a bone into the air and picked two off the deck before catching it.

"What are you concerned with now?" she asked her brother.

"Your hands are bigger than mine, Sissy," he complained, using his own endearing name for her. "It isn't fair. Of course you'll win."

"Is that so?" she asked. "I don't know; place your hand against mine and let's see."

She presented her palm to him, fingers spread. He glanced at her, uneasy that she wished to prove him wrong.

"Your hands are still growing," she explained. "You are sure to outgrow me soon. If you insist on a fair competition, we shall have to measure to see when I shall be able to play against you." She wiggled her fingers, encouraging him to raise his hand.

He did so, stretching out his fingers to their full length. The tips still fell a little short of her own. He huffed, dejected.

"Hmm. It looks like a scant inch left until you surpass me. By tomorrow, your fingers will have grown, and I can play with you."

Joseph giggled. "Of course my hands will not grow so quickly!"

"No? But I am so impatient to play! If you can carry all the bones one-handed, why should it matter whose are larger?"

"It will be more difficult to pick them up!" he protested, and began demonstrating.

She smiled, listening to him chatter. He had not wanted to leave their home in Dorking, and the thing which convinced him to come along was that there would be Indians in the New World. He knew of Indians and wanted to see them for himself. Priscilla had not much wanted to come along on this venture either. She had little choice. If she wished it, her parents might have let her stay in England with her half-sister's family. But Sarah was married, with child, and had been out of the house two years already. She would not appreciate Priscilla getting underfoot.

Priscilla glanced up and spotted Master Alden conversing with Captain Standish. His face was outlined by the sun, and she could just make out the shape of it: the brim of his hat, his flat nose, the square jaw now covered by a short brown beard that grew in patchy by the corners of his mustache. His stoic face was a reminder of her earlier indiscretion. She looked away and tugged at her coif, pulling it over her ears. Now he had spoken with her, and what could he think of her? Why had she spoken so freely? She always said too much, her mother warned her. A woman should be quieter. She supposed she would learn to hold her tongue. She had accomplished her goal and spoken with him, yet she felt herself even more silly in his presence than she had before. It was no use! Perhaps she was destined to look a fool in his eyes.

Chapter Three

The one side labored to have the right worship of
God, and discipline of Christ, established in the
church, according to the simplicity of the gospel:
without the mixture of men's inventions; and to
have and to be ruled by the laws of God's Word,
dispensed in those offices, and by those officers of
Pastors, Teachers, and Elders, etc. according to the
Scriptures. The other party (though under many
colors, and pretences) endeavored to have the
Episcopal dignity (after the popish manner) with
their large power, and jurisdiction still retained;
with all those courts, canons, and ceremonies... as
formerly upheld their antichristian greatness, and
enabled them with lordly, and tyrannous power, to
persecute the poor servants of God.

—William Bradford, *Of Plymouth
Plantation*, 1651

Sunday, 15 October 1620

On Sunday, John attended the Christian services 'tween
decks. The services were as proper as could be expected
aboard such a vessel, with such passengers as she carried.
Sundays came and went aboard *Mayflower* with little
argument between the congregation, who were of the
separated church, and the merchant adventurers, who
belonged to the Church of England. John found that many of
the merchants were, at least in part, sympathetic to religious
reformation, which eased the tension which would otherwise
have come between them. While the merchants may have
preferred to sit in a decorated nave and have the services done
with ceremony by proper priests, who wore vestments, there

was neither church nor priest here. Not even the Brownists'
pastor, John Robinson, made the voyage. He stayed instead
with the congregants who remained in the city of Leiden, in
Holland, until more ships could be got up for their passage.
So, the merchants stood together with the Separatists, as it
suited everyone better than trying to pray separately. It was
unthinkable to everyone to have no service at all.

John stood with the others who were shy of singing with
Separatists. His King James Bible was a last gift presented to
John by his master before he left Southampton. He imagined
it smelled of the cooperage. He feared his sense of home
might vanish with the turn of each delicate page. The
Separatists used the Geneva translation or Calvin's English
Bible. In the services John attended at home, there would be
hymns and recitations of the creeds and the Lord's Prayer.
His copy of the Book of Common Prayer would guide him
through each step of a never-changing journey. It was
something he liked about services back home: they were
reliable and familiar. He had not needed to take the Book of
Common Prayer from his sea chest for weeks. The Separatists
did things their own way. Their prayer was founded on the
Bible, and not supplemental texts prepared by church leaders,
which, they said, had no foundation in the word of God. They
believed that the individual could pray to God himself, not
rely on the hierarchy of priests and bishops and popes. The
Separatists thought people should join together to become a
congregation in belief, rather than depend on the established
hierarchy of the English church. John's congregation at home
was comprised of all his neighbors, the people around whom
he lived and worked day by day. Why would these men leave
their communities to seek out people who wanted a schism in
the King's church? People who would abandon their king and
their country, who wished to influence loyal Englishmen with

illegal and seditious materials? He shook his head in frustration.

Master Brewster led the prophesying, his voice passionate and steady. Separatist services tended toward extended interpretations of the text of the Bible and extemporaneous prayer. Brewster, an elder of the reformed church, was heartfelt in his appeals to God, but to John the words blurred together. The sermon turned to a faint hum, a lull; the sounds entered his mind but were not understood. From the rear of the deck, the squawk of chickens could be heard now and again, protesting their confinement. The pages blurred before John, and soon he did not even see them. He felt as though in a trance, aware of the rock of the ship, the lap of the waves against her hull, and the dull sounds of the Separatists' observation of the Sabbath. He waited, tired of these odd services which were spoken in English yet half understood. He waited, wanting to explain that this was not the way to God, that there could be no direct contact with God for any man on earth but King James and his bishops. That it was unlawful for any man to take upon himself the office of ministering without the authority of the Church.

Then the singing began. The Separatists did not believe in hymns with no basis in scripture, but in services they did sing the Psalms. A voice, sweet and soft and shaky, half hummed, half sang along with the raised voices of the congregation. It was not the first time he heard her tremulous voice, but now John recognized it. The singer was Miss Mullins.

Serve ye Jehovah with gladness.

Come before him with singing mirth.

His eyes shot up, and his hands snapped his Bible shut with more force than he intended. He sought her white cap amid the coifed heads of all the women aboard. A stray lock of dark hair caught his eye, and he followed it to her face. Her brows were furrowed in concentration. There were no hymn books, but there were a few copies of the translations of the Psalms by Master Ainsworth. Ainsworth had rearranged some of the psalms into metered verse to ease the transition to song. The words were familiar to those from Holland, but they were strange for those raised in the Church of England. Sometimes the Separatists set the psalms to familiar tunes, the tunes of hymns sung in churches back in England, and put the new words to them. It was confounding to John, yet Miss Mullins tried. She had been trying, all these weeks aboard, to learn the way the reformers sang the songs.

Confess to him, bless ye his name,
because Jehovah, he good is.
His mercy ever is the same,
and his faith, unto all ages.

John watched her silhouette, listening to the melodious voice fumble over the words. *It mayn't be so terrible*, John thought, unprompted, *to settle 'cross the ocean.*

His thought was broken by the sound of someone being sick into a bucket behind him. The sound made his own stomach turn over. At least if he stayed in the New World, he would not need to sail back.

Wednesday, 18 October 1620

Priscilla hummed to herself as she stroked Master Goodman's spaniel, who curled up beside her. His fur was long and tangled into filthy knots. She feared her own hair fared little better, after days tucked into her coif with little attention. It was difficult to maintain, in the dark dampness of the 'tween deck, so she kept it wrapped up under her coif and ignored it as much as possible. The dog rolled and stretched, the feathering from his front legs trailing across his belly.

"Be merry, my friends, and list a while unto a merry jest," she sang, working her fingers through the dog's fur. "It may from you produce a smile, when you hear it expressed."

He huffed a contented sigh as she scratched him behind the ears.

"It's of a young man lately married which was a boone good fellow, this song in his head he always carried when drink—"

"What are you singing?" Tilley asked, squatting next to her.

Priscilla jumped a little in startlement. She blushed. "Oh, it is nothing, I'm sure."

It was the first tune that popped into her head, but her father did not like her to sing drinking songs. It was not her fault that evening revelers wandered down the streets of Dorking singing them so she could not help but hear. The tunes echoed in her head until she needed to sing them to get them out. Tilley, who grew up in Holland, knew no English drinking ballads. It would not look well for Priscilla to teach her any.

The spaniel put his paw on Priscilla's wrist to remind her that she was busy stroking him.

"Would you mind going through one of the psalms with me, Tilley? It is so much more difficult to try to fit new words to a familiar tune than to learn a new song altogether."

Tilley smiled. She lifted her skirt and petticoat and sat down next to Priscilla.

"Aye. Did you have a particular psalm in mind? I know that the Ainsworth Psalter we use may read a little differently to the ones you are familiar with."

"There was one I enjoyed this past Sunday—oh, I cannot remember the number." She hummed a few bars. The tune they used was one she loved, and she would oft confuse the words if she did not concentrate. To be able to sing in church was one of Priscilla's joys. It was not strange to want to sing praises to the Lord, if one did so in an appropriate setting. Whether at St. Martin's Church in Dorking or here among the Separatists, the setting mattered less to her than the songs.

"I think that is number 23," Tilley said. "The Lord to me a shepherd is, want therefore shall not I," she began to sing. "He in the folds of tender grass doth cause me down to lie."

"Aye," Priscilla answered. "'Tis that one. Will you go through the lines with me?"

Tilley smiled. "It is a comfort to know the Lord is with us, is it not? To know that we shall dwell with the Lord eternally." She sighed. "It is a comfort. How much of it do you recall already?"

"I think a few repetitions would help keep it straight as one verse in my head, separate from any other words I might think of when singing that tune."

The Lord to me a shepherd is,
want therefore shall not I.
He in the folds of tender grass
doth cause me down to lie.

To waters calm me gently leads,
restore my soul doth he;
he doth in paths of righteousness
for his name's sake lead me.

Yea though in valley of death's shade
I walk, none ill I'll fear,
because thou art with me, thy rod
and staff my comfort are.

For me a table thou hast spread,
in presence of my foes;
thou dost anoint my head with oil,
my cup it overflows.

Goodness and mercy surely shall
all my days follow me,
and in the Lord's house I shall dwell
so long as days shall be.

Tilley's singing was not melodic; she was still quite young and did not have full control of her pitch. But she was sure of the words, and in their message, and the sound was sweet enough. At first, Tilley sang the lines one at a time for Priscilla to repeat. The lines were designed to be sung, so were written with meter and rhyme, which made them easy to remember. It took a couple of repetitions before the pair sang together, Priscilla stumbling but little over the words. Several of the women nearby joined their voices to the recitation, and soon they began singing other psalms to while away the afternoon. Even in the dark, in the midst of a storm, one could always sing. It was a great comfort, indeed, to be surrounded by familiar voices which all sang together.

Tuesday, 24 October 1620

A scream ripped open the night. John woke with a start, his heart racing. It was a woman's scream, and it came again. A horrible groaning cry. John recognized the sound and put his head between his hands. It was inevitable, alas. There were three women aboard round with child, and now one was birthing. He hoped the women might all last till land was sighted—it could not be long now—but nature did not slow its course for his comfort.

'Twas his misfortune it should be Mistress Hopkins, who lay not six feet from him. The close quarters did not provide any relief. As the woman let out another terrible sobbing shriek, John Goodman's spaniel began barking—frenzied, uncontrollable barks—until Goodman came and lifted his dog away to the other end of the ship. It was raining—of course—and there was no chance at all of being let onto the top deck. John stood, knocking his head against the low ceiling of the ship. Fumbling in the dark, he made his way through to the gun room and down the ladder whence he could descend into the ship's hold.

The memories started to come back to John, as he knew they would. The terrible memories. His mother, lying in agony, blood soaking her smock. The screams were bad, but worse was when they faded away. When she tried to scream but could not. Her voice was gone, her life going. He was in their house and could not escape it. The house was one room, shared with another family. His place on the floor afforded him a view of everything. The misshapen red thing which fell through his father's grasp. It did not cry nor wail the way a babe ought. His father sent John's sister out to fetch the midwife, but it was over by the time they arrived. The babe had not moved.

"'Twas like to have been born dead," the midwife said, when she arrived. "More like than not."

John stood between the barrels, tuns, and hogsheads that lay in the hold. The rocking of the ship lessened here. He began his by-now-familiar routine of work. He moved from each cask to another, checking for damage. The hold was well packed, the furniture and personal effects of the passengers stored with their provisions. Master Mullins' collection of shoes and boots caught his eye for a moment, but he focused his attention on the casks of seed and provision. The things which the Virginia Company, who financed the voyage, paid for. The weather knocked the goods about and kept John busy at his work repairing the wood to keep the contents well sealed. He fell into his labor and tried to block out the sounds of pain he could hear above him.

It was not long after his mother's death when his sister contracted the flux. It was not a week till she died. His father, with little enough control to begin with, gave in to drink. John supposed he should be glad his own contract to his master was made and he could go to live in the cooperage. John had been reliant on the master coopers who taught him ever since. He hadn't seen his father in all the years of his apprenticeship. He doubted the man yet lived. Though it was nothing so solemn as a vow nor an oath taken with himself, John was not interested in repeating his father's life. To be married and have children, but end up alone, finding solace in heavy drink, with all his family dead or gone? It would be unbearable to have such a thing happen to him when he'd already lost his family once.

A new cry broke through his self-imposed wall. A babe. A babe's cry. The relief flooded over him. The babe lived, at least so far. Mistress Hopkins' noises of continued struggle were welcome relief, too. Sounds of celebration were not oft heard 'tween decks, and it was joyous to hear it trickle down through the floorboards above his head. But the screams lingered in John's mind, and the sight of his mother's bloody body appeared before him when he closed his eyes. He would not sleep more tonight.

Chapter Four

At length, by God's providence, upon the ninth of November following, by break of the day we espied land which we deemed to be Cape Cod, and so afterward it proved. And the appearance of it much comforted us, especially seeing so goodly a land, and wooded to the brink of the sea. It caused us to rejoice together, and praise God that had given us once again to see land.

—*Mourt's Relation*, 1622

Thursday, 9 November 1620

"Land, ho!" came a shout from the deck above.

There were cannon ports 'tween decks, but they had been kept shut for the entirety of the journey across the ocean. The passengers instead rushed for the hatchway and scurried up the ladder. The sailors for once did not fault them, and they poured out to crowd at *Mayflower*'s rail, though there wasn't room for more than a third of them at a time.

There it was. In the distance they sighted a narrow strip of land, shrouded in the mist that rolled off the waves. Land. The New World. The place they all traveled such length to reach.

John looked about at his fellow passengers. The joy on their faces eclipsed the gloom of their destination. He caught sight of Christopher Jones, the ship's master, who sailed them across the wide ocean in safety. His face was pensive rather than joyous.

"We have yet reached the New World," Mistress Hopkins said. She appeared next to John in the crowd, her new baby, Oceanus, in her arms.

He looked down at her and smiled. "Aye," he said.

"I may not have had this babe delivered in Virginia, as Master Hopkins promised," she lamented. "But he will yet grow there, God willing."

"He will indeed," answered Hopkins, who, with his sheer bulk, forced his way through the crowd to stand beside her. His grizzled beard was a testament to the experience he'd already lived. He was, as far as John knew, the one man aboard who had visited the New World once before. Hopkins went to the Isle of Devils a dozen years ago, and from there to Jamestown. He spoke of his encounters with the Indians with enthusiasm, but every time John heard him tell them, the tales grew more embellished. He began to wonder whether Hopkins had ever even laid eyes on a savage. Furthermore, if Miss Mullins were to be believed, there was more to Hopkins' time in the New World than he'd told John. John knew not where Miss Mullins learned her information, but she knew a little of everyone aboard. She had whispered to him that Hopkins was part of a band of mutineers, stranded on an island for months until they built their own ship to sail to Jamestown. Whether true or false, it made John's encounters with the man a little less comfortable.

"Do you suppose there are Indians here?" John asked.

"Aye," Hopkins answered, "no doubt of it. There have been reports from Jamestown of the Powhatan. Our patent is for lands a sight northward of their settlement, at the mouth of the Hudson River, but there is no reason to suspect there are no savages here. It will be dangerous if we cannot either build some fortification or come to terms of peace with them. There are several different tribes of Indians who live in the area, and an alliance with one may mean war with another. And then there are cases like Roanoke." Hopkins grinned, baring his top row of yellowing teeth. Two were missing.

"Roanoke?" John asked.

"Aye. The lost colony. You've come all the way to Virginia and don't know of Roanoke? Though I suppose it all happened much before you were born, eh?"

"What happened? They were killed by Indians?"

"Well, that's what some people believe. From what I heard, though, they left a colony of men on this island, and when the investors came to visit, there was no one left. No bodies, no slaughter—but the men were gone."

Mistress Hopkins' smile faded. She bounced her babe a little and made soft noises in his ear.

"Hopkins," called Master Carver from behind them. Carver was one of the Separatist leaders, the man to whom Howland was indentured. From what Howland told John, Carver was an earnest man with an affable disposition, more inclined to making peace than to dispute.

"Pray, excuse me," Hopkins said, parting the crowd around himself with ease.

John turned his own attention back to the sight of land. They would no doubt be herded back 'tween decks at any moment, and he wanted to enjoy the sight as much as he could. Who knew how long he would be in sight of the New World, after all, before *Mayflower* took him back for the journey home?

The coast struck him as quite forbidding. It looked a desolate place, absent as it was of any friends, nor even any countrymen. He knew not what he expected, but the reports he'd heard of Virginia were all quite different from what he saw. He supposed the sailors who told him stories at the pubs in Southampton would not have mentioned the dreary days when the clouds rolled in and the sky looked little different than it did in England. He shivered a little at the chill and tucked his arms into his cloak. He expected Virginia to be hot, from all he'd heard, yet the wind off the sea pierced his skin.

"A shame it is already November," Mistress Hopkins said, echoing his thoughts. "Were it not for the delays in leaving England, mayhap we would have arrived when the weather was not quite so bitter."

"Indeed, Mistress."

She sighed. "If all went well in England, we may have had the little *Speedwell* with us, and all the friends and stores she could have carried, as well."

"Were not the pinnace's passengers of the reformed church, Mistress?" John asked, trying to gauge her sympathy toward the Separatists.

She gave him a sideways glance. "Though my husband may say otherwise, any man who would have accompanied us on this voyage would be counted as my friend, Goodman Alden."

"Aye," he conceded.

Speedwell had picked up the congregation in Holland and joined *Mayflower* at Southampton. She began leaking during the trip across the channel, and though they'd done repairs at port, *Speedwell* began to leak again almost as soon as they sailed out. The two ships turned back in concert to dock at Dartmouth, where *Speedwell* had been repaired again. However, when they set to sea a second time, the pinnace still took on water. The two ships docked a third time at Plymouth, *Mayflower* to load what goods and passengers she could from the smaller ship, and *Speedwell* to stay on for extensive repairs. *Mayflower*'s problems with overcrowding came in part from taking on some of *Speedwell*'s passengers. A number of the Separatists turned back to London rather than continue without both ships. The travelers had sold off quite a tidy portion of their goods and provisions in order to cover the repair costs and port fees. In the middle of an argument over the terms of their contract, their contact from the Virginia Company, a man called Weston, had declined to cover the costs of these debts.

"Well then, we must turn south!" Hopkins shouted, emerging from the main cabin. Mistress Hopkins took in a sharp breath at John's side.

"Indeed, Master Hopkins, and we shall," said Carver, who followed him. "Yet, with the weather so bad, we must accept that we may not reach Virginia."

Carver's voice was soft, but Hopkins' fury dampened the celebratory mood of the ship to a hush, and all the passengers looked up.

"You mean to say we have not made it to Virginia?" yelled a man in the crowd.

"No," Carver admitted with a sigh, "we have reached a point far north, a place called Cape Cod by the seamen in New England."

"A place," interjected Hopkins, "where our patent does not apply and where the Virginia Company has no authority to send us."

"Oh, dear," whispered Mistress Hopkins. She looked down at the babe Oceanus.

"We have discussed the matter with Master Jones, and he has agreed to attempt the journey south," explained Carver, who accepted that the news was no longer private. "But he has warned that our unseasonable arrival and the harshness of the weather make no easy task of it, and we may not be able to accomplish it. We will not risk the ship, nor her contents, for the sake of a patent."

That made sense enough to John. Though it would be a wrench to not, after all, see Virginia, he would see New England, which appeared to be a different sort of place altogether. Feeling the chill of his fingertips, he thought New England a sight less favorable. But what did it matter to John, when he would soon be bound for home?

"Best get yourselves down below now," shouted the ship's master Jones. "The winds are rough out of the bay, and we do not want anyone else goin' overboard."

This was a clear slight at Howland, and John searched for his friend over the heads of the company. It had been some time since they last spoke. The deck would not be cleared for several minutes, with reluctant passengers taking their time to descend. The murmurs over their strange arrival continued all around him, but John tried to ignore the talk. There was no use in speculation, after all. If they were able to sail south, they would. If they could not make the journey to their original destination, there was nothing which could be done to change their situation.

Friday, 10 November 1620

Priscilla sat with her brother, Joseph, on their pallets, laid out beside their family's heap of furniture and possessions. Her mother and father were sitting together on the other side of a six-board chest. They were murmuring together about the news. There were many other soft words being spoken between spouses around the 'tween deck. There were so many whispered conversations that the susurrus replaced the background noise of skimming waves that had accompanied them across the broad ocean. They should all have learned by now that there were no secrets on a ship such as *Mayflower*.

"What will we do if we cannot reach Virginia?" Priscilla heard her mother ask.

Joseph was lying on his stomach on the straw mattress, his head shoved into his pillow, kicking his feet into the air and down into the floor. He looked bored.

"Joseph, how much has your hand grown since last we checked?" Priscilla asked, trying to distract him as well as herself. He paused his kicking. "If it has grown enough, then we can play a game of knucklebones together," Priscilla goaded.

He came out from his pillow and pushed his hair away from his eyes. "Yours will still be bigger," Joseph muttered, glancing at her from under his fringe.

"Well, I want to see how much closer you've gotten. It can't be too much longer before we can play again."

"You said Mama didn't want you to play with me."

"Mama does want me to help look after you. Besides, at the moment, she and Papa are too busy to notice if we play a game or two."

Priscilla did feel that she was too old to be playing games with her brother, that encouraging him to play with her was not because she herself wanted to play but rather because it would make his time on this ship a little more bearable. There were other children he played with—two of Master Hopkins' children were about his age, and he and Tilley were closer in age to each other than either was to Priscilla—but at the moment every family had retreated to its own corner. So, she took it upon herself to entertain Joseph for a while.

He held up his hand, a little worried to see what might have come from their two weeks of growth. Priscilla laid her hand against his and leaned in close to examine the result.

"It's still smaller!" Joseph said, trying to snatch his hand away, but Priscilla held fast, saying, "No, no! Look how your finger is now longer than it was before. See? Last time, I swear, your finger didn't even reach this line, and now look!

Your hands have definitely grown." She squinted her eyes hard at their hands, as though to give them closer scrutiny. She saw Joseph smile.

"Really? Has it grown that much, Sissy?" he asked, excited.

"I think so. What do you think—another two weeks before I can play knucklebones with you?"

Joseph shook his head.

"Longer than that? Well, what shall we do until then? Shall we play noughts and crosses?"

Joseph nodded his head in the affirmative.

Priscilla opened the six-board chest to see what they could use for tokens. She saw one of her mother's aprons folded up, with the edge worn to fraying. Her mother had a habit of picking things apart with her hands whenever she lacked something to put together. Priscilla could pluck out and resew the hem in an hour, but her mother would, at any spare moment, just pick it up and start fiddling with it again, folding it or wringing it or ripping out the tiny weave of threads, piece by piece.

Priscilla pulled out an engraved box carrying spare buttons, needles, and little strips of ribbon. The box was inscribed with a simple floral pattern. She found four spares of the buttons that held together her red waistcoat. They bought the buttons at a good price, because they were engraved with Tudor roses, and bought spares because Mama liked to have a few matching extras of anything around. Not that they carried all Mama's extra bits and bobs on this voyage, unless they were both small and practical.

"You have your knucklebones; I have my buttons. Would you like to be noughts or crosses?"

"Crosses!" Joseph said with excitement. He took his leather pouch of knucklebones from under his pillow.

Priscilla drew lines on top of the pallet with her finger. "From here to here, and here to here."

Joseph nodded, then he looked down at the invisible board, concentrating. His tongue stuck between his teeth through the hole where his tooth had not yet come in.

"Will it be so different, in Cape Cod?" Priscilla heard her mother murmur on the other side of the six-board chest.

Joseph placed his knucklebone in the top left corner of the board. Priscilla placed a button beside it.

Her father's voice, now. "After all, they have formed the Council for New England now, and I believe Weston has a hand in it."

Joseph placed another bone below the first. Priscilla blocked his row by placing a button in the bottom left corner. Weston? Hadn't she heard that name before?

Her father continued. "Weston is with the Virginia Company; I am sure he can arrange a new patent for us in New England, and they will still send us supply once they know where we have settled."

Joseph placed a knucklebone in the center square, and Priscilla blocked his diagonal row by placing a button in the bottom right corner.

"Ah well," she heard her mother say on the other side of the six-board chest. "I suppose wherever we end up, we must make do."

It was a tenet of all the women Priscilla had ever known that, if anything went awry, 'we must make do.' It was a very sensible approach. After all, what else was there? But to her it seemed repetitive and disheartening to always be saying one must make do.

Joseph placed a final knucklebone in the center right spot, crossing their imaginary board with a line of bones.

Saturday, 11 November 1620

Master Carver, to whom Howland was indentured, approached John with a weary smile. "Goodman Alden, would you come down to the hold? We need to look over the stores, and you are most familiar with our provisions."

"Aye." John nodded. Carver was accompanied by the ship's master Jones, Master Hopkins, and Captain Standish. John led the way into the gun room, to the hatch through which they descended by ladder into the hold.

The first things they saw were barrels, laid on their sides, stacked in neat rows. They contained beer, biscuit, salt, peas, salted beef, and pork. There were smaller firkins of butter and larger hogsheads of oats, rye meal, and vinegar. The ship also carried pickled eggs in tubs and pipes of aqua vitae and Holland gin, which they hoped to use in trade with the Indians.

The different-sized casks were stacked to accommodate the curvature of the ship's hull, and everything was packed together, no space between left empty where it could be filled to stabilize the cargo. John's main duty as ship's cooper was to maintain these casks, but there were also sacks of onions, turnips, and parsnips, and boxes of smoked herring, dried neats' tongues, and salted cod. They carried both English cheese and Holland cheese, which John helped to load when *Speedwell*'s passengers and goods came over to *Mayflower*.

There was little room for John to move about down here, but he did not mind the close quarters when he was alone. The hold was comforting, filled as it was with the scents of wood and rope and the beer, which was most under scrutiny today. The presence of four other men made the confined space stifling, even more so than the deck above where a hundred men and women lived with most of their possessions.

"We need to maintain a supply of beer and provision to keep the sailors fed on the return journey," said Jones. "It's near two hundred nautical miles to reach the Hudson, best I can judge, and with the shoals and breakers we encountered yesterday, we'd either need to travel slowly and sound our way or risk going farther out to sea. We don't have enough beer to keep us traveling that much longer, and we aren't going to risk the ship on those shoals. The weather is already disagreeable, and the winds might try to guide us right back into that treacherous stretch of shore. We'd have to put out into the Atlantic a fair way, and we'll encounter more storms there as will put us off course."

"It is already November," agreed Master Carver. "There is barely time for us to build some shelter before winter will set in, and none at all to plant crops, even if we stay."

"The patent the Virginia Company authorized extends to the northern parts of Virginia. If we settle here, we are outside of the boundaries of the colony the King has permitted," Hopkins argued.

"We do not know this land, nor what savage peoples it may harbor," agreed Captain Standish. "We may be walking into even worse danger from the Indians here than we would be in Virginia."

Carver sighed. "We repeat our discussion from yesterday. We resolved to journey southward and to settle at the Hudson River if we could. Master Jones attempted the voyage but found it too dangerous."

The ship's master nodded.

Carver took his assent and continued. "It would be dangerous to try to travel near the coast, and we would risk much by going farther out to sea. Master Jones has said it is not feasible to make the journey. As I see it, we have no choice but to settle at Cape Cod. Mayhap it was God's intention that we make our plantation here instead."

"It is my intention to settle in Virginia. If you choose to do otherwise, you will do so without my family," said Hopkins.

"If you should head south by land, you and your family would doubtless perish!" argued Standish, making John, who was listening, uncertain on which side of the issue he stood. "Whether we like to settle here or not, it is unwise to separate from each other. We know not what lurks beyond the trees, whether there be lions or wolves or savage men." Standish picked up a rope coiled on top of the row of barrels and ran a length of it through his fingers, forming a noose.

"If you choose to settle beyond the bounds of the patent that the King has authorized, you no longer have power to command me," Hopkins retorted. "I shall use my liberty to find my own way to Virginia, where men do not so blatantly flout the authority of my King."

John, who had busied himself pretending to check the casks, turned to look at Hopkins. His attitude gave a ring of truth to the tales John had heard of his mutiny, but it was also clear he bore no love for the Separatists.

Carver tried to calm the angry merchant adventurer. "We shall no doubt be able to acquire a new patent for land near Cape Cod. You know Master Weston has been our ally in this effort with the Virginia Company. Weston long encouraged our congregation to settle in New England, rather than Virginia, and he believes there is much profit to be made from fishing here. Before we left Southampton, I believe he and some of his fellows obtained a large grant from the King for the northerly parts of the country, namely New England, which encompasses this Cape Cod."

"I have no desire to settle in New England, whether with a patent or without one. Whether or not there is profit to be gained by fishing here, no colony started in the northernmost parts of this country has yet succeeded. Fishermen go by Damariscove and Monhegan and return to England for their profit. Why settle when we have no patent and no notion what villains may await us?"

"We will perish if we do not hold together!" cried Carver. "It was not any of our intention to settle in New England, but God seems to intend it for us. You say that none have yet succeeded in planting a colony in this northern region—well, we shall not succeed either if we separate. We must stay together, or there is no chance of survival. We must bind ourselves together, in agreement to settle here, until Weston can help us obtain a new patent. If we stay together, mayhap our venture can yet succeed. There is no alternative which poses less threat to us!"

"How will we bind ourselves in a manner that will maintain loyalty, when your congregation cannot even keep loyalty to the King?" spat Hopkins.

"Master Hopkins, the reason we are here is *because* we crave to show our loyalty to King James. We do not wish to live in Holland any longer, where our children will grow to see themselves as Dutch, and not as Englishmen."

None of the other Separatist leaders would have responded to Hopkins' comments with such composure, but Carver was a man skilled in keeping peace. John was sure that Carver had much more to say on the subject of his loyalty to the King, but he did not further defend his congregation. There was a long moment of silence.

"Well," Hopkins permitted, "if we can write something down, an agreement that we shall obtain a patent from Weston as soon as we can, if the others agree, I'll sign and stay with ye until such time as we receive—or don't receive—a new patent." He pounded his meaty fist against a nearby barrel, making John flinch. The barrels needed to be kept stable, else the whole cargo hold would fall apart.

"An agreement should state that we will stay together, despite the circumstances," argued Carver.

"That all will submit to the law and respect those in offices meant to enforce it," added Captain Standish.

"That we have faith and loyalty to King James." Hopkins' gaze bored into Carver, who looked away, at their surroundings.

"We ought to call more men together, and there is not space to do so here." Carver gestured at the confinement of the hold.

"Aye, you can use my cabin to draft your agreement. We should leave the cooper to his work." Master Jones nodded to John. John returned the nod and watched the men ascend one by one through the hatch into the gun deck above.

John wondered what difference a patent could make for such a settlement. It would take six months or more for word to pass from their plantation to London and back again, wherever in the New World they settled. There was little enough the English might do to control them, whether they settled in Virginia or not. Even if they settled at the Hudson as planned, their proximity to Jamestown would not have been such that they might make easy communication with one another.

John whiled away some hours in the ship's hold, checking their dwindling stores. He made sure each cask was secure, in particular the ones that Hopkins and Standish touched. After the buffeting *Mayflower* endured the day before, extra caution was needed to ensure the safety of their provisions and the security of their packing. While he was at work, the principal men of both the merchants and the Separatists huddled together over papers, arguing between themselves. These men concluded their debate exhausted, but in agreement. John finished his work satisfied that their provisions would keep. All the better if they remained anchored in the relative calm of the harbor.

Everyone gathered 'tween decks when Carver called for their attention.

"Master Jones has informed us that we cannot sail south. It is too dangerous to attempt to reach Virginia. As you know, we have landed in a place beyond the authority of our patent. Nevertheless, we are bound together in this venture, and we can succeed if we stay together. In this New World, our fortunes and misfortunes are each other's."

There was a general murmur of assent. John was curious what these men wrote, after leaving him in the hold. He looked at Hopkins, who stood with his arms crossed and legs spread, as though daring anyone to challenge him.

"We intend to apply for a patent that will grant us legal authority over the land where we choose to settle here, in New England. Until that time comes, we have written a compact that will join us all together as one body, so that we might keep governance over ourselves. We ask that every man of legal age on board will sign this document, that we might be bound together in our venture."

Carver held the document in front of him to read aloud.

"In the name of God, Amen. We whose names are underwritten, the loyal subjects of our dread sovereign Lord King James, by the grace of God, of Great Britain, France, and Ireland king, defender of the faith, et cetera.

"Having undertaken for the glory of God and advancement of the Christian faith, and honor of our king and country, a voyage to plant the first colony in the northern parts of Virginia, do by these presents solemnly and mutually in the presence of God and of one another"— he paused again to look about, encompassing all the gathered crowd in his gaze—"covenant and combine ourselves together into a civil body politic, for our better ordering and preservation and furtherance of the ends aforesaid; and by virtue hereof to enact, constitute, and frame such just and equal laws, ordinances, acts, constitutions, and offices, from time to time, as shall be thought most meet and convenient for the general good of the Colony, unto which we promise all due submission and obedience. In witness whereof we have hereunder subscribed our names"—Carver gestured at the page—"at Cape Cod, the 11th of November, in the year of the reign of our sovereign Lord King James of England, France, and Ireland, the eighteenth, and of Scotland the fifty-fourth. Anno Domini 1620."

John nodded. He had no notion of law, but it sounded proper and persuasive.

There was a general agreement to the terms, and the men began to crowd around a table, unearthed from a pile of possessions for this purpose. John had gathered with the rest to hear Carver's speech, but now he found himself in the midst of the signers. He tried to extricate himself but ran into Master Carver.

"Goodman Alden," Carver said with a smile, "do you not sign the compact?"

"I know not that I should, Master Carver. I am the ship's cooper and am like to return with her to England."

Carver frowned. "Did we not extend an offer for you to stay and settle with us, if you should wish? I believed it was part of the arrangement when you were hired on."

"Indeed, Master Carver," John confessed, "an offer was made, but if I am as like as not to return with *Mayflower*, ought I to be on the compact?"

Carver smiled as though he understood. "Aye, well, the document is a sign of good faith more than a contract which must be followed. If you were to stay, it were better you sign it than not, is it not so? And if you do go on with the ship, what harm is done by your name on it?"

John nodded. Why not sign it, to please Master Carver, who was a kind man and a good employer to his friend Howland? He found himself back in the line of signatories, and, when it came to his turn, he signed his name. He was proud enough to be able to do so, that he learned to write as well as read from his master. More than one man on board could do no more than make his mark.

John leaned against the ship's rail and looked at the shore with a new eye after his conversation with Carver. He tried to examine it as a potential place for settlement. There was plenty of wood, at least. John mulled over the question of settling. Master Mullins was startled that John planned to leave with *Mayflower*, and Carver seemed to agree. Why would John travel all this way and then go back to England? After hearing Hopkins' arguments, John wondered why he should want to stay. Carver saw a vision of a home here, beyond what John could see.

The land John saw shared no character with the land they left behind. There were no buildings, of course, and no other ships. While he knew in his mind there would be none, John never realized before how much difference buildings made to the character of a shoreline. There were no open fields, nor cattle, nor any other sign of habitation. The coast was overspread with trees. The trees were not even in the full bloom of spring, nor crowned with the green leaves of summer. They were a dull, leafless mass of gray wood, branches creaking in the cold wind off the sea. The tree line ceased near the beach, a narrow strip of dense, earthy sand. The whole view was gray, the lowering clouds and the lapping sea framing the land on either side, shades of gray converging until the whole world looked gray.

Miles Standish sidled up to him and leaned against the rail. His cutlass was strapped to his side as usual. His large-brimmed felt hat sat snug against his head and hid his mass of red hair, but not the matching bristling mustache.

"Alden, have you had much use of a musket?" the captain asked, apropos of nothing.

John shook his head, wary. Standish's face dropped. Why the captain thought a cooper might need a musket, John refrained from asking. Silence was often the best method of communication with Standish.

"Ah, well. You shall have to learn with the others. A cutlass for now, then, and we'll see if anyone at all can take arms." He spoke more to himself than to John. "Mistress Standish has insisted that bearing arms can wait, but I aim to take account."

Standish would not much succeed at finding soldiers here, John reckoned, nor so much weaponry as he might prefer. Many of the congregation took up trades as printers and weavers in Leiden, taking whatever work they could, so they might live in the city.

"Now that we have settled in the northerly reaches, we are even less prepared for the Indians than we would have been at the Hudson. To change our destination—if we had known, I could have perhaps obtained a copy of Captain John Smith's book, *A Description of New England*. I believe he even writes about Cape Cod. So, perhaps the Indians will not be too startled to see us, having met with Englishmen before. Of course, in the case of Jamestown they came to open fire within a week of first landing. Ah, but look upon it, Alden." Standish swept an arm across the bleak vista in front of them. "'Twill be a perilous spot, I've no doubt."

John imagined—nay, hoped—that Standish would be disappointed by the threat he found on land. From John's view, it looked barren. Such an empty place could hold no armies. How could a land so devoid of life be perceived as a threat?

"The Powhatan at Jamestown are familiar enough. Reports of their relations there reach England, but who could say what beasts lie thither? It is a menacing spot, Alden, do not you agree?" Standish's questions rang with a hint of glee in John's ears.

John nodded, paying little attention, instead trying to guess the quality of the wood in the forest. He said nothing, but silence was the kind of company that Standish most enjoyed.

"Good man." Standish clapped him on the back. "I shall look to you to bear arms alongside me." The short man strode off to harangue another hapless passenger.

John gazed out to the land. He tried now to see it how Standish did. It was a very different view than Carver's. Menacing, John could agree. A land without people, without homes, without warmth—it appeared to him it may even be a land without God, whatever the Separatists said. It was a land without churches, and so how was God to find them? A land without priests, as they brought none with them, not even the Separatist pastor. How would they speak to God, even if he were here? It was quite impossible, John decided, that God would take any notice of this land at all. It reassured him to remember that he would return to England with *Mayflower*. Yes, that was what he needed to do—return home. Back to a place with pubs, and with hearths, with a church and a community.

Many passengers spent the afternoon on deck, enjoying the relative freedom of the ship at anchor, despite the chill in the air. Some of the men went ashore in *Mayflower*'s longboat to inspect the land and fetch wood and fresh water. Priscilla took advantage of their absence. The 'tween deck felt different now that they were in the harbor. The hatches and cannon ports stood open, and light filtered in to the still-dank, still-gloomy space. Few passengers remained confined to their beds with the seasickness; the ship rode steady now, at anchor in the bay. The quiet clucks of the chickens in the rear of the deck were reassuring, and the sound of sea birds could be heard outside. It was peaceful, but Priscilla could not enjoy it. There was too much uncertainty weaving itself through her head.

She could not approach her father with her suspicions; his overheard conversation with her mother made clear his own faith in Weston and the venture. Hopkins shouted his objections to their situation with such vehemence that everyone on board knew his stance on the matter, but Priscilla was not eager to approach him under any circumstances. She could have spoken with Mistress Hopkins, but that lady wanted nothing more than for things to be settled, and to make do.

She'd watched Goodman Alden go belowdecks to the hold with the men who she knew had written the agreement. She'd watched him hesitate to sign the compact. Perhaps he was not content with making do? If so, perhaps he would be receptive to her qualms over their arrival at Cape Cod, instead of Virginia.

She found Alden sitting on his mattress, leaning into the ship's hull, his eyes closed. He opened them as she approached, and she froze a few feet away.

"Miss Mullins?" Goodman Alden inquired.

She opened her mouth, then closed it. Pursing her lips, she took a few steps closer.

"Goodman Alden," she replied, biting down a rush of other thoughts.

Her height meant she was unused to looking down on anyone, and she watched with fascination as he rose, unfolding himself from the floor around her skirts to stand above her and rest his arm against the timber beam overhead. He was too tall to stand to his full height 'tween decks. She felt her heart beat faster, seeing him loom over her, and she glanced down, away from his face. Now was not the time to be distracted. How could she frame this so that he might heed her? Their conversations in the month since their walk together on the top deck had been brief. He was not an extravagant conversationalist, but his taciturnity was inviting, an opening that seemed to allow her to speak as she would.

"Goodman Alden," she repeated, fidgeting with her red waistcoat. "I..." She paused. Her eyes flicked around the interior of the ship. She was worried about being overheard. "I am concerned over our landing here," she said in a whisper.

He looked surprised, but he nodded. "It is a different land than I anticipated, too."

"Yes!" Priscilla cried. "We were promised land in Virginia. My father and the other merchant adventurers applied for a patent there. Without a patent here, we have no legal rights to settle on Cape Cod."

Goodman Alden blinked. "There seem not to be any here who will dispute with us over it," he said, alluding to the barrenness of the land.

"No, indeed," she snorted. "Though Master Standish seems keen to find someone with whom to fight."

She paused and looked away. A flush rose in her cheeks as she remembered the last time she spoke to him of Standish. "Pardon. I ought not to insult your dear friend."

"Your father has signed the compact," said Goodman Alden, ignoring the slight to Standish.

"Aye, and such is the cause of my worry. How does he not have more concern, after all we have been through since this voyage began? Since—" but she stopped herself before she could elaborate.

He thought for a moment, seeming to recall all the delays and troubles which afflicted their adventure. "I know not what we have undergone which might have been prevented."

She sighed. He'd had as much opportunity as anyone to listen to the rumors on the ship. "Do you not recall that back in England, Master Weston has joined the Council for New England?"

Alden stared at her, uncomprehending.

"God's wounds! Do you listen as little as you speak?" she demanded. "Before the congregation of Separatists made their agreement with the Virginia Company, they talked of building their plantation in several places. Some liked Guiana, others preferred Virginia. Weston encouraged them to choose New England."

"Aye," Goodman Alden agreed. "Carver said he believed the area profitable for fishing." He was at least engaged in the conversation.

"As that may be, the company chose instead to settle in Virginia, and they obtained a patent to do so. Yet, just before we leave England, we discover that Weston and his lordly friends have acquired a grant from the King for lands more northerly, which they control under the title of the Council for New England." She paused, examining his face to see if he understood. "Weston helped to charter the ship, including her master. He took control of land in New England before the ship he chartered sailed across the ocean. Although the ship was destined for the mouth of the Hudson, we inexplicably landed far north of our target, in the lands now under Weston's own influence. And, says the ship's master, sailing south from here is impossible. Weston has argued against my father and the Separatists before, regarding the terms of their contract, and he knows that there are points these men will argue and points on which they will concede. As one may expect, given Carver's nature and the recognized authority of the ship's master, we agree to settle, which will require us applying for a patent from Master Weston! Despite the decision they made, *Mayflower*'s passengers nevertheless end up with our plantation in the lands where Weston desired us to go."

She waited two beats, hoping the idea would sink into Alden's mind.

"You believe," he asked, "Weston redirected our course so he might profit from our need of a new patent?"

She nodded.

"But has he not invested in the success of this venture? If the plantation fails, is it not a loss for him as well? If he has sent *Mayflower* north, he must believe you can still succeed with a plantation here—nay, it seems he thinks you are *more* like to succeed, with the profitability of the northern lands."

"Mayhap we would, if Master Reynolds had not been so self-indulgent," Priscilla muttered.

"Master Reynolds? The ship's master of the pinnace *Speedwell*? What has he to do with Weston?"

"Do you not think it odd that the *Speedwell* was made to turn back twice, even after having repairs done in Southampton?"

Alden shrugged. "The pinnace took on water. We should all have preferred her here," he said.

"If, indeed, it was leaking on its own and not sailed beyond her capability so as to take on that appearance. And if we departed at the first in August, without turning back, without the delays which kept us from leaving England an extra month, we would not have met with such fierce storms to 'blow us off course.' We'd have landed a month sooner, and in Virginia as we intended," Priscilla concluded.

"Miss Mullins," Alden protested, "you cannot think Weston the cause of all our troubles? I have heard that Weston refused to pay your debts at Southampton, and whilst it seems he seeks for his own profit, I cannot see how he turned back *Speedwell*."

"No," her reply came sharp, "I believe Master Reynolds did not desire to be left with us in the New World for a year, so he arranged a means to back out of his agreement."

"For that I cannot blame him, Miss Mullins. As you may know, I too intend to leave the New World and return to England with *Mayflower*. After seeing for myself the land where your father intends to settle, I am if anything firmer in my conviction to go back."

Frustrated, Priscilla swept the coif from her bundled hair. "So you cannot believe that Weston intended to send us here instead of to Virginia?" she asked as she replaced the white cap over her dark curls and tied it at the base of her neck.

"Whether he sent us here or not, I cannot think that with such a decision he believed he would condemn us. Nor do I know what you hope to gain from revealing such suspicions to me. I may be the person on this ship least concerned with the permanence of your settlement. But, after all, perhaps it is best you confide these suppositions to those who are least affected by them. If you were to say such things to those who have spent their day designing a compact to bind us together, I do not think they would appreciate the strife this conjecture would cause, not when they have just settled some semblance of peace between them."

It was the longest thought that Goodman Alden had ever articulated in front of her.

"Mayhap you ought to consider the welfare of those who live around you, and not your own interest," Priscilla could not help but say before turning on her heel and sweeping away across the deck.

She tore the coif from her head again. No matter what she did, the strings pressed against her skull and the flaps irritated her ears. Her head itched and she scratched it, flecks of dead skin flaking off under her fingernails. One nail was broken, and her fingertip was sensitive. Could nothing go well today? At least she became so irritated with the conversation that she had forgotten to notice the beating of her heart and the flush on her cheeks.

The worst of it was that he was right. Whether such suspicions were merited or not, what good could they do in the ears of others, under these circumstances? If the ship's master, whether under Weston's influence or not, would not sail southward, nothing would change, and her accusations could not alter that fact. She should learn to gird her tongue. After all, now that they were here, and Weston still in London, what further damage could his influence have on them?

Chapter Five

> Being thus passed the vast ocean, and a sea of troubles before in their preparation... they had now no friends to welcome them, nor inns to entertain, or refresh their weather-beaten bodies, no houses, or much less towns to repair to, to seek for succor.
>
> —William Bradford, *Of Plymouth Plantation*, 1651

Monday, 13 November 1620

On Sunday, they held their Christian services 'tween decks. Work was prohibited on the Sabbath, and no one was permitted to leave the ship. On Monday, though, there was plenty of work to be done and plenty of passengers eager to do it. Priscilla helped her mother sort out a scant armload of spare shirts and smocks and then carry them up through the hatch. For the first time after two months at sea and more than three months on board, the women were going ashore. The ship's longboat had been lowered into the water on Saturday for the men to fetch wood and fresh water.

Priscilla looked down and saw the boat returned, bumping against the side of the ship, drifting against its mooring beneath a rope ladder. The sight made her stomach churn a little, but it did not lessen her joy at being allowed to leave *Mayflower*'s belly. She tossed her armload of washing into a net which was suspended above the water by a block and tackle. Throughout the day, the men would unload tools, armor, weapons, and pieces of the shallop, the small boat which lay 'tween decks and was in need of serious repair. For now, the washing filled the net in a filthy heap. Priscilla took a sailor's offered hand with her right arm, turning around so she would face the ship on her way down the ladder. She felt nervous; the ship's longboat below her kept floating away, leaving a gap between itself and *Mayflower* before being pulled back to bump *Mayflower*'s side once more. She bent, snatched at the rope ladder, and got herself down. She made it to the third rung from the bottom before she tripped on her own petticoat.

The longboat would be rowed back and forth across the bay to *Mayflower* several times today, transporting men to explore farther and collect more wood and fresh water. Captain Standish insisted he would accompany the women ashore, and he sat like a figurehead at the fore of the little vessel, as though he anticipated an onslaught. His wife sat close behind him, but they did not speak.

"Is he not admirable, dressed in his armor and helm?" Tilley whispered to Priscilla, nodding at Captain Standish.

"He is too proud to be admirable," Priscilla whispered back, eyeing the short man.

"His eagerness to defend us from Indians cannot be taken as fault?" Tilley asked.

"It is not his profession to which I object, but the lack of any humor in him. When he behaves as though he is leading the charge of battle, with no enemy in sight, I cannot but see it as funny. Yet I am sure he would chastise me for my laughter."

"Priscilla," her mother chided. She accused Priscilla of spending too much time engaging in frivolous gossip. It was time which could be better spent. As the Bible said, "Let no corrupt communication proceed out of your mouth, but that which is good to the use of edifying, that it may minister grace unto the hearers."

They fair flew across the harbor, the wind a little blustery this November morning. Priscilla felt the sharp sting of it against her face, but the sting was wonderful, as it meant she was free from the confines of the ship. Soon, the boat's bottom nudged the silty earth of the beach, and the sailors hopped over the gunwale to push it a little farther up, so the boat would be lodged in the shallows for the duration of their disembarkation. Mistress Chilton brought her little daughter Mary, and one of the sailors offered the girl his hand, helping her to step out onto a large rock so she wouldn't wet her stockings. Priscilla, planning to wash her stockings anyway, hopped over the gunwale herself, reaching back to help her mother over the edge. The water was colder than she expected, but her chilled feet did not dampen her spirits. A mess of arms dug into the pile of laundry until every scrap of linen was plucked from the boat. The women splashed through the shallows, laughing and chattering, carrying their filthy bundles. They'd all lived in their clothes for months without respite amid the rank filth of the 'tween deck. It would be a pleasure to have a clean smock.

The sailors pushed out the longboat to turn back to *Mayflower* and gather the men. The women settled around a shallow tidal pool, rocky and ideal for washing. Captain Standish marched a little farther down the beach, bending over a trickling stream, and raised a cupped handful to his lips.

"It's fresh water," he announced, looking past the edge of the pool to where the water trickled in a running stream. "The stream comes from inland." The men would gather more wood and fresh water to bring aboard the ship tonight.

The women sat around the pool, removing their shoes and stockings. Priscilla untied her coif, then dipped a washcloth into the water and scrubbed her face and neck. The coldness of the water made her skin tingle. She used to bathe her hands and face before meals, when they lived in England. The ship carried but little fresh water, and not enough for the luxury of washing. Any water kept aboard would have become brackish or sour after a few weeks, kept so long in the hold.

"Ah, it is good to be on land!" cried Mistress Standish. There was a cheer of assent from the women.

"Though we are perhaps even wetter than we were aboard ship," added Mistress Hopkins in jest.

"Aye, at least now we might keep open the gun ports and get some fresh air and light 'tween decks," said Priscilla's mother. She was concentrating on the pile of linen in front of her, submerging each piece in the tidal pool until it was completely soaked. Uncoifed, her mother's once-dark hair was now streaked with gray. Her forehead, too, was lined with signs of age. She looked weary.

They brought some lye and washing bats to scrub the clothes, but most of the women still focused on removing their collars and coifs and enjoying the small pleasure of washing their faces for the first time in ages.

"It will be lovely once we can leave *Mayflower* for good," said Tilley.

Priscilla nodded, dipping cloth in the water to follow her mother's example. She was determined to do better in taking her place working among the women, rather than in frivolity with girls.

"We shall need to make more lye, once we have settled in," said Mistress Carver, examining a container of the black soap.

"There will be so much to do, once we have settled on a place; I know not how we will manage it all," agreed Mistress Tilley.

"Let us hope for now that the rest of our company can cease to dispel their meals at every toss of the waves, now that we sit at anchor." Mistress Hopkins stripped off her waistcoat, revealing her smock and kirtle. The women would, of course, not immerse themselves in water—doing so could leave them open to any manner of disease—but Priscilla wondered if any would desire to strip off and wash the smocks they were wearing. After three months at sea, they all endured closer quarters than comfort or propriety dictated. Mistress Hopkins gave birth on a ship crowded with men. She had not even been able to keep away her husband, who by all rights should not have been allowed to witness it. Now they at last had space of their own to bathe. Priscilla looked around for Standish, wondering if he intruded on this moment. She found him positioned toward the tree line, on the lookout, as ever, for savages.

There were others aboard *Mayflower* eager to be on dry land. A party of men also departed the ship to explore the area and gather wood and water. John's purpose ashore was altogether different. The passengers brought with them a shallop. They would use the small boat for exploration, fishing, and navigating by water. They'd stored the boat 'tween decks in four pieces for the voyage. During the course of the journey, the crowding of the passengers was such that some chose to sleep in the pieces of the shallop. The pieces were also tossed about in the tempests at sea, and now the small boat required extensive repair to be reassembled. John surveyed the pieces with an uncertain eye.

Carver had asked John to assist in the rebuilding. "We cannot decide on a place for settlement without first exploring the coast and the rivers, and to do that we need our shallop."

John nodded.

"Master Eaton is a house carpenter, and Master Tinker is a wood sawyer. Your experience would be most helpful to them. Eaton has been doing the work of the ship's carpenter during the voyage, but houses and ships require quite different skills, so he says." Carver looked lost.

John nodded again. Tinker was a small man, but cheerful. As a wood sawyer, he was eager to get to felling but hadn't the least idea how to go about their repairs. Meanwhile, it was an understatement to say that the skills Eaton would have learned as a house carpenter would not translate to ship repair, much less ship building. Neither did a cooper's skills lend themselves to the construction of a vessel, though at least John had experience in curving wood and making casks watertight. Shipwrights had their own sets of specialized tools, which John had seen from time to time, his cooperage being situated near the docks, but he had never used them. It seemed the passengers did not bring such specialized tools with them. But John resolved to assist in whatever way he could. He was hired on by the passengers, after all, not by the ship. There would be no use in staying aboard, as his work in the hold had diminished with their arrival in a calm harbor. And, after all, the sooner the passengers found a place to settle, the sooner John could return to England. He did not wish to spend the whole winter in this desolate place. Besides, it was bound to be more pleasant working out on the beach than trapped 'tween decks, even if the job he faced was daunting.

John looked down the beach toward the women, who went about their labors chattering and giggling. His collar itched with dirt and sweat built up over three months. His doublet weighed on him with the heft of damp wool, though the weather was cold enough that he would not have given it over, even to have it back clean. He, like many others, took to wearing both his shirts under his doublet and cloak for the sake of what warmth they lent him. He pretended to look out over the sea, but from the side of his eye he could see Miss Mullins' curvaceous figure bent over the edge of the water in her blue skirts. Her head was uncoifed, and her dark ringlets glimmered with wet in the weak morning sun.

"Oi!" A shout came from behind him. He turned to see John Goodman bent over a muddy pool, his brown-and-white spaniel sniffing at the ground beside him. Goodman raised his fist into the air in triumph.

"Mussels!" he shouted, holding a small mollusk aloft.

The other men in the adventuring party bent to the ground to search for other treasures at their feet. John glanced at Tinker and found him ambling toward the shellfish. All three would-be carpenters left their heap of wooden ship pieces to join the adventurers searching in the mud.

"Aye, there are crabs here, too," shouted Hopkins, who moved closer to the edge of the water.

John bent down and examined the ground. There were blue mussels there, heaps of them. He pried one from the ground and cracked the shell. There was meat inside, sure enough—raw, fresh meat. After months of salted meat and biscuit, John did not resist the temptation to swallow it right there. The passengers had not been able to cook much during their voyage due to the rough storms. He saw the men around him cracking open crab legs and mollusk shells to devour the fresh meat. Tinker pulled a mussel from its muddy bed, waving it around in his excitement.

"Needn't they be cooked?" Eaton asked, a little wary of the strange new food.

"Aye, mayhap. I know not the process of cooking such things," replied Goodman, as he swallowed a mouthful of the little creature's innards.

The men collected them in buckets and in armloads, to carry over to the women in order to share their bounty. The women were pleased with the offering and just as eager to sample them as the men. The group set about lighting a fire and filled a bucket with water to boil the little creatures. John ate, unused to the odd sensation of the slimy object sliding into his mouth. He chewed with trepidation. The boiling did not do much good. The meat was gritty, as if grains of sand were lodged in it, but it was fresh, and different from salt pork.

"How do you like the taste, Goodman Alden?" Miss Mullins asked, approaching him with her hair still uncoifed and wet. Her smile was tentative.

John's fingertips were cold, exposed to the wintry air off the sea, but as she came toward him his chest grew sweaty under his layers of clothes. He reached up to remove his cloak, at least.

"If I am to be honest, I must admit I do not care for it, Miss Mullins."

She raised her eyebrows for a moment, then allowed her smile to strain the muscles in her cheeks. "I do not think I have ever heard you offer such a negative opinion, Goodman Alden."

Hadn't she? Had not their last conversation strayed near to argument?

"Even in our last conversation, were you not optimistic over our strangely altered fate?" she asked. She seemed shy of him, compared with her previous forthrightness, and he wondered if she was hesitant because of their difference of opinion. Her fingers were buried in her hair, combing out the tangles piece by piece.

"You have a strange view of optimism, if you see it in my saying that coming here has strengthened my resolve to return to England."

She looked at him. "Were you not resolved before?"

He shrugged. "There has been no particular reason to alter my plan to return, but that our shipmates keep suggesting it." He reached for another mussel.

"Although you do not care for the taste, you would continue to eat them?" Miss Mullins asked.

He turned the food over in his hands. "I had not given it much thought. Oughtn't I?"

She picked it from between his fingers. "Nay. Leave them for those that enjoy the luxury of eating something new." She cracked the shell apart and plucked out the little piece of meat, popping it into her mouth as she rejoined the women by the fire.

John sat for a while with the other men and listened to the gentle lap of waves. The extreme stillness of the New World unnerved him. Southampton was a constant bustle of activity. The noises in New England came from the passengers or from the breeze that clattered together the branches of the trees.

In the afternoon, when the sun approached the tree line, the work on the shallop ceased. They'd done little that day. Tinker bounced off to locate a good tree for felling; oaks and pines were the commonest about. The frame of the shallop seemed to be a hardwood, while the planking was soft. Would they need a hard oak or a soft pine to join them? John began to plane and smooth the edges of the first two pieces, still unsure how they were to keep the thing together. Some of the planks needed to be replaced, as the passengers sleeping in them had caused much damage. John had never needed to join such large pieces of wood before, nor such a complex shape. *I wonder if Master Eaton has devised a plan for the procedure?* Some of the tools they'd brought were transported without handles, and new ones would need to be shaped from the new felled timber. Though John was anxious over the nature of the labor, he was grateful to use his muscles once more.

He watched the longboat sailing across the bay, coming to bring them back to the ship. John's stomach churned. He ought to be used to the sea, but now that he'd spent a day aland he had no desire to return to the ship. *Would it be so bad,* he wondered, *to stay in New England if it would spare a three months' journey across the ocean?*

His stomach began to burble with greater intensity, and John felt as though he might be sick. The feeling was familiar after the bout of seasickness he'd experienced in their first weeks on the open ocean. But why? There was no unruffling motion on this shore. Could he be sick from leaving the sea, as the shift to life on the waves made him retch? He ran up the beach toward the tree line, a bowshot from the shore. If he were to vomit, he could do so away from the pile of fresh wood shavings he would work with tomorrow.

His bowels began to clench, and he realized his illness would not be limited to upheaval. He could see the men on the beach gathered by the shallop. Goodman was speaking with Master Eaton; as he spoke, he doubled over and spewed into the nearby water. Hopkins also headed for the wood. *We cannot all be land-sick,* John mused, right before he felt the bile rise up his throat. As he cast the contents of his stomach into the underbrush, it occurred to him—the ones who were suffering trouble were the men who ate the raw mollusks. The damned shellfish had poisoned them.

Friday, 17 November 1620

"Can you not complete the work on the shallop any faster?" Standish asked John on Tuesday, impatient to begin his exploration of the coast.

"Could you build it more quickly?" John asked, irritated at the constant pressure from all sides. He was a cooper, not a shipwright, and if he blundered this task, the shallop would sink as soon as she was put in water.

Instead of offering his assistance, Standish gathered a party of fifteen men to accompany him on an exploration by foot. They set off on Wednesday, Carver and Howland looking as uncomfortable as most of the men in their corselets and helms, marching with muskets at their shoulders. Hopkins was an exception; he looked well suited to his arms.

For almost three days, the shipbuilders worked in relative peace. They were efficient at the parts of the job they knew how to do well—sawing, splitting, and shaping wood—but were confounded by how to assemble their pieces to keep the shallop together. Tinker's good humor seemed boundless, and he kept John and Eaton in good temper, though he did little to help with the actual repairs.

On Friday morning, the explorers lit a signal fire, indicating their intention to return. That afternoon, John's work was interrupted by their arrival. It was a sight to see Carver and Howland carrying a large basket between them and Hopkins on one side of a great iron kettle filled with seed.

"Savages, Alden!" Standish shouted as they approached. "We espied five or six of them with a dog on the first day. They ran when they saw us, ran off into the woods, and we tracked them, but they run fleet-footed through the forest. Though we could not catch them, we followed their tracks and found an abandoned settlement which they left behind!"

"What is this seed you've found?" John asked, gesturing to the baskets the men were loading into the longboat. A dour man was staring at him and Standish, and he approached them when John waved at the cargo. John recognized Master

Bradford, another of the Separatist leaders. He was well respected among the congregation, though less even-tempered with the merchants than Carver. He was stout, with black hair reaching near his shoulders and a thick black mustache. He was a silk weaver in Leiden, and John heard he'd been imprisoned with other religious dissenters during his first attempt to flee to Holland.

"The Indian corn! There were bushels of it buried there, ripe for the taking. We could not carry it all with us, and so we need the shallop repaired." Standish clapped John on the back. "How long now? It has been five days; is the work near finished?"

John gave Bradford a dubious glance as he joined them. He ran a hand through his hair, wondering where he'd left his hat. "Aye, well, perhaps half-done," John said, looking over his shoulder at the shallop. It still lay in pieces as though someone had taken a hatchet to it.

"Do you mean to take the rest of the corn as well?" Bradford asked Standish. "Was it not enough to rob them of this much?" His tone was frigid, and John could tell he'd started this argument before and been outnumbered.

"We are in need of local corn, Bradford," Hopkins shouted from the boat. "We know not how our seed will fare in this more northern clime. The Indian corn will feed us when we would otherwise starve."

"We have acted as common thieves," Bradford continued despite him. "We have made no recompense for it but taken what we saw before us as though we were criminals. How can you account for such behavior?"

John could not help but think that Bradford *was* a criminal, that he had been arrested, that he committed treason every time he prayed, and yet he did not see those acts as worthy of the same disparagement as one necessary to keep a hundred people fed.

"We can, I think, repay the debt." Carver joined the conversation, having stowed his basket of seed in the boat. "Once we can discover to whom the corn belonged, we have plenty of goods to truck with the Indians. We will make recompense then. For now—it has been done, Master Bradford, and in the best interest of us all, lest we otherwise starve come spring."

Bradford curled his lip in disgust, but nodded. It was one of Carver's greatest assets that he could reassure both Separatists and merchant adventurers with his calm, even tone and endless reasonableness.

"The iron kettle is the thing, Alden, that interests me," Standish said, leaning closer to pick up the thread of his interrupted story. "They have not learned to forge iron, so these Indians must have had some contact with other Europeans. Of course, Captain John Smith encountered Indians during his travels in New England, and we know that English fishermen visit the northern stretch of the coast. Nonetheless, I did not anticipate finding iron goods in an Indian camp, beside their bows and arrows and their earthenware pots and woven baskets."

John nodded, wiping his tools with a rag before packing them away. If Indians were nearby, perhaps he would have the chance to see one before *Mayflower* departed. With this confirmation of their presence, though, the passengers would be even more keen to decide on a place to settle, necessitating the shallop's completion as soon as possible. John would be hard-pressed to finish the work, even in another five days.

The men finished packing the longboat and boarded, ready to return to *Mayflower* and share the tales of their expedition with the rest of the passengers. While Standish was eager to recount their close encounter with the Indians, Bradford sat stone-faced. Some of their company would doubtless agree that taking the corn was a sinful act and should not have been done. John hoped Carver and Hopkins could convince them that the sin was necessary, lest the whole company starve. None imagined that in their new life the first choice might be between sin and starvation.

Chapter Six

Whilst some of us were digging up this, some others found another heap of corn, which they digged up also, so as we had in all about ten bushels, which will serve us sufficiently for seed. And sure it was God's good providence that we found this corn, for else we know not how we should have done, for we knew not how we should find or meet with any Indians, except it be to do us a mischief.

—*Mourt's Relation*, 1622

Monday, 27 November 1620

It began to snow, and for more than a week the stormy weather prevented much progress on the shallop and inhibited the intended exploration of the coast. The passengers all remained aboard, crammed together 'tween decks as they had been for months. A cough was spreading, which irritated Master Jones. He threatened to leave them all and their luggage ashore and depart back to England rather than wait much longer for them to find a place for settlement. More delay would risk *Mayflower*'s supply of provision for the return trip, and Master Jones wanted to avoid any illness spreading to his sailors.

It took more than two weeks, but at last the work on the shallop was complete—or complete enough for the boat to be taken down one of Cape Cod's rivers. The pieces were each snugly fastened to their neighbors by use of refitted sections of the keel and top rail.

"One of us should accompany the exploring party," Master Eaton suggested when Standish came to look the boat over. They stood on the beach, all three would-be ship's carpenters together with Standish. Tinker looked delighted and was about to open his mouth when Standish interrupted.

"Aye, Alden, come and venture into the land of the savages with me!" cried the captain, clapping John on the back.

John glared at Eaton. The house carpenter knew that Standish would choose John, so he waited until the captain was present before making his suggestion. Eaton smiled, feigning innocence. Tinker grinned, and John saw that the pair of them set him up. Tinker no doubt wanted to go back aboard and see his wife and son. In truth, Eaton was more frustrated than John to be working on a project so far from his realm of expertise. The continuous requests for the boat to be complete and inquiries as to its progress irritated all of them. Though it was near done, they wanted one and all to wash their hands of it. If something went wrong with the shallop during the expedition, it would be down to John to see to its repairs.

So now it was John who stood on the beach next to the shallop, uncomfortable in a corselet and with a cutlass swinging from his side. He dropped the musket Standish thrust at him onto the pebbly sand. The other men in the expeditionary party were wandering the beach, waiting for the longboat to return from *Mayflower*, waiting for the shallop to be ready. John checked over all the joins and crevices to see if he could spot any flaws in their work. The wood would at least swell in the water, preventing any leaks.

"I hope our journey proves less dull for you than working on this boat has been," Standish said.

"I should enjoy it if it were dull, provided I am able to leave the forest still in possession of my scalp," John replied.

Standish laughed at the comment. John could not prevent a thrill of pleasure at having amused the captain, but he squashed it under the weight of his concerns. That the man took such delight at the prospect of a scalping was alarming enough. Rumors about the Indians spread among the passengers since the first exploring party's return. Most of the speculation was based on news they had heard in England or in Holland about the Powhatan near Jamestown. Someone brought aboard a copy of *A Description of New England*, but the information it contained gave them more cause for questions than it gave answers. *Mayflower* carried a copy of John Smith's map of the region, but the inland area of the cape was covered by a large coat of arms, and no detail was made of its rivers or coast. John heard a rumor that the Separatists considered hiring Captain John Smith himself, in place of Standish, and wondered how the fiery-haired captain ended up on the expedition instead.

Standish and some of the others helped John carry the shallop to the water. As they dropped it in, John waited for it to begin leaking. The cold water of the bay lapped against his calves and a chill crept up his legs. To this he was accustomed, having plunged his legs knee-deep into the cold water near every time he'd leapt over the gunwale, traveling back and forth to shore. After a wait of what seemed an eternity, Standish said, "Well, she seems water-fast to me, Alden," and began to load it with men.

They carried little provision with them, some biscuit and a little Holland cheese. John supposed they were trusting in their ability to find wood, water, and food on their way. It was a lot of faith for Standish to put in a group of men who took up trades as printers and weavers to get by in their Dutch city. He thought the merchant adventurers were little better prepared, looking to his left and finding Master Mullins struggling with his sword belt. A cordwainer was no more suited to adventuring than was a cooper. John knew not whether to be worried or relieved that he was not alone in his ignorance.

To John's annoyance, *Mayflower*'s master Jones decided to join the passengers on this venture, bringing both his longboat and some dozen of his sailors. *If he is willing to use the ship's boat for this expedition,* John thought, *why did he not offer it whilst the shallop was still undergoing repair?* It would have taken some of the pressure off Eaton, Tinker, and himself if Standish was able to take the longboat out exploring. Together, the two boats carried more than thirty men out into the bay, stiff in their armor and unsteady with their muskets.

Rough winds blew them from their intended course at once. The shallop was fitted with a mast and sail, but the wind tore at the ship too hard for the sail to be useful. The longboat, smaller than the shallop, could not keep pace. They made for a rocky beach, unable to sail as far as the mouth of the river which would take them inland. Even as they tried to navigate toward the shore, the fierce wind buffeted the boat away, and with the oars they struggled to make land. John hopped over the side with a few others of the party and pushed against the wind. Frigid water soaked his legs, past his knees. His stockings clung to his skin, and the hair on his legs prickled at the chill. The wind tore at the little boat he'd helped to mend. After much exertion, they were able to drag her to shelter amid the rocks.

"What now?" asked Bradford, panting.

"Most of us must march on," demanded Standish. "We shall have to leave men with the shallop until the weather has quietened. A few of the party can remain with it for now, and follow with the longboat to meet us where we camp in the morning. We have a duty to continue, to find a place fit for settlement."

They all nodded assent. John was, of course, left to mind the boat while other men marched off into the woods. A few of the sailors were left with him, but they made conversation among themselves. Though he did not mind the wait, it did seem the woods would have at least offered cover against the day which blustered about him. Indeed, it soon began to snow again, and his wet stockings froze, encasing his legs in ice. He huddled into the boat to sleep in his cloak.

Aboard *Mayflower*, Priscilla sat in an energetic circle with Joseph, Tilley, and Constance and Giles Hopkins, who were of a similar age. Being the eldest of the group made Priscilla wonder whether she had been left to look after the children, or if she was seen as one of them. Though she got along well enough with her brother, and Tilley was a dear friend, she did not want to be grouped together with them as though she were still twelve years old herself. Priscilla's mother had taken the cough that was spreading around the ship, and her father was abroad with the exploring party. Tilley's father had gone with the explorers too. Mistress Hopkins was nursing young Oceanus, and so Priscilla took Giles and Constance under her wing along with her brother and Tilley. She was grateful that these four, at least, seemed to be in high spirits. Many of the children were ill and coughed and sneezed alongside their mothers.

The children were playing draughts with a board and pieces Master Hopkins brought with him. Constance and Tilley were teamed up together against Joseph and Giles. The girls were winning, with one two-tiered king and three more pieces on the board than the boys. Priscilla watched her brother screw up his face and stare at the board. He kept trying to stick his tongue out through the gap in his teeth, but his new tooth was starting to grow in, and the gap was too small for anything but the very tip of his tongue. He was trying to find a way to salvage his situation, but there was little he could do. He moved one of his white pieces diagonally forward, and Priscilla could tell he had erred by the look of savage delight that crossed Constance Hopkins' face. She double jumped her king backward over two white pieces, plucking her trophies from the board and adding them to a growing pile. Giles shouted, "No fair!" at his sister, who responded by biting her thumb at him. Priscilla was alarmed at the rude gesture.

"Now, you still have a few turns, Giles; what can you do in the game?" Priscilla asked, trying to calm the children down.

"It's not fair—she's always black, and black always goes first!" complained the little boy.

"Well, when we finish this game, we can start a new game, and you can be black," she suggested.

"Papa says that it's rude for a gentleman to take his turn before a lady," Constance bragged.

"Perhaps we've had enough draughts for one afternoon," Priscilla suggested. "Would you like to hear a riddle instead?"

This caught their attention. Four faces turned toward her, draughts board forgotten between them.

"All right, let me think," she said, trying to remember one of the riddles her father liked to tell her when she was young. "What is ten men's length and ten men's strength, yet ten men cannot stand it on its end?"

She saw Joseph's face brighten as he recognized the rhyme. "Oooh!" he cried out, pumping a fist.

"You can't have guessed it already!" Giles exclaimed.

"Joseph," Priscilla said, giving him a warning look. "Let the others guess first."

He put both hands over his mouth, as though the answer wanted to physically escape him.

"Ten men's strength," mused Tilley out loud. "Ten men's length..."

"Is it a tree?" asked Constance.

"You can't stand a tree on end, you dunderhead."

"You can too!"

"It isn't a tree in this case," Priscilla tried to mediate. The group fell into silent thought.

"Is it a whale?" Tilley asked.

"Whales—" Priscilla began to answer, but she was interrupted by a loud shriek from behind her. It was not the usual distressed sound of the sick passengers.

Priscilla stood, searching the ship for the source of the commotion. Mistress White was on all fours on her mattress, Mistress Hopkins and Mistress Carver rushing to her side.

"Someone fetch the ship's surgeon!" called Mistress Carver.

Priscilla turned back to the children as Mistress White let out another loud moan. Constance and Giles looked terrified.

"What's going on?" Joseph asked.

"Mistress White is going to have a baby," Priscilla explained. "Remember when Mistress Hopkins gave birth to little Oceanus, whilst we were still at sea?"

"Is she going to die?" asked Constance.

"Our mother did," said Giles.

Their faces showed fright at the sudden alarming noise, but also worry borne from long experience.

"I'm sure the ship's surgeon Master Heale will take care of her, and Mistress Carver as well. Mistress Carver has some experience in midwifery, so I've heard, so I'm certain they'll make sure she and the babe are as well as they can be. After all, your stepmother delivered your little brother Oceanus well, didn't she? And that was whilst we were still at sea."

Most of the adult women aboard ship had some experience with childbirth, aiding their neighbors as well as undergoing the experience themselves. Priscilla was curious what it would be like to have a baby; she knew she would someday be making such sounds herself, and she wondered whether she would be ready. She knew that sometimes women died, but Mistress Hopkins was so happy when she held Oceanus that Priscilla felt it would be worth quite a deal of trouble to have a babe of her own sometime.

Looking down at Constance and Giles, she was not sure she was ready to have a child of her own just yet. Perhaps watching the children was a test, so her mother could determine whether or not she was ready to be married. Would she succeed? She'd kept them from their argument before. What more was needed to rear children? She had been helping to look after Joseph since he was small; had that given her the experience she needed to be a mother? She felt it wouldn't. At least her own mother would be there to help her, when it was her turn to bear children. She would have her family with her and would not have to go through it alone.

"So, Joseph, would you like to share the answer to the riddle?" Priscilla asked, sitting down again and trying to gather the children in around her so they might ignore the loud moans of Mistress White's pain.

"Aye, Sissy! It is a rope!" he shouted, remembering his earlier restraint.

"A rope?" Giles said, disbelieving.

Tilley nodded, and Priscilla wondered if she had guessed it while they were distracted.

"I want another," demanded Constance.

"All right. Hmm... When I did live, then was I dumb, and yield no harmony: but being dead, I do afford most pleasant melody."

They passed the time with riddles and jests until, at last, the wail of a babe's cry broke the tension aboard, interrupting the intermittent coughs of the passengers.

Giles smiled in relief. Joseph looked at Priscilla, inquiring. He had spent a little time with Oceanus, and he was fascinated with the child. She was sure he wanted to visit the new baby too. Joseph was eleven, and already he was eager to be a father. Did she have so far to go before she would be ready herself? She bade the children wait a while, to let Mistress White rest. She managed to hold them at bay for an hour before their restlessness wore her down.

"Would you all like to meet the little White child?" she asked.

A round of nods answered her. She took Joseph's hand and led the rest through the crowded 'tween deck. As they made their way forward, Priscilla saw a tiny, ugly thing wrapped up in swaddling, held against Mistress White's chest. She had seen babes before, and she never overcame this initial reaction that their faces were too scrunched up to be beautiful. But the feeling always disappeared when they moved their little fingers or opened their eyes.

Joseph pressed his way right up to Mistress White's side, dragging Priscilla behind him. She felt the smallness of his hand folded into hers.

"Can I touch it, Mistress White?" he asked.

Mistress White smiled, though her face looked weary. "Aye, young Mullins, but take care. He is still quite delicate."

Joseph stretched out a finger and poked the babe's little hand, peeking over the rim of his blanket. The fingers moved a little in response to the sensation, though the babe did not wake.

"Was I like this, when I was born?" he asked Priscilla.

She tried not to laugh. "Indeed, you were. But that was a long while ago—just look how much you've grown!"

Joseph was unsure whether to be amazed or scornful at her patronizing him.

"What's more, someday you'll have a babe of your own, and you'll be his father like Master White is to little Peregrine," Mistress White told him, smiling.

Joseph's eyes widened. He shook his head. Priscilla could not imagine it, despite sharing the thought herself. Joseph, a father? Joseph, all grown tall and bearded, with a babe in arms? It was too far-fetched to be possible.

"You have grown so much since you were a babe, I imagine your hand is even bigger than mine now, don't you?" she asked, holding up her palm. He raised his hand against hers. She tried to ensure that her palm was not quite aligned with his, to give him the advantage.

"I think you've nearly caught me up, Joseph. Soon I shall at last be able to play knucklebones with you again!"

He smiled, showing the hole in his mouth where his new tooth was growing in.

Tuesday, 28 November 1620

It wasn't until the next morning that the wind settled enough for John and the sailors to navigate the shallop. The longboat caught them up the previous afternoon, and the two boats followed the signal sound of gunshots until they reached Standish's camp. A thin layer of snow coated the ground all about them.

The men weren't cheerful. The coughing that had spread aboard *Mayflower* worsened overnight, and the commonest sound from any of the men was hacking or a wheeze. John's stomach ached with hunger, for his ration of biscuit did not keep him satiated. The cold penetrated through his cloak, doublet, and both shirts to his skin. He shivered and wrapped himself deeper in his cloak. The two boats rowed in company downriver until they came to a fork, where two creeks flowed in different directions.

"A bad harbor," shouted Master Jones at them from the longboat.

"Mayhap, for a ship like *Mayflower*," shouted Standish, "but the shallop will do well enough, and the ship's boat."

"Would it be wise to make a plantation in a harbor fit for small boats?" John asked Hopkins, who sat next to him in the shallop.

"Nay, but it is close enough to Cape Cod to be accessed by a multitude of ships. It is more important to find a source of freshwater and a place that is defensible. The Indians here have the advantage over us wherever we decide to dwell, so it is good for us to scout ahead to see whether we can find any living nearby. If we do, we can ask them to recommend a place to settle. If we are met with violence, we will know to go about our own way."

Some of the men disembarked to examine the land, while others remained in the boat with John to navigate the waterway. John assessed the land they sailed past. The woods were made of sturdy trees, good oaks and pines that would do well for staves, were a man inclined to build a cooperage here. *I pity the man who does*, he thought. He huddled into his knees. He was grateful for the company of the other men in the boat, who were close on either side and shared their warmth. Master Mullins sat beside him. John could not help feeling awkward; their first encounter ended when John realized that Mullins was a Brownist sympathizer, and they had not spoken with each other since.

"It's growing dark," Jones called out to them in the evening. "We should explore this area more when it is light again. The hill there may make for an admirable settlement."

Standish grunted, but agreed to follow Jones' orders. They pulled the shallop and longboat to shore, and some men set about making a fire. Standish took Hopkins and a few others out to hunt for their suppers, and they returned with three geese and six ducks—a feast, although it was to be shared out among thirty men.

John warmed his feet by the blaze, grateful for the respite from the chill that began to seep into his bones. He wiggled his toes, watching the fat drip from the birds roasting on a makeshift spit. The men cleaned them in a hurry to eat, and bits of downy fluff were burning off the skin as the birds cooked. Standish sat beside John, drinking cool, fresh water from his mug. One of the Separatist men, Master Winslow, sat across from them, on the other side of the fire. Winslow was a printer by trade, even before he joined the Separatists in Leiden. He'd used his skills to help produce religious tracts and pamphlets that they'd smuggled into England. One of his confederates was arrested, but Winslow looked more like a schoolteacher than a traitor. He even wore a pair of eyeglasses when he was writing. His narrow nose was underlined with a thin mustache and pale brown goatee. He was now engaged in examining a leaf by the light of the flames.

"How well do you like the spot, Captain?" John asked Standish. He wondered how Standish was evaluating the land, and whether by the same criteria as Hopkins.

"We shall have to examine it in the morning," the small man replied. "'Twould be unwise to settle far from such a creek, or another source of fresh water. The hill provides a good vantage. We have yet to see any savages, which would be all to the good for a permanent settlement," he admitted. "Your thoughts, Goodman Alden?"

John shrugged, surprised the captain would ask him his opinion. "I've no notion how to pick a place, though there seem to be fine trees in all directions. There's so little underbrush, it makes the wood easy to pass through."

"It seems to be the work of Indians," Winslow cut in, unprompted. "I know not the particulars of this kind of forest, but we've seen enough of their settlements nearby to think that they have lived in this area. They'd clear the undergrowth to make it easier to hunt and travel." Winslow did not look at them as he spoke but continued his examination of his leaf, turning it over and squinting.

"Mistress Standish has been good enough to remind me we ought not to have the settlement too near any camp of Indians," Standish snorted. "As though I wish to live any nearer them than she. It is not a desire to live near them which keeps me alert to their presence." As he spoke, he scanned the woods, searching, as though a party as large as theirs, and making so much noise, would not warn off any creature that approached.

"It would be better for us to make peace with them than to stay as far away as we can," Winslow said, looking up at the trees and stroking his goatee. "The French have cultivated a network of Indian tribes up and down the coast, with whom they trade for furs and other oddments. If we do not find Indians with whom to trade, we shall have a much harder time finding valuable skins to send back to England to pay down our debts to the Virginia Company." Winslow's eyes darted from tree to tree around their campfire.

"How do you inten—"

"Winslow!" A call from Bradford interrupted Standish's reply.

Winslow looked John in the eyes for the first time and smiled before standing to join Bradford. John was surprised to find his eyes a clear, cold pewter, like burnished spoons.

"Peace with Indians," Standish scoffed as Winslow walked away. "They are a danger to us, Alden, take heed. They mean us no good. There is no escaping them, however far off we live, but peace?" Standish shook his head. "They cannot be trusted. Master Winslow is a good man, I've no dispute, but it strikes me he may be more keen to convert the Indians than to kill them, should the need arise."

John considered this. He had never thought Winslow to be worth any kind of notice, despite his being a noticeable sort of man. He seemed always to be in mid-conversation with himself. John had seen men behave that way when they grew feeble-minded, but Winslow could not be many years older than John. He was not yet a man of thirty, yet he was somehow lost to this world. He was not inattentive—his wife did not complain he would not heed her, nor that he would not attend her—it was that, while his body was present, his mind was about something else. This made him rather peculiar to carry on a conversation with, as John experienced. Could his aim be to convert the Indians to his perfidious religion? Was it possible that that was the goal of these Separatists—to expand their subversive sect by recruiting the savages? He shook his head. The notion was incredible.

Wednesday, 29 November 1620

Though their intention was to continue up the river, they found in the morning they did not like the area.

"It is too hilly," Mullins assessed.

"And the soil will not do for crops," added Bradford. "It is as infested with rocks as anything."

Standish stood for a moment, surveying their location near the creek.

"Let us cross over, then, to the other branch of the river and gather up the corn which was left there on the previous expedition," he suggested.

"You are familiar enough with our location to know how to reach Corn Hill from here?" John asked Standish, impressed.

"From the path we took on our previous journey, and the distance we've covered in the shallop, I believe we are quite close. If we go back a little way and take the other creek, we shall come to it, by and by."

It was indeed a short journey by water before Standish and Hopkins recognized their location. They moored the boats, and John climbed alongside the others, his legs unsteady on the frozen ground. They came to the crest of a hill, where the frame of an old Indian house was collapsing into the earth. He'd been exerting himself working on the shallop, but climbing uphill used muscles that John hadn't needed since he boarded *Mayflower*. He felt invigorated, though shorter of breath than he would have liked. Several of the men stopped to rest. Months in ship's quarters did no good for their constitutions.

Atop the hill, they searched for the buried cache. They did not bring spades or mattocks on their expedition, so the men cleared the snow and attacked the frozen ground instead with their cutlasses and short swords.

"It is about here," Standish muttered. He looked at the chunks of frozen earth with distaste. His sword was not meant to be put to this purpose.

John dug, his hands red from the cold and his fingers tingling. He thrust his blade into the ground, chipping away chunks as though it were ice instead of soil. The corn was buried a foot deep, and the cold made it difficult to find. It began to snow again, too. At last he uncovered a pile of small seeds, red and yellow and blue-black. He dug with more care, excavating around the heap until the stockpile was all revealed.

"Bradford will not be pleased," Alden thought. He did not realize he'd voiced the thought aloud until he heard the snort behind him.

"The man is pleased with little other than prayer; and even then, if it is not his own way, he tends to fault it." It was Hopkins.

"It may be, but he has the ear of the governor," John replied. After the signing of the compact, Master Carver was elected to the office of governor for the term of one year. It was a good choice, and John could not fault the decision, although the man was a Separatist. Many of the merchant adventurers bore Separatist sympathies in any case, and John could not think of none among them who could reason with the congregation without being a member of it.

"Aye, he does, and his intent may be true enough for his own people. Where does that leave the rest of us, I ask you?"

John nodded.

Hopkins appraised him with a new eye. "And who might your people be, Goodman Alden?"

John grimaced. It was clear that, in the view of this man, John was not part of his own group, even if they stood together in their views against the separated church.

"I have no people, Master Hopkins," said John. "I am left to myself now. And yours?"

Hopkins smirked, showing the gaps where his teeth were missing. "I may not be a part of Bradford's congregation, but it does not mean I am a part of the rest of them. My tribe is me, my wife, my children. It's enough." He paused in thought. "Although I do not understand them, nor their urge to separate from the King, they have a streak of independence to them that I cannot but admire. Carver had the right idea about the compact. Here we all are, miles from any authority that can dictate what we do, and they go and set up an independent government. One wonders if it wasn't their plan from the beginning, to settle outside of the bounds of the Virginia territory."

John raised his eyebrows. He'd now heard two theories suggesting that their arrival in New England was not a mistake, but intentional.

"Whoever's idea it was to land us in New England," John said, "we're all a part of one civil body politic now, aren't we?"

"At least until you leave us to return to England, Goodman Alden." Hopkins gave him a squint which may have passed for a smile on a less aggressive visage.

Thursday, 30 November 1620

On the fourth day of their exploring party, John's feet started to ache with the chill. He was grateful to be riding in the boat rather than following the tracks of Indians, searching for an Indian encampment or a place for settlement. It snowed six inches the night before, and his stockings and breeches were frozen with his periodic submergence in the icy water. His nose began to drip every few minutes, and he couldn't feel his ears.

"At least you are not on *Mayflower*," he muttered aloud to himself.

"That's right," chimed in Hopkins, who always seemed to be about when John was talking to himself. "Something for which to thank God every day," he grinned.

John was uneasy about the man and knew not whether to agree or laugh. He settled for a kind of broken nod and turned back to face the river. Since he saw the light of mutiny in Hopkins' eyes, John was unsure whether to see him as a friend or an enemy. His outright insult to the Separatists intrigued John, who thought he might have an ally among the merchant adventurers, but Hopkins' acquiescence to their terms, and the admiration he'd confessed for their independent spirit, gave John cause to rethink the matter. Perhaps it was best if he stayed unaffiliated with either party, as he had till now.

An unnatural bird call echoed through the forest.

"Light your matches," Standish commanded, halting.

John fumbled with his musket. He reached for the length of cord which hung about him—somewhere. He glanced around at the other men. Some handled their task with ease and grace, but most, like him, tried to remember their brief instruction in musketry. He found the match cord and positioned it into the jaws of the serpentine attachment, careful not to let it dangle long enough that it might touch the pan.

He looked up. Standish stared at him.

"Alden," he shouted in his attempt to whisper, "you haven't lit the match cord." John winced.

After fumbling for another minute, all the men were ready. Their matches were lit, their belts of powder and shot positioned for easy reloading. They looked about themselves with a newfound alertness. Standish looked as though he were in physical pain from their slowness and clumsiness, but all in all John thought they'd done quite well. After all, most of them had never had much cause to hold a musket above a week or two ago.

Their renewed caution made each step forward a possible step toward scalping, an arrow in his eye, or a battle for his life. John tugged his helmet farther down over his hair. It was too small, and he'd been content to let it rest atop his head rather than fitted around it. No longer.

They continued, the light chatter of their earlier progress gone. All eyes were keen and trigger fingers nervous. They may not be soldiers, indeed, but they were men who crossed the ocean to begin a hard life, and they intended to continue in their lives as long as they may.

"I imagine the savages were alerted to our presence by the utter incompetence of weaponry this group displayed," Standish huffed.

The assembled men were torn between embarrassment and fury, but their captain spoke the truth. Still, at the comment their fingers relaxed, and the muskets drooped to their sides.

John took to carrying out conversations in his own head, most of them about what life would be like when he returned to England. *Oh, yes, there were savages, of course. We tracked them into the wood,* he'd say. And then what? *We found no sign of them* would not do, nor *I set off my musket at a squirrel.* Hmph. While part of him hoped he should not have to learn to use the musket, it would not be amiss for something of excitement to happen on their journey, so he could spin a tall tale out of it for retelling at a pub.

"Halt!" He heard the shout from the front of the party and once more gripped his musket tighter, but the Indians they stopped for were no longer living. The men gathered around a few wooden boards which lay across uneven ground.

"They are like the graves we found in the previous expedition," Winslow said as he knelt by them. He reached to turn a board over.

"Wait," cried Bradford. "If it is a grave, oughtn't we to leave it be?"

"We know not whether it is a grave or if it may be another cache of corn," said Hopkins.

"Mayhap we ought not to interfere with either," snapped Bradford.

"Mayhap we ought to know what kind of savages we propose to settle near as neighbors," Hopkins replied.

The rapid discussion ended when Standish reached down and tossed the board aside as if it were a misplaced child's toy. Hopkins stepped forward to help uncover the rest of the site. Bradford stood by, his arms crossed over his chest.

A woven mat lay underneath the rough boards. It concealed a treasure trove of oddments. Bowls, trays, dishes, and a fine bow lay jumbled on the ground. Standish and Hopkins reached for the items, to Bradford's audible exasperation.

Beneath the pile of oddments lay another mat, which protected a carved wooden board. It was painted with a fine design of many colors. Winslow took a long moment to examine the piece before Standish grabbed it out from under his nose and tossed it to the side with the others. Hidden beneath this decorative board were two cloth bundles.

It was so odd a sight that even Bradford quieted his protest, curious to see what lay inside these wrapped cocoons. John helped Standish and Hopkins lift the bundles out of the ground. Winslow edged forward and unwrapped the cloth from the larger. A quantity of fine red powder spilled out and marked the snow about their feet with color. John was not alone in his sharp gasp when the contents were revealed. Standish reached in and extracted a skull, still covered with pale golden hair. The remainder of the man's skeleton was nestled in the sack. Pieces of flesh still clung to the bones. He'd been buried with an English knife and several items made of iron.

"God's wounds," Bradford cursed. "We ought not to have disturbed this sepulcher."

"Do you suppose, Bradford, that God will look down on us because this was the grave of a European, and not a savage?" Hopkins asked.

"The canvas is a sailor's cassock," murmured Winslow as he peered at the cloth in which the man's remains were wrapped. "And his breeches, too."

John looked at the smaller bundle unraveling beneath Hopkins' fingers, and he stepped back, unsure he wanted to see what was inside. He wiped his dripping nose against the sleeve of his doublet.

"It is a child," Hopkins said. "It has been buried with care," he added, turning the bundle in his hands.

John stepped away to lean against a tree. A cough rose in his throat.

"Is the child Indian or European?" Winslow asked.

"How could we tell? Indian, from the burial," suggested Bradford.

"But the man was a European. No savages have such light hair," said Hopkins. "More likely they killed him and buried him this way as a celebration."

"Then why bury the child with him?" retorted Bradford. "Do you not suppose he was this man's child?"

As the debate sprung up around him, John helped to re-wrap the skeletons and return them to the earth. He noted with distaste that the items which were buried with them were now in the hands of Jones' sailors. He may not have been of the Holland congregation, but he was still a Christian, and it was not right to pilfer grave goods of the dead at rest.

The discoveries sparked a new liveliness in the explorers. They scouted ahead farther, looking for more graves, more corn, more Indian goods to take as their whims dictated.

"Oi, what's there?" one man shouted in the distance as he clambered up a frozen hillside.

"It is a dwelling," Standish said, chasing after him.

The rest of the party trailed along in his wake. John climbed the steep, snow-covered hillside with slow, deliberate steps. He stopped to breathe, frozen air pricking like icicles at his lungs. He started coughing hard, and he bent double, clinging to a nearby sapling to steady himself. His heart raced and his sight blurred. He closed his eyes.

When he opened them, his vision was hazy. He stepped forward and heard a crack, felt something crunch under his feet. The snow underneath him drifted in jagged patches. He leaned closer, willing his eyes to see true. It was not snow at all. Bones lay scattered in a random jumble about the ground. Unburied, multitudinous human bones. Skulls with empty eye sockets stared out at him. Ribcages, empty of organs and bleached white with sun, protruded from the soft white ground. He turned away and saw yet more bones on the ground farther off, unmistakable now for what they were.

He must have groaned, made some unpleasant noise, because Hopkins drew to his side, musket raised.

"What is it, Alden? What have you seen?"

"The... the bones." John hated the way his voice quavered.

"What?" Hopkins frowned at him, then followed his gaze. "Ah. Yes, we encountered this on our first expedition. They do lie about, here. It is curious why these are not buried, whilst we've found others in graves," he said.

John did not reply. He was having enough trouble staying upright. Hopkins stared at him a moment longer, then turned away.

"There are two huts ahead, with hides and baskets and such. I ought to see to them." He strode away and gave John a moment to try to regain his composure.

"Bradford says that it is God's will which has cleared the land of the previous inhabitants, so that we might reside here without fear," an inquisitive voice said behind him. John turned to see Winslow peering down his nose at the ground.

"It looks to me rather that God has cursed this place, if he has aught to do with it at all," muttered John. His voice shook.

Winslow cocked his head to the side. "It does seem less like the work of God than of the Devil, to have reduced a village to bones."

Chapter Seven

Also, cold and wet lodging had so tainted our
people, for scarce any of us were free from
vehement coughs, as if they should continue long
in that estate it would endanger the lives of many,
and breed diseases and infection amongst us.
Again, we had yet some beer, butter, flesh, and
other such victuals left, which would quickly be all
gone, and then we should have nothing to comfort
us in the great labor and toil we were like to
undergo at the first.

—*Mourt's Relation*, 1622

Saturday, 2 December 1620

John stood at *Mayflower*'s rail next to Hopkins and watched
the whales. The great beasts visited the ship every day and
frolicked in the waters about her. Today it was a mother and
her calf. The sun shone warm, and John felt the heat of it
penetrating his doublet. It was nice to feel warm, for just a
moment. These days he often found himself wracked with
chills he could not shake off. The mother whale was enjoying
the sensation as well, for she sunbathed along the top of the
water. She lay so still for so long that he began to wonder if
the whale might be dead. She floated so close by the ship that
several onlookers, passengers and sailors alike, came on deck
to stare.

"D'you know 'ow much it'd be worth, back 'ome?" said
one sailor to another, who sighed.

"Don't suppose any of this lot would 'ave brought an
'arpoon wiv 'em, do ya?" he replied.

"No, indeed," said Hopkins with equal wistfulness. "It'd be mighty good, too, to send back oil and start to pay down our debt."

The sailors looked over at Hopkins, then back out at the whale. One clapped the other on the shoulder and they disappeared into the crew's cabins. John wondered how they would have gone about harvesting the whale, even if they were able to kill it. It was so large that he couldn't envision the force of men it would take to move it.

"Oh, it has been an age if it has been a day since I last saw you," came a familiar voice at his shoulder. John's heart skipped a beat. He turned and wiped his dripping nose on his sleeve. There stood Miss Mullins. She looked drawn, but she smiled at his face. The sight of her made him smile, too.

"Aye, and how do you fare, Miss Mullins?"

"Well enough, though I wish for a few days' leave of this wretched boat, as you have just returned from," she admitted as she looked out at the coast.

"It may not be so pleasant as you imagine," he murmured. The memory of skulls littering the ground made him shiver.

"'Twould no doubt be lovelier than this place," she replied without hesitation. "Have you not seen the situation 'tween decks? Every man and woman coughs without ceasing, and the children grow worse by the day. I've not much hope for little Peregrine."

He furrowed his brows in confusion, and she recognized his startlement.

"Ah! 'Tis right, you were away. Good tidings, then. Mistress White was delivered of a boy, and both lived. A few days past now, and healthy enough at the birth, but the sickness spreads so. 'Tis a troubling time to have a babe in arms."

John's relief overwhelmed him. He was spared the agony of witnessing another birth, and his gratitude now extended to Master Eaton and Standish for suggesting that John accompany the exploring party.

"I should hate to have such a sickness rampant when I have my own children to care for. It would be terrible to see your own child undergo such a thing, would it not, Goodman Alden?"

John blanched. His own children? Perish the thought. It would be nightmarish to have a child survive birth and then be struck ill in the first days of life. How could someone bear to lose a babe in arms just days after bringing it into the world? It was monstrous to have children at all if you could not protect them.

He was spared the need to make any response by the reappearance of the sailors with muskets in hand. They laughed as they approached the rail. One raised his weapon and sighted at the whale, floating at the surface of the water.

"You talk of 'ow nice it'd be to 'ave the plunder from such a prize, but you do naught to take it in your grasp. What use are ya?" the sailor asked. He took his sight off the beast and tore open a pouch of powder and shot.

"There is no purpose to shooting at it; it will wake and swim elsewhere," protested Hopkins.

"It lies 'alf a musket shot away. It looks dead already, lyin' there so quiet like. If I can startle it awake, then we will know for certain whether it yet lives, and if it is dead then all shall be richer men." He loaded the musket. The match cord was burning, held a quarter inch away from the pan.

"It yet lives—just look upon the thing and you can tell. Even if it were dead," Hopkins argued, "none of our men know how to harvest the oil from it, nor could we float it to shore from this distance." *Mayflower* was at that time anchored about a mile from shore. Nevertheless, the sailor shrugged this off and took his aim at the creature.

"What use is that?" Miss Mullins demanded, marching toward the sailor just as he lowered his finger to the trigger. John heard an explosive crack and, without thinking, grabbed Miss Mullins about the waist and swung her around, turning his back to the musket. She yelped a little, surprised at the sudden contact, but he had grown familiar enough with the sound of a musket shot to recognize that this one went awry.

"You would have him shoot at it for no purpose?" she demanded, wriggling away from him.

Her elbow made contact with his ribs when he seized her, and he coughed, trying to shake his head. He stepped away from her and gestured at the sailor.

The musket had backfired; the barrel and shaft were held apart in his hands. His face was streaked with powder, but no serious harm had come to the man. At the noise, the mother whale snuffled at the water's surface, flipped herself over, and swam away, her calf close by her side.

Miss Mullins looked back at John, crossed her arms, then dropped them and fidgeted with the waistband of her apron. Her expression was strange, and she seemed, for once, to have nothing to say. His own arms felt warm where they held her. It was necessary, of course. To keep her from harm. It was to protect her that he did such a thing. He struggled to articulate this thought through his subsiding cough.

"I would not have had you nearer that blast."

She glanced at the cursing sailor and back to John.

"It is the will of God," she said, "which protected the beasts and injured the man. It's just as Bradford said, when that other wretched sailor died. It pleased God to smite him."

Looking at the sailor, singed and irate, John would have enjoyed thinking that God intervened, but he could not bring himself to believe it. After all, God did not intervene on behalf of the countless people from the village just a few miles inland. While the villagers may have been heathens, they could be no less faithful to God than the huge, mindless beasts in the water. There was no path he could follow to reach the Separatists' way of thinking. But Miss Mullins seemed to embrace their tenet of God's direct involvement in everyday life. He raised a hand and massaged his chest. Perhaps the blow to his ribs was harsher than he'd realized, for there was a throbbing pain in his left breast for which he could think of no other attribution.

Thursday, 7 December 1620

John's cough worsened by the day. He moaned and rolled over on his mattress. The soreness in his throat spread to an ache in his bones. Even if he wished to go, he was in no state to join the third exploring party. He was just one among many men who had been on one of the first two expeditions but were now in ill health and could not venture forth again. The party was much reduced: fifteen men, including several sailors. The sailors went in the hope of finding Indians with whom they could make trade. Though all were bone-weary, Governor Carver, Standish, Hopkins, and Bradford went, determined to find a place for settlement, and sickness would not keep them confined to their straw-stuffed pallets. Howland accompanied his employer, Carver, leaving John with no friend to aid him through his sickness.

When the shallop left on Wednesday morning, the explorers carried with them a small body wrapped in canvas. Jasper More was a child who, along with his three siblings, was placed in the care of the Separatists. Miss Mullins told

John that the father of the four More children paid for their passage. The father believed the children were the product of his wife's affair, not his own flesh and blood. He divorced their mother and, when he took custody of the children, he shipped them off. This man abandoned his family to the will of God and strangers, and now his son was dead. He would never hear of it; he had no intention of discovering even if all his children were to die. It was unbearable.

John groaned at the fire that spread through him. His fingers tingled, and he could not tell if they were hot or cold. He could not feel his toes. A wave rolled the ship, and pain shot up his back from his buttocks. John detested this ship. He was beginning to dread the months-long return trip to England. Perhaps he ought to choose to settle, instead. He needn't endure the hardships of the travel back, the poor rations, the loneliness, the inevitable scurvy which already beset the crew. But then, once they reached England, there would be fresh food and beer and the company of civilization, which could cure all ills. Arrival back in Southampton would herald a warm bed, a decent meal, a mug of good ale, and the hope of lasting good health—at least, a better hope of it than had anyone in New England. *Mayflower*'s gray arrival here was the dreary precursor to argument, cold, sickness, and two deaths thus far. More death would follow.

Images came unbidden into his mind: the faces of those he knew, blanched and weak. He saw Howland's body, stiff and unmoving. Standish's head, red hair trailing, buried with a fine bow in an Indian graveyard. Miss Mullins...

John was infuriated with the Separatists and all their claims of God's intervention. Was it God's plan that so many of their own people should fall ill in this accursed harbor? If God watched over the Separatists, could they not see he was angry? That he did not approve of the ways of the reformers?

Nay, nor of those who ventured alongside them. John, too, was ill, with the sickness that caused two deaths already; would he die in this godless place? Sickness plagued them, and alongside it the threat of the Indians loomed ever more dangerous in his thoughts. Whether by savages or by sickness, John could see in his mind the deaths that awaited all aboard. He saw Bradford's black mustache, stark against the bloody snow after an Indian attack. Mistress Hopkins cradling her poor sick babe.

A scream aroused John from his half-dreaming nightmare. His body was soaked, and he could not tell if it was from sweat or the sea spray. The dampness 'tween decks, always troublesome, had worsened since they came to anchor. The passengers needed to find settlement, so they could all leave this dreary ship empty and ready for John's return to England.

Another scream and a shout from above focused his mind again. He sat upright, blanket clutched around his shoulders, lank hair tangled in his face. It had grown too long in his months at sea. He swept it aside and tried to stand, but as he rose, he found his vision clouded by black spots. He paused, crouching, and took a long breath in and out. He clutched at the hull of the ship lest he lose his balance in his blindness.

"Goodman Alden?" Miss Mullins asked.

He blinked, the darkness clearing away, and looked up at her. Her concern for his well-being was evident in her blue eyes. Lines crossed between her brows, and her lips were pursed. Despite her apparent anxiety, her presence was solid and reassured him. She did not tremble from chill or cough. She looked far from the death he saw in his nightmares. He wanted to reach out to her, to touch her, to hold her close. Whether for her comfort or his own, he knew not. But, that would not do.

She somehow understood. She grasped his arm and helped him lie back against his pillow.

"What happened?" he asked, remembering the shout that caused his alarm.

"Mistress Bradford has fallen overboard," Miss Mullins told him. "She has drowned."

Mistress Bradford? That shy, petite woman who said little that was not in praise of God or her husband?

"Where has she gone?" he asked, his fevered delirium confusing his words.

She laid a wet cloth on his forehead. It was cool, and he closed his eyes in relief.

"She is on the deck, awaiting the exploring party's return. They will take her to shore to bury her, as they did with little Jasper More when they departed."

"No," John said, opening his eyes to squint at her. "Her soul." What would happen to his soul, if he died here? There was no priest to say a litany over his body. The Separatists did not even believe in saying services over burials.

"She awaits God's final judgment, as all of us must."

Feeling dizzy, John closed his eyes again. In darkness, he felt her hand stroke his hair, felt the cool drip of water from the cloth fall onto his earlobe. Was dying here any different from dying in England, if Jesus would come to earth to judge the living and the dead? If, at his coming, all people would arise and give an accounting of their own deeds, and those who had done good would enter eternal life, and those who had done evil would enter eternal fire? John felt the fire inside him growing, threatening to swallow him and take him to damnation.

"I believe in God the Father Almighty," John said, reciting the Apostles' Creed from the Book of Common Prayer, "maker of heaven and earth."

He heard her voice join his recitation from memory, despite not having looked through his book for weeks. They were familiar words, comforting words, words in which the Separatists put no belief. It was relief to hear her speak them, to believe she might still have faith in the King's church.

"I believe in the Holy Ghost; the holy Catholic Church; the communion of saints; the forgiveness of sins; the resurrection of the body; and the life everlasting." He took a slow, deep breath. Perhaps if God were to take him now, he would know at least that John bore faith in the English church. "Amen."

Priscilla left Goodman Alden sleeping, her face hot. She fanned herself with her hand, but the action was ineffective against his suffusive warmth. It seemed as though his fever burned her. Her palms sweated, and her cheeks flushed every time she went near him. Even after their numerous encounters, how could she still feel so? She feigned normalcy in his presence, tried to act as she did with any other man, but she could not remember where to put her hands, how to pitch her voice. She wanted to speak to him all the time, but when she worked up the courage, found herself stupid, with nothing of interest to say. Her heart pounded in her ears with so much force that she could not think. She was conscious of every movement, yet her hands reached for him unrestrained.

She could not help but wonder what he thought of her. Did he think of her at all, the way she did him? When he was on board ship, she was often aware of his presence and stole glances at him. There was no purpose in these looks, yet she felt compelled to watch him, to engrave on her memory the prominent line of his nose, the round folds of his ears, the calloused pads of his fingers. She often caught herself doing this, and her throat constricted and her chest tightened and she forced herself to look away.

She flopped down onto her stomach. The stiff buckram of her kirtle pressed into her chest and her abdomen, several inches below her belly button. It was uncomfortable, but she did not mind the discomfort—at least, not enough to move. Instead, she settled into herself, mind drifting until she could feel the firm, supportive garment shift with each of her slow breaths.

"Priscilla?" asked Elizabeth Tilley from above her head.

Priscilla closed her eyes, took a deep breath, then rolled over to face her friend, hugging her pillow to her stomach.

"Are you poorly? You look quite pale."

"Tilley," Priscilla moaned, "why do I feel this way? I do not understand it."

"How do you feel?"

"As though Goodman Browne's mastiff has sat on my chest and squeezed all the breath out of me."

"Is your kirtle constricting? Should it be loosened?"

"Hah. No, it is comfortable enough. In any case, I feel it whether I wear it or not. It is what I am thinking about that makes me feel so, not what I wear."

Tilley did not seem to understand. "What is it you are thinking of, when you feel this way?"

"Not what, dear Tilley, but whom."

Tilley gasped. "Do not tell me you are love sick?"

Priscilla scoffed at the idea before she'd even given it consideration. "How can I be love sick when it happened even on the very first occasion of our meeting, without having spoken a word aloud to one another?"

Tilley shrugged her shoulders. "Your feelings seem to fit the description of love sickness, though I do not know how you could be in love and not know it for yourself."

"It is not love sickness, Tilley. It is not sensible to love him, and I refuse to do so. It would do no one any good to be in love with him."

"Then, what will you do? You cannot live with short breaths under a mastiff's rear forever."

"If I do not think about it, it will go away," Priscilla said. "And soon enough, he will go too, and I shall have no more chances to think upon him."

"So, it *is* Goodman Alden you think about?" Tilley asked with a sly grin.

Priscilla sat up and stared at her friend, wide-eyed.

"Priscilla, he is the one man around whom you are not quite yourself."

Priscilla flung her pillow at her friend. "I am always myself. In any case, as I said before, I do not love him. God help me, what can I do?"

"Perhaps God *can* help," Tilley suggested. "Remember Psalm 23? 'The Lord to me a shepherd is, want therefore shall not I.'" She hummed the tune.

"The Lord to me a shepherd is, want therefore shall not I," Priscilla repeated. She scrunched up her nose. "Tilley, I do not see how this verse refers to a cure for love sickness."

"I think it refers to everything," Tilley replied. "If you fill your heart with the Lord, you shall have no room in it to want anything besides."

Priscilla chewed on her lower lip, thinking this over.

"Well, what of you? Do you not blush and giggle when even Goodman Howland's name is mentioned?" Priscilla asked, wanting to embarrass her friend. Sure enough, Tilley's face glowed, and she buried it in her hands.

"How can I help it when he is so charming?" asked Tilley. "At least I do not deny that I think him so. And handsome, too! Is it not miraculous to think that he has been touched by the hand of God and saved from death?"

Priscilla groaned, teasing Tilley further. Howland and the miracle of his saving was one of Tilley's favorite subjects to discuss.

"Of course, of course, because God saved him just so that he might become your husband, Miss Elizabeth?"

"I do not see why not," Tilley said. She tried to hold her head up high but dissolved into a fit of giggles. "I cannot imagine it, Priscilla. He would want someone far more interesting and capable than me."

"Who is more interesting than you? You have lived in England, in Holland, and now will settle in the New World! You've seen more of the world than I," Priscilla huffed, feigning jealousy.

"But you are so comely. And you sing so well!"

Priscilla laughed. "Are those my finest attributes? I shall be quite useless to a husband."

Wednesday, 13 December 1620

The triumphant air of the returning exploring party was devastated upon their arrival. The death toll doubled since their departure, and two bodies awaited them: those of Mistress Bradford and of Master Chilton. His young daughter Mary held to her mother, as his body was passed over to the longboat for burial ashore. Bradford's face was stony, and he was silent. He disappeared after the ceremony and stayed out of sight. The other passengers let him be.

In spite of his solemn reception, Standish would not be put off. He settled himself next to John, who lay recovering from his ailment. John's cough faded, and his nose returned to erratic dripping rather than congestion, but he was haggard, exhausted from a lack of sleep. Though his nightmares started in delirium, even after his fever broke he continued to dream either of the dead and dying faces of his friends or of the agonies of eternal fire.

"Well, Goodman Alden," Standish said, as he removed his helmet and ran a hand through his sweat-darkened red hair. "We shall need your helpful hands to once more mend our shallop. Her mast broke into three pieces, and we are lucky to have kept her steady enough to bring her back."

John grunted, sitting up on his pallet. He had no desire to lay his hands on the shallop again.

"We shall be in need of it, in good repair, once we come to our new harborage."

"You have found a place, then?" John asked, his tongue thick with disuse.

"Aye, though Carver wishes to discuss it before it is decided. It has a small brook running by, and abandoned Indian cornfields that we may plow over to plant our own crop. The harbor is a good depth for ships, and there is a fair hill on which we can mount our ordnance."

"You are certain the cornfields are abandoned? There are not Indians nearby?" John asked, alert. Would the passengers settle in an Indian village? Was the ground there, too, littered with bones?

"They are absent from our proposed place, but they live a day's sail away. Far enough, says Hopkins, though they fired many arrows upon us when they met us at our encampment." Standish's eyes gleamed. He'd reached the part of the story he wanted to discuss further, but waited for John to ask for more.

"You were attacked by savages?" John asked, willing to play along to hear more of Standish's story. An attack by Indians was worthy news indeed.

"Ah, Alden," Standish cried, warming up to his role as storyteller. "They came upon us, whooping and hollering, making their fearsome noise. The men had put half the guns in the shallop already." He sighed and shook his head. "I was prepared with my snaphance musket and got off a shot at them at once, which I dare say did startle them. And yet, there was one such hale and hearty young man, he would not fall even after three shot of musket hit him, and instead yet ran away! And wearing naught but a loincloth, even in the snow and chill." The admiration in his voice was unmistakable. "Still, then he called them all off, and they scampered away. We picked up a great number of their arrows, tipped with brass and hart's horn and eagle's claws. At least I'd insisted we prepare a barricade, for we'd heard the hideous cries of wolves or foxes in the night. Some men's coats were hanging off it, and Howland can show you his shirt was shot through and through with arrows."

"Is settlement so close by these savages wise?" John asked, troubled. Had he been among the explorers, no doubt his musket would have been one of those unready.

"It is fifteen leagues or more by boat, not an easy journey to make overland. Carver insists that if we can truck with them, we may be able to come to some peaceable arrangement. And, in any case, as Bradford says, it pleased God to vanquish our enemies and give us deliverance. How can we fear the savages, when we have God's providence to aid us?" He smirked, his faith in the Separatists about as deep as John's. He cared not for religion of any stripe, but for the things he could accomplish with cutlass and musket. It seemed to John that Standish respected the Indians, but in the way that a hunter might respect his prey. In a way that meant when he was able to kill them, he would be proud to display their carcasses.

"It will be good to have a place to settle," John said. Once the passengers found a place for their settlement, he could unload the ship and be on his way back to England. Whether their plantation was in the midst of a den of savages or not, John would not tarry there long. Soon he would be on his way home.

Chapter Eight

There was but 6 or 7 sound persons; who to their great commendations, be it spoken, spared no pains, night nor day, but with abundance of toil and hazard of their own health, fetched them wood, made them fires, dressed them meat, made their beds, washed their loathsome clothes, clothed and unclothed them. In a word did all the homely, and necessary offices for them, which dainty and queasy stomachs cannot endure to hear named...

—William Bradford, *Of Plymouth Plantation*, 1651

Friday, 22 December 1620

The passengers carried with them a map of the New World which was made by the famed explorer Captain John Smith. On it, their chosen harborage, discovered by the third exploring party, was called "New Plymouth." It was a fitting designation, for their last departure in England was from Plymouth. It was where they left their companion ship *Speedwell* behind, along with their country. Plymouth would now carry another meaning, the appellation for their new home, the place where many of the passengers would begin again. *Mayflower* weighed anchor from her place in Cape Cod Bay. It was but a short voyage to Plymouth Harbor. Two natural spits of land stretched out on either side of Plymouth Bay and enclosed it in a near-embrace. There was a single point of entry between them, through which *Mayflower* passed. To their right rose a high promontory covered with pine trees; to the left, a narrow strip of rocky sand.

The passengers were kept aboard in their new anchorage for two days, due to vicious storms. The ship rocked in the wind, and the cover of clouds sank them into darkness even during the middle of the day. In the midst of all this turmoil, Goodwife Allerton's birthing pains began. Priscilla, who was *not* looking at him because she was in love with him, saw the horrified expression cross Goodman Alden's face. She was shocked to recognize the look of terror in his eyes. She tried to recall where she had seen it before—so much misfortune plagued their company these last months that it took a moment to remember. But of course—it was during that other childbirth, the one when Goodman Alden was off ship. She saw the same look on the faces of little Constance and Giles Hopkins. They were terrified because they had seen their mother die in childbirth—and now Alden shared the same expression. Her heart squeezed, making her chest ache. What had the man experienced, to give him such a look?

She watched Alden retreat to the hold. She hesitated a moment before following after. He had fainted from his illness in front of her just two weeks before, and though he was much recovered, he still did not look well. He often nodded off in conversation, and his eyes were bloodshot and underlined with dark crescents.

She had never been in the hold before. The space was well filled with furniture and crates, sacks and barrels. Goodman Alden hunkered down in a corner between a row of barrels and the giant hogsheads. Priscilla sat against the ladder, wishing to lend him some strength but unsure how. She did not even know if he realized she was there. They listened to the cries from above, muffled by the distance Alden put between himself and Goodwife Allerton.

As these things go, the birth was brief. It was Goody Allerton's fifth child, and she was well used to the process. Priscilla waited for the wail that would signal a healthy babe, but it never came. Instead, weighty silence descended. The silence was worse than the howls of pain. Priscilla knew what it meant without needing to be told.

Alden stood and banged his fist against the large cask. It was then that he noticed Priscilla. His face was red and shiny with unasked-for tears. His jaw worked as though he was restraining himself from shouting. She watched him fight to regain control of his features.

"Do you not think this a bad omen?" he asked her, but he did not leave her time to reply. "These Brownists, they are arrogant enough to think that God would follow them here. Does this seem like the symbol of a God who is watching over us?"

"Not all babes in England live either. Mayhap God desired to spare him this imperfect place."

"Imperfect? We have navigated to a place barren of the life it once housed in plenty. A place where bones litter the ground, and, instead of the new life we expected, our arrival is met with more death." He shook his head in his fury. "God is absent from this place, and we have none with us who are able to reach him. This is the place where you wish to bear children? How can you desire so foolish a thing, when the threat of death looms ever closer over you?"

"You believe the desire for children to be foolish?"

"Aye, if you cannot safeguard them. What is the purpose of trying to have a child if you will lose it in childbearing, or days after to sickness or an Indian attack?"

"I am not so afraid of loss that I will not try." Priscilla stood and took a step toward him. "There is no guarantee that any of us will survive. If this sickness kills me, would you blame my parents for having birthed me? Would you rather they lived childless, to protect me? On the contrary, the concern you bear for your unborn children means you would be their staunch protector. Do you not trust your own hands to safeguard your children?"

John sniffed. His face was still wet, and he rubbed his cheek with the cuff of his shirt.

"It matters little what I think. We have found a harbor and a place for your plantation. Once Master Jones has left you all ashore, I will depart this accursed place and no longer obscure your mind's idyll with my opinions."

He brushed past her to ascend the ladder to the gun room. She looked after him, a muddle of emotion. It was possible, after all, that Tilley had been right. If that was the case, the pain in her chest made perfect sense.

But, Priscilla had been right, too—Goodman Alden did not desire children, thought her foolish and incapable, and did not even intend to stay in the New World. What use was it to love such a man as him, who would leave her brokenhearted?

Monday, 25 December 1620

"It seems not right," said John, "to be at such labor on Christmas Day." He sat with Howland on the beach, drinking fresh water out of wooden mugs.

He was still tired, not sleeping well at night. His cough returned, though his fever remained at bay. Today, no man who could work was permitted to rest, for they were felling and riving and hewing timber to provide themselves with building material. Despite his weakness, John did not object. He felt it would benefit him more to use his body than to sit aboard the plague-ridden ship. There was pottage for breakfast, made of poultry bones and water. He devoured his ration.

"Aye, it may seem so to you," Howland agreed. There were days when John forgot his friend held to the Separatist ideals.

They all observed the Sabbath the day prior, remaining on board the ship. But today, they set to work as though it were any other day, not minding the fact of Christmas. It was Christmas already. Five months had passed since John left home.

"So long as Jesus dwells in your heart, does the day make much matter?" Howland asked.

"Where was Jesus when Goodman Prower died yesterday?" John bit back.

His comment met with silence.

John cursed himself and ran his sleeve across his nose. The bottom of it burned with the tenderness of this oft-repeated motion. He wished for companionship in his beliefs but had once again sought it from the wrong source. Even the merchant adventurers did not object to working this day. The passengers—now colonists—desired to begin their efforts without delay. They had settled on a site for their plantation at last and would soon begin to build. They longed to disembark from *Mayflower* once and for all, and to no longer rely on the good will of Master Jones. John willed it too, that he might soon be free of New England.

"How do you fare?" he asked, hoping Howland would forgive his hasty remark.

It was not without real concern for his friend. The sickness had spread throughout the congregation, and with ever more deadly consequence. Howland was a hearty man, but he had been weakened by his fall overboard.

"Oh, I imagine I fare as well as any," Howland replied with a small smile. "Indeed, there are many who do worse."

Indeed. Six of their number had perished already.

"Alden! Howland!" Standish shouted at them. "Are you about the ordnance platform?"

"Aye, Captain." It was the second day they were felling timber, but their work had been interrupted by the cry of Indians in the wood, which caused them all alarm. Even now, John picked up his musket from the pebbled sand next to him, as he rose, and followed Standish up the hill. They needed to build a mount for their cannons as soon as they could.

"The hill is defensible. There's a clear field of vision all ways round, as far as the trees allow. We'll get the ordnance pieces from Jones when we have somewhere to put them, and I don't much take to the idea he might sail off and leave us without any means of defense against the savages."

John trudged up the hill after the little man who, short though he was in stature, was quick and sturdy. John's breathing was rough even after such a short exertion, and he stopped to cough. He was still astonished that the settlers chose to build here, but, he reminded himself, it was none of his concern. He would help do what he could, so that they could unload *Mayflower* as soon as may be.

"There's no doubt we'll want a proper fortress, a place wherein the women and children may go in event of attack. For now, though, Governor Carver insists the common house and other dwellings take precedence," Standish snarled. "So, for the moment it will suffice to build a platform, so Master Jones will let us have our ordnance off his ship."

The labor force was split between the common house and the ordnance platform. Without a proper defense, time spent building houses might amount to time wasted, if the Indian threat became any more tangible than hollers and cries in the forest. But Carver was addressing the settlers' more urgent need for shelter and a dry place to store their provision. This very evening some of the men working on shore would stay overnight without shelter from the snow.

"It needs to be taller than the surrounding grounds and strong enough to hold our cannon," said Standish, once again rousing John from his thoughts. "We should be able to keep a lookout and have the firing advantage over any of those savages who come this way."

Master Eaton, being a house carpenter, was downhill overseeing the building of the common house.

"We'll need to fell more timber before we can build a frame," said John.

Standish nodded. "Join Goodman Tinker, then; he's the wood sawyer. When we've hewn enough to start with, come to me, and we can measure out the place." Standish was no good with tools, but he was so accustomed to command that he was quite out of place trying to find something to do among the woodworkers. He accompanied them to the site where Tinker shouted directions, often sitting on a stump to cough. The small man had lost some of the vim and vigor he had exhibited when they worked together on the shallop, but he knew his craft and directed the operation well, despite having caught the sickness. He waved away concerns with a smile, and John let him be.

John joined a small group of men who worked on a cluster of pine trees. There were not enough tools for every man to work at once, but the labor was difficult, and they were glad of the breaks. Once a few of the trees were felled, they were stripped of their branches and hewn into rough squares fit for use in framing dwellings.

John took up an axe and chopped at the broad trunk of a pine tree. The bark was thick and scaly. The upper branches swayed with the force of his efforts. There were, in fact, many broad trees about. He was eager to examine the grain and weight, once a few more trees were felled, to assess the quality of this New World wood. The colonists needed to use the wood right away, but John wondered in the back of his mind if some might be set aside, to be well seasoned and dried. If anyone were to begin a cooperage here, he would need a store of well-dried oak. Fresh-cut staves would lose moisture as the wood aged, which would damage casks. Casks made in this way would be unreliable for holding beer or water.

He shook his head. *What thoughts, to imagine building a cooperage here.* He tried to rid himself of the very notion.

Tuesday, 16 January 1621

The unskilled crew worked and learned through many failures how best to build something from nothing. Eaton taught John the essential knowledge of building a house, and John tried to teach the men who worked with him. The work crew changed, day by day, as the sickness kept more men aboard ship and the common house grew and required more attention. On many days, it rained hard enough that the weather prevented them from work. In time, the frame of the platform was raised, and planks were laid, piece by piece, to create a floor. In the evenings, tired though John was, he welcomed the aches in his muscles. It was the kind of pain that resulted from good work, and not from illness, though his breath grew shorter and his cough worse from each day to the next.

In mid-January, the common house was complete, and the working men could stay ashore overnight without freezing. The wattle-and-daub walls kept the interior warm, and they'd coated paper with linseed oil to serve as windows. They packed as many beds inside as could lie by one another, and it was crowded with people. All were sick to some degree, though most were still able to work. Most space not filled with beds was occupied by muskets, cutlasses, and a small portion of their store of provisions from *Mayflower*. Half of one wall was set back, with an opening in the ceiling acting as a chimney. A grate made from stones created a space for a kitchen fire, and within a few days, the wall behind the hearth was blackened with smoke. The corner of one wall was also blackened near the ceiling, where the fresh thatch had caught fire. They'd worried, at first, that Indians had fired the building, but it was revealed the fire in the hearth had not been banked; a stray spark was the probable culprit. New thatch was laid to replace the burned portion, and John marveled at the neatness of the building they created, despite the general lack of skilled woodworkers in their midst.

John rose one morning in these accommodations, his head pounding a little before the day even began. He refused the stew offered to break his fast, though it contained some fowl which was killed the day before. He felt that anything in his stomach was bound to make him sick. He had sweated through his shirt overnight, kept warm by the closeness of so many bodies in the common house, and when he went outside the chill pierced through the wet garment to his skin. He breathed and felt the familiar piercing cold in his lungs. It seemed to replace the sickly, stuffy air inside the common house. Hard work kept him warm, day after day, and he set about clearing a fallen tree of its small branches. After an hour, sweat poured into his eyes, and his vision blurred. He sat on the tree's trunk and took a drink of water.

At midday, he felt well enough to eat a little of the stew left over from the morning. The common house was set close to the shore, and John, who ate outside, was the first to see

Mayflower's longboat approaching the beach. Standish rode along with a couple of sailors and the all too familiar sight of a canvas-wrapped body. Their toll now numbered eleven dead. John walked toward the beach to greet the incoming party.

"Ho, Alden! I take it Browne and Goodman have returned from their adventure?" Standish asked, by way of greeting.

"Indeed they have. Just imagine, they were not kidnapped by Indians at all, but lost their way in the snow with their dogs. They sit by the fireside, warming their feet even now." He jested, but the disappearance of two of their men terrified everyone in the plantation. For two nights they were missing, and everyone was on edge, imagining an Indian attack was imminent. John's belt of powder and shot was always about his hip, in addition to the musket he carried everywhere.

"Are Master Bradford and the governor about?" Standish asked.

"They've both taken ill and lie sick in the common house. If they be awake, you can go in and speak with them. Is there news from the ship?"

Standish spent the last few days aboard, caring for all the sick who still lay there, including his own wife.

"Aye. Master Jones wants the governor informed that he's decided he will not leave for England until spring." John's mouth opened, and his eyebrows rose. "He says too many of his men have taken ill, and he'll wait until their condition improves. The winds will also be more favorable for an eastern journey in two or three months' time."

John felt his head swimming. He was to remain in Plymouth for two or three more months? How, when an Indian kidnapping or burning of their buildings was sure to come any day?

"You may yet have the opportunity to aid me in quelling the Indian threat, Alden." Standish grinned.

"Aye," John acknowledged, "if the sickness does not kill us all first. Who have you there?" He pointed at the corpse.

Standish's smile drooped into a dejected frown. "It is Goodman Tinker. What's more, his wife and son are soon to follow."

John clenched his jaw, but he was not surprised. The sawyer had stayed on land until three days ago and had been getting worse all the time.

"Bury him tonight, once it has gotten dark," Captain Standish advised. "We do not want the Indians to see how many of us perish. They are sure to take advantage of our weakness if they know of it."

"Do you think they watch us so persistently?" John asked.

"I've no doubt of it." Standish raised his eyes to the tree line. "Even now, there are doubtless eyes upon us."

Standish clapped him on the shoulder as he strode past and went into the common house. John shivered. He felt the back of his neck prickle, as though he could feel the gaze of Indian eyes upon his nape.

It took an afternoon's work before John accustomed himself to the idea that he would not be leaving Plymouth for some months yet. At least conditions would improve, now that they had built the common house. Since the ordnance platform was also done, they were at work now assembling a frame for the next dwelling. Carver planned for nineteen homes to line a broad main street, going downhill from the ordnance platform to the harbor, where the shallop could dock. He could almost see it, looking down the slope from his vantage point at the top of the hill. The abandoned Indian cornfields stretched out to his left. They would, in spring, be planted with the seed of Indian corn and English barley and peas. They could complete half a dozen houses by April if they kept this pace. The sickness was so rampant now, that they must have reached the peak of its danger.

John hefted his axe over one shoulder and picked up his musket. Dusk was beginning to fall, and it was too dark to continue hewing timber. As he walked downhill toward the common house, he imagined a fair street lined with neat and tidy houses. All the chimneys would be spewing smoke, the way the common house's did, for if this land had anything in plenty it was wood. No matter the weather outdoors, the inside of a home would be cozy and warm, with the corn they raised cooking in a pottage or a loaf. He could see Miss Mullins, sitting by the hearth, stirring the contents of a great iron kettle, looking up with a smile as he came in the door. Cold wind whipped across his face, and he shook his head. It was mere fantasy, to think that way.

He dropped his axe by the common house and leaned his musket against the wall. He bent and, in one swift motion, hefted the canvas-wrapped body of Goodman Tinker over his shoulder. His head spun at the sudden weight, and he leaned against the common house wall to allow the blackness clouding his vision to clear. He picked up his musket and hooked his fingers through the handle of a spade.

They buried their dead at the top of a small hill which sat just across their future main road from the common house. The hill abutted the water and looked out over Plymouth Bay. Trees were sparse enough that John could see the last remaining crescent of the sapphire sky, fading upward into a band of royal blue before being overcome by the darkness of space. John carried Tinker's body to the top of the hill, breathing hard. At the crest, he dropped his tools without ceremony but took care to lay the body down on the solid earth. He stayed bent over his knees for few moments, his lungs burning with exertion. He had grown so weak since this journey began. To not even be able to lift this small man, made frail by weakness and hunger. Tinker had laughed with merriment when they worked together, when trying to fit the pieces of the shallop had seemed the foremost of their concerns. John picked up the spade and tried not to think about it.

The ground was frozen, and he struck it hard, digging in. His shoulders burned with the strain he'd exerted on them all day, but he continued to pierce the ground, lifting chunks of dirt away from a widening hole. He hoped his shovel would not hit the frozen corpse of another *Mayflower* passenger, for their graves were left unmarked to keep the Indians none the wiser. He dug deeper, spadeful after spadeful of dirt, coming swifter and easier as he moved past the top layer of ice. He felt lightheaded from the exertion. His next thrust into the darkness missed its mark. It felt as though he heaved at nothing. He staggered, balance lost. The world was obscured by dark spots which swelled in front of him. He floated for a moment until his shoulder collided with the frozen ground.

Monday, 29 January 1621

Joseph cried. His shrill whine of pain woke Priscilla from her doze, and she crawled from her pallet 'tween decks and moved closer to him, to stroke his head and murmur meaningless assurances. He clutched at his ear, tugging at it and folding it over, manipulating it in any way he could think of, to try to relieve his pain. Priscilla pried his fingers away to examine it. The yellowish-white pus was starting to leak out of it again. She sighed. Joseph had not shared a silly face or smile with her in days.

The ship's surgeon, Giles Heale, had attributed the pus to an excess of yellow bile, and he offered a remedy of warm mustard water. This was an emetic and, true to its purpose, made Joseph cast his breakfast into a bucket. It seemed his humors were still not balanced, for the oozing pus had returned. Perhaps today Joseph would be able to eat some boiled turnips, which were hot and wet and would offer some countermeasure to his choleric disposition.

Priscilla's mother had also taken to lying in bed at all hours, unable to shake the alternating fevers and chills that came over her. Even Priscilla's father coughed now, but none of the passengers were without a cough, these days. Master Mullins and his servant, Robert Carter, spent their days ashore, laboring to fell trees and build the first dwellings in New Plymouth. Tilley was nearby, her father ailing too, her mother weak but trying to sustain him. Tilley helped her and tried to keep everyone on board cheerful with prayer and hymns. Tilley was humming a tune now, and Priscilla picked it up, stroking Joseph's head. She hoped the soothing melody would help stop his crying. It took a moment to realize which hymn she was humming. Once she did, she smiled and sang a few lines.

> *The Lord to me a shepherd is,*
> *want therefore shall not I.*
> *He in the folds of tender grass*
> *doth cause me down to lie.*
>
> *To waters calm me gently leads,*
> *restore my soul doth He;*
> *He doth in paths of righteousness*
> *For His name's sake lead me.*

She remembered the green meadow at the edge of Pipp Brook back in Dorking. Of course, there was the tannery next to the water in town, but the parsonage grounds upstream were lush. The soft grass slipped under her feet, and as she approached the riverbank in spring, the mud would ooze through her toes. Perhaps, one day, Town Brook, which ran parallel to the proposed main street of New Plymouth, would be lined on either side with tender grass, sparkling fish swimming beneath the clear surface. Plymouth would grow more beautiful as the weather warmed and the trees began to bud. The shades of gray and brown would be replaced by bright green and the white and pink of spring flowers. She could almost feel the tickle of the grass against her toes, when a loud whine from her brother interrupted her idyll and brought her from the meadow to the damp, creaking interior of the plague-ridden ship.

"Hush now, Joseph," she said, resuming her stroking of his hair. "Master Heale will be along in a while, and we will boil you some turnips for you to eat, so that your ear will feel well again."

Priscilla, Heale, and the others taking care of the sick did what they could, which seemed to amount to very little. She wiped fevered sweat with cool wet rags and gave the shivering patients blankets, where there were any to spare. If there were, they were the blankets of those already dead. She washed the sweat and stench out of what clothes and bedclothes the sick could spare, when there was so little to start with. Through dry, cracked lips, she spoon-fed thin pottage or boiled turnips, or whatever else Master Heale suggested might balance their humors, if there was anything in their store of provision which might be used. Everyone was mindful of the stores, knowing they might remain their primary supply of food until they could plant and harvest their crop. The ship's surgeon would also recommend emetics, laxatives, diuretics, or bloodletting, which he would carry out himself.

Priscilla's mother had been wracked with fever, and Heale bled her. It worked for a while; she grew clammy and shivered until Priscilla wrapped her up with blankets. In a matter of hours, she was feverish again. Priscilla was frustrated. It felt like there was nothing at all she could do to help her family. Tilley helped her mother tend her father, and she looked on the verge of tears each time her father's condition worsened. Mistress Hopkins, caring for her four children while her husband was on land, seemed to be at her wits' end. The one caretaker who did not seem to be overwhelmed was Captain Standish.

Standish, to Priscilla's surprise, took on the role of his wife's keeper with steadfastness. To her greater surprise, he extended the role to any on board who required his aid. He assisted Master Heale in bloodletting, helped with cooking and washing, and even tended to the ailments of the sailors, which grew greater by the day. She found him a reassuring presence, and she caught herself looking for him when she needed to find some point of constancy.

Joseph tugged at his ear and squirmed, but he did not whine. He knew that his crying out made everything more difficult, and he was trying all he could to keep it in. Priscilla stood and grabbed a stiff, dried-out rag from the corner of her mattress. She went to the bucket of fresh water that was carried aboard by the most recent longboat trip to shore. The freezing air outside penetrated through *Mayflower*'s belly, full as she was with people suffering fever. It was not cold enough today to leave a film of ice on top of the bucket, but it was enough to keep the water frigid. She dipped her rag inside and carried it, sopping wet and dripping between her fingers, over to her brother. She sat and laid his head on her lap, then brushed the cool cloth over his face.

"Sissy, when will it stop?" he asked, while she rubbed the cool rag around his ears.

"I'm certain, if we do as Master Heale suggests, you will soon be feeling better again," she reassured him, although her faith in Heale was waning.

It was agonizing to watch him lie there, when he was once so animated and quick to laugh. She hoped that the boiled turnips would help balance his humors. There was so little else she could do.

In the afternoon, Priscilla climbed up the ladder to the top deck to spend five minutes in the salty sea air. It refreshed her after the putrid stench of the 'tween deck where Master Heale's emetics, diuretics, and laxatives took their effect. She was happy to stretch her legs, too, after sitting so long with them folded under her and Joseph's head nestled in her lap. Hoping for five minutes without interruption, she slumped over the rail to regain her composure.

When she looked up, she spotted the place on deck where Goodman Alden had wrapped her in his arms to protect her from musket fire. It sounded so much more appealing when said that way than "he seized her and dragged her away from a coward's misfired shot." However it was said, she felt the warmth of his arms around her and could not help but smile at the memory.

No! she reminded herself. *It is no use to be in love with Goodman Alden. He is leaving New England with* Mayflower, *and in any case, he thinks you are a fool and does not return your interest.*

She spun about in a circle, her skirts flaring up beneath her, giggling at the impossibility of thinking about love when her family lay among many others, sick and dying on the deck below. She heard that even Alden himself was laid up in bed with fever, in the common house on land. How strange she was to have such frivolous thoughts at such a time. Her mother was right all along, and Goodman Alden too. She was a fool.

She stopped her twirl in time to glimpse Captain Standish climbing up the ladder. His head hung down, and he did not seem to have noticed her. She approached, never having seen him so dejected.

"Captain?" she asked. "What is wrong?"

He looked up at her, and she saw teardrops running down his face. He was without his corselet and helm, and his red hair glowed where the sun struck him. He blinked hard, each closure of his eyelids releasing more tears down his cheeks, but he did not weep or sob.

"She is dead," he said, "and now nothing can be done. What was the use of it all, of everything I did, if she is dead?" He sat down hard on the lid of the main hatch, which was perhaps a foot taller than the scrubbed wooden deck. His knees were level with his armpits, and he rested his elbows on them, lost in thought.

"Oh dear," Priscilla said, sitting next to him. Without thinking, she reached up an arm and stroked his head. It had become her automatic response to sadness, these past weeks. He did not seem to notice her. His hair was coarse and firm, very different to hers. She marveled that hair could even feel so different on a person outside her family, and realized it was the first time she had touched the head of a stranger.

"There is no purpose in it," he repeated, still staring into the empty space in front of him.

"Shh, it will be all right," she said. "She is in the hands of the Lord." Priscilla took his head and leaned it against her shoulder, still running her hand through his hair, and began to sing Psalm 23.

The Lord to me a shepherd is,
want therefore shall not I.
He in the folds of tender grass
doth cause me down to lie.

To waters calm me gently leads,
restore my soul doth he;
He doth in paths of righteousness
for his name's sake lead me.

And despite her resolution, despite the man now crying on her shoulder, despite her own foolishness, or perhaps because of it, Priscilla found that she wanted nothing more than the feeling of Goodman Alden's arms wrapped around her again.

February 1621

John opened his eyes to find the fiery red mustache of Miles Standish mere inches from his face. A low groan escaped him, but he could not find the strength to make his alarm more apparent. A warm spoon was pressed against his lips. His eyes fluttered shut.

When they opened next, it was brighter, and Miss Mullins sat by him, her eyes red and her cheeks streaked with dirt. He tried to lift his arm, to touch her cheek, but the cursed thing weighed as much as a hogshead full of oil. A cool cloth was pressed against his forehead, and he succumbed again to slumber.

He drifted in and out of consciousness, sometimes shivering, sometimes with his body on fire. Always his muscles ached, and his limbs felt too heavy to move. His nightmares were lurid, garish displays of the worst of his imagination. He saw a party of Indians, and though he knew not much what an Indian might look like, he knew that was what they were. They were lit by the torches they carried. They had come to burn the settlement. The torches went out, and all was blackness, until the cold, dead face of Goodman Tinker appeared with clumps of black dirt piling on top of his white corpse.

Sometimes these scenes were interrupted by the pleasant image of Miss Mullins, sitting in a chair by a fire, sewing in her hand. She laughed and her smile felt warm, and John reached out his hand, but as he stretched out his arm, her smile turned to a scream and she clutched at her protruding belly, round with child. He could not reach her, and she screamed as a pool of red grew, painting her smock red. Her screams stopped, just as the mangled body of an infant appeared, leaving his ears echoing in horrible silence.

These new visions joined his old, familiar nightmares, the memories of his mother and the scenes he had concocted during his last fever, of the deaths by sickness or murder of everyone he knew aboard *Mayflower*. Flashes of everything muddled together in a horrific stream, never ceasing but for his occasional brief consciousness.

He woke at last with a sense of clarity, the befuddlement of his restless sleeping gone, a residual ache lingering in his head. He sat up, and the world spun about him, his vision going dark and starry once more.

"Zounds," he croaked.

"Alden!" came a cry from nearby. "You waken at last!"

Howland came into John's view, kneeling by his side. "How do you fare?" Howland asked, his expression intent.

"Well enough," John murmured, one hand shielding his eyes.

"Aye, well, 'tis good to hear so. We were afeared you may pass along, for some time," Howland said. "The sickness has taken so many."

"How many?" John asked.

"Fifteen or sixteen now."

John sat up again, without repercussions this time, and looked about him. He was inside the common house on a pallet and surrounded by half a dozen men in the same situation.

"Standish?" he asked, remembering his presence but not seeing the captain in the room.

Howland's face creased with sorrow. "He is well, but Mistress Standish... she went to the Lord. The captain had been caring for her and many others, but she succumbed to it. There's naught he can do for her now, of course, but it doesn't stop him from railing about and fretting. He has taken to venturing into the woods to hunt for Indians."

John cursed. His head ached. He leaned into his hands until the pounding lessened.

Howland blanched. "Ah, pardon, Alden, you oughtn't to be worrying over this yet. You ought to sleep more and recover your own self."

"Aye," John agreed, grateful he need not say it.

He slept. When he woke, he knew not how many days or hours had passed. It was daylight. It was daylight when he'd spoken with Howland, but was this the same day, or the next? It was confounding to waken and not know whether a night had passed.

He looked up at the ceiling, breathing in and out. The scent of fresh wood filled his nose. How long had he been ill? It must have been a week, at least. The oiled-paper windows let in little light, but dust motes floated through the weak sunbeam. He remembered for a moment the daydream he'd indulged in before he collapsed. A daydream of a Plymouth that looked like a village, rather than a couple of ramshackle buildings. A daydream wherein Miss Mullins was pleased to see him. The nightmarish vision of her screaming and screaming interrupted the daydream. He pressed his palms against his eyes, willing the scene to disappear. How long would it be now, before *Mayflower* set sail? He had almost died in this godforsaken place. If he had, he'd have been buried without ceremony with all the others, in an unmarked grave under frozen black soil.

Friday, 16 February 1621

John rested and slept as best he could. There was not much food; thin pottage was all he could rely on to gain back the strength he'd lost, though sometimes fish or fowl was hunted and shared with the ill. After a few days, he itched to be away from the groans and restlessness of the sick. Though he knew he'd been just the same, now that he had recovered his senses he flinched at the sounds of dying men. He worked wherever he was needed, chopping wood, cutting notches, raising frames. He spent many nights on the hill by the water, burying an ever-growing number of bodies. A few other bodies, though, that were still living but too sick to work, were also put to use in Plymouth. The sick men were set up with their backs to trees, and muskets were put into their hands. In their growing fear of the Indians, they hoped this would put off an assault a while longer.

John woke early one morning, stretched his arms above his head, touching the ceiling of the common house. He would yet spend another month or two on land, before they would sail back. At least here there was room to stand. He blanched at the thought that there were still passengers aboard the gloomy *Mayflower*. Miss Mullins was there, tending to her sick father, mother, brother, and even their family's servant, Carter. There, on the plague-ridden ship at anchor, she sat surrounded by the dead and dying. He ignored his creeping doubts about spending another two months on the ghastly ship for his return to England. There would at least not be one hundred other souls packed 'tween decks; there might even be room for him to sleep in the crew's quarters. If the sailors began dying at the same rate as the colonists, would there even be enough men to bring the ship back? He could learn something of the sailor's work, to be of some use until they reached Southampton. Once there, he could return to the cooperage, return to the settled life he'd had before embarking on this godforsaken adventure. His thirst for independence was well sated, and he longed for the comfort of his master's reliability.

He stepped outside into the light of day. Snow blinded him, the outdoors bright compared with the dim interior of the common house. The snow was tamped down into mud where marching feet had walked. There was activity out here, men carrying logs, splitting wood into clapboards, smoothing rough-cut beams with planes. The frosty smell of winter was cut by the scents of sawn wood. Howland and Carver sat together on a felled log, each with a mug of watery stew.

"Is there aught I can do to be of use?" John asked.

"Aye, if you—"

"Savages! Savages in the wood! Approaching the settlement!" Hopkins' shout interrupted.

John looked about for a musket. There was none at hand, and he dashed into the common house to seize one from the settlers' store. He grabbed a stand as well and patted himself down, reassuring himself that he had dressed with a belt of powder and shot as part of his daily wardrobe. He rushed out of the common house again and spotted Hopkins forming a line of defense in front of the ordnance platform. Bradford was on top, standing between the small pieces of ordnance that had so far been delivered. He squinted out into the forest, anxiety twisting his features. Standish was out in the woods, working, and he was not yet returned.

"What did you see?" John asked Hopkins, as he stuck his stand into the ground and rested the long barrel of his musket atop it.

"A dozen of them, crossing the creek in our direction. More following; I could hear them. I could smell them." He sniffed to emphasize his point.

John loaded his powder and tamped his shot down into the barrel. He repositioned the barrel on the stand and lit his match cord, positioning it in the serpentine lock.

"I saw them coming. Standish will be sore when he's missed it," Hopkins said.

John waited with Hopkins, Bradford, Howland, and Carver. Their ranks were swelled by men who heard the cry coming in from their work in the woods. Standish came running, so hurried in his eagerness that he left his sickle behind. Nothing had yet happened. Still, the settlers waited on Hopkins' word that the Indians came this way.

At once, John saw a flash of movement in the wood and pressed down on his trigger. Nothing happened. He cursed and saw a brown bird take off from the branches he'd been watching.

"Standish, it would not fire," he called to the captain. Standish, impatient of waiting but unhappy to be distracted from it, came to look over John's musket.

"Your powder is wet." He removed the match cord and put out the lit end, then turned the gun and shook until the powder came falling out in clumps.

"My pouches are dry," John said, lifting his belt to show the captain.

"It is the musket which is moist, and therefore out of temper." He raised his voice. "Does anyone else have a musket that's been left out in the rain?"

Several of the men picked up and turned over their guns, confused. Standish sighed and began, one by one, to take account of which guns had trapped their moisture.

The Indians did not appear that day, which at least gave John plenty of time to clean and oil his musket. In the afternoon, Standish went back into the woods to his work, but returned fuming.

"They have been in the woods, Hopkins, and they have stolen my sickle!" he shouted. "When will they cease this endless taunting from the forest and come and meet us like men?"

That evening, the Indians sent them another signal: a large fire in the place where Hopkins claimed he saw them.

"They'll approach any day, perhaps tomorrow." Hopkins and Standish seemed to agree.

So, in the morning, John watched with peeled eyes and kept his clean musket close. Governor Carver was talking to Standish by the ordnance platform, when John saw two figures appear on the next hill. It was certain they were Indians, for no English men went around bare-chested, bare-legged. They were jumping and whooping, trying to get the Englishmen's attention. As though this were some kind of game among young men, to see who could approach the English camp without coming home with bullet wounds.

"Captain!" he shouted so that Standish would hear.

Standish, who had held on to his musket all morning, leapt forward to look where John was pointing. John's finger trembled.

"Aye, savages," Standish said, staking his own stand in the ground next to John's. He propped his musket on it but did not initiate fire. He waited, watching the Indians. They waved at him, jumping with glee.

"Hopkins!" Standish shouted without turning around to see whether Hopkins was nearby. "Come with me to see what it is they want."

"At last," said Hopkins, who came at John's first cry.

The two of them marched down toward the creek which ran between the two hills. John kept his musket barrel in the stand, though the Indians were at least twice the distance he could shoot with any accuracy. With his aim, he'd as soon hit Standish as he would an Indian. Still, it was the first time John saw a savage, and he strained his eyes to see them better. His breath hitched. All his muscles were tense, trained on keeping his musket level.

Hopkins and Standish approached Town Brook. To John's surprise, Standish relinquished his musket and raised his arms in a gesture of peace. John heard a great whooping cry, a much louder noise than two men could make. He strained his eyes, looking for a great many Indians to arrive on the crest of the opposing hill. None came. In fact, as Standish and Hopkins approached closer, the two Indians who had beckoned to them turned and ran, leaping out of John's range of sight in an instant. Standish also lost track of them and ran up the side of the hill. As he reached the top, John saw him stamp his foot and pick up a rock to fling after the retreating Indians. They had come so close, but there would be no parley today.

John's heart drummed a rapid beat in his chest. The Indians were gone, for now, but who was to say they wouldn't come back in the night and fire the settlers' houses in the dark? When would they return, to kill the Englishmen and leave their bones to bleach in the sun?

Chapter Nine

But that which was most sad, and lamentable, was that in 2 or 3 months' time half of their company died, especially in January and February, being the depth of winter, and wanting houses and other comforts; being infected with the scurvy and other diseases, which this long voyage and their inaccommodate condition had brought upon them; so as there died some times 2 or 3 of a day, in the foresaid time; that of 100 and odd persons scarce fifty remained...

—William Bradford, *Of Plymouth Plantation*, 1651

Wednesday, 21 February 1621

Priscilla's father coughed and spat out a wad of wet phlegm. His condition had worsened in the past two days, and Priscilla was distraught with panic. She tried not to let her worry show.

"Papa, please, do eat something hot." She tried once more to offer him a spoonful.

"The soup ought to help a little, with the added mustard seeds," said Master Heale at her back, where he was preparing a glass of yellowish liquid. "Mustard seeds are hot and dry, to balance his phlegmatic condition."

Priscilla nodded. She had heard various recitations on the four humors and how to balance them for the past two months, and she knew it all as well as Master Heale did, she was sure. She was more enthusiastic about implementing changes in diet before, but despite his numerous recitations and application to their treatments, the men and women in their care continued dying.

"It is our misfortune that we arrived so late and could not build a garden," Heale continued. Priscilla nodded, a dull throb starting up in her temples. She had heard this part before, too. She began to understand the adage 'we must make do'—at least making do with what they had was better than complaining over what they had not and could not get. 'If we could have some basil or tomatoes, their cold and dry properties would combat her sanguinity,' did not help a woman burning with fever. Conversely, hearing him say 'of course they became sick, mussels are cold and dry, they would do nothing but increase the imbalance of black and yellow bile,' did not make suffering through the expulsions to restore balance any easier. They could wish all they wanted, but what provision they had was guarded. Much of what they carried over was intended for use as seed, and if it were eaten now, they would have nothing to plant in their fields and gardens. They also needed to ration their food to make it last until their first crop could be harvested. When they set out from England, they hoped to arrive in September, in time to plant at least something in Virginia. But New England in December was not receptive to growing things. Master Jones was also stingy over the use of any beer, meat, and biscuit, which his crew would need for their return journey.

She looked up and glanced about the deck, searching. She realized after a moment that the face she was looking for was Captain Standish's. He became such a fixture when he was aboard, and she had grown accustomed to his presence. He was always willing to converse with Master Heale at length on topics which bored her, too, which saved her and the other women from feigning interest. Not that Priscilla ever feigned her interest well.

She threw her spoon back into the bowl and wiped her nose on her apron. She stood and went to warm her hands over the cooking fire, which burned low and smoked too much. There was some dry fallen underbrush in the woods, which the men collected from time to time, but all the wood they felled was green and did not burn well. It was another case where they would have to make do until they could build a store of dry wood to burn.

At least the fire gave off sufficient heat to warm her fingers. Her hands were always cold and dry. *If I had some warm bread, then perhaps my hands would not feel the chill of the air.* She grinned at herself, the silly thought coming into her head unprompted. The thought of a hearty crust of warm bread made her long for England. She had never in her youth thought that she would someday yearn for a simple hunk of fresh bread and cheese. Meat, too, though not at every meal, was something that could always be obtained with enough wealth in Dorking. It had never occurred to her when they began this voyage that she would not taste beef for months on end because it could not be gotten. When they ran out of *Mayflower*'s stores, there would be no more until, somehow, they got some cows to New England. And who could have predicted that she would drink water more often than beer? Perhaps her father had, but it had never even crossed her mind. The water here was cool and clear enough, and she had become accustomed to the taste, but it was very odd to be drinking water when all her life she was told it was unhealthsome.

Her stomach burbled at all these thoughts of food, and she realized she had not eaten anything all morning. *Perhaps I will have some of Master Heale's mustard seed soup, if Father will not eat it.* She turned away from the fire, letting it warm her back for a moment before making her way back to her family. Her mother and Joseph were each asleep on their pallets. Joseph had not been at peace for weeks, and she feared that whatever disease afflicted him caused his left ear great damage, for he could not hear well out of it, and it still gave him pain. Her father's indentured servant Carter, too, was taken ill and laid up nearby. The soup, which was an approximation of a recipe learned in Holland, was quite tangy and toothsome. It warmed her within, as the fire warmed her without.

"Priscilla," her father said, reaching up to touch her elbow. "I think you must call for Governor Carver."

A chill shot up her arm and into her heart. "Why so, Papa? Master Heale has made a fine soup that will help your constitution improve."

"Nevertheless, it would be well to have him here, to take down a few lines for me, as he did for Master Martin. I think it is past time I wrote a will. 'Tis better to have it done than leave it too late, my dear."

"I should not like to leave you, Papa. I can go and fetch the governor in a while, if you should still want him, but try to rest a little first."

"If rest has not improved my condition these last weeks, I cannot see how it will help me now. I would not put it off, now that I have resolved to do it, so please, daughter. Fetch him to me, if you can."

Priscilla stood and sought the eye of Master Heale. He noticed her anxiety and came closer.

"My father has requested I seek out the governor," she told him. "I think he means to have them write something up for him. I am not sure..." She hesitated, looking back and forth between them. She did not wish to leave him.

"I can keep an eye on him, Miss Mullins. Worry not. I believe Governor Carver is up on deck with Master Jones, if they have not already left for shore."

Priscilla climbed the ladder and found the governor on the top deck.

"Aye, if that's all right with you," he was saying to Master Jones. "I should like to look in on the progress of the houses they've begun to build."

"It is no burden to us to take you, so long as you don't mind sharing the space with the ordnance pieces."

"Miss Mullins?" Governor Carver asked, noticing her. "Is there aught amiss?"

"My father has asked for you, Governor. He hopes you will take down his will for him."

"Aye, I'll come—the boat won't depart for shore for a little while, will it, Jones?"

The ship's master shook his head. "The men must still go 'tween decks to retrieve the cannons. I'm afraid it will disturb the sick a little." He did not look too remorseful; though he was less rude than some of the other sailors, he did not like keeping so many sick aboard his ship. He became a little more friendly and gentle to the passengers, though, after they tended his crew in their sickness as they did their own people.

"We'll need another witness, if you'd come down with us, Jones."

Jones agreed, and Priscilla led the men to her father's side. She curled up on Joseph's pallet, trying to keep out of the way but unwilling to be too far from him. Joseph woke from his stupor and coughed, clutching at her hand. His hand felt so small in hers.

"Sissy," he said, "my ear hurts."

"I know, Joseph; it'll be all right soon." She petted his hair, as her mother did for her when she was young. Though his ears no longer leaked pus and he did not wail at the sharpness of the pain, the ache in his left ear persisted and he had developed a deep cough. He put his head in her lap, resting on his right side to relieve the pressure on his ear. He saw the crowd of men gathered around their father. Heale joined Master Jones and Governor Carver.

"What's wrong with Papa?" Joseph asked in a small voice that did no justice to his character.

"They're looking in on him. I'm sure all will be well, once they have seen to him."

"What?" Joseph asked. He shifted his head, so he was looking up at her, and coughed. "I couldn't hear you." He started having trouble hearing from his left ear some days before. Priscilla felt as though a knife stabbed her in the chest.

"All will be well," she lied. It was a comforting lie at least, one that would reassure him. "Now hush—Papa needs to speak to the governor, and you must not interrupt him."

Governor Carver sat by her father's bedside and took his dictation.

"I leave my wife ten pounds," his voice quavered. It sounded nothing like the voice of the man who, for Priscilla's whole life, was so straight-backed and stern. "My son Joseph, ten pounds; my daughter Priscilla, ten pounds." Priscilla sniffled. What would she do with ten pounds in Plymouth? There wasn't an amount of money her father could leave her that would make her life easier than if he were still here. Without him, whose hands would shape her future and Joseph's? Yet she could not convince herself that this was a precaution; too many of the sick had died already for her to think her whole family might be spared.

He continued his distributions, including several items to his eldest children, Priscilla's half-siblings. William and Sarah chose to stay in England with their spouses, and Priscilla didn't know how they would get the bequests taken care of, across the ocean. But Governor Carver was nodding with every line; perhaps he would know what was to be done. Priscilla felt a droplet of water land on her hand and realized she had started to cry. What would she do without him? He was the very reason they were all here, in a place where they had no shelter, no means of buying food with whatever money he left them. If he were not here, how would she take care of Joseph and her mother on her own?

"To my wife Alice, half my goods, and to Joseph and Priscilla, the other half, equally to be divided between them." As a cordwainer, he brought merchandise of shoes and boots along, and he gave those to the company, that they might be sold for more shares in the venture. He distributed these shares, too. Shares, boots, stakes in the venture; what did any of these words matter? She was in Plymouth, now, and had no means to go anywhere else. What meaning did shares have here, in a world where your life was in the hands of God and Indians, when anything you needed you had to make yourself?

"Also," he said, breaths shallow, seeming to be near conclusion, "Carver, I would give you twenty shillings if you would keep an eye on my wife and children, and be a friend and father to them. And," he sighed another breath, "a special eye for my man Carter." It was a request, and the governor nodded his acquiescence.

Priscilla tried to keep her tears confined as Master Heale, Master Jones, and Governor Carver signed the will as witnesses. Joseph clutched her hand, his short fingers interlaced with hers. She could not keep her sobs in any longer, and she was found crying into her apron by the sailors who came down to hoist the cannons from the gun room up to the top deck for delivery in New Plymouth.

Master Jones' arrival on shore made a considerable commotion. At the harbor, the longboat pulled up bearing a 1200-pound cannon, along with a few sailors and the ship's master.

"Ah, the minion is here!" Standish exclaimed and scampered off down the hill, shouting over his shoulder, "Alden, come help me bring it up!"

John wiped his hands on his breeches. The minion was the largest of their ordnance pieces. Several of the smaller guns had already been mounted on their crude platform. John scrutinized the behemoth, unsure if the platform he had cobbled together would hold its weight. Perhaps Standish had another strategic location where they could place this one. John wandered toward the harbor, in no haste to lug the heavy object up the hill. The growing armament atop the platform eased his mind a little, but since the two Indians came and taunted them, he felt a nervous tension running through him. Before, the savages kept their distance. Now, it felt real—he had seen them with his own eyes approaching the settlement. They knew the English were here, and they were confident enough to taunt them with broken invitations.

He joined Captain Standish, who bounced with excitement over the arrival of his cannons. Standish had long desired their full complement of guns ashore, and this was the last of them. Master Jones and the sailors helped them roll the 1200-pound cannon over the well-trodden ground of their developing main street. At least the ground was still frozen hard, though the air was starting to thaw. If they had attempted this later in the spring, the cannon would no doubt have been lodged in mud. John heaved, straining the muscles in his back and legs. Was it necessary, he wondered, to mount this cannon at the very top of the hill? Perhaps they could have mounted it halfway up the hill, near the governor's house, instead?

When they'd delivered the minion to the top of the hill, John slumped onto the ground and lay flat on his back, arms and legs flopped out like a five-pointed star. He closed his eyes against the sun and listened to the rapid rhythm of his heart. His let his breathing slow. He felt the warmth of the sun penetrate through the front of his clothes, just as the icy chill of the frozen ground seeped in through the back. He would soon be cold and filthy. Nevertheless, he waited a few moments longer, until someone crouched over him and blocked the sun from hitting his face. He blinked his eyes open to find Standish grinning down at him.

"Worn out already, Alden? I expected you to have better stamina."

John waved his limp arm an inch off the ground, then pushed himself into a sitting position. Standish helped him up, then slid an arm around his shoulder, directing him toward the ordnance platform once more.

"There is much to do, Alden, to prepare ourselves for the next onslaught."

In the afternoon, John was repositioning one of the smaller base cannons when Governor Carver approached the platform. Howland, Standish, and Hopkins were all about the work of setting up the best arrangement of cannons for a full range of protection over the village.

"Can one of you help with the burials tonight?" the governor asked, weary and too accustomed to the words. "There are two bodies that the sailors will bring over from the ship."

"Who?" Hopkins asked, hopping off the platform to converse with Carver.

"Mullins and White."

"Mullins?" John asked, looking up in alarm.

"Aye. He called me to write his will not an hour before. 'Twas fortunate I was on the ship at the time."

The father then, not the daughter.

"I'll aid in the burial," John volunteered. Carver nodded at him with gratitude.

John thought of Miss Mullins, still confined to the dingy 'tween deck with her sick mother and brother and servant. How did she fare now, her father gone and family in ill health? Was she sick now, too? Did she still smile at all? He could not think of the last time he saw her face, and the desire to see her rose up, like a coiled snake, in his chest. He allowed himself to imagine it for a moment: the laugh on her lips, the warmth of her as she leapt into his arms.

"Oi," said Hopkins, dropping a five-pound cannonball into John's empty hands. "We have more work to do."

The chill of iron against his skin brought John back to the present. Right. He was preparing a defense against an Indian attack. He was here to help the colony until *Mayflower*'s crew were strong enough to sail her home. He had no business thinking fantastic thoughts.

That evening, John accompanied the pair of bodies to the little hill by the water for burial. Miss Mullins and the babe Peregrine both lost their fathers that day. He dug his spade into the frozen ground. The earth was not as tough here as it was on the main road: softened, rather than hardened, by constant use. Of late, they buried bodies every day. John's bones ached with chill, and he was so tired his eyes swam, but he dug nevertheless. Those with a body fit to work must use it, else all would doubtless perish.

Thursday, 22 February 1621

When the sun disappeared behind the trees the next evening, John was drawn like a moth to the lights of the common house. The warmth he knew to be inside invited him to sit on his pallet and take off his boots. He would take off his sweaty stockings and stretch his weary toes. He wondered what they put in the pottage bubbling over the fire. As he opened the door, he was startled to see Miss Mullins kneeling on the floor by the hearth. She looked up as he entered, and smiled. It was the vision from his daydream brought to life, though she looked more careworn than he ever imagined.

"I was glad to hear of your recovery, Master Alden."

"I was sorry to learn of your father's passing."

They spoke at the same time. Miss Mullins' lips tightened.

"Some of the sick here are sleeping; would you accompany me outside? I grow weary of seeing these four walls each time I come ashore."

Though he had just come in from a day spent out in the cold, John nodded his assent. She stood and took her cloak from a peg by the door. John had not warmed up much, but as he stepped outside again the cold wind off the sea bit into his exposed cheeks afresh. His nose dripped, and his ears were so cold he could no longer feel them. At least his capotain hat kept some of the warmth in his head. Miss Mullins raised the hood of her cloak, so he could not see her face.

"I believe they thought that sending me ashore today would help to clear my mind of the memories of yesterday. But I think I worry more, being unable to see how Joseph and my mother fare."

They strolled down the broad main street, the dirt below their shoes packed under the memory of many footsteps. Pale pink streaked through the darkening blue of the evening sky.

John longed to sit by the fire, to get off of his feet and into the warmth. But Miss Mullins should not be left unaccompanied, so he would stay with her as long as she wished.

Tonight, the moon was the faintest of slivers, and the world around them grew ever blacker. When they came to the edge of the water, Miss Mullins found a large boulder and scrambled up to sit atop it, drawing her knees to her chest. John regarded the rock for a moment, then pulled himself up and sat, putting both his musket and some distance between them. She stared out at the sea, at *Mayflower*, at the spit of land called Gurnet's Nose which interrupted the flat line of the horizon.

They sat in silence for a few minutes. John looked up. Stars were beginning to emerge as the sky grew darker. He was always astonished by the multitude of stars that could be seen here. There were never so many stars in England, not that he had noticed. He wondered if they were the same stars that shone down on Southampton, on the cooperage. He never took much interest in astronomy before.

"Goodman Alden," she said, breaking their peace. "Will you pray with me?"

"Pray?" he asked, apprehensive of her expectations.

"Aye," she said, not looking at him. "I want to thank God for taking my father away from his suffering. And to ask him to look after my mother and Joseph and Carter, if they are to follow soon."

John did not know what to say. Pray to God? It was the Separatist way. He could not pray here, on a rock by the side of the ocean. He did not have even a symbol of a saint through whom he could channel his prayer. A direct prayer to God was too intimidating to contemplate. He tried to think how he could articulate these things to her. How could he say that he did not think God could even see them, here? Then he saw the tears on her cheeks. They shone in the faint moonlight. She did not want a theological discussion. She did not need debate. She desired companionship in her fear and loneliness.

"All right," he said.

Her hands clasped in a tight knot. She pressed her knuckles into her nose and forehead, her cheeks resting on her knees. She rocked a little back and forth, and he could hear her murmuring, but he could not make out the words.

He looked again toward the sky. To the growing body of stars. God created the heavens and the earth. John folded his hands in his lap. God created these stars, which looked down on this land of heathens. He must have created the savages, too. The wolves, the lions, whatever other unknown beasts populated the New World. If God created the world and everything in it, how could he not be watching them here? But if there was no church, perhaps he could not hear them?

John's head ached. He closed his eyes. He listened to the rhythmic splash of the water. He listened to the rustle of the trees. He listened to Miss Mullins, who sat beside him, praying. Her father had died. Her brother and her mother were sick. Had he not suffered this once himself? Had he not lost his own family? Had he prayed for them? He could not remember.

Miss Mullins' breath grew ragged, and her tears came faster. John did not know what he could do. He could not hold her in his arms. Here in the wilderness, he was yet ruled by what propriety he knew. Her shoulder pressed into his arm. He could feel her shaking. He stilled, allowing the point of contact, but not increasing it. He waited. The warmth of her arm weighed against his. Her shuddering subsided. They sat together a moment more, just breathing.

Monday, 26 February 1621

John and Howland raised a beam and slotted it into the frame, then hammered it in place to secure the ends into their notches. They were helping with the construction of another building for common storage. Some of the men who were still walking were working on building their own houses, but as John did not intend to stay in Plymouth, he helped where he was needed. He did not mind asking Eaton for advice and learning needed skills. He enjoyed his usefulness; it was better than being confined to the ship while he awaited her departure.

After raising the beam, John employed himself in cutting strips for wattle. The work was less precise than coopering, and he tended to take more care with it than he needed. He lined the sharp side of his froe against the end of a long block of wood, near the edge, then hit the back with his froe club. The tool bit into the wood, splitting the strip from the trunk as John twisted the froe away. It was calm and slow work, just the kind of steady chore that John enjoyed.

In midafternoon, his peace was broken by the arrival of the longboat. John exchanged a wary look with Howland. Most often of late, the boat came bearing the bodies of *Mayflower*'s dead. Miss Mullins and Miss Tilley were both tending their ailing families. The Mullins' servant, Carter, passed yesterday. John stood, leaned his froe against a length of wood, and left Howland to continue the work.

Master Bradford was coming ashore carrying a corpse. John recognized the wasted body of Mistress Mullins. She had not long outlived her husband. He blinked twice, but he could not even feign shock. Now, Miss Mullins' brother was all the family left to her in the world.

"I'll—" John offered, reaching for the woman.

Bradford, eyes marked with tiredness, handed over the body in gratitude.

If there is aught that could have joined us with the Separatists in fellowship, John thought, *it is this.* Not the compact they all signed. No piece of paper could bind men together as did this shared experience. Those lucky enough to be left standing cared for those who were struck down. The sickness took men, women, and children, indiscriminate of religion. The need to care for the sick and tend to the dead was felt by all those who were able, without regard for their differing beliefs.

Despite his own keen desire to be of use, as more and more days passed, along with more and more of the passengers, his longing to be back aboard *Mayflower* and headed for England increased. He wanted to turn his back on this place and leave it in his past. More than three dozen lives had been lost since they anchored here, and many still lay sick.

John could not believe that God had a presence in this place. God could not hear their prayers, for the Separatists prayed without ceasing. If he could see them, why would he have allowed such atrocity to afflict them? Even the Separatists did not deserve to be left as nothing more than dry, white bones upon the earth. John shuddered at the memory. Either God could not hear them, as they had no intermediary to speak with him on their behalf, or this was a playground of the Devil, and God could not reach them.

It was this place. Plague visited the Indians here, and instead of taking the omen as a warning that the Devil ruled, the Separatists took it as a sign that God made the land ready for them. Such conceit from men who walked away from the Church of England, who sailed across the sea so that they would not be ruled by their king. John dreaded the thought that they did not cross an ocean but had instead crossed into Satan's hands. That they, too, would meet the same fate as the Indians, and soon none would be strong enough to bury the dead.

It had not happened yet. John carried Mistress Mullins behind the common house. He would, of course, wait until dusk to bring the body to the little hill by the water for burial. Silent, dark, one- or two-man burials, with no litany, no service, not even a grave marker. All to keep their dwindling numbers and weakness from the Indians. John feared their position enough not to argue. If Standish believed that watching them bury their dead would give the Indians the confidence to attack, John would keep digging in the dark. It would not matter much longer, if the sickness kept spreading. He shook his head, glancing away from the body. He ought to get back to Howland. He tugged the rolled-up sleeves of his doublet down to his wrists—he'd taken off his cloak in the sweaty heat of his morning efforts, and now the chill began to seep in. They'd try to finish preparing the frame tonight, so they could enlist others to help raise it on the morrow. He turned his back on Miss Mullins' mother, regretting that he ever sought an adventure in the New World.

Wednesday, 28 February 1621

Joseph coughed, and streams of blood dribbled down his chin. Priscilla wiped them away with a damp rag, patterned already with red patches.

"If you do that, it is like you have not grown at all since you were a babe who could not eat his meals properly," she admonished. Tears slipped down her cheeks, chasing each other down familiar paths.

He tried to smile, but the movement constricted his throat, and he coughed again, spattering more blood. The ship's surgeon, Heale, had drained him of a cup of blood already, yet more blood kept coming every time he coughed. He was pale and looked almost blue in the faint light of the 'tween deck.

"Be well, Joseph, be well," she begged him. "We're meant to play a game of knucklebones, when you grow big enough—did you forget?"

He raised his hand to hers, laying it palm to palm. She shook with sobbing, closing her fingers around his. He opened his mouth, but as he tried to draw in a breath Priscilla could hear a faint wheezing sound, as though no air could enter. His eyes grew wide and he choked, blood dripping from his mouth, but he could no longer cough because he could not draw in breath. His hand tore away from hers, clutching at his chest, his throat, trying to breathe, but he could not.

"No, no, Joseph!" Priscilla cried, digging her fists into her apron, but she knew there was nothing she could do. Not all of those who died on *Mayflower* died this way, but enough had that she knew it was the end. At length, his movement stopped.

She picked up his hand between hers again, clasping it, snot and spit covering her mouth and chin as she cried. She felt unable to stop, unable to breathe through the sobs that wracked her. Had he grown at all since Peregrine White was born? Mistress White had said that someday, Joseph would be a man with a child of his own. Yet he was still a child himself, and he would grow no more. He would not again look upon a newborn babe in fascination, could no longer answer riddles or stick his tongue into the gap of his teeth. He could now do nothing but await the day when Jesus would come to judge the living and the dead. She cried until she felt weak and dizzy, then she laid her head down next to Joseph, still holding his hand.

When Master Heale came, he spoke to her, but she could not concentrate on what he said. It was as though there were an insect buzzing in her ears. She blinked up at him, then looked back at her brother, the last remaining member of her family. His hand grew colder between hers, even colder than the winter air 'tween decks. She felt as though she was frozen in place. When someone came to take Joseph away, she watched as her arm raised up, still clutching on to his hand, until they carried him too far and her arm fell back to her side.

She tried to think, but her brain was as frozen as her body. The strength she had found to mask her worry ran out. There was no need for a mask anymore. She had no one to pretend for. She blinked, aware of the sensation of her eyelashes closing on each other. Her arms felt like jelly, and her legs were starting to tingle with pins and needles, protesting having been locked in one position for so long. She turned her head to look for Tilley, who sat by the side of her own sick mother. Tilley's father had succumbed a few days before Priscilla's, and now her mother was close to dying too. It felt like a year had passed since Priscilla's father died, but she had lost her whole family in just a week.

She wondered what would become of her now. What would she do, when *Mayflower* departed and she had no place to live? What worth were her shares in the venture, if she had no way to hunt for food or build a timber frame? Mistress Carver, the governor's wife, took charge of Mary Chilton when her mother died in January. Mary had been orphaned for near a month. Priscilla had been orphaned for two days.

The weight of it settled on her at last, now that there were no more pressing needs to attend.

Hands descended onto Priscilla's shoulders and wrapped around her in an embrace. Tilley had left her mother's side a moment to give Priscilla some comfort. She clutched at the arms encircling her, clasping them tighter. There was someone left who cared for her, someone in Plymouth who would look after her. She relied on the strength of a thirteen-year-old girl who would, more like than not, be orphaned herself in a matter of days.

"Yea though in valley of death's shade I walk, none ill I'll fear, because thou art with me, thy rod and staff my comfort are," Tilley whispered into her ear. "Do not forget what a comfort it is to have God with us in our hours of need."

If I put my faith in God, will he be as father and as mother to me? Will he care for me and make sure I am well fed? Will he build me a house to live in and cut me firewood to keep me warm? Will he darn my stockings and hem my petticoats? Will he ensure a good marriage for me, through which I can give him healthy children?

Priscilla sang with Tilley to stem the flow of worries entering her mind.

> *The Lord to me a shepherd is,*
> *want therefore shall not I.*
> *He in the folds of tender grass*
> *doth cause me down to lie.*

> *To waters calm me gently leads,*
> *restore my soul doth he;*
> *he doth in paths of righteousness*
> *for his name's sake lead me.*

> *Yea though in valley of death's shade*
> *I walk, none ill I'll fear,*

*because thou art with me, thy rod
and staff my comfort are.*

She would not want. God would provide for her. God would protect her in this valley of death.

Winter's end was in sight, and the chill in the air was starting to depart during the warmth of midday. Snow was scarce on the ground, and though there were no green things yet peeking from the frozen earth, it would soon be time for planting. They planned to sow their fields with the Indian corn they took from their anchorage at Cape Cod, as well as the barley and peas they carried over from England.

When John learned that Miss Mullins' brother died, it struck him harder than he expected. There had been so many deaths already, and so little rest for those living. Between caring for the sick and trying to build some kind of settlement, everyone was exhausted. Joseph was just another body, wrapped in cloth, so small and delicate that John could lift him in one arm. Yet for one moment he thought how terrible it was that one so young and lively should live no more. Under the dark night sky, he carried his corpse to the burying grounds. He tried to find a place on the hill where the earth was not yet turned. Here, he had dug a grave for Master Tilley; there for Master Winslow's indentured boy, Elias Story; and under that tree he had placed the bodies of Mistress Tinker and her son. John had buried so many, he could not remember them all. It was so black here, without a moon, the cloud cover obscuring even the stars from view. It wasn't that the night was blacker here than in Southampton, but that there was no way to escape the darkness of it. There was no friendly pub with candlelight shining through its windows, inviting you in, out of the night.

The darkness overwhelmed him. He could feel nothing; his capacity for fear and sadness was stretched too far. Now, his life was work. He would dig. Then he would sleep. Then tomorrow he would cut trees and trim boards and start to build a frame for a new house. Then he would be needed to dig again. Miss Mullins was the sole member of her family left living. Yet, the rest of the company fared no better. Death followed death, leaving Miss Mullins an orphan, Master Bradford a widower, and few families intact. Tinker's family had been decimated. John was fair sure that he was not alone now in missing the comforting lights of home, the warmth and company, and the food. Food. Oh, how nice it would be to sup in a pub with a mug of beer and a fire. Oh, how he longed to return to his comfortable life in England, to go to a proper church on Sunday and not sit in a huddled tangle listening to Brewster profess his seditious sermons. John yearned to go back to his life, to forget the staring eyes of the dead he buried. He wanted to escape the turned-over heap that was once a simple hill by the water, where now the names of the dead ran together like the soft dirt that covered their bodies.

Saturday, 10 March 1621

After Joseph's death, Priscilla took on the fever which she fought all the time she cared for her family. For a week she lay abed, sweating and shivering by turns, as she had seen her mother do. She did not want to be a burden to Master Heale, Tilley, or whoever else might take care of her. However, she was unable to muster any strength. The will which had kept her busy for the past six weeks evaporated.

Tilley's mother died the first week in March. After, the girl spent much time curled by Priscilla's side. They had lost all else and clung to each other as barnacles clung to *Mayflower*'s hull.

"Priscilla," Tilley said one afternoon, lying beside her on her pallet, "Governor Carver's house is complete, and Mistress Carver has invited Mary Chilton and I to go ashore and live with them. Will you come and live there with us? They mean to move all of us ashore as soon as they can, and all our goods, so that *Mayflower* can make ready to sail back to England."

Carver, keep an eye on my wife and children, and be a friend and father to them. It was one of the last things her father said before his death. She was alone now, of those named. Would the Carvers take her in as one of their orphaned girls? She was years older than Tilley and Mary, but unmarried. She could not live on her own. She did not think she would know how.

"Aye," Priscilla answered, stroking Tilley's hair. "I believe I shall."

"Good." Tilley snuggled closer to her friend. "I should hate to go without you."

Priscilla gathered her strength in the following days, but still she could not bear to face the mountain of possessions that she had inherited. When they left their house in Dorking, Priscilla despaired at how much they sold or left behind. She could not even remember now what items she was so worried she could not live without. They had packed and carried with them the essentials for a family of four, and now Priscilla was left to handle it all herself.

"Tilley, I cannot face it. How am I supposed to know what to keep? What shall I do with all the things I no longer need? The governor's house is not so big that it will fit my family's things, and yours and Mary's, along with everything Mistress Carver brought for their household already."

"Do not fret so, Priscilla. We shall take a few things of yours ashore for now, and when the common storehouses are finished I'm sure we can move the rest. *Mayflower* will not leave without our knowing. You will have time."

So, Priscilla carried ashore a small selection of the belongings which came to her when all her family perished: her own clothes, and any of her mother's clothes which fit her, her mattress and bedding, and the small leather pouch containing Joseph's knucklebones. She clenched her fist around it, remembering the hours her brother spent at play with them. She would keep them, to remind her of those more carefree days. Tilley assured her that Mistress Carver had sufficient skillets and dishes and other household sundries that Priscilla needn't worry over bringing hers; if they should need them, they could ride in the shallop back to *Mayflower* and retrieve them. Tilley's family and the Chiltons, too, had left the girls with more kitchen tools and washing supplies than any household needed. After so many deaths, those who survived were left with plenty. Though it was morbid to consider, everyone was a little less worried about starvation than they were before. There were now so many fewer mouths to feed.

Carver's one-room house smelled of fresh-cut thatch mingled with the muddy odor of daub. The Carvers' bedstead took up one large corner of the room, farthest from the hearth and chimney. A large six-board chest squatted at the foot of the bed, the open lid revealing folded clothes and bedding. A writing cabinet took up the wall opposite the bedstead. The sturdy table by the fire was obscured by a pair of wide boards, leaning against it, waiting to be mounted as shelves. A pile of dishes and candles sat heaped on one of the chairs, ready for the shelves to be completed. Priscilla's mattress was stowed in the loft, a storage space built by adding a flat wooden ceiling at the bottom of the roofline. A gap was left between the low ceiling and the peak of the pitched roof.

The house bustled with pleasant activity, sorting and cleaning and setting up house. At one point in the afternoon, Howland came in, and Priscilla remembered that he was Carver's indentured man. No wonder Tilley was happy to come to the Carvers' home. Tilley tugged at a loose strand of her hair, looking around the room as she spoke to him. The three girls helped Mistress Carver where they could, and Priscilla felt her age as they went about their tasks. Mistress Carver did not organize things the same way as Priscilla's mother, and Priscilla kept fumbling over herself, trying to do things right. She knew she would always worry about trying to do things well in the Carvers' home; perhaps if she had a home of her own, she would feel less insecure.

By the time night fell, Priscilla was tired. Though the busyness of the house was homey and sweet, she desired a few moments of peace to be by herself. She took her cloak from the back of a chair (for the coat hooks were not yet installed) and wandered down the street toward the shore. It felt odd to be on land overnight. She had spent every night but one of the past eight months sleeping on *Mayflower*. Now, she could see the ship at its anchor, floating far off in the bay. The hill where their dead lay buried loomed over her as she approached the harbor, and she turned away from it.

She untied her coif and let the sea breeze rustle through her long hair. The moon glowed, a waxing crescent, and shone a path of light across the rippling surface of the bay.

She spotted the same large boulder, perched by the edge of the shore, on which she had sat and prayed with Goodman Alden. Her evening prayer brought her some strength before; perhaps it could give her some solace now. She hoisted herself up onto the rock and nestled into its curves. But she found she did not want to pray. She just waited.

Lapping waves caressed the sides of her large throne, making a soothing rhythmic noise. It was interrupted by the crunch of boots walking across the pebbled shore. Someone else had come down to view the harbor at night. She felt his presence approach her, but she did not have the energy to be startled. Goodman Alden climbed atop the rock beside her and sat down. She noted with a small smile that, though he still kept a careful distance between them, it had shrunk since the last time they'd sat together. It seemed he had become as aware of her closeness as she had been of him all the time since they'd first met. He smelled of wood shavings and freshly turned earth. It was a pleasant scent, and she wished she did not know that it meant he had just come from digging graves.

They sat in silence for a long time.

Chapter Ten

In his person he is a very lusty man, in his best
years, an able body, grave of countenance, and
spare of speech. In his attire little or nothing
differing from the rest of his followers, only in a
great chain of white bone beads about his neck...
his face was painted... All his followers likewise,
were in their faces, in part or in whole painted,
some black, some red, some yellow, and some
white, some with crosses, and other antic works;
some had skins on them, and some naked, all
strong, tall, all men in appearance.

—About Massasoit, *Mourt's Relation*, 1622

Friday, 16 March 1621

At midday, John left his work in search of a meal. Through
the winter they hunted fowl, when there were enough men
standing to spare in hunting. As spring came on, the fowl
grew scarcer. The men set about clearing their fields for
planting. Herbs and berries were not yet in season. So they
were caught between the difficulties of winter, when too
many men lay dying to send many out fowling, and the
difficulties of spring, when the men who yet lived were at last
recovering, but there seemed little yet to hunt.

John carried his musket down the main street, admiring
the neatness of the dwellings he had helped to build. There
were four homes done, with a fifth framed, and three
buildings for the common use. They stood in pretty rows on
either side of a well-worn thoroughfare. The cannons on their
platform sat as unyielding sentries, overlooking the whole
from the top of the hill. Governor Carver's house was
halfway down the hill, on the way to the common house

where John was quartered. Most times of day, all the homes bustled with activity. Now, however, Carver's house seemed quiet. John peered through the half-open doorway.

The shutters were open, and weak light filtered in through the oiled-paper window. Miss Mullins sat in a chair by the hearth, her head bent over a stocking. It was the very image of her from his nightmares, and he felt dizzy for a moment, waiting for the blood to come. Her coif was askew, and black curls fell across her face. She pushed them away, squinting at her work. He let out a breath. It was not a nightmare; she was real, and breathing, and safe.

"Where are all your boon companions?" he asked, startling her into pricking herself with her needle.

She yelped, looking up at him with fury. He hid a smile. It was good to see her face enlivened again, even with anger. She had been so tired and dull since the deaths of her family.

"John!" she shrieked, alarmed into the impropriety of using his Christian name. "Whatever do you mean by startling me that way?"

"Miss Mullins," he replied, pushing open the door with the butt of his musket. She reddened at the reminder of her own informality. "I wondered what happened, to leave the house so unusually still?"

She huffed a little, blowing the curls out of her face. "Do not you think it nice to have silence now and again?"

He stepped back toward the door. "If you wish for solitude, I will leave you to your mending."

She put the stocking in her lap and drew her feet up on the chair to sit with her knees to one side. "No, no," she sighed. "I am but content with it when it comes. Do you seek the governor's attention?"

John shook his head. "I have no need of him, just thought it strange to find you alone and wondered where they had all gone." There were at least eight people living in the Carver's home. To find them all out but Priscilla was near miraculous.

"Did you not know? The governor wanted to conclude the establishment of our military orders." She looked up at him with one eyebrow raised. "I am surprised Captain Standish did not tell you."

"Oh. I suppose they need to finish, having been interrupted by the shouts of savages in the woods the last time. I suppose it is not my concern, as I will be departing with *Mayflower* in a fortnight or so, when she is ready."

Miss Mullins pressed her lips into a line and glanced at the window. John felt uneasy. Was she discontent with him leaving? Or was this just a return to the pensive mood she had been in since her family's deaths? He took off his hat to scratch his head, unsure what more to say.

"I suppose you have a place awaiting you, in England." She did not look at him as she spoke.

"Well, I suppose I will return to my master's cooperage for a time. He has always afforded me a place when I have needed it." John felt a little squeeze of guilt. He had not considered that his departure may have burdened his master, who always treated him with kindness. He had encouraged John to go, of course, and pushed him out of the door with a smile. John wondered if his bed had been filled by a new apprentice since he left. He'd desired to save his master and the cooperage from the burden of continuing to care for him; he'd wanted to prove that he could care for himself. And now he desired to return to the safe, comforting bosom of home.

"I cannot imagine you at a cooperage," she said, "nor any place in England. I am too used to seeing you here, on the beach or in the wood."

"I do not know that I would be so different there than I am here."

"Would not you be? I think I was different, in Dorking, before Papa decided to come here. Joseph and I would go down to East Street on market days and run through the crowds of people come to buy our Dorking fowl. Our chickens are five-toed, instead of four, and among the best breeding stock there is. Papa's shop was on West Street, and the market was on East Street, by St. Martin's Church. It wasn't far, but Mama didn't like us to run about like children."

She smiled at the memory. It was a trace of the joy that had once been there, before. He wanted to reach out to her, to touch her face, to welcome her back to the world of the living. But Mistress Carver might return at any moment, and Miss Mullins would no doubt find such a gesture odd. He put his hand in his pocket instead.

"From the market square we could go down Mill Lane to get flour. Sometimes we'd buy bread from the miller's wife. It was just downstream from the tannery and dye house, so the stench could be incredible, but somehow bread always tasted better when the miller's wife made it than when Ma—"

"Savages! Indians!" The sentry's cry interrupted Miss Mullins' thought.

John bounded out of the house, musket in hand, and raced uphill toward the ordnance platform, but he found the Indian in the street, walking in the same direction. John stopped and fumbled with his belt of powder and shot, trying to pluck his match cord free. The Indians came closer each time they approached, but they'd been quiet some weeks. Now one stood in the street, men gathering around him with muskets raised. The Indian raised his bow high in the air, as a gesture of peace.

He was tall, with black hair that reached down his back to his waist. It was cut short in front of his eyes, and the man had no hair on his face at all. He wore no clothing except a span of leather about his waist.

John's heart hammered in his chest. He looked around the street and saw Captain Standish in the half-circle of men who intercepted the Indian. John stared at Standish, looking for a signal. He could smell the slow burning of the match cords.

"Englishmen," the savage said at last, "I bid you welcome."

"This place—Patuxet," said the Indian, his gesture encompassing the fallow fields and the hill on which they stood.

His name was Samoset. He knew some broken English, which was easy enough to understand. He'd come from a village in the far north, Monhegan Island, where many Europeans fished and traded with his tribe.

"There is village. Here," he continued, pointing out into the woods a short way. "Then, plague. All die."

John shuddered.

"Then there are none to hinder our possession of the place," said Master Hopkins.

"It would seem not," Bradford agreed. "God has indeed led us here."

John held his tongue. It was distasteful to him that they had chosen to settle in a sepulcher, but he would bite back his opinion. Soon, he would be gone, and they could live where they wished. His ears twitched. A chill wind whipped all around.

"We must have a spare coat, do we? Would you like some food, Samoset?" Governor Carver inquired.

"I like beer," Samoset answered. He accepted a red horseman's coat with delight, pulling the sleeves over his arms.

"I am afraid we have not any. What of strong water? Aqua vitae?"

Howland, who was at the governor's side, went off to fetch refreshment.

"Are there none of the Patuxet people left?" asked Winslow, who stared at Samoset in fascination.

Samoset shook his head. "Only Tisquantum. He captive. Brought to England. But he return. Speak good English. Live with Massasoit."

"Mah-sah-so-it?" Carver asked, sounding out the name.

"Massasoit. Great *sachem*." Samoset thought for a moment. "King. King of Pokanoket."

"Poh-kah-no-ket," repeated Carver.

"They are nearby?" Standish asked, still holding his musket ready, though pointed away from Samoset.

"Yes. Near." He thought for a moment. "Nay-bores," he said with a twisted tongue, the word unfamiliar, not often used.

"Are they the ones who shot arrows at us, when we first came here to investigate by shallop?" Hopkins asked.

"That was a day's sail east of here," Bradford doubted.

"Nauset," said Samoset.

"What?"

"East. Shoot arrows. You shoot three times one *pniese*." He tapped his chest. "Pniese. Warrior. Soldier."

"How do you know of that?" Standish demanded. The barrel of his snaphance musket wavered.

"They take tools. In woods."

"They're taunting us!" Standish shouted. They were his tools that the Indians had stolen.

"Who does these things? Who was it we fought with, and who took our tools? Mah-sah-so-it?" Carver asked.

Samoset shook his head as Howland rejoined the party, carrying a mug with aqua vitae and a plate with biscuit, butter, and cheese, as well as a tender piece of mallard. John's stomach growled. He'd forgotten that he'd come back from work to eat.

"No. Massasoit king of Pokanoket. Aspinet king of Nauset. Pokanoket north. Nauset east. Paomet more far east. You steal their corn."

Bradford took in a weary breath. Hopkins snorted.

"Oh! We mean to make recompense for the corn, if we can. We can truck with them and repay them the debt," Carver offered. They had brought English beads, knives, copper and iron, strong drink, and victuals to trade.

Samoset took the mallard between his fingers and tore off a strip to eat.

"Then, if Massasoit is not the one who attacked us, will he have peace?" Bradford asked. John could see the hope shining in his eyes as though he were an urchin looking upon the face of the Lord.

Samoset thought for a long time, chewing on the offered food. At length, he nodded. "Peace. Yes."

The questioning continued all through the afternoon, but John soon found himself lost. *Peace.* Was it true? Might they not need to fight after all? The notion made him lightheaded. Or was that the lack of food?

Monday, 19 March 1621

The Indians had been in Plymouth now for four days, and Priscilla was nearing her wits' end. Mistress Carver told her it was inappropriate for a young woman to see such men—for Samoset left on Saturday, to return on Sunday with five more Indians! They were all quite tall, with long black hair that shone in the sun, decorated with ornaments of feathers, and quite broad chested, as she could see because they wore leather trousers and naught else—for of course Priscilla did what chores she could outdoors to get a glimpse of them, even fetching water, which was often done by younger girls. It was nonsense to expect her to shield her eyes for four days for the sake of modesty. She had seen more obvious displays on market days in any case. She suspected the directive was aimed more at Tilley and Mary, anyway, and less to protect their virtuous eyes than to hide them from the Indians. The visitors were sent away from the settlement on Sunday, it being the Lord's day and not good to trade, but Samoset still stayed—excited, now that he had come, to eat their English victuals. If this sort of thing continued, Mistress Carver could not expect them all to stay indoors forever.

But, for now, Priscilla was confined to the house, as she was trying—for the most part—to be obedient to the mistress of the household. Mistress Carver took Mary and Tilley to the ship, to sort through the rest of their belongings. The settlers were bringing over their possessions from *Mayflower* a shallop at a time, preparing the ship for her final departure in the next week or two. Priscilla was taking in one of her mother's waistcoats, which was too large for her to wear. Governor Carver sat at his cabinet, reading from a pamphlet of some Separatist leader or other. She couldn't quite keep track. She held the waistcoat up for inspection, flapping it in the air so that everything would hang flat. It was green, a pleasant pale green that would soon be matched by the budding leaves of the trees along the coast.

"Fie!" She noticed a missing button on the right cuff. Carver glanced up from his desk.

"I shall need a new button for this waistcoat. Oh!" She jumped up from the table. "I have just remembered—I brought my mother's buttons off the ship. They are just in the loft; I shall retrieve one."

She scrambled up the ladder to the loft, where the things she most desired to keep of her family's goods were stored, along with Tilley's and Mary's things. She picked her way across the loft. The floor was sturdy—it held the weight of all the belongings stored there, including some barrels of provision. But somehow she felt uneasy crawling on the ceiling. Her family's things were kept in the six-board chest, which was pushed to the side to clear the path for the pallets which were put up in the mornings and taken down again at night for sleeping. She opened the lid. There, her mother's apron, frayed a little at the hem. Here, her father's awl, which he liked to keep with him in his pouch 'just in case.' Nestled in the corner, Joseph's bag of knucklebones. She touched these things, one by one. Her mother's box of notions was not to be found. Priscilla lifted everything out, depositing them in stacks on the floor around her. At the bottom of the chest, she retrieved the box. She ran her fingers over the simple floral engraving and sighed.

She was just placing the last of the items back into the six-board chest when she heard the door open in the house below.

"Governor Carver?" Captain Standish's voice floated up through the boards. Priscilla dropped the bag of knucklebones onto a stack of clothes with a soft plop.

"Aye, Captain. What is it I can do for you?"

"Aye, well. I was curious… are you now acting as guardian for Miss Mullins?" Was it just the cushioning of the floor that made the captain sound so hesitant? Priscilla froze, her hand on the lid of the chest.

"I don't believe the arrangement is so formal, nor know if it will be. We will send word of Mullins' will with *Mayflower*, and a list of all the dead. I've been meaning to discuss it with her." The tone of his voice changed, as though he looked up toward the loft.

Priscilla lowered the lid so the hinges would not squeak, and closed it on the tips of her fingers.

"Aye, that's... well. It's well."

"Is there a reason you ask, Captain?"

"I wondered if you might have plans for her marriage, Governor. She... well, she's a very marriageable prospect, with her inheritance and..." He paused and continued in a gentler tone. "With so few unmarried women in the colony, now."

If you counted women of marriageable age, there was one, Mistress White, who had been widowed in February and left with her infant son Peregrine. There were two other girls around Priscilla's age: Desire Minter, a brash girl who complained without end, and Carver's maidservant, Dorothy, who was so shy and timid that she did not speak unless spoken to, even to Priscilla, who lived in the house with her. But Standish wasn't talking about them. He was talking about her. She held her breath, waiting for Carver's answer, the musty smell of dried thatch filling her nose.

"Well, I hadn't given it much thought as yet, Captain Standish. She is not yet of an age to marry."

"I see." Standish sounded a little crestfallen. "Well, it is not—I imagine there will be— several men may ask you, so— it is something to consider."

"Aye. I'll give it careful thought, Captain."

Priscilla heard the door shut. She sat for a moment, considering. Marry Standish? The thought had never crossed her mind. But it did not seem such a terrible thing. She remembered the weight of his head against her shoulder, the bristly feel of his hair, and blushed. He could not have been considering such things mere moments after his wife's death. That moment had been consolation, the same as Priscilla gave Joseph. A motherly instinct, if anything. But, marriage? It would give her her own household, her own definite position in the community. The captain's wife, no less.

She heard the creak of Carver's chair as he pushed back from the table and walked across the room.

"Are you still with us, Miss Mullins?" he asked at the foot of the ladder.

"Oh, yes, of course. Excuse me. I'll be right down." She picked up the box of notions and crawled back across the loft to the ladder. When she hopped onto the floor, she found Carver standing at the doorway, looking after Standish's retreating back. She ducked her head and put the box on the table.

"I imagine you'll get more offers than that in the next year, Miss Mullins. As Standish said, there are not many marriageable women in the colony. Not that there are many marriageable men, either, but a much greater proportion. If no one has asked yet, I think it is as I said to the captain: you won't reach marriageable age for some time." He sighed and turned away from the door to face her. She was looking down at her hands, fiddling with the box on the table. She was sure her face was scarlet. It felt hot.

"I urge you to consider going back to England, Miss Mullins. Your father stated in his will that he was leaving some bequests to your older brother and sister. I am sure your father had his own reasons for coming here, but you yourself did not, and if you should like to go back and join your brother and sister, I am sure Master Jones will take you in *Mayflower*." She looked up, startled, to see his face was serious. "As I'm sure you know already, we look at a difficult life here, Miss Mullins. It will not be easy, if you choose to stay in Plymouth. Of course, as I said to Standish, I am not your legal guardian. I will not ask you to go, when it was your father's will that I watch over you here. As long as it is in my power to be a friend to you, I will do so. But if you have any desire at all to return home and live with your sister or your brother, it may be the best course for you to take."

After Captain Standish's revelation, this was too much. She sat down and missed her chair, landing instead on its arm. Return to England? After all she went through to come here?

"Will you urge such a decision on Miss Tilley or Miss Chilton?" she asked. Desire Minter and Dorothy had both traveled to Plymouth in Carver's household, so though they were unmarried, their benefactor at least yet lived.

"Miss Tilley and Miss Chilton have no family in England, Miss Mullins. As members of our congregation, their family is either here or is in Leiden and will soon be joining us. They belong in New Plymouth, at least until they are of an age to marry, which is some more years off for either of them. Your inheritance will of course be compensated, and I believe Goodman Alden still intends to return with the ship, so you would not be alone amongst the sailors."

Ah. That was right; Goodman Alden was to leave. Soon. Ought she to go back to England? She remembered her life in Dorking with great fondness, but if she went back, it would not be so carefree.

"I do not think there is a place in England that would much welcome my return, Governor. My father's other children are less family to me than Tilley is." Priscilla's half-sister Sarah had little interest in Priscilla even before she married, and none afterward. To go all the way back to England, to live at her house? And William was ten years her senior. He was amiable enough, just more or less a stranger to her.

Carver nodded his understanding. "As Standish said, your father has at the very least left you well settled. It means very little now," he chuckled, "but in a few years, when the town has grown, it will be of value to you, and to your future husband. As Standish said, it is something to consider."

Priscilla agreed. She would think of little else for days.

Thursday, 22 March 1621

John worked his hoe into the earth, pulling weeds and turning over the soil. The fields near the settlement had been lying fallow too long, and they needed to be weeded before planting. It felt good to be digging in anticipation of new life and growth, rather than for burial. The trees, though still barren, were beginning to show small buds of growth along their branches. Sweat dripped down his forehead, despite the fact that the weather was still chilly.

His desire to work was fueled by his continuing conviction that God could not hear them, could not reach them in this Devil-ruled New World. He wanted to aid in the construction of houses, that those who remained might have shelter, and to aid in the clearing and the sowing of the fields, that they might have food. The last of the passengers and their belongings had been rowed off the ship in the last few days, and all were settled ashore, albeit in less comfort than they might have wished, with no more than five houses yet raised.

"Savages!" came the now-familiar call of the sentry at the ordnance platform. John's heart still leapt a beat. This time, would they attack? He took up his musket from the edge of the field and dashed toward the settlement.

By the time he'd reached the main street, Standish was already welcoming Samoset, rifle raised, much more relaxed with him after near a week of his company. Samoset was accompanied by four other Indians, one standing apart from the rest. He looked about their village with great curiosity.

"They've left their arms a quarter mile away from town, as we agreed," the sentry told Standish. The captain nodded and adjusted his helmet.

All the Indian men were about John's own height, taller than most of the English. They wore long leather hose down their legs and breechcloths at the waist, with deer skins draped about their shoulders. Their long hair in particular was adorned with fur and feathers. Their faces were bare of hair but painted with stripes of black and red paint in varying patterns.

"This Tisquantum," said Samoset, gesturing to the man who stood apart from the rest.

Tisquantum had been the subject of much discussion since Samoset's first visit. He was the last surviving member of the Patuxet, who once occupied the land where New Plymouth now stood. His hair bore a single feather, hanging sideways from a knot in his hair. His face was painted with four stripes of red paint in the center, drawn from forehead to chin. He looked about with curiosity, John realized, because this had been his home, before he was kidnapped and taken away into slavery by an Englishman. John wondered how he found his way back home.

"Tiss-kwon-tum," Carver said, testing out the strange syllables.

Tisquantum smiled. "The English call me Squanto," he said, formal, more cordial in attitude than John expected.

"Squanto, then." The governor nodded. "You hail from Patuxet?"

"Yes," Squanto said, spreading his arms out wide. "This was our home."

"How terrible for you, to come back and find them gone." Bradford's face was sympathetic, although his words were indelicate.

Squanto nodded, as though his head was bent under the weight of great sorrow. "Massasoit's people were once a thousand men. Now..." He shrugged. "You can see them, across the hill."

John's head snapped to the hill across the brook. As though on cue, a rank of Indian warriors rose onto the crest of the hill. He gripped his musket, aware that it was not loaded, his match cord unlit. Had Samoset come in peace to lower their defenses? Had he, as Hopkins suggested, scouted out their camp to tell their weakness to their enemies? Would John die, now, at the hands of these Indian warriors?

"They cannot approach the camp armed," Standish said, almost before Squanto finished speaking.

Squanto shook his head. "Massasoit will not come into your village," he said.

Carver frowned. "He will not come?"

"No. Too much danger from the English."

"Well, then we must go to him," Carver said.

"You cannot go, Governor," Bradford put in. "If their lord sees danger for himself in our camp, there will be danger for you in his."

They intended to parley? There were many more men in Massasoit's retinue than there were left in all the English company. The Indians could overwhelm them without sweating, despite the English's advantages of guns and cannons. There were still living in the settlement perhaps twenty men, and a handful of teenage boys, most of whom were still as inept as John at bearing arms. He estimated at least twice that many Indians across the brook, and they were just those he could see. How many more were waiting out of sight, in the woods or down the slope of that hill?

"Well, I will go," volunteered Winslow.

John stared at him, wide-eyed.

"Aye," Carver agreed, still assessing the opposite hill. Squanto nodded also.

Carver began making preparations, talking to Howland and Winslow about what victuals and goods they could present to the Indian king. Squanto observed, his eyes flicking back and forth between the English settlement's leaders. John approached him, curious about this sole survivor of his obliterated people.

"How do you bear it?" he could not help himself from asking. "Being here again?" He remembered the village they found, with bleached-white bones, scattered where too many ill had not had the strength to bury the dead. After the number of graves he dug that winter, he could well understand the despair, the knowledge that, soon, the plague would come for you and kill you too.

"Whether they are here or not here, this is their land," Squanto said. "Although they are all gone, I can feel their presence."

This was contrary to John's own experience. He felt no sign that God watched over them here. Perhaps it was true that the spirits of the Indians still lingered, and that was why he could not feel God? Nonetheless, he felt pity for Squanto, who was left alone in the world of all his people.

Howland ran off to pick up some biscuit, butter, and aqua vitae, while Carver handed Winslow a few English-made knives and jewels to be presented as gifts. "You must express to them that we want peace, and to truck with them and have a favorable relationship," he said. "We do not come here to harm them." The former printer nodded, accepting the things with care. He trooped off with Squanto and Samoset, down the slope, across to the hill where Massasoit and his company waited. John's stomach turned at the array of fearsome visages and bows that waited there. Winslow was either quite brave, or even less in touch with the world around him than John believed. He checked that his belt of powder and shot was ready, although his match cord was still unlit, and the time he took to prepare the weapon would be insufficient if they were attacked.

"We ought to prepare, in case he comes. Goodman Alden, you were helping to unload the shallop of our things from *Mayflower*—can you not make Winslow's house look comfortable, and fine? Bring in cushions and things, so he may be comfortable."

Winslow's house was the newest built, and, as it had two rooms instead of one, it was much larger than some of the others. It had also taken longer to build and was not yet thatched, so it was not yet furnished.

"Aye, Governor."

John remembered a green carpet he carried off the shallop and deposited in the common storehouse. As the governor watched the retinue approach, men scampered about collecting food and drink on his orders. John went to the storage shed. In addition to a hogshead of meal and their stolen collection of seed corn, they filled this space with some of the excess household goods of the dead. He dug under a stack of books—these Brownists did carry a lot of books—

and found the rug he sought. He shook it out and glanced around for cushions or other rugs which might be pleasing to a savage king. Then, arms loaded with soft rugs and cushions, he made his way down the street to Winslow's house. The news of Massasoit's imminent arrival spread through the entire population of the town already, and the street was filled with people pressed together in excited whispering.

He grunted and heaved the items into a formless heap onto the dirt floor of the new house. Sunlight streamed in through the wood framing of the roof. He picked up the rug to spread across the floor.

"Joseph would have adored this," murmured a soft voice at the door. He turned and saw Miss Mullins watching him.

"Aye?" he asked.

She nodded and came inside to allow Master Goodman past her, carrying a small cask of aqua vitae. "He was so excited to come to the New World, to see the Indians. It was all he talked of for weeks. Father got upset with him. I believe he thought that Joseph's tales of scalping were frightening my mother and me."

John raised a quizzical eyebrow. "Were you not frightened?" he asked. He was wary enough of the idea himself.

"I heard the stories before. I was not afraid, knowing my father would be with us. Now that he is gone, and Mother, and Joseph too, there is naught that frightens me. For the worst that can be in this life is to leave it, and once I do, I will await God's judgment with them."

"Hmm," John murmured, turning back to his task.

Miss Mullins came forward to help him lay the cushions around the rug. More and more people were crowding into the house, and John began to feel his heart hammering in his chest. His eyes strayed to Miss Mullins, who fluffed a pillow to perfection. Her figure was not so robust as it was when they began their voyage, her complexion no longer genteelly pale. She had grown gaunt, her face drawn with the horrors of grief, with the agony of so many deaths. Her hair hung in lank threads from her coif. Her blue petticoats hung in dirty tatters about her shoes. Her hands were raw from rough labor, and dirt collected under her fingernails. There was room in her bodice where there used to be none, and the hunger that wore them all down was evident in her narrow frame. Even like this, his desire to see her smile increased day by day. Her thinness made him feel the pangs of hunger in his own belly. It would soon be spring. There must be fish and fowl in spring; there must be salad greens that could be eaten until the harvest, when they could at last make bread.

They? He would not wait in this place until the harvest. He was to leave, as soon as Jones gave word. He would go with *Mayflower* and go back to England, where he belonged, where he need never worry about the dangers of Indians, nor this terrible disease, nor starvation. Yet there, also, he could not look back at this dark-haired maiden with bright blue eyes.

John felt cornered, crowded into Winslow's house with both the principal of the English and Massasoit, Samoset, Squanto, and several of his warriors. The rest were left outside, but at least sixty men came in Massasoit's retinue, numbers which easily daunted the English. Two tall Indian men stood at John's right side, their faces streaked with yellow, white, and black paint. One wore a fox tail hanging from his hair, the other a fan of feathers at his crown. John was unused to meeting men of his own height, and he liked it not. Their presence unnerved him, the more so because their bare flesh showed their muscles, while John felt that his own muscular cooper's body had withered and shrunk during their long confinement and his subsequent illness.

He held his musket and would not relinquish it, despite the close quarters and the fact that it would be useless if fighting broke out inside Winslow's house. Somehow, holding it reassured him. He started to understand Standish more and more. Hopkins' presence on his left reassured him further.

Howland presented a mug of aqua vitae to Governor Carver, who raised a toast to Massasoit. The sachem drank from his cup, draining it in a single draught. Massasoit was a young man, with his forehead painted red all the way across. He was dressed much like any of his men, with leather hose and feathers in his hair, but he bore the skin of a wildcat around his arm and a great chain of white bones about his neck. His countenance was grave, and though he was dressed alike to all his men, he carried power about his shoulders with as little effort as he did the cat's skin which draped them. He had the bearing of a man used to being obeyed.

"As to the terms of our agreement," Carver began, looking back and forth between Massasoit and Squanto, who translated his speech into the Indian tongue, "we should of course like to have peace. No violence between us, between any of our people."

Massasoit nodded and spoke, staring at the governor and not sparing a glance for his interpreter. His forehead was breaking out in many beads of sweat. John attributed it to the great quantity of aqua vitae he consumed without pause.

"Massasoit would also like to be an ally to the English. To have peace between you, and your support against his enemies."

"Enemies?" Standish asked. "The Nauset? The Paomet?"

Squanto shook his head. "The Nauset and Paomet are Massasoit's people. Their sachems are under Massasoit. It was the same with my people. We were not of Massasoit's tribe, but he is the grand sachem over many."

"So, if we have peace with you, will we have peace with the Nauset and the Paomet also?" Carver asked.

"Samoset told us the Nauset have fired upon us and stolen from us. They may not mean to be our friends," Standish said, still miffed about the tools that were stolen from him, although Samoset had returned them on his second visit.

"We do mean to make recompense to the Paomet for the corn which we took on Cape Cod," Bradford put in, ensuring that point was made clear.

Squanto sat in long discussion with Massasoit. The beads of sweat now dripped down the sachem's forehead, marring the neat red paint which adorned it.

"The Nauset do not like the English, because many of their men were taken away by Englishmen and sold as slaves. If you make peace with Massasoit, they will understand that you do not mean to do them harm. Massasoit will speak to Aspinet and tell him you mean peace. He will tell the Paomet you mean to repay the debt of the corn you have taken. Then you may have peace."

Bradford sighed with relief.

"If the Nauset are not Massasoit's enemies, against whom are we meant to defend him?" Standish demanded.

"When the plague came, it killed many of Massasoit's people. He was once at great strength and feared by all the tribes around here. The Massachusett also suffered, and they would not act against him, but they have made many threatening speeches against you already. He would help to defend you against them."

Carver nodded.

"Their intelligence must be good, for Squanto to know what all the other tribes are thinking," muttered Hopkins at John's side.

"You do not think they share such information in the open?" John asked, whispering. "Samoset also knew about our many encounters with the Nauset and the Paomet."

"If they heard the Massachusett making threats against us, it was because the Massachusett asked them to join in threatening us."

"Are there tribes against whom Massasoit would seek our protection?" Standish continued his interrogation with a little more arrogance than John could credit. How would such a man, with such a force of warriors, seek protection from their weak and much diminished company?

Squanto hesitated. "The Narragansett make great sacrifices to our god, and because of this they were spared the plague. They still number many thousands, and they seek to dominate Massasoit, who was once their great enemy."

Massasoit looked at Squanto at the name of the Narragansett. It was one he recognized, and not information he'd asked Squanto to divulge. What did that mean? Was Squanto warning them of the danger they would be in by entering an agreement with Massasoit?

"It is clear," said Carver, wresting control of the conversation from Standish, "that we both would benefit from an agreement. Mutual protection. Let us lay out some terms in writing. I think, firstly, that we shall agree not to do harm to one another. No injury by any of his people to any of ours, yes?" Winslow, who sat next to the governor, wrote this down. He was prepared with paper and ink and quill, and even with his glasses, which he affixed to his forehead, their ribbon threaded through the nose piece and tied at the back of his head.

Massasoit nodded. His forehead was now wet and shining with his sweat. He said a few words to Squanto.

"He adds that if any man of his should do harm to yours, he will send them to you to be punished according to your custom. It is a common thing amongst the people here, that an offender be punished by his sachem."

Carver nodded. "Aye, it is right that such an offender should be punished. And we shall do the same for any of ours who might offend him."

Next to John, Hopkins grunted.

"Any of our tools or other things that get taken by any of his people should be returned," interjected Standish. Carver sighed.

"And we should return to them anything we take, as well. Like the corn from Cape Cod," Bradford added.

Carver closed his eyes. He had not the face for cards; he hid nothing well. "Yes. Any theft on either side should be returned or repaid, to each side's satisfaction. Yes?"

Massasoit agreed.

"Then, as we have discussed, mutual protection against any who should war against us. If the Narragansett should make war on him, or the Massachusett on us, or any others, we should come to his aid, and he to ours."

"He says that he should also speak with Aspinet, and the other sachems under him, and ask that they make peace with you also. If they know you have made peace with Massasoit, it will ease your path."

Winslow scratched away at his paper, filling in the terms the pair named.

"Aye. Are there any other terms that should be set?" Carver asked, opening the floor for Standish.

"We should formalize our agreement that they leave their weapons before they come to our door."

"Massasoit asks that you should do the same, with your guns, when you come to visit him."

Standish snarled, but Carver agreed, quieting the fierce captain.

"It is good we are agreed. We should each sign, when Winslow has finished transcribing for us. King James will esteem you as his friends, as you are our allies." Carver smiled. "When you return to your home, how will we reach you? As our allies, we should like to send messages and to trade with you, to visit you."

Squanto seemed to have an argument with Massasoit as he discussed this dilemma, but when it was over, he presented a careful smile to the governor. "Massasoit wishes that I stay with you and teach you our ways, to help you grow your corn, and so you can send messages to him through me."

Chapter Eleven

John Alden was hired for a cooper, at South-
Hampton, where the ship victualed; and being a
hopeful young man, was much desired, but left to
his own liking to go or stay when he came here...

—William Bradford, *Of Plymouth
Plantation*, 1651

Saturday, 31 March 1621

"Corn, squash, and beans are three sisters," Squanto said,
showing them seeds of all three crops. "We plant the corn
first, with the bodies of eels or fish in a mound of dirt, with
the seeds." He took a dead eel that he captured in Town
Brook and dug a little hole in the dirt of the field. He put the
eel inside, buried five or six seeds of corn with it, and
mounded the dirt until it was a small pile with a flat top.
Priscilla watched his hands. He handled the seeds with care.
A large gathering of the English watched Squanto as he
buried the seeds in the dirt. Even the children were watching,
and the older ones would be expected to help in the planting.

"When the corn has begun to grow, we will plant the
squash and beans around her. The corn will help the beans
grow tall, and the squash's broad leaves will protect the
corn." He took another eel and built another mound of dirt,
planting the seeds inside. "You need to sow the ground with
fish, or nothing will be able to grow."

"We've seen but a handful of cod in the bay, and naught
but eels in the brook," complained Master Hopkins. His
young son Giles stood by him, arms crossed over his chest in
imitation of his father.

Squanto smiled. "The fish will come. Just when it is time for planting, they come in great numbers down the water."

"Won't animals come to eat the dead fish? If we fish for them and bring them in, why should we put them in the ground for lions instead of eating them ourselves?"

"Wolves may come, yes. Would you rather eat the fish now, while it is plentiful, or use it to help your corn grow, so it can feed you through the winter?" Squanto asked. "You must defend your fields against wolves, so that you can eat the things you have sown."

They set about planting, digging up small holes of dirt and burying eels, which Squanto captured for them with the help of some of the boys. Priscilla worked her fingers into the dirt, enjoying the coolness of it while the sun shone hot on her back. She would need to work in the Carvers' garden soon, and plant some herbs and greens from the seeds they carried with them, along with the ones that Squanto showed them grew wild in the forest.

Mistress Carver had given up on keeping the girls from seeing Indians. After the conference with Massasoit, several of his men tried to stay at Plymouth again, for several days. It was determined, too, that Squanto should settle there and live among them. Under these circumstances, Mistress Carver realized it was impossible to keep them from the Indians. It was just as well, for any hands that could be used in planting could help their crop at harvest time.

Mistress Hopkins knelt in the field, across a row from Priscilla. Her stepdaughter, Constance, was helping her, though Giles stuck like glue to his father. The babe Oceanus was already five months old and lay cradled by his mother, trying to sit upright.

"It is good to be at work outdoors," Priscilla said. "Much more pleasant than being aboard ship, even if we are burying rotting eels." She picked one up and entombed it in a mound of dirt.

"Aye," said Mistress Hopkins, distracted by her babe. Oceanus grabbed her sleeve and pulled it toward him.

"Would you ever want to sail back across to England?" Priscilla asked, unable to cease thinking about the idea.

"What? Why should we want to leave, when we have just begun our plantation?"

"Carver has asked me if I wish to return to England," Priscilla confided.

Mistress Hopkins paused, pulling the infant from her lap. "Do you wish to go?"

"I..." She poked a few seeds into the middle of the dirt heap. "I have no particular desire to return, nor to live in my sister's house, but..."

Mistress Hopkins raised her eyebrows. "You have some reason you wish to go? Or, rather, a reason not to stay?"

Priscilla smiled a little, thinking of Goodman Alden carrying a pile of pillows and rugs so high he could not see around them. "I think it is a foolish reason," she admitted.

"Do you concern yourself so over a man?" Mistress Hopkins kept Oceanus in her lap with one hand, using the other to dig up the soil.

Priscilla felt herself blushing. "Two men, in fact," she admitted. "I—well, Captain Standish has proposed to the governor that he might marry me."

Mistress Hopkins snapped her head up. "And the other has not made such an offer?"

Priscilla shook her head. "He intends to go back with *Mayflower*. I do not think the idea of staying has even crossed his mind."

"So, you have the choice to stay, and perhaps marry Standish, or go, with a man of whose feelings you are unsure?

And you do not wish to go, apart from your interest in this man?"

She nodded.

"It seems clear to me, Miss Mullins, that you have a preference for this man, and not for the good captain."

"I have no quarrel with Captain Standish. His offer well surprised me, but it did not make me feel glad."

"Have you perhaps spent too much time at the theater, where marriages are determined more by feelings than by sense?" Mistress Hopkins asked. "Feelings carry you so far before they change, and you are left wondering why you made such foolish choices."

Priscilla pursed her lips. She was frustrated, for she had some inkling that Mistress Hopkins was right, but she could not help her feelings.

"I have been orphaned by this New World and lost my family," Priscilla said. "I thought I was alone, but Miss Tilley, who was also orphaned, stayed close to me. To leave that and go back to England, where the people are known to me by blood but not such experience—I find the idea absurd."

"That decision, then, is dictated by your feelings for a friend, rather than for a nameless man who would leave without a second thought. Would he not think to stay here, because this is where you are? Do you not want a man who would give you at least as much consideration as you are giving him? If you are thinking of sailing to England for his sake, even though you do not wish it, ought he not to consider staying, because that is what you want?"

Priscilla's eyes widened. "Are there such men, that take their wives' wills as more than whims?"

Mistress Hopkins laughed. "Although you have suffered much this winter, my dear, you are still too inexperienced in the ways of the world. You need to wait some time before deciding who to marry."

"About a year, before Carver says I am of appropriate age."

"You are in such haste to be married as soon as you can?" Mistress Hopkins sighed and shifted Oceanus so that he sat in her lap with his back to her stomach. She bent and laid a kiss on the top of his head. "I suppose it cannot be helped, now that you have no father living. What would he say of the man you desire? And your mother?"

"That he is not as respectable as the captain, I suppose. That he may not make good use of my inheritance of shares in the venture, if he is so eager to fly this place. Those thoughts make no accounting for the urge I feel to stand beside him, when I can. A desire that does not arise with Captain Standish."

"So honest!" Mistress Hopkins let Oceanus tug at her sleeve and put it into his mouth. "You should consider those things, before you decide who to marry. A reason as rash as young affection will not sustain you through a marriage. Young as you are, it is difficult to see that marriage spans the course of a lifetime, which is far longer than you can imagine. If feelings fade, what benefits or harm to you are there in this union? If he is to be in charge of your inheritance, ensure he is the kind of man who will use it to provide for you."

Which was all well and good, but left Priscilla feeling no surer about making a decision than she was before.

Monday, 2 April 1621

"Do we not hate Spain already?" asked Goodman Alden, laughing.

Priscilla was on her way back to Carver's house when she found Alden laughing at Goodman Howland in the street. Tilley stood beside Howland, swaying side to side a little, making her skirt weave patterns through the air. She was not often parted from his side, these days, at least when Howland was in town.

"Why should we hate Spain?" Priscilla asked, joining the group and threading her arm through Tilley's. It was rare to see Alden laugh.

"Because Spaniards kidnapped and sold your family into slavery," Tilley said, giggling.

Priscilla raised her eyebrow and looked between the three of them. She shrugged. "It is reassuring to find you all laughing over such a thing." She did not see the joke.

Howland was not laughing. Instead, his ears were reddening.

"It was an example, so that we might see their point of view," he protested. It seemed Tilley and Goodman Alden were teasing him.

"Whose point of view?" Priscilla asked, trying to catch up.

"The Nauset. Goodman Alden says they mean us harm, and I thought rightly so, after the ills the English have inflicted on them."

Howland's embarrassment made Tilley giggle harder. She covered her mouth with a pale hand, but she kept looking at his face. The flush spread to his cheeks, seeing her laugh at him.

"Well, what business have you all, about the street in the middle of the day?" Priscilla asked, to give poor Howland some relief. "Oughtn't you to be building something?"

"I have come after the governor's attention, but it seems he is not at home," Alden answered.

"Goodman Alden, you find me returning," called Carver, who came up the road behind him. "You have a question?"

"Aye."

Priscilla caught Alden casting a wary glance in her direction. "I saw you spoke with Master Jones this morning. With the ship empty of passengers and taking on ballast, I wondered how soon he plans his departure?" Why did he look at her before saying such a thing? Did he worry what she thought of his going? Her heart picked up a beat.

"Yes, *Mayflower* will sail in three days' time, if all goes well with lading her, and the weather doesn't turn on us again." The strength of Carver's gaze on her made Priscilla uncomfortable. "Master Jones has offered to take back any of the colonists who wish to go. I don't imagine there will be many who take him up on the offer, but those who are in a position to go back to England might consider it." She frowned.

"Only three days?" Goodman Alden asked.

"Aye, three days. Though, with all the preparations being done, you knew the day approached, did you not, Goodman Alden? If there is aught you need do to prepare, I would not keep you laboring at our dwellings and in our fields. You've done far more than you were hired on to do, and I'm sure the company appreciates your efforts."

"No, no. Nothing to do but pack my things together. I am surprised to find I have grown used to this place."

Used to it? It was the first time Priscilla heard him waver in his conviction to be gone from Plymouth. Did he have some inclination to stay, after all?

The governor clapped him on the shoulder, having the same thought as Priscilla. "Goodman Alden, do think that you can reconsider. There is room enough for you to stay, and we would not let your hands stay idle long."

She wondered if the hope shining from her was visible to others. She was not the one to propose it, but would he consider staying?

"Master Jones has said they might make good use of me aboard," Alden answered. "I should hate to leave him shorthanded."

What kind of a reason was that, to want to leave? When a week ago he told her he would return to his master's place in England, and he was less than certain of his welcome there?

"If that is what you wish, though I am certain we would make much greater use of you here."

Goodman Alden smiled, but made no answer, and after a moment, Carver went inside his house. Carver was so straight-backed and smiling when they left England, but Priscilla found he seemed every day more stooped and sorrowful under the weight of the colony's responsibilities.

"Do you still intend to return to England with *Mayflower*?" Tilley asked Alden, frowning. "Why do you not mean to settle here?"

"It was always my intention to return, and Master Jones lost many men in the sickness. I can be of use to him, and I have already been away longer than I'd imagined. By the time *Mayflower* returns to England, I'll have been absent a full year."

"We shall miss your presence here," said Howland. "Our losses are uncountable, but they have been relieved in some measure by your hands."

She saw Alden look at her again. What was he thinking of, always glancing at her like that? The man needed to decide whether he desired her company or not. All these sidelong glances gave her hope that he might feel some affection for her, as she did him. Her heart hammered in her chest. Should she say something of the governor's proposition? He had looked at her with such meaning that someone must have noticed it. She took a deep breath.

"The governor has suggested that I consider removing to England as well," she said, staring at Alden's face.

"What?" Tilley shrieked beside her, caught by surprise.

"Aye!" Goodman Alden yelped. His eyes were bright.

What had Mistress Hopkins told her, just two days ago? If he would not stay for her sake, when she would go for his, was he a husband worth having? He would have her go with him, but he would not consider staying? Her mind rushed with questions unanswered by his response.

"You would leave me in Plymouth without you?" Tilley asked, injured at the perceived betrayal. "I thought we might stand by each other."

Priscilla squeezed Tilley's arm. She had not meant to injure Tilley's trust in her. They had stood by each other so far. She did not mean to leave her, without family or friend. Did she?

"It was an idea of the governor's," Priscilla reassured. "Not one I should relish abiding."

She glanced at Goodman Alden again. His eyes were glued to her face, but he did not ask her to go with him, did not expand on his single positive exclamation with any reason why she should travel to England.

Would he speak his mind if she told him of the captain's proposition? Would he be glad for her, or disappointed for himself? Would he not say something, if he had a rival for her affection? She felt pain in her chest. How could the very act of making a statement be so difficult?

"If I should go, then I cannot fulfill the expectations of the captain."

"Expectations?" Tilley asked, leaning her head against Priscilla's arm.

"Indeed. He came to the governor asking about his plans for my marriage."

Miss Tilley gasped, eyes seeking out Goodman Alden. "Captain Standish has asked for you in marriage?"

"Not in so many words. He pointed out to the governor that I will be a very marriageable prospect, when I am of an age to marry." She stared into Goodman Alden's eyes. He looked dumbfounded. Did he seem distressed? Why did he still say nothing? Would he not make any argument at all that she should go with him?

"Captain Standish would at least safeguard you from the Indians," he said at last.

Her jaw dropped. She looked at him in disbelief. Did he have no interest in her at all, that he would offer her to Standish without hesitation?

"If you are to marry here," he continued, "you could do worse than to marry the captain. He is strong, after all—did he not survive all the winter, without falling ill even once? Did he not spend his time tending the sick alongside you? He has much to recommend him." Alden's voice was flat as he rambled on, as though he could not stop the stream of praise flowing from his mouth, as though he could not believe himself saying it. "He is well respected, the military leader of the colony. He's loyal, and he would be a boon protector. You should have naught to fear from the Indians, if *he* were your husband."

"You would have me marry Captain Standish, while you sail away to England?" Priscilla cried. "You would stand in front of me and list his praises, while planning in two days to leave without looking back?" She could feel tears welling in her eyes. How could she have been so wrong? How was it possible that she felt so much in his presence, and he felt nothing for her? "Go, then," she said. "Go back to

Southampton, if you would speak so admirably for the captain. Go to your master's cooperage, and leave me to marry Standish." Her voice choked, and she turned away, tugging Tilley with her. They started down the hill, but she could not help but turn and look at him once more.

"Why don't you speak for yourself, John?" she asked, her voice tinged with all her bitter regret.

Priscilla rushed down the street, Tilley dragged along in her wake. She felt her heartbeat in her ears, felt the pounding of it. Of all the things in her life, that had been the hardest for her to say. Yet she dared herself to speak, and he still spoke on behalf of Captain Standish, rather than in his own interest. She must have mistaken his intentions. If he could make such a recommendation, there was no way he felt the same quickening of breath, the same heat that she felt whenever she thought of him. She felt as though an invisible cord tied them together, and that, while she could keep a certain distance from him, she could not sever it. Yet, he wanted to cross the ocean, to leave Plymouth forever, and he did not even care whether she accompanied him or not.

"He can leave, then, if all he wants is to go back to England!" she shouted at the ocean before flopping down onto the pebbled beach.

Tilley squatted beside her and rubbed her back. "It is what he intended, all along. I forgot that was his plan." She looked at Priscilla. "But you remembered, otherwise I do not believe you would have even considered the governor's suggestion."

Priscilla groaned and pulled her apron up over her face. "Why would I consider such a foolish plan? My sister does not want me in her house any more than I want to leave Plymouth."

"You cannot live all your life with a mastiff sitting on your chest."

Priscilla rolled her head to the side to look at the ocean. The large rock where he sat with her hove into her view. She groaned.

"Do you think that if he leaves, I will forget about him?" It did not seem possible, when every inch of Plymouth reminded her of him.

"Do you wish to forget him, if he leaves?"

Priscilla sighed and lay back on the beach, knocking her head against the ground. "The worst of it is, I know not that I do. How can I wish to forget him, when his mere presence makes me feel so discomposed?" She shook her head. "At first, I just felt so nervous and dull-witted around him, and it was not pleasant at all. But then, as we spent a little more time in each other's company, the beating of my heart became more joyful each time I saw him. These feelings tell me that he is nearby, and that somehow reassures me. How can I stay here and marry some other man while the man who makes me feel this way sails across the sea?"

Tilley was silent for a long moment. When she answered, her voice was fluid with tears.

"If you want so much to be beside him, I will fare well enough on my own." She was trying not to cry, trying to be as strong as she had been through her mother's illness. "Priscilla, I do understand. You have been love sick for him so long, you oughtn't to let him leave you."

Priscilla bolted upright and took Tilley in her arms. "Of course I will not leave you, Tilley. For, while seeing him makes my heart thump harder, seeing you makes me calm. You have been beside me through all my troubles, and he suggests I marry another." Tilley's tears made Priscilla start to cry again. "I would be a fool to consider leaving you for such a man as that."

The two orphaned girls held each other and cried over all they had lost.

John and Howland were left standing outside Carver's house, watching Miss Mullins and Miss Tilley run off.

"Does she not want to marry Captain Standish?" Howland asked in confusion.

"I am sure I cannot say," said John. "The moment before, I thought she wanted to return to England."

Howland shook his head. "I do not think she has aught in England to return to, Goodman Alden. Many of us here do not."

John shook his head. He felt lightheaded.

"What have you in England, that makes you so eager to return there?" Howland asked. "It seems that many here would have you stay."

"I admit my reasons for leaving have carried less consequence for me, over the past weeks. Yet, the reasons are still there. I cannot just put aside the desire to go which has been plaguing me since we landed here."

Howland nodded, considering, though John had not answered him.

"What happens to my soul if I die here, Goodman Howland?" John asked, surprising himself. He had not thought to share this question.

"Is there some difference in dying here than dying in England?" Howland asked.

"I do not think God is in this place." John shook his head, adamant, not to be persuaded that this conviction, on which he'd based all his decisions, was false. "And here there are so many threats to life. If you die where God is not present, how will he know to call you, to meet your judgment?"

"How do you claim to know that God is not here, when you will not seek him out? Do not your thirty-nine articles say that you must receive God's promises as they are sent to you in scripture?" Howland asked. "If you are expecting a priest to appear and absolve you, to tell you that you will be saved, I do not think you will find any. But does not the King's church also preach predestination? Whether Jesus judges you saved or not, does not rely on your location on this earth." Howland shook his head. "If you are so afraid to die here, is it not because you are afraid to die at all?"

"And here there is more risk."

"You still think so, even after we have made peace with the Indians?"

"As I said, there are still threats from the Narragansett and Massachusett."

"Yet you would leave us all to our fate? Do you think that if I die here, I will be damned? Does the choice of salvation or damnation not still reside in the hands of God?"

John scrubbed his hands across his face.

"Would you leave Miss Mullins to such a fate, whether or not as the wife of the captain?" Howland asked.

"If she wishes to be the captain's wife, it is not my place to dissuade her."

"It seemed that she wished for something else entirely."

"Did she mean that she hopes for me to ask to marry her?"

"If that is what she hopes, does it in any way alter your decision?"

Marriage? If he married her, would that not lead to childbearing? How could he put her at such a risk?

"Are you content to go and leave her to marry the captain?"

If John did not marry her, then she would marry another. And she would still bear the risk of childbearing, at the side of someone else. He felt his temper flare at the idea of her beside Standish. Standish? How could she think to marry Standish? Had she ever laughed beside Standish, ever told him her suspicions of plots and conspiracy, ever shared her tales of her home in England? Standish was a fine man, but was he distracted from all other thought by the sound of her singing, did he put his arms around her to protect her from a musket blast, or sit beside her by the ocean, her strength in her grief pulling him from the brink of his own despair?

Had Standish put his arms around her? *Had* he felt the comfort of her hand upon his brow?

"How can she marry *him*?" John asked.

"Whether or not she chooses to marry him, if you sail on *Mayflower*, she will not be able to marry you."

And John found he hated the thought of losing her. Of rowing out to *Mayflower* and seeing her standing on their rock, looking after him. It was hard to think that once he'd sailed, he would never see her again. It was hard to bear, but not impossible.

For he well remembered his nightmares, which still shook him awake from time to time. How many bodies had he buried here? He knew that if he stayed, he might someday have to bury her. And that thought was beyond his ability to bear.

Wednesday, 4 April 1621

It was the last day before *Mayflower*'s departure, and the ship's longboat was taking the final lading from shore: her crew. John's sea chest sat in the bottom of the boat. The governor handed a packet of letters to one of the sailors to be delivered in England. John knew that one of them accompanied the will of Master Mullins.

He had not seen Miss Mullins in the day and a half since she had questioned him. *Why don't you speak for yourself, John?* The question still echoed in his mind. There had been mere hours to mull the question over, and in the end his indecision led him to the longboat. Following the path of least resistance, the path he had been planning on for months, but for his brief moments of daydreaming. He could not follow the daydreams which were so effectively chased out of his head by nightmares.

The ship was due to sail with the morning tide, and the colonists were gathered to say a last goodbye to the ship's men whom they had come to know. Master Heale, the ship's surgeon, was among the last to leave, and some tears were shed at his going.

"Alden," Howland said and pulled him into an embrace.

"Fare thee well," John told his friend.

He could not believe what was happening all around him. He had anticipated it for so long, part of him thought that the day might be forever delayed and never come. He thought that there would be something that would prevent him from going. Did they not keep saying that they needed him here? Did they not need another man for the militia, another pair of hands to work wood? Was he going to go aboard that ship and never return? But Carver had left this choice to him. John was allowed to make his own decision, and now he stood on the shore, looking up at the little town into which he had poured his sweat, his strength, all he could for the past five months. It looked different, now, than the gloomy, intimidating, barren place he'd first viewed with skepticism from *Mayflower*'s deck. The trees budded with green leaves and spring flowers. Smoke rose from the chimneys of the dwellings he helped build. His gaze slid to the hill by the water, where half their friends and neighbors lay buried. He shuddered and focused on his resolve to go.

The governor gave him a fond farewell, but John was looking about for the one person he longed to see. She was not there. He had half thought that, if she wanted to marry him instead of Standish, she would take up the governor's offer to return to England. Would Miss Mullins rather stay in Plymouth, with the bodies of her parents?

Heale murmured to him that it was time to go, and John stepped into the longboat. He gazed at the crowd, searching one last time for her face. When he didn't see it, he returned Howland's goodbye wave and took up an oar. They pushed off from the shore. He pulled back on the oar and the boat slid through the water. The gathering of colonists grew smaller and smaller as they retreated into the bay.

"*Mayflower* is taking the last of her lading today," Tilley told Priscilla.

She nodded acknowledgment. He had not come after her, had not spoken with her. Well, that was answer enough, was it not? He did not want her.

"Shall we go down and see them off? This is the last opportunity to say goodbye to anyone departing with the ship," Tilley wheedled.

Priscilla shook her head. They both knew there was but one person boarding the ship today that either of them would miss. She still couldn't quite believe that he was going to leave.

"Come now, Priscilla. You will not even wave goodbye? It will be good for you to see him leave, to know that he is going."

"Why *is* he going?" Priscilla burst out in a fit. "He has not even spoken to me in two days. Why should I see him off, when he does not want to talk to me?" Priscilla knew that Tilley knew she was avoiding Goodman Alden at least as much as he was avoiding her.

"Then at least let us go and watch the boat depart. We do not need to say goodbye, but you should see it off, Priscilla."

When Priscilla still refused, Mary Chilton butted in from her spot on the floor by the hearth. "Why do you worry so over whether to go or not to go? What does it matter if a bunch of sailors take some beaver pelts back to England?"

"I do not wish to see him off!" Priscilla protested.

"Well, I do not wish to have you shouting in my house!" said Mistress Carver. "It would do you well to take in the fresher air, so go out and see them off and leave me in peace."

Tilley took Priscilla by the hand and dragged her toward the door.

"I'll go, I'll go, unhand me," she muttered. She took the time to fasten her cloak about her shoulders, although the weather warmed enough that she didn't need it. She wanted to feel enclosed and hidden, wanted the comforting heft of the wool weighing on her shoulders and around her skirt.

As they came out of the house, she looked down the street toward the water to find that they were already too late. The longboat was pulling away from shore. She could see Goodman Alden, his brown felt capotain askew on his head. He was bent over his oars, concentrating on rowing away.

She broke from Tilley and dashed down to the beach, weaving around the gathered crowd of well-wishers until she was at the fore. She watched him row: strong arms, strong back, pulling against the water to draw him farther and farther from her. She stared after the boat as it grew tiny, until it bumped up against *Mayflower* and began unloading its passengers. She stared at it even after the other settlers turned away to leave.

Tilley took her arm and led her back up the hill. Priscilla nodded, blinking to keep her tears from falling.

"He left," she said.

"Aye. He's gone."

Mayflower loomed above John as the longboat glided into place beside her. A block dangling a woven net hung from the spar above their ladder for ease of loading the cargo. The rope ladder slapped against the hull in the breeze. John pulled his oar in and stood, grasping for the side of the ship to steady himself. The seamen moved about with ease, loading his belongings into the net. His stomach churned and he tried not to look at anything.

"Go on," a burly man said to him. "We'll need to load the boat on deck soon enough, and we can't have you standing about in it."

John nodded and gripped the ladder, hauling himself up to the top deck. He'd no sooner set foot on deck than a bucket of water splashed over him. He looked up to see a mouth of sparse brown teeth grinning.

"'Pologies, mate," the sailor said. "Gots to wash the deck, y' see."

John grimaced. He was still unsure where he was meant to sleep; he was beginning to think the sailors wouldn't take to his presence aboard with as much enthusiasm as he had hoped. He set off toward the main cabin, seeking after Master

Jones. To his startlement, he saw Standish and Bradford already standing with the ship's master.

"You are not returning to England as well?" he asked, gaping.

Bradford laughed. "Alden! Good to know you've made it aboard. No, indeed, we were paying our last respects to the vessel and her master. *Mayflower* has been a great help to us, and so has Master Jones."

"The shallop is waiting below to take us back, along with Hopkins," Standish explained. He reached up to fix John's hat, which was close to falling off his head.

Standish, who sought to stand beside Miss Mullins in marriage? And until that time, John thought the man a friend, or at least a comrade. He could not very well express his newfound distaste, but neither was he inclined to sociability.

"Ah. I see."

Master Jones stared at John, unblinking, in a way that suggested he disliked John's presence on his ship.

"Do you have some concern for my attention, Goodman Alden?" Jones asked.

"I do not know where I am to sleep, Master Jones."

Jones blinked and then sighed. "Apologies, Goodman Alden, the thought had not crossed my mind. Three quartermasters and the boatswain died in sickness, and I imagine there is some lingering disorder. I was more concerned over the loss of the cook, as the men are all experienced enough to know their places aboard. Give me a few moments to conclude my discussion with the captain and Master Bradford, and I will see to it."

John nodded his thanks and fled from the cabin. So, his presence on board was forgotten even by the ship's master. The deck was a bustle of activity, and he could see nowhere he would be out of the way. Even the hatches were occupied, as stores were moved down to the hold and 'tween deck. Still, he thought he might at least look in to see how the casks were laded. They would be his main responsibility.

He slipped down the hatch between loads of cargo. He was transfixed by the sight of the 'tween deck, empty. No people, no piles of straw mattresses or stray cupboards. No blankets tacked to the ceiling for a semblance of privacy. It was just empty.

He shook off the eerie feeling and went down another level to the hold. Hopkins stood chatting with the sailors as they piled beaver skins in a heap.

"How do you fare, Hopkins?" John asked, inserting himself into the circle of conversation.

Hopkins' eyes flashed onto him. "Alden! Bound to sail off to England once more, are you? I imagine you've come to check the casks."

"Indeed. It is my purpose for being aboard, is it not?"

"Aye, 'tis well." Hopkins clapped him on the back, following him through the strewn pelts toward the stores. "Will you not miss our fair city, with all she has to offer a young man such as yourself?"

"Is it yet as beautiful as Leiden, do you imagine?" John asked with a smile, bending over the nearest firkin of butter. Bradford loved to speak of Leiden, calling it 'a fair and beautiful city' so often that John wondered why he did not stay there.

"Not yet, alas," Hopkins said, growing serious. "But it will be. Do not you wish to stay and see it happen? What waits for you in England that is worth more than building a new place of your own?"

Hopkins appealed to his sense of independence. Did he expect it would fare better than the other volleys against which John steeled himself? He busied himself about his work. Hopkins clucked his tongue.

"I would not sail again with such as these. Nor would Mistress Hopkins let me. Alas that you have no wife to keep you from their sordid company," Hopkins mused.

Unbearably, the face of Miss Mullins arose in John's mind. She had not spoken to him in two days, and yet he expected to see her at the shore. Why had she not come to say farewell? If he saw her face, he may not have had the will to leave it. Was that what he'd imagined? Did he need her to make a final plea, before he could abandon his pride and stay beside her?

"You cannot like to stay, amid the Brownists?" John asked. What repercussions could there be now for speaking his mind?

Hopkins grunted. "There are far worse men in England, and indeed aboard this vessel, than those men of God ashore. They may have their strange habits, but what difference should that make to me?"

"I…" John hesitated. "I do not want to see more harm befall the men and women there," he said.

Hopkins laughed. "Do you think you can escape death anywhere on earth? Is it not better to die in the arms of a loving woman, than to do so surrounded by wretched sailors?"

John looked up in alarm. Something in Hopkins' tone suggested that he knew of John's predicament.

"You assume there is a loving woman awaiting me ashore."

"It is not an assumption, when she has as much as confessed it to my wife and daughter."

John's heart beat faster. Had Miss Mullins spoken to Mistress Hopkins of him? But—never mind—she had almost confessed as much herself to him, and yet his feet had taken him to the shore today.

"How could I bear to bury such a woman?" It was the question that most weighed on him.

"Goodman Alden, I have seen the grave of the mother of my eldest children, and yet I stand here talking to you whilst my five-month-old son suckles at his mother's breast." Hopkins shrugged. "My first wife pleaded with me not to sail to Jamestown. She thought that if I left, I would ne'er see her again. I left her with reassurances, but our ship wrecked on the Isle of Devils, and I was stranded for ten months. By the time I again reached England, she had died, without my knowing. Would you rather be stranded at sea with these men than by the side of Miss Mullins, even if she lies dying?"

"Do you taunt me for sport?" Alden asked, wretched at the images Hopkins was putting in his head.

"It is not my purpose, Goodman Alden, but an amusing perk."

"What is your purpose, then?"

Hopkins shrugged. "I seek the happiness of my own wife, little as it is compared to all that I promised her when we set sail. She is the reason for my being here, and well worth the loss of any life I might have had instead of marrying her."

"Hopkins!" Standish's bark came from above. Hopkins gave John another clap on the shoulder and walked back toward the sailors.

"The shallop will return to shore in short order, Goodman Alden." He flashed his wolfish grin, showing his two missing teeth, before ascending the ladder through the hatchway.

John's heart beat against his chest with such rapidity he clutched at his doublet. Did Master Hopkins speak the truth?

He dashed for the ladder above decks, hauling himself up.

If she loved him, would a life full of Miss Mullins be worth even seeing her die?

He dashed around the ladderway to climb up the second flight to the top deck.

If she married Standish, would his misery be bearable?

Even as his mind filtered through the questions, his body answered them. He knew what his choice would be, even as he doubted it. Bradford and Standish were standing by the ladder, making their last polite farewells.

"I'm coming back with you," he panted to them.

Standish's eyebrow rose in bemusement. Did he realize, as Hopkins did, that John was going back for the sake of Miss Mullins?

"You wish to stay in Plymouth?" Bradford smiled. "Praise be to God. We shall be grateful for your presence, indeed."

"Do you leave us, Goodman Alden?" asked Master Jones. He was not smiling.

"I…" John knew not how to answer.

"Aye, he will be of more use ashore than here, I don't doubt," Hopkins cut in with a grin. "He knows not e'en how to fasten the topsail halyard to the topsail yard, do you, Alden?"

John shook his head.

"And he was sick for a month, once we'd left Southampton. I doubt he'd be of any use to you at all, Master Jones," Hopkins continued, "but the plantation is yet growing, and he's become quite a master at fitting up dwellings."

Standish grinned, amused at the abuse Hopkins was casting on John's character. The captain could not know that John meant to marry Miss Mullins in his stead.

"Aye, well, we'd best be off to shore. Leave you to your last preparations. Fare thee well, Master Jones." Bradford doffed his cap and leaned over the ship's rail. "The shallop awaits." He swung his leg over the side and began his descent down the ladder.

John gazed out to the shore and saw the large rock, where he and Miss Mullins had sat together, protruding from the sand. Was there a flash of blue upon it? He shook his head. He could not let himself think of it. He could do as Hopkins instructed, not thinking at all, moving one step at a time, one foot after the other down the ladder, as his sea chest was loaded once more into the woven net and lowered with the block and tackle. They shoved away from the side of the ship and opened the shallop's sail.

What had he done? Had he just thrown his God-fearing life away for the hope of a woman's affections? A woman who had not spoken to him nor looked at him since she told him she had been made an offer of marriage by another! What was more, his rival sat beside him in the shallop, cheerful and smiling at John without concern. John wondered if he could yet go back aboard, apologize, and ignore Hopkins' words. He knew he would not, even if he could. He had to go to Plymouth. He wanted to go to Plymouth.

The shallop drew ashore at the usual spot. No one remained there, waiting, the leave-takers all dispersed. John jumped over the gunwale and splashed through a few feet of water. He leapt onto the earthy shore and started jogging up the hill. He heard Standish shout after him but took no notice. Hopkins would deal with it. Or not. It didn't matter. All that mattered was that he see her, as soon as possible. He had taken his leap of faith. He had turned away from his future. He needed to know what for.

He burst through the door of Governor Carver's house, sweat dripping down his face. He tried to breathe, tried to slow, but found he had little control over his legs.

Miss Mullins sat by the hearth, sobbing into a corner of her apron, Tilley's arm about her.

"John!" she gasped when she saw him.

"Priscilla," he replied and crossed the room to meet her.

She stood and threw her arms around him. It felt somehow right, more right than any person's touch had felt to him in his memory. Her face was buried in his shoulder, the soft wool of her red waistcoat under his hands. It warmed him, and he did not want to let go.

"You did not leave," she murmured into his shoulder, tears still in her eyes.

"I found I could not leave while you remained."

Part II: April 1622–May 1623

Chapter Twelve

May 12 was the first marriage in this place; which according to the laudable custom of the Low Countries, in which they had lived, was thought most requisite to be performed, by the magistrate, as being a civil thing, upon which many questions about inheritances do depend, with other things most proper to their cognizance; and most consonant to the Scriptures, Ruth 4; and nowhere found in the Gospel to be laid on the ministers as a part of their office.

—William Bradford, *Of Plymouth Plantation*, 1651

Monday, 1 April 1622

The bashful sunlight of a spring morning in New Plymouth fell around John, making him look radiant. Priscilla held his hands in hers. It had been a full year since he came back from *Mayflower* and embraced her by the hearth. In that year, much changed in Plymouth.

Carver died a few days after *Mayflower*'s departure, and his wife took a few weeks to follow. He did so much and took so little rest in the months he was governor of their little settlement; it struck them all hard to lose such a man. Bradford was elected governor in his stead.

"This decree or law about marriage was published by the States of the Low Countries Anno 1590: that those of any religion, after lawful and open publication, coming before the magistrates in the town, or state house, were to be orderly, by them, married to one another," recited Governor Bradford.

Priscilla saw John grimace, looking at Bradford. His face was so expressive, his mouth visible with his beard shaved off for the ceremony. It was not the way either of them envisioned a marriage, but the Separatists carried some of the customs of Holland with them to the New World. She tried to smile, to reassure him that this was at least a marriage.

"Banns have been read for the past three Sundays," continued Bradford, "and your troth has been known in the colony for near a year."

Priscilla expected little different from the ceremony, after the marriage of Mistress White and Master Winslow the previous spring. She and John witnessed the civil union with the rest of the colony. The thirty-nine articles abolished matrimony as a sacrament even within the Church of England, claiming the practice a corruption by the papists. Yet, she knew John found the idea of being married by the Separatist Bradford distasteful.

"As the local magistrate, representative of the law, I proclaim you joined together now as husband and wife," Bradford said, concluding the ceremony.

There was much congratulation from the gathered crowd of witnesses. Captain Standish came forward, grinning from ear to ear.

"At last!" he cried. "The long-awaited union, at last!"

Standish was a little put out when he first heard that John and Priscilla plighted their troth to one another, but he soon overcame his indisposition. There had been much else to occupy him last summer, as expedition after expedition to the Indians kept them all busy. Winslow and Hopkins went with Squanto to visit Massasoit at Pokanoket, but Standish was needed for the voyages to tribes who might mean them harm. He took ten men, including John, with him to the Massachusett to settle peace and make trade with them. John related to Priscilla that the English found the Indians shaking and trembling with fear, despite Squanto's claims that they made many threats against the settlers. Their sachem submitted himself to be a subject of King James, and they promised to trade with them again this spring. John also accompanied Standish on his voyage to the Nauset, which they undertook after one of the colony's children wandered too far off into the woods and ended up in their territory. There, they had the good fortune to encounter a representative of the Paomet, and they at last made recompense for the corn they stole in November. The English made peace with the Nauset sachem, Aspinet. As Squanto predicted, he was willing to make peace, knowing that the English were allied to Massasoit.

Standish accompanied John and Priscilla to their small wedding meal. Wild fowl were becoming less plentiful as the season shifted from winter into spring, but the fish started to come thicker and faster down the river. Their harvest in the fall was bountiful, enough that when Massasoit came to them, with ninety of his men in tow, they were able to entertain them well for three days of feasting and games. The Indians killed five deer over the course of their visit, and roasted venison became one of Priscilla's favorite delicacies. However, in November, a ship called *Fortune* arrived, laden both with thirty-five hungry men and women and with scathing words for the deceased governor from Master Weston in London. It was not laden with a supply of provision, and their bountiful harvest was stretched to cover the needs of the newcomers. Even though their rations had been halved all winter, their supply of corn would soon run out, and planting season was just beginning.

At the wedding table, Standish sat next to Hobbamock, another Indian who, like Squanto, was sent by Massasoit to live with the English. Hobbamock's wife accompanied him, and she regarded everyone but Squanto with kind eyes and good cheer, though she did not understand a word they said. Standish at once took to the Pokanoket warrior, who was one of Massasoit's best—a pniese could not be killed in battle, or so the Indians believed. Hobbamock looked as sturdy as a boulder, but his fierce aspect was somewhat softened in Priscilla's eyes when she watched Standish try to teach him English. Standish, who went about the most with the Indians, proved a competent linguist and picked up a little of the savage tongue. Hobbamock, it seemed to Priscilla, learned English with greater ease, perhaps by virtue of living in their plantation, when he was not accompanying Standish on expeditions. He grinned as Standish sat down beside him, quickly engaging him in a conversation of fluid language.

Tilley sat beside Priscilla, chewing a piece of duck. "I do hope the trading expedition to the Massachusett goes well, that we may soon have corn in our stores again."

"It would bode ill to have to wait till the harvest is ready," admitted Priscilla, "though last summer was sweet enough, with all the fruits and salad herbs that grew, both wild and in our gardens. And the river and bay abounded with fish! Though we lacked sufficient seines to catch them."

The summer had been warm and wonderful, and Priscilla's memory of it was hazed with the happiness of mutual love. John oft took her away from the prying view of the other planters to kiss her in fields, in forest, or by the rocky shore.

"Aye, God has well provided for us here, in satiety and in peace. For me a table thou hast spread, in presence of my foes." Tilley grinned, nodding at Hobbamock and his wife. "Thou dost anoint my head with oil, my cup it overflows," she sang, a little off-key.

Priscilla laughed. Hobbamock could not be considered a foe, but she knew it was by the grace of God that she could say so. Though there was not much abundance of food in the settlement, God spread a table for her in her matrimony. Though her parents and Joseph walked in the valley of death's shade, she had the love of Tilley, the love of her husband, the affection of the colony in her support. Her cup, it overflowed. She sang with Tilley, giggling over the fourth verse of their favorite psalm.

The Lord to me a shepherd is,
want therefore shall not I.
He in the folds of tender grass
doth cause me down to lie.

To waters calm me gently leads,
restore my soul doth he;
he doth in paths of righteousness
for his name's sake lead me.

Yea though in valley of death's shade
I walk, none ill I'll fear,
because thou art with me, thy rod
and staff my comfort are.

For me a table thou hast spread,
in presence of my foes;
thou dost anoint my head with oil,
my cup it overflows.

"Master and Mistress Alden," crowed Goodman Howland, approaching the couple with a jovial smile. Priscilla giggled at the use of her new surname. He held a mug containing a clear liquid. "Aqua vitae?" His ears reddened as he noticed Tilley sitting with them.

It was rare that any in the village drank anything besides spring water. Priscilla never expected to grow accustomed to the lack of beer, but she came to enjoy the cool, clear water from Town Brook. Nevertheless, she would not refuse so generous a gift.

"How have you obtained that?" John asked, suspicious. "Is it not meant to be saved as a gift for our Indian neighbors?"

Howland gave John a mischievous grin, though he was without a doubt the least mischievous man Priscilla ever met. He'd somehow charmed his way to the dregs of a small cask.

"What fear have we of the Indians, now that Massasoit and his allies are our friends? Indeed, what need have we for fear, with Squanto and Hobbamock living by our side?" Howland winked across the table at Hobbamock. Hobbamock looked up at the sound of his name, saw that Howland was only speaking of him and not to him, and returned his attention to his wife, murmuring something to her quietly. Howland's ostentatious behavior was, Priscilla did not doubt, in part for Tilley's benefit. Tilley's eyes followed him as he sat on John's other side.

Perhaps Howland got the liquor from the Indians. Perhaps some was stored away after their visit to Massasoit, or their trading mission to the Massachusett. In either case, one cup would not be missed. John took it from Howland and swallowed a mouthful of the strong drink. His cheeks turned pink as the liquor warmed him. The chill of winter was still upon them, but Priscilla was looking forward to a summer as plentiful as last year's. She took the cup from her husband— for he was, now, her husband—and enjoyed the sensation of burning trickling down her chest as she sipped it.

"Do you still think we have naught to worry over, with the Indians?" John asked, taking the jest to heart. "We have received a declaration of war from the Narragansett. Even if Bradford's return of bullets for their arrows has frightened

Canonicus, as Squanto says, they do not cease their taunting and their threats."

"After all the effort you put into building the impalement which now surrounds our fair and beautiful village," Howland said, gesturing at the fence, "do you not have faith that your own work will keep out Narragansett arrows?" Hewn of rough wood, standing much taller than John, with pickets close together, building the impalement had taxed John through many weeks.

"The fields where we plant our corn lie outside of the palisade," John pointed out, "and we constantly go in search of the Indians in their own territory."

"How can you be so confident in Goodman Alden's handiwork when there were not one, but two hostages taken last summer?" Priscilla asked, teasing her husband. The incidents both occurred before the palisade was begun.

"Ah, hostages!" Howland exclaimed, waving her concerns away. "You have a fanciful mind, Mistress Alden."

Priscilla giggled again at his extravagant politeness in using her new name. Tilley giggled with her, at his dramatic attitude.

"The boy wandered too far out of sight, and the Nauset kept him safe for us, until we made recompense for the corn which we took at Cape Cod."

"And Squanto?" Priscilla pressed, but she was smiling, enjoying Howland's high-spirited mood.

"Aye, Squanto had a rough time indeed at Corbitant's hands, sitting pretty at Nemasket while we wounded three of Corbitant's men, and Squanto returned without a scratch!"

"'Tis good indeed that he was not harmed, else the governor would have had Corbitant beheaded, despite his being one of Massasoit's sachems," John argued.

"That is part of our agreement with Massasoit, is it not? If any of his men do harm to our people, the offender is to be punished at our hands," Howland answered.

"And so we are glad that no punishment was needed," Priscilla broke in, trying to keep the conversation light and peaceable.

"Aye," John said. "Many thanks for the gift, Howland." He raised the empty cup in salute.

"May God bless your civil union," Howland said, and he left them with a bow. Tilley soon got up and followed him.

John looked down at Priscilla, his gentle smile growing more suggestive as he raised a hand to touch a lock of her hair which strayed from the confines of her coif.

"How now, husband?" Priscilla inquired; his joy was infectious.

He grasped her hand and drew it to his lips to kiss. Her eyes sparkled with delight.

"Just think, now all your shares in the venture are mine," he teased.

"Just so? All that land bequeathed to me by the Virginia Company? All that land, which they are bound to take away at any moment, as the colony fails to return their investment?" She sighed with mock weariness. "You may have it, if you wish, and take the burden of their expectations with it."

"Ah, but they counted not on my remaining here to till that soil for you. Have we not had good harvest? Have we not made good trade?"

"They counted not on our losing half of our people in the span of four months, and gaining back more men who ate up half our stores," she said. "But—aye, indeed, I see it now. You have the strength of fifty men, and all will be well."

"I have strength enough to care for thee, my darling," he promised.

"I doubt it not, my best beloved."

He spent much of his labor for the colony's benefit over the year since he decided to stay in Plymouth. With his decision, he changed his inscrutable attitude toward political affairs, proclaiming instead that he was a member of the civil body politic they formed with the Mayflower Compact, and as such he had a stake in the general good of the colony. She knew that his involvement in the Indian affairs and in the building of the palisade, and these days in preparing the fields for planting, were all for her good more than for the general colony.

When their meal was done and their table cleared, Priscilla carried a couple of large platters back to John's house. She remembered with another giggle that, as of today, it was *their* house. She would be the mistress of this household, which John shared with several unmarried and widowed men. Mistress Brewster, the wife of the elder of the Separatist congregation, took in Priscilla, Tilley, and Mary Chilton after the Carvers died. She and her husband brought their youngest two children, Love and Wrestling, over on *Mayflower*, but left the eldest three behind. Love was about Joseph's age and trying already to be a man.

Of *Mayflower*'s married women, four were still living. Each had taken on the responsibilities of caring for many men and children after the deaths of their wives and mothers. Priscilla today joined their ranks as a young wife. Priscilla helped with her household chores in Dorking, but she obtained, as they all did, a new education in the housework of a plantation. The work never seemed to end. They kept up with the mending and cleaning and cooking and childrearing but also spent much of the summer planting and tending to their kitchen gardens, helping to wattle and daub the new houses, and tending to their crops in the fields, which, in fall, they helped to harvest. The men worked beside them, building houses, weeding and sowing the fields, hunting and fishing, as well as making trips to visit and trade with their Indian neighbors, and honing their skills with muskets and swords. Since the threat came from the Narragansett, Captain Standish established four companies of militia, which drilled in the use of sword and musket.

Priscilla stretched, after putting her platters on the table, reaching her arms up to touch the exposed beam which ran across the ceiling. Her back ached from hours spent bent over seedlings the day before. The doorway darkened, and she turned to see her new husband enter, carrying an armload of napkins. Her cheeks tinged with pink. They were alone in their new home. He dumped the pile of napkins on the table and wrapped his arms around her waist, bending to press his cheek against hers. She felt again the familiar heat of adoration rise inside her and flush her cheeks. His skin was rough and bristly with the shadow of a new beard already growing, and hers prickled where it touched her. She drew back a little, her nose sliding across his cheek. His eyes flicked toward her mouth, and she stood on her toes to press a kiss against his lips.

Chapter Thirteen

At the spring of the year they had appointed the
Massachusetts to come again and trade with them;
and began now to prepare for that voyage about the
latter end of March; but upon some rumors heard,
Hobomok their Indian told them upon some
jealousies he had, he feared they were joined with
the Narragansetts and might betray them if they
were not careful; he intimated also some jealousy
of Squanto, by what he gathered from some private
whisperings between him and other Indians.

—William Bradford, *Of Plymouth
Plantation*, 1651

Tuesday, 2 April 1622

"I know not what we ought to do." Standish sighed, pouring
some water into a mug for John to drink. John took it with
gratitude. He was at work in the field when Standish called
him into town for a private discussion.

"Hobbamock has come to me with some suspicions of the
Massachusett. We are meant to leave soon on our trading
expedition, but there have been rumors that they have allied
with the Narragansett and mean to do us harm."

John choked on his water, getting spittle across his chin.
He wiped it on the back of his sleeve.

"Do you mean to say they will attack us if we go there?"

"*If* it's true, they mean to take advantage of my being with
the trading party, away from town, and have the Massachusett
kill the members of our expedition whilst the Narragansett
attack those who are left at home. In that case, what am I to
do?" Standish scratched a hand through his curly red hair,
leaving it sticking up at odd angles.

"We're in desperate need of the corn, Captain. How has Hobbamock come across these rumors? How sure is he of their veracity?"

Standish's head lolled back and forth like a slow pendulum. "It seems a habit of the Indians to deal openly about their plans—indeed, even to boast of their strength against an enemy they do not plan to fight. Since he has lived here, he has been excluded from the truth of things and cannot help but deal in secrecy, so he has no way to tell how true the rumor is." Standish snorted, laughing a little. "I'll tell you one thing he says: that along with these rumors came stories of Squanto, going to the other Indians and telling them we have the plague buried in the barrels in our storehouse. That we might release a plague upon their people any time we wished. Hobbamock asked me if it were true."

"What answer did you give?" John asked. Such a rumor was ridiculous, of course; the English could not carry the plague about with them to spread it to the Indians.

Standish shrugged, putting his feet up on the table so they nudged John's elbow. "That God alone can wield such power as directing a plague toward his enemies, or ours. I doubt the governor would condone a prayer requesting God to send a plague upon the Narragansett."

"Would it be a prayer, or a curse?" John asked, heaving a sigh. "That Squanto should spread these rumors is confounding, when he lost his whole tribe to plague, yet he lives among the English. But why would Squanto tell such tales to the other Indians, unless it is what he believes? If you told Hobbamock the truth of it, does Squanto not trust that we have no such power?"

Standish waved his arm about his head, as though trying to swat a pesky fly. "Hobbamock related several such stories. He tells me Squanto spreads these tales to Massasoit's people, claiming that he is using his influence amongst the English to gather their loyalty to himself instead of Massasoit."

John furrowed his brows. "Why should he want to undermine Massasoit? Is that not treason? What reason has Squanto to seek such attentions? With his own people gone, he cannot hope to stand against the grand sachem, so what purpose is there for him in spreading these lies?" He took off his hat to rub his forehead in confusion.

"That question is why I give little credit to these rumors that Hobbamock has brought me. And, as you said, we are in desperate need of the corn we get in trade. So, what am I to do, Goodman Alden? Credit the rumors, and stay to defend the plantation against attack by the Narragansett? Go, and let myself be killed by the Massachusett?"

"If we do not go, we will show that their rumors are enough to frighten us. Our need is too great to let them think we are so quickly cowed. But neither can we afford to leave you at their whims. We need to defend you better than that." John swatted his hat against Standish's boots, still resting on the table beside him. "You cannot go alone, or with just two or three men. At least since *Fortune*'s arrival, we have a better supply of men in the colony, though Bradford may wish more of them were his own, rather than those Weston chose."

"Ha! If it comes to that, I wish Weston would prize skill above brute strength or ambition in his choices. Did you hear that Weston sent a letter in *Fortune* railing against the late Governor Carver? And him long buried and no longer able to defend himself."

"What had Weston to say against Carver?"

"Complaints at *Mayflower*'s lack of lading. Accusations of weakness, even when he knows we buried half our company before *Mayflower* left." He jerked his head from side to side, refusing to credit such accusations. "I was never an admirer of Weston, but Bradford and the rest cling to him, as though he were their savior, Jesus Christ. As though he alone, and not the rest of the Virginia Company, was responsible for their being able to voyage here. And he encourages them, saying he alone will support them in their extremity, when the rest of the Company will quit the business. Saying that if he shared with them all the petty details of our agreement, the Company should not have ventured a halfpenny toward the procurement of the ship. And he says this all while casting aspersions on our character. It's a strange relationship they have, and no mistake."

"Hardly seems an admirable man, nor the kind that I'd expect Bradford to put faith in," John commented. Standish grunted an agreement and took a draught of water from his mug.

"But we have wandered far from the original question, Goodman Alden. Shall we sail to the Massachusett? If so, how many men shall we take, and which should we leave in the colony's defense?"

John thought it over. "We have the shallop, which will not hold above fifteen or perhaps eighteen men, and less if you succeed in trade and manage to carry some hogsheads back with you. If you take ten men, is that enough to form an adequate defense against an onslaught?"

"Aye, I think ten men will do. We need either Hobbamock or Squanto with us, too, to translate for us. My skill is not yet so great that I can negotiate a trade." He grinned, and nudged the toe of his boot into John's arm. "And you'll come, won't you, Alden?"

John hesitated. Go, days after his new marriage, and leave Priscilla to the whims of the Narragansett? How could he leave, when defending her against the Indians was now his responsibility? But if he stayed, was that not also a form of deprivation, to defend against a rumored attack instead of going to procure tangible corn, which they needed to survive the spring? Standish saw his hesitation.

"Your new bride will be well protected. We've forty men to leave in her defense, and you yourself led the effort to put up the impalement. The town is at least enclosed, and the men we leave behind are capable enough to defend her." He withdrew his legs and leaned across the table, pleading with his eyes. "And I need you with me, to watch my back."

John raised an eyebrow, unmoved by Standish's pouting face. "All right, I'll go. I'm amazed you have the confidence in my musketry to wish me by your side."

Standish threw himself back into his seat, fist in the air, laughing at John's easy manipulation. "Ha-ha, don't presume my confidence—I mean to use you as my shield. Though you have improved, since we formed our militia companies, and you've at last taken my instruction."

John grinned. The captain was too confident in his own tutelage, but his confidence at least made John less doubtful of his own abilities.

He left Standish's house and stopped by his own before returning to the fields. He found Priscilla working in the garden.

"How do you fare, Goodwife Alden?" he asked.

She wiped her sweaty brow with the back of her hand, leaving a smudge of dirt on her forehead. "I will fare better when we have done with the planting," she confided. "There is too much else to do, that I am constantly besieged and cannot seem to finish preparing the garden."

"I suppose I shall walk away, then, and take my conversation with me," John said, pretending offense.

She smiled and sat back on her heels. "Do tell me what conversation you have that is of more import than finishing the garden, dear husband."

"Your husband is to be amongst the trading party that goes to visit the Massachusett."

"Ah! At last we shall have full stores of corn again. 'Tis well to have you venture forth for our contentment. When will you depart?"

"In two or three days." He was unsure whether or not to tell her of the rumors. What if they were just rumors, after all? But Standish would set the men at home on guard, and she would notice it.

She must have seen the worry line his face, for she took his hand and smiled. "Do be safe, will you not, John? I should not like to become a widow quite so soon."

He grinned and chucked her under the chin. "I would not do anything to cause you such deprivation."

Thursday, 4 April 1622

John loaded a small bundle of knives into the shallop. They were ready to set off, waiting for Captain Standish to complete his inventory of their armory.

"Are we ready yet?" Hopkins asked.

"Aye, aye, if you would that every man has but a knife to keep him from the harm of the Indians," muttered Captain Standish in bad temper.

"I would if it meant we would be off in less than an hour," returned Hopkins.

"Well, then, let us be off, and be it on your head if we are all killed on the expedition," Standish growled.

They were to be accompanied by both Hobbamock and Squanto, that the one could be reassured in having his own eyes laid on the other. Hobbamock would not let them go with Squanto without his also being present. Squanto insisted that he needed to go, that Hobbamock's skill was not yet enough to help the English alone. Though Standish did not much credit Hobbamock's tales, the warrior himself was wary of Squanto, and he kept glaring at him as they prepared the boat to sail. His wariness put John on edge. From the start, John pitied Squanto, who lost everything to plague and to the English. Yet Squanto tried to help them, showed them how to survive here, and translated between them and Massasoit, no simple task. Standish and Winslow's efforts in learning the Indian language carried them but a little way, and it must have been a challenge for Squanto to relay not only the words but also their meaning between the English governor and his own king. Even if he considered himself alone, apart from the Pokanoket, Massasoit was still his sachem, and Squanto stayed with the English so that they might better communicate together. It made no sense to John that such a man would cause strife which could jeopardize his own delicate position.

They pushed the shallop out into the water, the sailing smooth in the bay. The Massachusett were a fair way off, near twenty leagues. They sailed out to Gurnet's Nose, the point of the long promontory that jutted into the harbor. The wind was fair and the water good, but the promontory was high and shielded the bay from the true nature of the ocean. As soon as they were past it, they were becalmed.

"Drop the grapnel," said Goodman Morgan, a sailor who came with *Fortune*. "We'll need to take oars to keep us from hitting those rocks."

John reached for the multi-fluked anchor, dropping it over the side.

"Now, push off from the port—" called Morgan, but he was interrupted by the loud blast of a cannon.

"It came from Plymouth," Hopkins said, alarmed.

"We must turn about," ordered Standish. "If it be the Narragansett taking advantage of our absence, God's wounds, I shall have their heads."

John strained his arms to pull up the grapnel again. The men all took up their oars. They muddled through some confusion over who was in charge of the vessel, but at last they pressed against the wind, back past the promontory and through the bay. His stockings were still damp, but John hopped back into the water to stick the shallop into the sand. The whole party took up their arms, Standish ensuring their match cords were lit and their muskets loaded before they started toward the eastern gate of the plantation. John's blood pounded in his ears. Was Priscilla safe? Had the men kept the Indians at bay? Were they in the town already, chasing down the women and children?

They threw open the door, poised to repel enemy fire— but none came. There were no arrows aimed toward them, no screams of fear, or even any strangers, except one Indian shouting at Bradford near the ordnance platform. A small crowd of English settlers were gathered behind the governor. John, still cautious, took up his well-practiced position behind Standish, falling into line with the other militia men, and they advanced up the hill, muskets at the ready. He looked around for Priscilla, trying to find her in the crowd, while keeping one eye on the foreigner.

"How now, Bradford?" Standish shouted, and the whole gaggle of onlookers turned to stare at the small militia.

As they approached, John could see that the Indian was young, perhaps a teenager, with half his face covered in blood. John also saw Priscilla, standing next to Tilley, behind Bradford. His tension eased. She was safe. For the moment.

"Tisquantum!" the boy shouted when he saw them approach. Squanto pushed past the Englishmen to meet him, and Hobbamock followed close behind.

"What's happened?" the captain demanded.

"He came to the gate, calling for Squanto," Bradford answered. "He's mentioned the Narragansett and Massasoit, and he seems to be saying they've both joined Corbitant at Nemasket and lie in wait there. That cannot be true!"

"Not true," Hobbamock agreed. "Massasoit not tell me." He shook his head. "Not true. Massasoit friend with English."

Squanto disagreed. "He has come running from the gathering and barely managed to escape, himself—he received this wound from speaking in favor of the English. How can you claim he lies, seeing the injury he received on your behalf?"

John longed to go to Priscilla's side, but his eyes stayed steadied on the stranger, and he kept his position, musket up, the match cord's burning in his nostrils.

"But I don't understand," Bradford said in desperation. "Massasoit is our friend, as Hobbamock says. He would have told us of any quarrel he had with us, to make him do such a thing."

"He says that Massasoit waited for the captain's absence from the town, so that you would not be well defended when he came," Squanto said.

John looked at Standish and found Standish glancing at him, too. It was the same rumor Hobbamock shared with them, but with the addition of Massasoit's involvement it seemed even less believable than before. What reason had

Massasoit to fight them, to break their treaty, without at least addressing the quarrel first? John thought again about the rumors that Squanto was dividing the loyalties of Massasoit's people. *That* could be an adequate reason, he realized, and scrutinized Squanto. The Indian's face was impassive and gave no sign of turmoil.

Hobbamock snarled at Squanto. "Lies. I am pniese. He agree with English."

"Would Massasoit tell you of it? You live amongst the English. It would benefit him to have you defend him and encourage them that he is faithful." He turned to Bradford. "Massasoit doesn't know that we have been forewarned. We have the advantage, now that Captain Standish has come back. We should go and surprise Massasoit where he waits."

"You would have us attack Massasoit?" Bradford asked in disbelief.

"Lies!" Hobbamock repeated. "Massasoit friend to English."

"Bradford," Standish said, "I may have some light to shed on this, if we could speak privately."

Bradford sighed. "Is now the best time, Captain Standish?"

"Now may be the only time, if you're at all inclined to follow Squanto's recommendation."

Bradford clenched his jaw, but he nodded.

"Alden, you keep aim on him," Standish shouted at John, nodding in the direction of both Squanto and the stranger. John took his meaning. He was to keep an eye on Squanto, as well as the newcomer. He trained his musket, the slow burning of the match cord sizzling in his ears.

The captain and the governor were gone for mere minutes, during which time Squanto patted the stranger on the head and murmured reassurances to him, the stranger looking back toward the main gate into town, eyes wide as though he suspected something would follow him here at any moment.

When they came out, Standish directed his squadrons to their guards.

"We cannot in good conscience launch an assault on Massasoit, with whom we have a treaty promising peace between us. But we cannot very well let Captain Standish, or any of us, leave on a voyage of trade whilst we may be under threat," Bradford announced.

The company dispersed, in preparation for attack. John darted for Priscilla.

"Are you well?" he asked, running his hands over her coif as though fearing she sustained some injury he could not see. He was fearful, worried that he almost left—that, if the wind took their sail, he might have been too late to come back and guard her against this attack.

"I'm well, John, as are we all. We fear that we may not be so much longer. Tell me it is not true that we are to be attacked by Massasoit?" Though she smacked his hand away from her head, she leaned in close and laid her fingers on his doublet, as though she did not want him to leave her sight. He put a hand on her back.

"I know not whether it is true, but there have been many strange rumors surrounding the Indians of late. I must find Standish and talk with him." But he made no move to leave her. He liked feeling that she was safe in his arms. If she was here, if he was here with her, then he could defend her. He was loath to go out of sight of her again.

When Priscilla at last went to sleep, John met for a quiet word with Standish. The men were still on guard, though no sign of assault followed the young Indian.

"Are we just to wait an eternity, or have you and the governor arranged some other plan?" John whispered, leaning close to the captain's ear to ensure they would not be overheard.

"Hobbamock has sent his wife to see whether Massasoit is at home, and, if he is, whether he bears arms against us."

"Can we trust her to tell the truth? Hobbamock is devoted to Massasoit; if there is an attack planned, would she reveal it to us?"

"Bradford believes she will, and I do also. Her loyalty is to Hobbamock, and he is here with us. If she comes back with an army, he would be at the very least our prisoner."

John thought of Priscilla. If they were living in enemy territory, and their captors asked her to go, to cross the lines of danger and face head-on the threat of an impending army, would he have the strength to send her? He thought Hobbamock must be very faithful, indeed, to believe Massasoit would do no harm to his wife.

"Besides, if you have not had the opportunity to watch Hobbamock try to tell a lie, it will prove an afternoon's entertainment for you." Standish sniggered. "The man will never enjoy a game of dice or cards. He cannot bluff to save his skin."

"And what of Squanto? I assume you shared Hobbamock's suspicions of him with the governor. If Massasoit is not coming to attack us, does the blame for this misunderstanding lie at Squanto's feet? Has *he* a face for deceit?"

"He's gained a face for politics through his travels, which I would wager is much the same thing." Standish spat a wad of phlegm onto the ground beside him. "I should have taken more care with Hobbamock's warnings, though the governor credits them as little as I did, on my first hearing. The rumors at least gave him enough pause to stave off an attack on Massasoit, until we've heard from Hobbamock's wife."

"Even if what Hobbamock said is true," John argued, "what benefit could come to Squanto by asking us to attack Massasoit?"

Standish tapped the barrel of his musket against his forehead. "That is the question, my dear Alden. If he means, as Hobbamock suspects, to divide Massasoit's people, taking some to himself, then to have us attack Massasoit, does it not seem that he wishes to raise himself as sachem in Massasoit's place? Hobbamock told me this afternoon that he heard from others hereabouts that they began to give Squanto gifts in return for his supposed protection against the English threat. I suppose they wondered whether Hobbamock might also offer them protection, but he would never take their tribute away from Massasoit. That taste of power." Standish clicked his tongue. "Perhaps once he'd had a little of it, Squanto desired more. It is the way of men and power."

Friday, 5 April 1622

In the morning, Hobbamock's wife approached the gate. She was hurried inside, and the gate closed quick behind her.

The news she brought was good for the English, but it shed uncertainty upon their faith in Squanto. Massasoit was at home, and all was quiet. The stranger was spreading lies, and John assumed it was at Squanto's behest, to further whatever it was he felt he was accomplishing by aggrandizing himself among the Indians.

"Goodman Alden! Are you willing to make the voyage to trade with the Massachusett in a few days?" Standish asked him that afternoon, when the men were convinced away from their posts.

"I..." John hesitated, unwilling to leave Priscilla to the mercies of God's fate a second time.

"You will do more good for her sake abroad than you will here, Alden," Standish said, reading his mind. "Now that we have proved there is no impending doom, and that Massasoit is still our ally. He will come to our aid if the Narragansett do attack."

Standish leaned closer. "I can trust you alone to watch Squanto; you alone know the full scope of his supposed treachery. At the same time, the governor insists that we cannot trust Hobbamock without reservation. That, if at any time Massasoit does bear us ill will, it seems that Hobbamock will side with him, rather than with us. He has decided it is best to keep both Squanto and Hobbamock at some distance, and yet for each to think us in his confidence." Standish gave him a significant look. "I trust you will watch Squanto for me, on our voyage? It is best if I take the part of Hobbamock."

John returned Standish's look, studied his eyes for a long moment before he agreed, persuaded once more by the captain's appeal to his usefulness.

Tuesday, 9 April 1622

Priscilla stood against the gate, gathering her courage. She could hear laughter and the murmur of soft conversation going on in the open yard beyond the palisade. She took in a deep breath, held it, and expelled it through pursed lips. She pushed open the gate and marched through, cheerful smile plastered on her face, basket of smocks, shirts, and monthly rags in her arms.

"Good morrow, Mistress Hopkins, Mistress Winslow," Priscilla greeted, nodding to each in turn as she set her basket on the ground beside a large wooden tub.

"Goodwife Alden, how do you fare?" asked Mistress Hopkins, cutting off her conversation with Mistress Winslow. Mistress Winslow (who had, until a year ago, been Mistress White) nodded at Priscilla's greeting but looked down to pick up her infant, Peregrine.

"Mama," the baby said, pointing at her nose. She cooed at him, taking his tiny hand in hers. Oceanus Hopkins, who was a month older than Peregrine, was up and toddling away from his mother, a leading string connecting his gown to her wrist.

Had they ceased their conversation because of Priscilla? Had she interrupted some talk between them which she was not supposed to hear? She thought that kind of thing might stop, after she was married. Her pulse was quick, and she strained her ears for any hint of conversation. She was too nervous! Why was she so nervous, to talk with women whom she'd talked with countless times? All that had changed was that she herself was now married.

Priscilla began dunking clothes in the tub. They'd carried water up from Town Brook to heat over their hearth fires and mixed in lye made from wood ash. They would soak the linen clothes in the warm lye water for a time, before taking them down to the brook to beat them with wooden paddles.

"Where is Constance today?" Priscilla asked Mistress Hopkins, who was tugging on Oceanus' leading string. It didn't help correct his balance enough, and the baby still tumbled to the ground. Mistress Hopkins stood and went to fetch him, bringing him back to her seat by the buck tub.

"She will be by; she has gone to collect the things that the widowers may need laundered." She sighed, putting a wriggling Oceanus on the ground. "Master Hopkins is displeased to have me tending to the household needs of so many men besides himself, but I do not know what he expects of me. We are a part of a community here, and they cannot do their wash themselves."

Priscilla nodded, stirring the lye water in the tub with a long-handled wooden bat. Her husband did not say anything to that effect, although she was working with the other women in the care of the whole colony long before their marriage. John had been one of the single men who benefited from the women doing work for all. Besides, he'd been her husband for a matter of days before he'd gone off to trade with the Massachusett, a voyage which would keep him away for several weeks.

"I am grateful that Master Winslow has taken so fondly to little Peregrine," said Mistress Winslow, cuddling her son. "He has taken him in as his own son, which I take as a kindness."

"He has grown so big since your marriage," cooed Mistress Hopkins, leaning over to tickle Peregrine's belly.

"No!" the baby shouted and tumbled out of his mother's arms, crawling a few feet across the grass. Mistress Winslow leaned over and seized him, dragging him back toward the tub.

"I shall soon need to sew a leading string into his gown," she admitted. "I have not found the time to do it yet, but I should before the spring planting begins in earnest."

Priscilla nodded again. Her nervousness settled, in this tedious talk of everyday. What was she expecting? In truth, she'd half expected at any moment that the talk would change—that it would turn to talk of married women, to which unmarried girls were not privy. But it was just the same. Talk of husbands and of babies, which Priscilla could not join in. Mistresses Hopkins and Winslow talked a little more of their babies, of what new words Oceanus and Peregrine began to say, of whether Oceanus slept through the night yet (he didn't) or Peregrine began to feed himself (he did). Priscilla looked at the small children and wondered when she might have one of her own. If she had a child, would she continue to feel so out of place amid these talks between Plymouth's wives? She hoped that once she was married, somehow it would make her position easier.

She saw Tilley walking past with Howland on the path from Town Brook to the southern gate, and she longed to be in her friend's company. Tilley would turn fifteen that summer. Though she still felt herself in love with Howland (and he seemed to be with her, the more they were together), her talk was more often talk of God, of curiosity of the New World, or of her parents and those she missed in Leiden. She would share stories with Priscilla about the customs of the Dutch, sometimes speaking a few words of their strange language, which made Priscilla laugh. Priscilla, meanwhile, would tell tales of Dorking, of life in a rural English market town, which was as foreign to Tilley as the New World. She left England when she was just a few years old and did not remember it well at all. Whatever they talked about, the subject mattered little. Priscilla was always entertained or cheered when in Tilley's company, and always out of place in that of the older women. She spent the last year living with Tilley and with Mary Chilton, first in the Carvers' house and then the Brewsters', being treated as an orphaned girl when she felt herself a grown-up woman. Now she was at last married and the mistress of her own house, and yet she still longed for the company of Tilley. Should she not spend her time instead with women in her own position? But did she share their position, when she had not a child of her own?

Chapter Fourteen

They began to see that Squanto sought his own
ends, and played his own game, by putting the
Indians in fear, and drawing gifts from them; to
enrich himself, making them believe he could stir
up war against whom he would, and make peace
for whom he would... which procured him envy,
and had like to have cost him his life; for after the
discovery of his practices Massasoit sought it both
privately and openly...

—William Bradford, *Of Plymouth*
Plantation, 1651

Tuesday, 14 May 1622

John rode in the shallop, returning home after several weeks
away in pursuit of trade with the Massachusett. There was no
threat of danger, nor any signs that an alliance with the
Narragansett had been made. Though Hobbamock proved
right in his mistrust of Squanto, the other rumors appeared
false. John was pleased with the quantity of corn and beans
they carried; trading had gone well. He saw the rise of
Gurnet's Nose ahead and felt joyous to be returning home. A
year before, he couldn't have imagined being so glad to call
their little plantation 'home.' The Massachusett were
hospitable enough, but their accommodation lacked
something—namely, Priscilla.

They harbored the shallop, and John lifted a large woven
basket of corn from the boat. He was chatting with Howland
as they passed through the gate, carrying their wares intended
for the storehouse, when a shout diverted their attention.

"Tisquantum!" bellowed Massasoit, who stood in the
middle of the road. John could see the chain of white bones

hung around his neck. He must have been visiting the settlement as they'd arrived and heard that Squanto was returned. A crowd of Plymouth's English settlers were gathered with the group of Indians at the top of the hill. John strained to see if Priscilla was among them.

"Massasoit, please," said Governor Bradford, who followed after him.

"He has cause to be angry," muttered John, eyeing the sachem with apprehension.

"Massasoit," Squanto greeted, coming up the hill to meet his lord.

A stream of angry speech came flowing from Massasoit.

"I believe he came intending to clear himself of that earlier trouble," said Governor Bradford to no one in particular. "He was calm and kind until we heard the shallop was back."

Hobbamock entered the fray. "He angry Squanto, not English," he explained. "Massasoit English friend. No plot. No danger."

"Of course," Bradford answered. "We understand his anger. It was a terrible misunderstanding, of course."

Massasoit threw up his hands and turned about, marching off up the hill and through the palisade with a few of his men trailing after him through the gate.

"He not want see Squanto," said Hobbamock.

"I'd say that much was clear," commented Howland at John's shoulder.

"Aye," John agreed.

Priscilla and Tilley came rushing down the hill to greet them, a little out of breath. "You are well!" cried Priscilla, reaching up her hand to caress his face.

"Aye, we're well. All went well with the expedition, and look!" He hefted up his basket to show her the store of corn.

She smiled. "All has been quiet here, too, except for that. Why is Massasoit so angry? Is it true that Squanto accused him of conspiring against us without foundation?"

"It seems to be so," John said, sighing.

"Do you suppose the excitement is over?" Howland asked. "I'd like to finish putting these away and get by a fire."

"Aye, we'd best get back to working. And you two, too— no hands to be idle while others do work." He grinned, patting Priscilla's coif. She harrumphed and took Tilley by the arm, but she looked back and smiled over her shoulder at him as they walked off. Howland sighed and pushed John by the shoulder to stop him staring after her.

They went back to the shallop and picked up another load of corn and animal furs. It was good to have some supply again, which might even last until the first of the crop was ready to harvest, if no more unexpected turns for the worse befell them.

"Do you think we'll have much time for building new dwellings, with *Fortune*'s men to help tend the fields?" Howland asked as John closed the door.

"We also have that many more mouths to feed," John answered.

"Aye, I suppose. It would be better to have a few dwellings more. We are a bit pressed together in our houses ever since the newcomers came."

"I wish for my wife and myself to build our own place as much as any man," John agreed, "though we must make shift in these temporary houses until the term of contract with the Virginia Company is up. If I must wait till then to make my own home which cannot be seized in repayment of our debt, then I must agree to wait."

They walked together up the hill toward the ordnance platform, where Bradford was getting a report of their journey from Standish and Hobbamock. As they arrived, an Indian came running up through the wood.

"He messenger from Massasoit," Hobbamock translated for them. "Massasoit want you kill Squanto."

When they left the two men, Priscilla and Tilley went to the Brewsters' garden to finish the work they began before Massasoit's visit. The season for planting was coming to an end, and they needed to finish setting seeds into the ground. Mistress Brewster, though very able, was already a woman in her fifties, and Priscilla wished to help repay the kindness she showed through the year Priscilla lived in the Brewsters' house. Besides, more than a month had passed since her marriage, and Priscilla still felt more at ease in Tilley's company than in any other woman's.

They sat at the edge of the garden bed, smoothing soil and planting seeds. She heard Tilley take a sharp breath and looked up to find Tilley's eyes directed behind her shoulder. She half turned, but before she could, she found John's arms around her. "John!" she shrieked, surprised to find him at her back. He buried his face into the crook of her neck, scratching her skin with the stubble of a short, growing beard. She felt the heat of his breath on her shoulder and blushed.

She tried to face him but knocked his capotain askew. "I thought no hands should be idle whilst others are at work?" she asked, her cheeks flushed with the rosy hue of embarrassment.

"I am hard at work, protecting you from Indian arrows. I work as your shield from harm."

Priscilla glanced at Tilley, confused, but Tilley shrugged.

"You were not so worried just after Massasoit stormed away." She reached up to touch his stubbled cheek with tenderness. "What has happened, since I saw you last, to make you so protective?"

"Massasoit sent a messenger to ask Bradford to kill Squanto," he murmured.

"Kill him? Surely he does not deserve so much as that?" Tilley gasped, horrified.

"The request is justified," said John. "If Squanto's plan worked, we might have gone to kill Massasoit. He has done other harms to Massasoit's authority as well."

Priscilla frowned. "But Squanto has been such a great friend to us, for more than a year while he has stayed here." She swatted John away, to get him off her back. This was not a conversation for tender touches, and in any case, such a familiar embrace was not appropriate in the garden, with Tilley right there. "If he did not accompany us, or translate for us, God alone knows what would have become of us."

"God worked through him to help us," Tilley agreed.

Priscilla's husband sighed, relinquished her, and crouched next to her. "Bradford has urged Massasoit's messenger to ask him to reconsider, as loss of Squanto would impair our good communications with him. Massasoit was so angry, I doubt he will accede to the request." He ran his fingers over the nape of Priscilla's neck, which made her shiver. "But that is not what I wanted first to say to you, when I returned after so long away," he said. Her neck grew hot under his fingers. It was not the conversation she looked for either, after his absence, but he was the one who brought it to her.

"Goodman Alden, I believe your hands are idle when they are needed elsewhere." She refused to look him in the eye. If she did, she might see his playful look and pull him into a kiss right then and there.

"In that case, I shall go where my hands are wanted." He stood and went to the garden gate. "And hope that they are better received by my wife at a later hour."

Her every inch of skin was on fire, and he had the gall to leave her with those words?

Friday, 17 May 1622

"Massasoit want peace," Hobbamock translated. "Squanto do harm. Punish Squanto. Else, break treaty." He made a motion with his arms, to signify the broken alliance. The messenger who came a few days before had returned, along with a large retinue of other Pokanoket warriors. Massasoit did not mean to let Squanto live this time.

John and Howland stood near the ordnance platform, muskets at their sides.

"He does deserve to die, for your respect, but I ask you please not to take him, so that we might better understand each other," Bradford said with desperation in his voice.

The Indian emissary took out a copper knife, which John recognized as one the English presented to Massasoit as a gift on their first meeting. He spoke in his own tongue, gesturing with the knife at his wrists and his throat. The meaning was clear enough without Hobbamock's translation. Massasoit sent the emissary to take the head and hands of Squanto and bring them back to him.

Another Indian came forward, arms loaded with beaver skins. He made a gesture of offering them to Bradford.

"Massasoit not kill Squanto without English willing," said Hobbamock. "Beaver gift. For agreement."

The governor snorted in disgust. "It is not the manner of the English to sell men's lives at a price," he said, gesturing that the beaver skins should be taken away. He stood for a long moment in silence, considering.

"Winslow," he said at last, "fetch Squanto here."

Winslow nodded, and the crowd of armed men parted for him to make his way to the place where Squanto lived. There was tense silence for a few long moments. John surveyed the party of Indians who were gathered beyond the open gate of the plantation. He, along with many others, worked to build the palisade which encircled the town. They did so after receiving a threat of war from the Narragansett. They did so to keep the Indians out.

Squanto, upon his arrival, surveyed the emissary and his followers with fear in his eyes, his nostrils flared. John's jaw tightened. He no longer pitied Squanto. He was not alone in this change of heart.

"These men mean to take you—your head—back to Massasoit, for the wrongs he perceives you have done against him," Bradford explained.

"Hobbamock has told lies about me," Squanto protested, desperation in his pitch. "It is Hobbamock who has said I have behaved with treachery, though he has no love for me and has never been a friend of mine."

Bradford's eyes flicked to Hobbamock. John could see his doubt. Bradford never believed that Squanto could betray Massasoit, could betray Plymouth.

Squanto saw his hesitation and acted on it. "However, Governor Bradford," he said, trying to take back control of his tone, "if you send me to go with them back to Massasoit—to meet my fate—I will do it, if you think that it is wise."

"We have heard from your own lips the accusation that Massasoit was allied against us," argued John. "We heard you suggest that we attack him, when he did nothing to merit such a response."

Squanto narrowed his eyes at John. "I was translating the words of the boy who came here," Squanto said. "I was doing what I always do—translating for you, to protect your best interest."

If Bradford refused this request from Massasoit, they risked losing their greatest ally. Their relationships with the other tribes—with the Nauset, the Paomet, even the Massachusett to some degree—came from the Indians' loyalty to Massasoit. If they refused to hand over Squanto, they would alienate the Pokanoket, but they would risk the loss of all their Indian friends. John shuddered, remembering the fears which dogged their every move upon their first arrival. His nightmares, of the deaths of his friends by Indian hands. Their tension, wondering whether their Indian neighbors would be friends or foes. But it would be worse than that. It would be worse, because they would *know* they had no friends among the Indians, and the question would be *when* they could expect attack. He could well imagine the Indians invading their plantation—he had imagined it, had seen it in his mind's eye when they were called back from their voyage to the Massachusett. He had imagined Priscilla captured, even killed. Yet Bradford still hesitated.

"We must hand him over, Bradford," said Hopkins.

"Do you believe that Squanto is of more use to us dead than he is alive? Do you not remember all that he has done for us?" Bradford asked.

"We are grateful for all that Squanto has done, indeed, but is a war with Massasoit worth our keeping him here?" asked Hopkins.

"Not just Massasoit," John reminded them, "but all of Massasoit's allies. The peace treaties that we have forged have all come from the faith that Massasoit put in us. No doubt some of those that forged peace with us would break it if they hear of our breaking off with Massasoit. Not least the Nauset, who, without his intervention, would long since have sought our deaths. They already attacked our exploring party at Cape Cod."

Bradford held his silence a long moment, looking at Squanto with anguish. At last he sighed. He stepped back, leaving Squanto alone between the English and the Indians. Squanto's eyes darted in terror between Bradford and Massasoit's messenger. He knew his time had come.

"We cannot—" Bradford began, but he was interrupted by the sentry, who that day was Goodman Browne.

"A ship!" Browne cried. "A boat approaches!" His mastiff barked alongside him at his shouts.

John turned and squinted out at the sea, raising his hand to pull down the brim of his hat and shade his eyes from the sun. There was something, indeed, beyond the southern spit of Plymouth beach.

"Is it French?" demanded Standish at once.

"I know not, Captain," replied Browne.

Bradford turned back to the emissary from Massasoit. He took Squanto by the arms and dragged him back into the safety of the palisade. "I must see who it is that approaches, before I can make any decision," he told them. Squanto smirked.

"For what reason do you put it off?" John asked in agitation. "What colors could that ship carry that would change your decision to go to war with Massasoit? Handing Squanto over now protects every person in this plantation from danger!"

Hobbamock was translating Bradford's words as best he could, but the signal he gave by turning away was clear enough.

"What if they are French, Goodman Alden, and in league with the Indians on some conspiracy?" Bradford asked, his hand still on Squanto's arm. "What if they are in combination with the savages and plan to fire upon us while we are busied at this horrid task?"

The emissary scowled and shouted something that John could not understand. He turned on his heel and marched off into the forest.

"That does not bode well," John muttered.

The boat did not prove to be a French warship, nor any other vessel one might suspect to be in confederation with the Pokanoket. It was an English shallop, come to them from a ship called *Sparrow*, which was set forth by none other than Master Weston. *Sparrow* was anchored at Damariscove, an island far up the coast to the north. It was near the island of Monhegan, where Samoset lived and where there were good fishing grounds.

"My name is Phineas Pratt," said a lanky man, as tall as John but skinny, with sandy brown hair that fell into his eyes. "Weston sent these letters for a Governor Carver." He held out a bundle toward Standish, the clearest figure of authority in the group of men who met Pratt's shallop on the beach.

"Then Weston had not yet heard from *Fortune* when he sent you," Bradford replied, snatching the letters. "I am governor here now." He broke them open and began to read.

"Are you sent to join our plantation?" Hopkins asked, one eyebrow raised, assessing.

"Ah…" Pratt looked about from one face to another, confused. "No, no. Master Weston has procured a patent for us to start our own colony."

Hopkins narrowed his eyes. "So why have you come here, instead of going straight to your plantation?"

"We seven passengers came ahead, aboard *Sparrow*. We wait for the two ships Weston is sending with the bulk of our company. He asks that you supply us friendly entertainment, that we will lose no time in felling trees to lade the ships when they arrive." Pratt gestured toward the letter in Bradford's hands. "It's all in there, he said."

Bradford was smiling at the letter. "Weston says he solicited the other merchants of the Virginia Company to send us resupply, yet they refused until the *Fortune* was received, although they expect her any day. He does ask that we supply such necessities as we can spare, which they will repay with a salt pan in our bay."

"Do you not bring even necessities?" Hopkins asked Pratt, who trembled under the grizzled man's imposing gaze.

"Only that which the shallop needs to return her to *Sparrow*. We were not supplied with more."

Hopkins flared his nostrils and drew back his head.

"He says they mean to send a small ship to abide by us, which he conceives will be a great help to our plantation," Bradford continued.

"It seems to me that he has sent these men to take from our plantation, not to aid it," Hopkins said.

John agreed. "If they bring no provision at all to supply them, how are we meant to feed them, less to house them? Our trading mission to the Massachusett did not procure us enough corn to take in another seven men. It is already past the peak time for planting; how will they survive the winter without relying on us to feed them? Them, and the others who are coming after?"

"How many do come after you, in Weston's other ships?" Hopkins asked Pratt, who kept raising his finger as though to interject, but was too timid to enter himself into the conversation.

"He estimated between fifty and sixty were to join us, in a month or so."

Hopkins cursed.

"Sixty men? How do you intend to survive the winter without provision?" John demanded.

"Bradford, you cannot mean to take them in," Hopkins said.

"I am sure Weston means to send supply with the next ship that comes." Bradford tried to calm them.

"We are meant to stay, so we can cut clapboards and trade until they come, so we can the more readily send the ship away with goods. I am sure we are meant to remove to our own place, when they come, but I know not for certain." Pratt offered this opinion as though it were not his own, stumbling over his words. "Weston's brother will come himself, in the later ship, and he will tell you when he comes."

"And without provision, how do you plan to establish your plantation, from June until next spring, when planting season comes again?" Hopkins asked. "Bradford, I warn that they will try to take from us all that they can when they arrive, and we will be left to starve."

"I'm sure we—"

"This doesn't concern you," Hopkins snarled at Pratt.

"Enough!" Bradford shouted in the most commanding voice John ever heard him use. "Now, we are Christian men, and these men here have been brought into our hands in need of aid and succor. Would you turn them out into the wilds of the forest, as alone as we were when we first arrived? If we found a steady plantation when we came, and they turned us out, would you not have railed against them and called them villains?" He looked back and forth between Hopkins and John. "Now these seven men have neither provision nor ship, once their shallop returns to *Sparrow*. What would you have me do with them—leave them outside our palisade to starve?"

"Let them go back to *Sparrow* and get their succor there until Weston's brother comes and can bring them to their new plantation," John said, gesturing at Pratt, who was twiddling his fingers.

Hopkins agreed. Bradford did not, and while he welcomed these friends of Master Weston's into their homes against their will, he also did not send Squanto back to Massasoit.

Chapter Fifteen

This boat proved to be a shallop, that belonged to a fishing ship, called the *Sparrow*, set forth by Master Thomas Weston, late merchant and citizen of London, which brought six or seven passengers at his charge, that should before have been landed at our Plantation; who also brought no more provision for the present than served the boat's gang for their return to the ship...

—Edward Winslow, *Good Newes From New England*, 1624

Saturday, 1 June 1622

John pushed open the door of Winslow's house and found the former printer of seditious tracts seated at his writing desk, glasses secured by ribbon to his head. Winslow held up a finger and shook it, begging John to wait a moment. John stood and waited while Winslow finished the page of the letter he was reading, then placed it down distractedly about his desk. He turned to look at John, retracted his head backward like a turtle, then, widening his eyes, lifted the glasses from in front of them to identify him.

"Goodman Alden," Winslow said. "What brings you... here?" and he glanced about the room, as though in doing so he could identify some object which was the reason for John's coming.

"I came to welcome you home from your voyage to Damariscove, Master Winslow." John spent much time with Winslow on their expeditions to the Nauset and the Massachusett, and he had grown used to Winslow's perpetual discombobulation. "I heard you procured some corn, of which we are in desperate need."

"Not enough," Winslow said. "Not half as much as what we asked, though they freely spared what they could give." He shook his head. "If in their resupply they would send seines!" He turned to make a note on a corner of a random piece of paper. As though he could forget the colony's need of nets and tackle, the lack of which let schools of fish swim free while they went hungry.

"Aye," John agreed, "I do wish soon to eat a meal without any shellfish in it. Since Weston's seven men came, we have run through all our store of corn, and without your mission we should have none."

Winslow waved this away. "We shall need once more to truck with the Indians, though with Massasoit still angry, I know not who will trade with us."

"Do you not think Weston will send us resupply?"

"No, indeed. I was just reading what he sent for the governor." Winslow shook his head. "It is a sad thing, his deciding to break from us altogether. He even encourages us to break from the rest of the Virginia Company!"

John's heart sank in his chest. He had not carried much faith in Weston since Priscilla first planted seeds of doubt and suspicion in his mind aboard *Mayflower*, but this was too callous after the hope Bradford put in him.

"He has broken entirely?" John asked in shock.

"Yes, yes, sold all his responsibility in the venture to the rest of them," Winslow said, turning pages over on his desk to try to find the one he just set down. "Here, see—'As for myself, I have sold my adventure, and debts unto them. So, as I am quit of you, and you of me, for that matter,' et cetera, et cetera."

John glanced at the paper with curiosity. "Does he still ask that we give friendly entertainment to his men?"

"Oh? Oh, yes, he says that he will send supply and compensate us for aught we have to spare. Yet, even though he has no stake in our successes anymore, he goes on to give us his advice, as he has often done since we began the venture."

"Do you think he means in his advice to do you good?" John asked. He stepped toward Winslow's desk, trying to read the paper Winslow had put down again.

"What else is advice, but guidance offered with regard to prudent future action?" Winslow asked, pulling the definition from some corner of his mind with a little smile. "Of course, with *Fortune* robbed by Frenchmen on her way home, we have no means at all to quit the venture, even if we wished it."

"Robbed?" John asked, dumbfounded.

"Has Bradford not told you? I suppose that letter came yesterday, with that ship bound for Virginia. It carried these new letters, from Weston, too." He shuffled the papers around and handed one to John.

> *Mr. Bradford these etc. The* Fortune *is arrived, of whose good news touching your estate and proceedings, I am very glad to hear. And howsoever he was robbed on the way by the Frenchmen; yet I hope your loss will not be great, for the conceit of so great a return doth much animate the adventurers...*

John's head spun. *Robbed?* And Weston so cavalier about the loss of five hundred pounds of lading, which John and others worked so hard to acquire? It would have been their first repayment to the Virginia Company, their first repayment of the debt which seemed to weigh ever heavier about John's neck since he married into the burden of it.

He bent his head to read further. Before his eyes, a plot unfolded. A letter had been sent to Plymouth from some of the Virginia Company merchants. The letter both proclaimed the company glad to be rid of Weston and warned Plymouth that Weston and his brother Andrew were plotting against their colony. Andrew Weston was expected to arrive at Plymouth with the other men destined for Weston's new settlement.

Weston found this letter, concealed on one of his ships, because he refused to carry correspondence or provision from the Virginia Company to Plymouth. Rather than destroy the letter, as one might expect, Weston enclosed with it his own response. He called the Virginia Company merchants unhuman and barbaric for advising Plymouth to no longer put their faith in him, and he went on to claim that the ship he sent with Andrew would help, not hinder them. As Winslow said, he concluded by advising the plantation to break with the Virginia Company.

Winslow was plucking through his papers and humming to himself, each random note tripping over the previous. John picked up a letter from Master Cushman, a member of the Leiden congregation, and well trusted by Bradford to represent their interests to the Virginia Company.

> *The people which they carry are no men for us, wherefore I pray you entertain them not. He hath taken a patent for himself; if they offer to buy anything of you, let it be such as you can spare, and let them give the worth of it. I fear these people will hardly deal so well with the savages as they should; I pray you therefore signify to Squanto, that they are a distinct body from us; and we have nothing to do with them—*

The letter was snatched from his hand by Bradford, who looked furious. "These were directed to me, Goodman Alden, and not to any other."

Startled by the sudden appearance of the red face above the bristling black mustache, John muttered, "Then you should not have left them in the care of Master Winslow, Governor."

"I never left them in yours."

John's anger got the better of his shock. "I can understand why you'd want to conceal such matters from the public. It could lead to confusion and panic, when we have no answer for them. But you should share them at least with some outside your congregation. Weston's betrayal affects us all."

"It is no betrayal," protested Bradford. "He was within his rights in the terms of the agreement, and with such unkind welcome as he received at the hands of the Virginia Comp—"

"How can you take his part, even in this?" John demanded.

"Without Weston's efforts, we would not have been able to leave Holland," Bradford said. John wondered if Bradford been shown so little kindness in his life that this one act—a mercenary one on Weston's part, John had no doubt—left such a lasting impression on him?

"But did he not promise in the letter sent in *Fortune* that he should not quit you, though all the others did? Is he not instead the first to abandon us?"

"He has left it for his own good reasons," said Bradford, "and still gives us friendly advice and means to repay us for any kindness we show to his men."

"Is pretty speech to your face all that it takes to distract you from the knife he has plunged into your back? Your own friend Cushman says we should not accept these men, should distance ourselves from them as much as we can. Tell me you plan to do that much, at least."

"'Blessed is he that hath the God of Jacob for his help, whose hope is in the Lord his God,'" Bradford said. "What would you have me do, other than help them?"

"We can help them find their own place," John argued. "But if they are as bad as Cushman says, we will soon regret even that decision. Perhaps we would at least regret it less than taking them under our own protection, which will signify to the Indians that we are one and the same. Have you not already stirred enough trouble between us and the Indians, without inviting more?"

"It is for the furtherance of communication with the Indians that I protected Squanto in the face of baseless accusations."

"It did not further our communication, since Massasoit does not speak to us at all since you refused to give him Squanto. You cut off our connection with the Indians, so that we cannot trade, and now you would burden us with the lives of sixty men for whom we can procure no sustenance?" John shook his head. "If you take in these men, any deaths that follow in *our* colony will be on your hands alone."

John came through the door and it slammed against the wall, startling Priscilla, who was sitting by the hearth. Summer came upon them in earnest, and she was sweating sitting so close to the fire.

"What fool hath dared to cross thy foul temper?" she jested, but he glared at her. "You will not be cheered today, I see."

"He is like a dog who loves his master even though when he approaches, he gets kicked!" John shouted at the ceiling, tearing his hat from his head with frustration after knocking into one of the low exposed beams.

"Who is?" Priscilla asked, surprised by her husband's fury. She dropped her long spoon into the iron kettle and wiped her hands on her apron.

"Bradford. Weston must have some kind of charm or curse laid on him. Though I am as loath to admit it as any man, Bradford is sensible in matters unrelated to religion. But any action Weston takes, Bradford says it is the right one. And any fault that Weston lays upon him, Bradford as good as takes it up."

He banged a fist against the beam. Priscilla raised her eyebrows. Since Weston's men arrived two weeks ago, John had been bad-tempered. She thought it more to do with their broken treaty with the Indians, than with Weston himself. To her knowledge, since their conversation on *Mayflower*, John had not thought of Weston in eighteen long months.

"You cannot think Weston the cause of all our troubles?" she asked, reminded of that conversation long ago when he asked her the same question.

He glanced at her. At last, his ragged breathing slowed. "Aye, Miss Mullins," he said, reminding her who she had been, aboard *Mayflower*, nervous to speak her mind to him. "Weston has been the architect of all our ills, since 'ere we landed at Cape Cod, though then you alone could see it." He still could not bring his temper down enough to smile. "And now he has sentenced us to famine, subjected us to plots, even broken our peace with the Indians, though that much I'll concede he may not have intended."

"Even I cannot think how he can be blamed for that." Famine? Plots? John was so distressed; he must have reason for these suspicions. Were more of Weston's men to come? Even if they did, Plymouth had no more corn to give them.

John sat down beside her at the table. He took up her hand and stroked his thumb across it. His touch was rough, hands used to wielding tools to house and feed her. Her, and the rest of the colony he took as his own when he left *Mayflower*.

"If his shallop had not arrived at the very moment—the *very* moment—that Bradford was about to hand Squanto over to Massasoit, we would yet have our alliance with the Pokanoket."

"Hmm," she said. "You have changed your tune enough to think him so wily? He has planned the timing of the ship's arrival in concert with Bradford's great dilemma? He must have quite an ally in Squanto, which meant that Bradford was right, and the boat was in league with the Indians all the time?"

He laid his forehead down upon her upturned palm, pressing her hand into the table. Her knuckles hurt, but she did not make shift to flee.

"What has he done now, that brings you like a blizzard into the house? Have the men arrived and brought no provision after all?"

"The ship that came yesterday on its way to Virginia carried a stash of letters which Bradford meant to conceal. I went to welcome Winslow back from his trip to Damariscove and found myself looking through them."

"Tsk," Priscilla said, stroking the back of his head. "You ought never to have read them, if Bradford meant to keep them hidden. Whether you agree with him or no, he is the governor. Did not your subscription to the compact bind you to obey those in elected offices?"

John snorted. "He has conveyed to us the pieces which paint Weston in a good light, which still did not convince us to Weston's favor, when there are seven men sitting in our houses and eating up our corn till it is all gone. And you, made to care for them, because they brought no women of their own. Because Weston believes a colony of single men is strongest."

Priscilla did not much mind helping care for Weston's men. What were another seven mouths, when she and the other four wives and the growing girls had eighty men and children to feed and clean up after? If she was capable of so much, did John think that a little more might break her?

"You don't believe it was best to keep the other parts of the letter concealed?"

"I do not think it should be made known to everyone, but I wish Bradford would share it with at least some of the men outside his own congregation. When Bradford insists to us that Weston will resupply us, does it not behoove him to let us understand Weston has quit the Virginia Company? That he means no more to deal with us, except to foist the men of his own colony upon us?"

"Would you have them left to live alone, without any help from us?" she asked, stiffening in her chair.

"I would that the Virginia Company would send us resupply, that I could afford to feed both you and any stragglers who wander into our midst. Since they do not, I told Bradford that perhaps we could help them find a place to settle, which is more aid than we had when we came here."

"They should at least be kept as safe as we can make them, and by the grace of God none should die in the extremity which left me without family." She pulled her hand away from him.

"But even Cushman said that they are such reprobates we should not associate with them! He fears the Indians may not take to them and will attack us both together." John sighed and took off his hat to run a hand through his hair. "Perhaps it is better if *they* do not associate with *us*. We have already antagonized the Indians, and perhaps in doing so have worsened other men's chances to get along well here."

"Perhaps it would be best, then, if we cared for them, since we have put them into such an unfortunate position."

Friday, 14 June 1622

A loud alarm echoed from the ordnance platform, and John dropped his three-tined hoe in the field and hurried to the western gate of the plantation. He searched for men at their muster stations but found no signs of imminent violence. Instead, he spied a ship in the bay, with a smaller boat approaching their inlet.

Many ships came that summer, in contrast with their first year of complete isolation. Now that news of their settlement's location reached England, fishing ships going from Damariscove to Virginia often stopped near New Plymouth. As the season lengthened into summer, they saw more and more new ships arriving. John almost grew used to the idea of new boats appearing without warning, even docking in their harbor, if they could. Someday the exchange of ships to and from England would become more regular, and they would not need to wait these interminable intervals for word and resupply from the Virginia Company. He did not expect supply to come; if anything, it would be another ship filled with hungry men and women but no provision.

Governor Bradford sent men to greet the ship, which, as it turned out, carried nothing worse than a message; the message was bad news enough.

Friends, countrymen, and neighbors,
I make bold with these few lines to trouble
you, because unless I were unhuman I can do no
less. Bad news doth spread itself too far; yet I will
so far inform you that myself, with many good
friends in the south colony of Virginia have
received such a blow that 400 persons large will
not make good our losses. Therefore I do entreat
you (although not knowing you) that the old rule
which I learned when I went to school may be
sufficient; that is, Happy is he whom other men's
harms make to beware.

"The Powhatan," said Hopkins, who alone of all men present had been to Jamestown.

"Yes. A massacre of the English settlement there by the Indians," Bradford explained.

"Four hundred lost?" repeated John.

"Aye," confirmed Bradford.

John fidgeted with the buttons on his doublet.

"How long will it be before the Nauset or the Narragansett do the same here?" Hopkins asked the room at large. "The Narragansett have seen our weakness, now that we have both lost Massasoit as our ally and run out of corn. They need not even attack us to watch us die; our starvation will be imminent, if Weston's ship brings men and no supply."

"We need to at last build a proper fortification," Standish asserted. "A fortress, on which we can mount our ordnance and into which we can send the women and children for protection, in the event of an attack."

"To do so now will divert many hands from attending to the crops," John protested, although he too wanted the reassurance that Priscilla would be safe if any Indians invaded Plymouth. "We are as much in need of a good harvest as we are of protection from the Indians. The palisade will stand, for now, and meanwhile we have no means but our own hands to get corn, since we have broken our peace with Massasoit." He glared at Bradford.

"If Weston's men come, then do we not obtain a supply of sixty men to aid us in our endeavors?" Bradford retorted. "Then we shall have hands enough to dress the corn and build a fortress. It can serve also as a meeting house, where we can hold our Sunday services with all the company present. We have been lacking a church of any kind for some time. As to the corn, we will send the shallop out to meet the ship which has delivered us this message and see if we can get any provision from her. What's more, we have as yet heard no threatening speeches from any Indians but the Narragansett. Even the Pokanoket have made no move against us."

"Though Massasoit has turned his back to us and has not sent word to us at all since your refusal to uphold the treaty," said John.

"The Nauset were eager for our heads even before we broke peace with Massasoit," added Hopkins. "I doubt they'd give us warning before coming to butcher us; they gave no warning at Cape Cod."

"Enough!" commanded Standish. "The threat from the Narragansett alone is enough to prompt us to build a stronger fortification. This word from Jamestown is just an additional incentive to do what we should have done long ago. The governor has agreed. Alden, I'll need you at work on the fortress as soon as may be. We'll keep as many hands to tend the corn as we can, and hope that the ship from Virginia has aught to spare, and that Weston's men carry supply with them, as he has promised."

So, John was set back to his work with wood, with his familiar companion Master Eaton. It pleased his hands to be splintered and rough, rather than covered in dirt. He'd learned many valuable skills from Eaton and the work he'd done on many of the other buildings in town. His confidence in his abilities grew, but he still wished that someday he might go back to his trained profession and make casks again. They had not yet set aside any wood to season; all there was to spare was loaded aboard *Fortune* or used in the building of the palisade.

The message from Jamestown gave him new nightmares of Indian attack. Though not borne of experience, these dreams were no less vivid than his nightmares of his mother's death, which he witnessed firsthand. He saw Massasoit pick up an adze and put it through Standish's skull. He saw Aspinet, sachem of the Nauset, draw back a bowstring and let arrow after arrow fly into Hopkins. He saw their fields of growing corn on fire. He woke from these nightmares anxious and sweating, unable to lie down again. At those moments, he looked at his wife, sleeping in her smock beside him. Her hair was unbound and lay about her head in a messy tangle. She sniffed and rolled over, dragging the blanket off him. He smiled, touched her face, then got up to work. If he worked hard to build this fortress, perhaps it could protect her from this Devil's world.

Chapter Sixteen

In the end of June, or beginning of July, came into
our harbor two ships of Master Weston's aforesaid;
the one called the *Charity*, the other the *Swan*;
having in them some fifty or sixty men, sent over
at his own charge to plant for him. These we
received into our town, affording them whatsoever
courtesy our mean condition could afford.

—Edward Winslow, *Good Newes
from New England*, 1624

Wednesday, 24 July 1622

At the latter end of June, two ships, *Charity* and *Swan*, came
to Plymouth, laden with the remainder of Weston's
complement of men. These men were put ashore by their ship
Charity, which carried other passengers who were bound for
Virginia. *Charity* then departed to deliver her freight, leaving
Weston's men in Plymouth. They asked, of course, that
Plymouth house and feed them while a portion of their
company used the smaller ship *Swan* to seek through the land
procured them by their patent for a place worthy of
habitation. John's and Hopkins' protestations fell on deaf
ears, and Bradford welcomed them.

The company was led by Richard Greene, whom they
chose as their governor and who was Weston's brother-in-
law. Joshua Pratt, Phineas Pratt's brother, was also among the
company, and the two walked together through town like a
pair of spindly cats combing the Southampton alleys. Some of
the men were sick and required Plymouth's women to
provide them medical attention. But the man John disliked
most was Andrew Weston, the brother of the London
merchant. Goodman Weston was rangy, with a bulbous nose,

narrow eyes, and a lascivious smile. His hair was an unprepossessing shade of bronze and coiled about his ears like snakes.

It was Goodman Weston of whom the merchants tried to warn the colony. They described him as heady, violent, and set on Plymouth's undoing. Heady, indeed, for his mere presence seemed to make all the women about act intoxicated with him. Constance Hopkins followed after him the way a drunkard chases his next drink. It was unseemly, for a man ten years older than John to encourage such a girl. Yet John could not ignore him; John, at least, heeded the warnings of the Virginia Company, since Bradford would not heed them and would not share them with the colony at large. Therefore, John kept his eyes on Goodman Weston.

He soon found Weston with his hands in the common store of corn, which they replenished from the ship that brought them news of Jamestown. The governor rationed this store, for it came not above a quarter of a pound per person per day. It was all they had to last until the harvest. The rate at which the corn was disappearing indicated that it was not Weston alone among the new company who stuck his filthy fingers in it. Even as they pretended to be at work in the field, they ate growing corn from the stalk while it was still green! John tore Weston from the store at that time and made report to Bradford, but speaking ill of Weston's men to Bradford was as useless as complaining to a river; the message was soon carried away from the center of his attention.

It was more than the theft that irked John about the newcomers. These men found, despite their warm welcome, much to mock and scorn in the way things were settled at Plymouth. They laughed at their short supply of food and claimed that they would do much better in their own plantation. They teased the children and made advances on their women, yet claimed that a plantation with strong men alone would doubtless do much better. If they believed such things, John could not fathom why they spent their days in lounging about Plymouth instead of setting off at once to prove their claims.

It was thus that John came to the field one day to find Goodman Weston with his fingers wrapped around a hoe, scratching at the ground, seeming to help with the dressing of the corn, but paying it no attention. His attention was instead focused on Priscilla, who stood beside him smiling, a bucket of water in her hands to offer drink to the men at work. Goodman Weston bent, leaned in close, and touched her hand. John's blood boiled, and he let the large cut of wood he was hauling back to the fortress fall. He leapt across the field and right to Goodman Weston's side, seizing his doublet.

"John!" Priscilla cried, dropping her water bucket and backing away from his sudden violent approach.

"Good morrow, Goodman Alden," said Weston with an amiable grin, unconcerned with the danger which awaited him.

John snarled. "What do you mean by touching my wife?"

"I meant no harm, only to get a drink of water. I've been at my labor in your field all morning, in the heat of summer, and she"—he leaned his head to the side and winked at Priscilla—"was kind enough to offer me refreshment."

John lifted the hand he had curled in Weston's jacket, bringing the man to his toes. "You mean us all harm here, you and your devious brother, who would smile at our faces even whilst he betrays us."

"He was taking water, John," Priscilla protested from behind him, but he could not see her. He could see the scoundrel in front of him, who did in his sight everything that his brother did from a distance: smiled, and laughed, and appeared merry, all while taking their corn and plotting their ruin. How could a man be so duplicitous?

"Betrayed you?" Weston asked with an air of innocence. "Were you so hurt by his leaving your merchant friends in London? Were you so reliant on his money to keep you going?" Weston frowned and shook his head. "You shouldn't have put yourself in a position where you need to cling to a better man's feet to give you your daily bread, should you?"

The urge to do violence to this man swelled in John as it never had before.

"John!" Priscilla's shout penetrated through his haze of anger. He threw Weston to the ground and stalked off toward the woods. Priscilla shouted, following after him, running in his wake.

Weston groaned, arching his back, and laid his hand on his side. John growled, foreseeing that his actions would someday earn him further trouble.

"Why would you do such a thing?" Priscilla asked, chasing her unfathomable husband through the woods. "He was taking a drink of water. Remember that Governor Carver took his death from heat in our fields. These men are here as temporary guests, at the governor's insistence. They need our aid and our support, not our brutality!" She dashed around rocks and fallen tree branches, holding her skirts aloft.

"If he's in so much need, why doesn't he ask his scoundrel brother to buy him food and shelter?" John groused, still walking away, with one hand searching his head for his capotain, which he lost at some point in the skirmish.

She jumped over a felled log and caught up to him. The trees above them rustled, in full green leaf.

"You cannot injure someone just because you do not like his brother," she said, touching the back of his doublet.

"I also do not like him," said John, shrugging off her hand. "He is shiftless, he is greedy, he is salacious, and, what's more, he aims to bring about our downfall and smiles at us while he does it."

She grasped his coat and tugged. "And how will he do that, pray tell? By taking the water which flows freely down Town Brook?"

He smacked her arm away from him but stopped walking. "I know not how, but the merchants of the Virginia Company wrote to Bradford that Weston and his brother plotted together for their own ends, which would be our undoing."

"What more can they have meant than that he intended to set up his own plantation for his own profit?" she pleaded. "You know I do not trust that Weston does anything without regard for his own profit from it, but I do not think he acts solely out of intent to cause us harm." John tried to interrupt, but Priscilla kept talking. "I do not argue that he has betrayed us sorely, but he did so in the pursuit of his own gain and not out of any ill will. Could that not be all the other merchants meant, when they wrote to say he was pretending to act for our good?"

John sighed and leaned back against a tree, crossing his arms over his chest. She could smell his sweat on the air, mingled with the scent of disturbed leaf litter and the bitter tang of juniper.

"Whether or not the brother in London means us ill, the brother who shares our roofs is naught but dishonest and harmful. He takes our corn, he antagonizes our men, he…" John looked at her, then looked away and muttered, "he seduces our women."

"Ha!" She snickered, not being able to help it when he said something so ridiculous. "Do you think me seduced by Goodman Weston?"

"I do not think he has any right to make you laugh," he said. She laughed again. "It isn't funny!" John complained, taking a step toward her to take one of her hands. "He has not the right to come so close by you, to touch you. What should I do, when he takes such liberties with my wife?"

She let her hand be taken, felt the tender touch of his rough skin, expressing with his fingers what he could not say in words.

"Do you say such things because you see he is handsome?" Priscilla asked. "Are you so worried I would fly from you at the first sight of an attractive man?" Goodman Weston *was* handsome, indeed: lean, with a piercing gaze and hair that shone like burnished metal. His smile could pierce the knitted brows of stern matrons and raise the hopes of a gaggle of young maidens. Yes, he was handsome. But handsome meant little compared with a husband who gave up a voyage across the sea to settle here in Plymouth for her sake.

John flinched at her accusation. "He is not handsome," he grumbled. "He is a rake. A debaucher. A dissolute rogue."

She considered this list. "In order for him to be all of those things, does he not need to be handsome?"

"Is that the quality in him which made you smile so brightly?"

"Does it matter what about him made me smile, when you are my husband, and I am bound to you?" She pressed his hand in both of hers.

"If you find being bound to me so distasteful, then I am sure, degenerate that he is, that he would comfort you."

She scowled. Her husband was a fool. "Do you have so little faith in the troth I pledged to you?" she asked, trying to soothe his jealous pride.

"If it is to me alone then why, day after day, must I watch you do service for other men, dressing their meat, washing their clothes?" He squeezed her hand too hard.

"They will soon be gone, off to their own plantation." She still tried to assuage him. "They will leave, and all will be well."

"How soon? They have lingered here near a month already, and no word comes of a place for their settlement. It is a kind of slavery, that you must work for so many for so little, and I find it difficult to tolerate, for *those* men in particular."

"I can bear the work as well as any woman," she said. "I am not so weak that I am fit to take care of one man and no more. We have not even any children for me to look after."

John released her and stepped away, crossing his arms over his chest again. "Nor would I that we have any, if I could spare you the burden of such a thing."

"I am as capable of that as any other woman, too!" she burst, shouting at him. "Do not think that you must spare me from such a gift from God as having a child would be. It is not in your hands, and you knew when you stayed to marry me that, sooner or later, it would come!"

"If I did not, you would have borne the risk at the hands of Captain Standish," he shouted back.

"Captain Standish?" She was taken aback. "First you accuse me of consorting with Goodman Weston, and now you hark back to the offer made to me by the captain?" She threw her arms up in the air. "What is it I can do, when all these men make me advances, to show that I only ever desired to marry *you*?"

"You can outright refuse them, and not taunt me with their proposals, or act giddy when they lay their hands upon you." And he stormed off, away from her and deeper into the woods.

Chapter Seventeen

Then by [Weston's] direction, or those whom he set over them, they removed into the Massachusetts Bay, he having got a patent for some part there, (by light of their former discovery in letters sent home). ... but of their victuals they had not any, though they were in great want, nor anything else in recompense of any courtesy done them; neither did they desire it, for they saw they were an unruly company, and had no good government over them, and by disorder would soon fall into wants if Mr. Weston came not the sooner amongst them; and therefore to prevent all after occasion would have nothing of them.

—William Bradford, *Of Plymouth Plantation*, 1651

Friday, 2 August 1622

A few days after their argument, John, who was avoiding Priscilla and spending all hours at work on the fortress, came forward to apologize to her.

"I ought not to have said such things to you, when it is Weston who frustrates me so." He ruffled his brown hair with one hand, looking awkward and unhappy.

It left her still in some doubt as to his faith in her, but by that time there were larger matters to worry over, so she let things lie between them. Soon, she would need to cause him further distress.

From time to time she'd missed her monthly bleeding since *Mayflower* came to Cape Cod. She had been afraid to tell her mother, because her mother told her that happened when a girl lost her virtue. Though she did not believe she'd acted outside the bounds of propriety with any man, Priscilla feared she had made some mistake and somehow gotten with child. She asked instead Mistress Carver, who was the most experienced with midwifery. Mistress Carver, trying to hide a smile, reassured Priscilla that it wasn't impropriety but lack of proper sustenance which made her miss her bleeding. Priscilla hadn't raised the issue with the ship's surgeon, but through Master Heale's instruction on the four humors, she learned that women carried a plethora of blood, which men did not, due to men's hard work. She concluded that her difficult labor in building the new colony, combined with their lack of proper meat, beer, and bread, caused an unusual balance of her blood with the other humors.

However, when the second month came and went without the expected bleeding, Priscilla began to grow anxious.

"I am fair sure you are with child," said Mistress Hopkins, when she asked.

"Do you think so?" She did not know whether to be pleased or terrified. Her own desire to have children grew as she spent more time around Peregrine and Oceanus and their mothers. Her unease was obvious.

"You may wait a few weeks more, to be sure, before you tell your husband," Mistress Hopkins said. "Sometimes in the first few months, things can go badly. Or, as Mistress Carver said, it could be an imbalance. Perhaps you need to eat more things which are hot and wet, to be certain."

So, Priscilla tried to eat more spring onions and turnips. They had not any bread, nor mutton, butter nor milk nor cheese, which were all the usual things to bring on sanguinity. Corn was cold and dry, and fish was cold and dry, except when added to hot water or to salt, so she added a little more of their ever-diminishing supply of salt to her portions of corn pottage. She even picked some particular herbs before their season, including thyme, which grew that summer in her garden. Still, her courses did not come.

Monday, 19 August 1622

In the second week of August, *Charity* returned from her voyage to Virginia and carried Weston's men north. The men aboard *Swan* identified a place suitable for their plantation, in the heart of the Massachusett territory, a place that the Indians called Wessagusset.

Before his departure, Goodman Weston made a point of exaggerating the injury John had done him, to get out of doing his part in dressing the corn or working at the fortress. At the last, he made sure to take Priscilla's hand in John's sight. John was surprised Weston did no worse. His wife snatched her hand away and glanced at John with wary eyes. She kept more distance from him since their argument in the woods, and he was distressed that even his apology did not reconcile them, as they were before.

It was not a week since Weston's men set forth for Wessagusset that an Indian messenger from the Massachusett approached Plymouth's enclosed settlement. With great caution, they allowed him to enter.

"He says that the men at Wessagusset are stealing their corn," translated Squanto, who still lived in their midst and had not left the English encampment since Bradford almost handed him over to Massasoit's messenger. Hobbamock, who stood by Captain Standish, did not take his eyes off Squanto.

"They have stolen from us, too," said John, hoping still to indicate to the Massachusett that Weston's men were distinct from them, for all that they lived six weeks together.

"Does he come to us as ally, seeking our aid?" asked Bradford.

Squanto spoke with the man and told them, "He is your ally, yes. You have made peace with the Massachusett, and their sachem Obtakiest would not break that peace. But if these men continue to steal corn and to do harm to the men of the Massachusett, there will be trouble from some of Obtakiest's pnieses. They took goods from some Frenchmen who shipwrecked on their shore, and made the Frenchmen their slaves, and will do the same to Weston's men at Wessagusset, if they do not treat them according to your peace."

"We cannot speak for the men at Wessagusset," John said again.

"But we would trade again on good terms with the Massachusett," added Hopkins, who saw an opportunity to make good some part of their Indian relationships. They were in desperate need of it; yet, they were nearing the last of their English goods to trade. They long awaited any resupply from the Virginia Company, which would have provided them with English-made knives, jewels, and other things they could give the Indians in exchange for corn and beans and beaver and otter furs. But, while they waited with dwindling hope for that resupply to come, anything they could trade with the Massachusett would be welcome. Even with Weston's men gone, and harvest mere weeks away, they yet lived on quarter rations and what few fish they could catch with their few and broken nets. They subsisted for the most part on groundnuts and mussels.

Bradford glared at them. "We shall send word as we can to Wessagusset, and advise them not to steal, and send them some reproof for the action they have already taken."

The messenger did not seem convinced, but it was all that Bradford felt he could offer. Squanto persuaded the man that it was as much as they could do for the present, and he went away dissatisfied.

"It would be well to trade once more with the Massachusett," Bradford said. "We should not make assumptions that all our good alliances have broken off. We have not received word from Aspinet, after all, that he is no longer our friend. Perhaps we can go to trade with the Nauset, or even the Paomet, too, when harvest time is over?"

John just shook his head, speechless at the governor's optimism.

Thursday, 29 August 1622

By the time she missed her third monthly bleeding, Priscilla began to vomit after waking up and to feel nauseous at the strong smells of cooking fish or mustard seed. Soon, Mistress Hopkins told her, her belly would start growing, and she would no longer be able to keep it secret from her husband. Priscilla resolved to tell John, before she lost her nerve.

She went to find him at the fortress, at which he worked diligently since the message came from Jamestown, eleven weeks before. It still stood hollow, the framework more involved with this than with their houses, and a great part of their attention being diverted in caring for the corn and other crops. Weston's men, as John said, though they seemed to aid in the colony's labors, departed with little more done than when they came.

She did not see him by the fort, so she went out by Plymouth's west gate to see if he was in the forest, gathering a new supply of wood. She found him at his work with

Master Eaton. He was surprised to see her and came forward a few steps to greet her, wiping the sweat from his forehead with his sleeve. He was stripped to just his shirt, uncomfortable wearing a doublet in the summer heat.

She meant to lead into it, but she could not find the words. "I am with child," she said instead.

His eyes widened, and he took her arm and led her farther away from the hearing of Master Eaton.

"With child?" he asked.

"Aye," she confirmed. "Like to be born next spring."

"How…" He raised his hands to press his palms against his eyeballs. "Why now, with Indians at our door making threats against our neighbors, and no store of corn to keep us through the winter?"

She pried one of his arms away from his face. She was prepared for him to react with anger or horror at the thought.

"I cannot help that it is now, and not some other time," she told him. "But, tell me, when would you have preferred? It seems that we encounter trouble after trouble in this New World, and now seems as good a time as any."

For a long time, he gave her no answer. He took off his hat and scratched his head, wandered in a circle, and kicked at loose rocks on the ground. She waited, listening to the chitters of the birds in the summer trees. She watched a squirrel dart from one trunk to another and climb, balancing a corn cob from their field in his mouth. It weighed him down on one side, but he scampered up the tree without hesitation.

"How can I protect you from that?" was the question John used to break their silence. "I am building a fortress to protect you from attack. I work when I can in the field, to tend crops to protect you from starvation. But this?" He threw his hands up in the air, defeated. "I can do nothing. I know nothing of midwifery, and even they sometimes can do nothing. How can I defend you against such a menace?" She saw he was starting to panic, words leaking from him like a faulty bucket spilling water.

"Shh," she said, taking his face between her hands. She could smell his sweat, the proof of his labors, on him. "Shh, John. There is naught you can do. But I am strong. I am able. God has given me birthing hips, and they shall ease the passage of our child into this world." She smiled at him.

"It will be hard, here, harder than in England."

She laughed. "It will not be so much more difficult," she said, "and no worse for you!"

He touched her hair and brushed back her coif. She felt it fall, heard it land on the carpet of leaves beneath them. She felt his fingers tangle in her hair, and he drew her face up so that she looked into his eyes.

"I do not want to bury you, Priscilla." He was as serious as she had ever seen him.

"Why are you so afraid that I will meet that fate?" She put her arms around him, rubbing circles into his back. She did the same for Joseph, when he cried of his pains before dying.

He hesitated. "My…" He gripped her shoulders till they ached, but she did not brush him away. "My mother died in childbirth. Before my eyes." He closed his eyes as though he were remembering. She recalled his face when Goody Allerton gave birth aboard *Mayflower*. She recalled his tears, his panic, his distress. His anger that anyone would have a child they could not protect. She understood.

"You have lost your mother, and I have lost mine, too," she said. "Through one means or another, death comes for all in time. But you are strong, and I am strong, and our child will be strong too. And though I am sure I have the strength to live, if I do not, I know you will protect our babe. You will build a fortress. You will sow the fields and dress the crops and harvest every morsel you can. You will fight, if needs must, against our foes. And I will fight against the hand of death that comes to every mother in her childbed. And all will be well, for I will not let him take me from you or our child so soon, as he took my mother from me and yours from you." And she rubbed circles into his back, and he held on to her until his fear subsided.

Chapter Eighteen

Now the welcome time of harvest approached, in which all had their hungry bellies filled. But it arose but to a little, in comparison of a full year's supply; partly because they were not yet well acquainted with the manner of Indian corn (and they had no other) also their many other employments, but chiefly their weakness for want of food, to tend it as they should have done; also much was stolen both by night and day, before it became scarce eatable, and much more afterward...

—William Bradford, *Of Plymouth Plantation*, 1651

Monday, 16 September 1622

They could tell as soon as they started that their harvest would be insufficient for a year's supply of corn and barley. Their English grain grew indifferently in this New England, and their harvest of peas was poor. Though the Indian corn grew well, their work on the fortification drew many hands' labor away from their fields. Worse still, the sixty men of Weston's came into their fields and ate pleasant green cobs right off the stalk. Again and again, throughout their harvest, John came upon half-chewed ears of corn lying rotting in the field between two rows, which could not now profit anyone.

Despite all this, for a few days at least, their harvest provided a relative feast for the inhabitants of Plymouth. While they gathered in the corn and beans to be dried and stored, they were at last able to make bread from the corn and wheat that was collected in the prior weeks. They'd grown squash together with the corn and beans, after the Indian fashion. It would keep for several months into the winter. For now, their hazy summer days grew shorter, and the nights grew cooler. Fowl came often about their plantation, pecking at the ground and leaving themselves targets for the settlers' dinner. Hopkins even went out into the forest and got a deer. For a few days, their tables could once more be laid with a proper diet of bread and meat. Their bellies were full, and their spirits were joyful.

"It compares not with the harvest feast of last year," said Howland with a grin, as he tucked into a hunk of the mealy corn bread and some venison.

"Aye, not well at all," John agreed. Last year's harvest festival spanned three days, and Massasoit came with a retinue of ninety of his men. They brought five deer to eat, and their tables were laden with meat and fish, lobster, oysters, squash, and corn, as well as dried berries and nuts. They laughed together, the Indians danced, and it felt like peace.

"Do you imagine we shall be friends again with Massasoit?" asked Tilley, leaning forward from Howland's other side.

"I think not, until Squanto is dead," Howland answered.

"You think we might yet have peace if Bradford were to deliver Squanto to the Pokanoket?" John asked.

"Aye, right enough. Why, do you not think so?"

"Have things not gone too far for that already?" asked Priscilla. "Men do take these things seriously," she added in an aside to Tilley, who giggled.

"Treachery and disloyalty are serious matters," responded John, though with such a look of haughty contempt that he succeeded in making his wife laugh. It was a lovely sound, though second to her singing.

"Such a feast," sighed Tilley. "I should hope they could make up, so that we may have such a feast again."

"I am glad we do not have quite so many guests to tend to," Priscilla moaned. "My fingers were so sore from plucking fowl's feathers that I could hardly lift a spoon to my mouth after."

John smiled, the ease of chatter surrounding him, his stomach settled and not grumbling. How pleasurable it was to feel content.

Monday, 23 September 1622

John's contentment, as ever, did not last. As they brought in a greater and greater portion of their harvest, it grew obvious that they would need to trade with the Indians to survive the winter. Yet they had no more goods to trade. They were saved, in this desperate strait, by a ship sent out by English merchants to discover all the harbors up and down the coast. They were at last able to buy some English beads and knives, though they bought them at a dear price, for this ship's master was the last supply the planters would get that season. So, they dug themselves deeper into their debt and purchased what they could, that they might use it to buy food with which to survive the winter.

No sooner did they hear of these new acquisitions than Weston's men at Wessagusset sent Goodman Phineas Pratt to Plymouth.

"Governor Greene would like to suggest a joint trading expedition," he said.

Though they had been away less than six weeks, Pratt's doublet looked a little tattered about the cuffs, and each of his stockings bore a hole or two.

"We should send our men in *Swan*, which you could use to carry more goods. We would repay the use of your goods in trade when Master Weston sends the salt pan he has promised, or when other supply comes to us from England." Pratt scratched at his hair, which kept falling into his eyes.

"You mean to offer your ship, but no funds nor any goodwill with the Indians toward this expedition?" John asked, incredulous.

"We carry little enough goodwill with them ourselves," said Hopkins, sighing.

"But they have already antagonized the Massachusett, and stolen from them," John argued.

"As we ourselves stole from the Paomet when we first came," Bradford reminded him. John ignored him.

"Were you not left well provided when *Charity* returned to England?" Hopkins asked Pratt.

"Aye, on her return from Virginia, *Charity* did leave us with some supply, but Master Greene would have us supplied with enough corn and beans to last at least until next year."

"We ought not to covenant with them, in this or any other venture," John objected.

"We are in as much or more need of trade as they are," protested Bradford.

"It is because of their thieving hands and shiftlessness that we are desperate," John retorted. "And even now, they suggest further thieving and have the gall to dress it up as support." Pratt raised his finger to refute this point, but John talked over him. "We ought to trade on our own and leave them to do what they will with the gifts that Weston left with them."

"If they are in such need that they steal from the Indians, I do not see how that can be helped by refusing to aid them in securing to themselves more corn." Hopkins looked at Pratt.

"If Weston says he will repay us, it will be on your own heads to ensure that you do, when he next sends you supply."

Pratt nodded, still a little afraid of Hopkins, even after he lived beside him in the colony all summer.

John shook his head and muttered, "Weston will never send you resupply if he can help it. Not when it will cost him money."

Pratt's eyes widened, and he looked between Bradford and Hopkins to see if either would confirm it. Neither denied it, which John thought was enough. But he was outnumbered in the argument. If they needed to trade with tribes who might be hostile, it was better to have more men with guns to go along with them. It would leave more men at Plymouth to build the fort and finish taking in the harvest.

Wednesday, 25 September 1622

A bulge was starting to show in Priscilla's abdomen, and she began to loosen her kirtle a little more. She held her stomach with a sigh of contentment, though a hint of worry crept into her mind again. She had hoped that one day she would be with child, and that her mother would tell her of the trials and pleasures that were in store for her. But her mother was now dead, and her best friend was still an unmarried girl. It was near a month since she told John, and she was beginning to show signs. Soon, the whole town would know one way or another. Mistress Hopkins already knew; perhaps Priscilla could ask Mistress Hopkins and Mistress Winslow for their advice, in place of a mother? Perhaps now that she was with child, Mistress Hopkins and Mistress Winslow would take her into their confidence and divulge to her all the secrets of childbearing.

With this in mind, she took, one chilly morning, a dense loaf of corn-baked bread to Mistress Hopkins' house. Though it was yet too early for snow, a nip of frost visited them overnight, and she could smell the sharpness of it in the air. The first few of the trees began their journey from green to red or orange or yellow, then to brown to litter the forest floor.

As she often was, Mistress Winslow was with Mistress Hopkins; and Peregrine and Oceanus, both almost two years old, sat next to each other on the floor, one squeezing a ball, the other chewing on a husk left over from their harvested corn. The two women gave thanks as Priscilla broke bread with them, then Mistress Winslow returned to stripping dried corn kernels from the cob, and Mistress Hopkins went back to pounding the corn into meal with a mortar and pestle.

"I am with child," Priscilla told Mistress Winslow, expecting she'd heard the news from Mistress Hopkins. She had, but Mistress Winslow smiled anyway and gave congratulations.

Priscilla's nerves hummed up again, as she tried to fortify herself to ask her next question.

"As you both know, my mother died in the first winter. I have little idea of childbearing, and I wondered if you both might tell me more of it? Of what will happen, until birth, and then what I am to do when the babe comes?" Thinking so far ahead, about how much she did not know, began to overwhelm her.

Mistress Hopkins and Mistress Winslow exchanged raised eyebrows. Mistress Winslow jerked her head toward Priscilla and jutted her chin forward, querying. Mistress Hopkins shrugged. They both turned to her with wicked smiles.

"Tilley," Priscilla cried, throwing herself into her friend's arms, "I do not wish to be with child anymore."

"Why, why? Why the alarm?" Tilley asked, brushing Priscilla's frazzled hair away from her face.

Priscilla breathed hard for a moment and wondered what to say first. The women told her so many terrifying things about how her body would soon change, things she had not even thought to imagine before. But then she remembered one thing above all, which was that *she could not tell Tilley.* They shared with Priscilla at last all the secrets that they did not tell unmarried women, for fear that girls would never marry if they knew what awaited them in pregnancy and birth. If she survived (which she saw as much less probable now than when she'd reassured John she would), Priscilla would have a babe in arms whose value to her would exceed all pain and all the trouble it took to get there. They told her it was something that a woman who was not already going through it could not understand. Touching her swollen belly and remembering the nausea, the morning sickness, the tenderness and aches she felt in her body already, she thought they might be right.

"No, I…" She sighed and cuddled deeper into Tilley's embrace. "I was afraid, for a moment. Do not mind it."

"You have been trying to befriend Mistress Hopkins and Mistress Winslow again, I suspect," Tilley teased. "Why do you keep trying to abandon me, to be friends with women who would so frighten you?"

Priscilla shook her head. "I know not why—my head tells me I should, when of course I long for nothing more than your good company."

"I ought not to forgive you for trying so often to leave me, after our solemn promises aboard *Mayflower.*" Tilley huffed an exaggerated breath of indignation.

"Oh, Tilley," Priscilla begged, "please forgive my indiscretion! It was a moment, a moment, that my thoughts strayed away from you! Be merciful in my hour of need."

"You have had so many hours of need, and I am fair sure I have shown you mercy through them all. But, very well— one last time, I shall forgive you. Does not the Lord teach forgiveness, and mercy too?" She hummed the old familiar psalm, and Priscilla joined her in singing until they reached the last verse:

> *Goodness and mercy surely shall*
> *all my days follow me,*
> *and in the Lord's house I shall dwell*
> *so long as days shall be.*

And Tilley smiled, and Priscilla giggled and felt more at ease about bringing a new child into this world, through all the strange changes and pains that it would give her.

Chapter Nineteen

It may be thought strange that these people [Weston's men] should fall to these extremities in so short a time; being left competently provided when the ship left them, and had an ambition by that moiety of corn that was got by trade, besides much they got of the Indians where they lived by one means and other. It must needs be their great disorder, for they spent excessively whilst they had, or could get it.

—William Bradford, *Of Plymouth Plantation*, 1651

Sunday, 20 October 1622

In the month following Pratt's visit with Wessagusset's offer, Bradford tried three times to send Captain Standish with Squanto and *Swan* to barter with the Indians. On the day before their first proposed departure, Wessagusset's governor Richard Greene, who was Master Weston's brother-in-law, fell ill and died of a fever at Plymouth. Bradford insisted on giving him a proper burial, and they waited for word from Wessagusset on whether to proceed. By the time the trading party set out again, the winds grew so fierce that the ship was blown back into the bay. Before they could set out on their third attempt, Captain Standish fell ill with fever. He still lay abed with it, unable to venture out at all.

It seemed like the will of God was upholding John's desire not to treat with Wessagusset and preventing Bradford's want to go, which confounded John as much as it irritated Bradford. John, despite his staying with them at Plymouth, was not yet persuaded to the Separatists' view of things. He maintained his faith in the King's church and would not pray to God, but with his wife he attended the community's religious services.

One Sunday in late October, on their way to the half-completed fortress, John watched Priscilla bend down to pick up a large, red maple leaf from the ground. The five veined limbs stuck out like the spread fingers of her hand. The maple leaves were a rich red color, though they were less common than the orange oak and yellow hickory and beech leaves which littered the ground. The evergreen of pine trees interspersed the flood of autumn color. He saw her twirl the leaf between her fingers as they ascended the hill. He watched her more, of late, as her body began to change and grow under his gaze. She seemed content today, happy that two weeks had passed without vomiting. He could not comprehend that she was carrying their child, yet. When would the hope start? The joy? For now, all he felt was worry.

The meeting house was framed now, the lower beams like trees, spreading branches out to support the floor above. The floor between the first and second stories was laid with beams and crosswise floorboards to support the weight of men and cannons. Though still a skeleton, they took to gathering in the fortress for their Sunday services, using it for its secondary intended purpose: a meeting house. There was not another place large enough on the plantation, and no place not in constant use with casks and boxes next to beds and tables, filling up the whole of the space. Here there were piles of wood waiting to be used, stray tools careless men left behind, and a collection of musket stands by the palisade wall, in case of Indian attack.

John stood beside Priscilla as they gathered. How long was it now that he'd been without a proper service? Without a proper priest, without a proper church? While new men kept coming, landing on their shore, there were none who might lead a separate service for the Church of England, none who could walk John through his half-forgotten Book of Common Prayer, which lay neglected in some chest in the loft of his shared house. He tried, since his decision to stay, not to dwell too much on whether God could see them—or whether it mattered if he couldn't. Howland's argument that, wherever they died, their fate rested in the hands of God alone, sat between John's shoulders, prickling him. Was it not said that a body should be buried whole, for God to find it? That the heathen practice of cremation left you in too many pieces to be recognized by Jesus? What, then, of a skeleton picked bare of flesh and left to bake above the earth with no living soul to bury it? What of a pile of bodies buried in an unmarked mound of dirt? What of dead men left propped against trees, sitting at their posts, muskets in their cold, unmoving hands? It was not right, not right, to die in such a place as this.

Elder Brewster professed at the head of the group of worshipers. "There is no rule nor example of the Book of Common Prayer in God's word," he said. "The Nicene Creed, the Apostles' Creed, Athanasius' Creed, and the so-called Lord's Prayer: they direct the faithful to look down, to read the words that men have written, and do not leave one open to God."

John looked over at his wife to see her fold the leaf in her hands in half along the vein and tear it apart. She was busy, these days, in managing their overlarge household. It was difficult for her to take these days of rest, but there was no work done on the Sabbath in Plymouth. For their dinner, in the break between morning and afternoon services, they would have cold meat and day-old bread. At least it was now autumn, and the fowl came out in droves to be killed for their suppers.

Governor Bradford spoke to the questions which Elder Brewster raised in his reading and exposition.

"So, also, is false the assumption that Christ and his Apostles used set forms of prayer. Does it not say in Romans, 'for by the Gospel of Christ the righteousness of God is revealed from faith to faith: as it is written, the just shall live by faith'?"

John saw Priscilla tear the leaf in fourths, halving each of the smaller sections along their primary veins. Two or three more of the congregation would no doubt add their thoughts to this subject when Bradford finished. John never joined in this part of the service, though he was tempted when they so railed against his church. On one occasion he left the service, and on another came not to it at all. But it was not right, to be alone on Sunday. It was no more right to sit at home than it was for a body of men to revel in extemporaneous debate over the merits of his King's church; and so John was caught between a choice of lesser evils. He clenched his fists and gazed out the open hole in the side wall, ignoring the discussion in favor of planning the wall's construction in his head.

Winslow was extemporizing now upon the use of set forms of prayers in the Bible. "It is shown in Mark, in Matthew, and in Luke, that Christ prayed and spake different words upon each occasion. Had our Savior used the very same words verbatim, upon the same occasion, what would this have proved?"

Winslow's inquisitive nature made such questions feel like a discussion, open to John's beliefs to answer, more so than Brewster and Bradford's statements of his church's erroneous practices. He knew from experience that this feeling was not true. The Separatists were no more open to discussion on the use of the Book of Common Prayer in their services than John was. But in Plymouth he was outnumbered, and he had no viable alternatives.

He felt a cool finger run over the back of his hand. He looked down at his wife, who crushed the remnants of the maple leaf in one hand and reached out to him with the other. She sensed his unease, it seemed, and sought to comfort him. He smiled, which made her smile in return.

Wednesday, 25 December 1622

Priscilla cupped her hands around her mouth and blew into them. Her fingernails were starting to turn blue from the cold, and she knew the worst of the winter was yet to come. Tonight, all seemed quiet in the settlement. Smoke rose from chimneys of Separatist and adventurer homes alike. As she peered up the quiet street, she saw no fir garlands hung from doors and saw no revelers dance.

John ducked out of their house and shut the door. Priscilla took his arm and tugged. She did not jump up and down, because she felt her belly had swollen in the past few weeks, and her feet began to swell too. They crept up the street, the blanket of snow muffling their tread across the ground. But when John pushed open the door of Hopkins' house, the pair were met with warmth and light and laughter. Merriment abounded within the confines of the house, which was occupied by men and women who felt that Christmas should not go unrecognized. A pine bough decorated the mantle above the hearth. Priscilla smelled the scent of roasting goose. Dried-up kernels of Indian corn were scattered on the table, being used as chips in a game of chance still underway. Though they liked the game, there was nothing of value with which to gamble.

Priscilla hugged and greeted her way across the room to join Mistress Hopkins and her stepdaughter Constance by the hearth. They offered her a cup of aqua vitae, which she took with gratitude, not asking where they'd gotten it. She sat, one hand balancing her incomprehensible girth. She held the wall for a moment as her vision went dark and hazy. She was often dizzy or faint of late, and it was frustrating to feel so overwhelmed by this infant who was so small yet wrought such great changes on her.

"It will pass, in time," Mistress Hopkins said, smiling at her. Priscilla narrowed her eyes. She had not forgotten the detailed list of torments that awaited her, explained with such care by Mistress Hopkins and Mistress Winslow. She wanted to know what was in store for her but did not expect quite so many changes to all the parts of her body, nor the side effects to her cheerful disposition.

"Have you heard the talk of Governor Bradford's return?" Constance asked, interrupting Priscilla's pessimistic mood.

"Briefly." She smiled at the girl. "Why don't you tell me more about it?"

After Captain Standish's illness, Bradford grew impatient of delays and ventured out himself with Squanto and the men from Wessagusset, to procure for them some corn and beans by trading with the Indians. Although Priscilla had heard John's lengthy opinions on the subject, she could tell Constance was eager to talk about it. Constance heard news later than anyone else in the colony, and Priscilla was pleased enough to hear a different person's view of things than her husband's.

"Well, of course he went to trade with the Massachuset and the Nauset, but when he was with the Nauset the shallop broke!" Constance was, like a child, excited over this loss of such a useful vessel, not seeing the consequences. "And

Governor Bradford, not being a carpenter himself, and having Squanto and the Wessagusset men with him—wait," she turned to her stepmother, "did he have Squanto with him then, or had Squanto already died?"

Priscilla raised her eyebrows at the simple manner in which this young woman spoke of death. Constance had seen much of it, in her young life: first her own mother and her elder sister back in England, and then of course the many other passengers who passed away on this very shore. As Priscilla understood it, Squanto took an Indian fever on the voyage, and he died asking Bradford to pray for him to the English God. As though it were so simple as having one English God and one way to pray to him.

"Well, he had not any carpenters with him, and so he was made to leave the corn he bought with the Indians, and leave the shallop with them, and he himself was made to walk the fifty miles through the snow back to our plantation!" Constance squeaked in her astonishment. The news was new; Bradford arrived back two days ago. "Fifty miles by foot in the snow! I do not think even Father would like to make such a journey."

Mistress Hopkins agreed. "I do not think Governor Bradford *liked* to make the journey, but there was little other choice, dear Constance."

"In any case, now there will be another expedition to the Indians to get the corn which the governor left there," Constance concluded her recitation.

"Let us hope that, since Captain Standish has recovered from his illness, he can go and get it for us soon," Priscilla told her.

"Aye. Do you think the Indians will be at peace with us again, Goody Alden, since Squanto is dead? That is what Father says."

Priscilla flicked her eyes up to look at Mistress Hopkins. Mistress Hopkins shrugged, helpless to control her husband from voicing his opinions. That was something Priscilla well understood, and she smiled in sympathy.

"I hope we shall have peace with them again, but death is not often the way to mend relations which have been broken," she told the girl.

Constance chewed her lower lip.

"And does Bradford's trek through the snow mend the breach he has with your husband, over going out at all?" Mistress Hopkins murmured to Priscilla.

Priscilla looked for John among the crowd. He was grinning, talking with Captain Standish and Master Hopkins. Master Hopkins held young Oceanus in his arms, while Giles stood stoic by his father's side, head about the height of Hopkins' shoulder.

"As I understand it, he did not wish to stop Bradford going, for he knows that we need corn. He wished we would not do so in concert with the men from Wessagusset, and I know of naught that can mend the rift that the very name of Weston seems to drag between my husband and the governor."

For it was not a question of religion, anymore. John's rift with Bradford had become something that Priscilla understood one-sidedly. Whether the good that Weston did the colony was worth the limitless faith that Bradford put in him, she did not know.

It was refreshing to Priscilla to chat with Mistress Hopkins. In their usual routines, Mistress Hopkins was with Mistress Winslow, or Priscilla was with Tilley, and they rarely spent time alone together. Now, Mistress Winslow was not present, nor was Tilley, as both belonged to the separated church and did not recognize Christmas. Priscilla did not much mind the tenets of the Separatists, and she liked Tilley's faith in God that was so simple and so close. It felt comforting to know that God was near, as opposed to John's belief that God was far away, unreachable by man alone, hidden somewhere within an organization of priests and kings and churches. She'd grown up in the Church of England and, though she suspected her father of Separatist inclinations, she'd never paid much mind to spiritual matters. Church was a place you went to connect to things you could not see, could not touch, so Priscilla felt the spirit move her through music. The practical world was much easier to understand, with things laid out in front of you. Tilley's God was one who could be reached, and in whose praise you could find comfort, but John's was too distant for Priscilla to comprehend. She did just wish the Separatists were not so opposed to Christmas. Priscilla liked Christmas well, for the festive mood was infectious and the songs were plentiful.

As the night wore on, they did indeed start singing. The songs moved from spiritual ones such as "A Great and Mighty Wonder" and "In Dulci Jubilo" to more secular tunes such as "The Boar's Head Carol" and "The Gloucestershire Wassail" before devolving outright into drinking songs.

> *Wassail, wassail all over the town,*
> *our toast it is white and our ale it is brown,*
> *our bowl it is made of the white maple tree,*
> *with a wassailing bowl we'll drink to thee.*

She sang, able in the joyous mood to cease feeling the ill effects of her pregnancy. Soon the singing turned to dancing, and the dancing grew rowdy in their close quarters. It was not until the festivities were ebbing that John and Priscilla tumbled from the house into the snow and the chill night air.

"John," she said, her cheeks still glowing with the warmth of the indoors.

"Priscilla," he said, holding her close against him.

In the middle of the snowy street, in the middle of that midwinter night, they kissed in their dark, cold settlement on the edge of a vast and unknown country.

Tuesday, 25 February 1623

The winter dragged on, cold and wet. Fires burned smoky inside, oiled paper covering the windows, doors shut tight against the harsh winds off the sea.

In February, a messenger came to them from Master Sanders, the man who replaced Weston's brother-in-law, Greene, as governor at Wessagusset. To John's surprise, Bradford called for him to discuss the letter's contents.

"Sanders does not know what he should do," Bradford sighed, leaning back in his chair and stretching his arms above his head so that the letter dangled in the air. "He says that his men will not quit stealing from the Indians, breaking their ground and taking from their hidden caches. They have stocked and whipped the men that steal the corn from the Indians, but the Indians still threaten them unless they punish the offenders further. They've impaled their settlement around already, and staked the entrances, but they still feel some threat from the Massachusett. Still, they've used up all their corn—"

"Already? After they were left competently provided by *Charity* and by our trading with them over winter?" John interrupted.

"Already, aye, Alden, for Governor Sanders' leadership has led to great disorder amongst them. After Master

Greene's death, it seems, they have fallen into great want. Sanders must not have rationed the corn they got from trade with us, of which we still have not yet even retrieved the greater part." Bradford tapped the letter on his forehead, deep in thought. "They ask the Indians for more in trade, but the Indians will let them have none."

"Reasonably enough, since we spent all the winter trading with the Massachusett, and they've given us what they could in trade already. Besides which, if Weston's men are stealing from them, as his letter indicates, why should they trust them to deal honestly in trade?"

"I take your point, Goodman Alden." Bradford raised an uneasy eyebrow at John. It was a long while since they'd agreed on anything, and they'd never agreed on anything to do with Weston at all. Bradford sighed. "Know I tell you this because I trust that you will tell me what I should say to them, and in this case, I do not think that any leniency is justified." He put his elbows on his writing table and steepled his fingers together. "Sanders asks whether they should do violence against the Indians, in order to obtain some of their corn."

John tried to answer with care, to push back his first thought and give instead a considered reply to which Bradford might listen. He had been good at concealing his own opinions when he meant to stay in the colony for a short time, but he had not much practiced reticence since he decided to settle. As a member of this civil body politic he did not hold back.

"What good would it do them, to instigate such action? If they do that, they will gain as much corn as the Massachusett have left in store, which is little more than they need for seed in spring. Once that is gone, for I think you are right and disorder rules amongst them, what shall they do? Start a fight with the Massachusett, when the Indians are already bringing threats against them and have been complaining to us ever since they removed to Wessagusset? It is shortsighted and will do them harm. What's more, we at Plymouth may also be hurt by this action. The Indians may consider us their enemy as much as Wessagusset and come against us too." John remembered Cushman's letter, half-read, urging them to signify to the Indians that they and Weston's men were different. Urging Plymouth not to take the men in, lest just such a situation as this should arise. Cushman and the Virginia Company both warned them that these men would be their undoing.

"To my surprise—and yours, I'm sure, Goodman Alden—I agree. Sanders says he plans in any case to take *Swan* to Monhegan, where Samoset lives, to trade with the fishing ships thereabouts. He seeks to steal corn to tide the company over until he should return."

"That's insanity," John said, voice raised, but he bit his anger back again at the governor's wary look. "I mean to say that it would be unwise to begin such trouble with a strong enemy to stave off hunger a few days or weeks. The Massachusett may have been as affected by the plague hereabouts as the Pokanoket, but they have more warriors to fight than Governor Sanders does. The more so, if his men are as weak from lack of corn as you describe."

"He says they are in great want, and his men are daily falling and some dying without bread. Some have gone so far as to fetch wood and water for the Indians, that the Indians might spare them a meal, which work would be better spent in gathering clams and mussels and groundnuts, the things which this country affords in plenty. If they spent their efforts more toward their own preservation and rationed out the use of their corn, as I suggested, they would not be in these straits. They are not so ill situated that they may not, with some little effort, feed themselves upon the land without such base behaviors."

John could see that the governor was in frustration over having his own advice ignored, as well as loath to speak ill of the men whom Weston sent. John never thought that he would fault a man for thinking too kindly of others, but in Bradford it was fault brought to excess.

"In any case, it would be unjust for Sanders to steal more from the Massachusett, and worse if violence became necessary. Any officer sent here by His Majesty or by the Council for New England would see Sanders hanged for it. We can spare him a little corn, for now, if he needs enough to subsist until he can come back from his voyage to Monhegan."

John bit into his tongue in trying to hold back his immediate response. For once he was having a fruitful conversation with Bradford, whereby the governor was swayed to his position. Could not his powers of persuasion extend to one more point?

"Governor, do you think it wise to send him more, when you know that they distribute it foolishly? We cannot so easily spare any until we retrieve the corn that was left with the Nauset."

Bradford took up his quill and smiled at John. "Well, then it is good that the work on the meeting house is nearly done, so that you and the captain can make haste to retrieve it, Goodman Alden. We'll need you to go along and make the repairs to the shallop, so the captain can bring her home. I am sure Governor Sanders would be happy to stop here on his way to Monhegan, to pick up the corn and bring you men to the Nauset, so that *you* don't need to walk all that way through the snow."

To which John could do nothing but suspire and nod his acquiescence.

Chapter Twenty

News came to Plymouth that Massassowat was like to die... Now it being a commendable manner of the Indians, when any, especially of note, are dangerously sick, for all that profess friendship to them to visit them in their extremity, either in their persons, or else to send some acceptable persons to them; therefore it was thought meet, being a good and warrantable action, that as we had ever professed friendship, so we should now maintain the same, by observing this their laudable custom...

—Edward Winslow, *Good Newes
From New England*, 1624

Tuesday, 18 March 1623

John bent over the shallop, working to fix the damage done by the squall Bradford encountered. He was unhappy to leave Priscilla, whose belly was swelled to the size of a firkin. She woke in the night more often than he did, these days, to use the chamber pot or scratch her giant stomach. Her feet were also swollen, and she breathed hard even to ascend the hill to the fortress. He was worried that her labor would soon come, but Mistress Hopkins reassured him that it was still some weeks away. Governor Bradford left him little choice but to go. At least the fortress was complete—complete enough that the cannons were mounted on top. Complete enough to safeguard the women and children inside, in the event of an attack.

John, Howland, Hobbamock, and Standish rode with *Swan* and came to shore in her ship's boat before watching her depart northward. John hoped that Sanders would get much store of corn from the fishing ships at Monhegan and Damariscove, so that his men would no longer feel the need to steal from the Indians and jeopardize all the English in New England. The mending of the shallop would at least be quick work, and he and Howland and Standish could take the store of corn awaiting them and soon be back at Plymouth. Hobbamock would act as guide and interpreter. They made but a small company, and John hoped their work would soon be done.

"Finished yet, Alden?" Standish shouted to him from across the rocky beach.

John raised his head from within the depths of the boat to peer above the gunwale. "Nearly. Do you mean to take me from my labor?"

"If it is aught that can wait until the morrow. Aspinet has invited us to his home to sup."

John put down his chisel and the block of wood he was holding. "We'll finish on the morrow, then."

It was cold out on the beach, and the late afternoon sun pushed weak rays through the dense clouds. Standish looked eager to eat with the savages. As prepared as he was at any moment to encounter an Indian attack, Standish was the best linguist among them and had taken much time conversing with Hobbamock and the others on their voyages, once peace was established. They would spend at least a day or two here in the Nauset's company and in lading the corn once the shallop was complete.

John walked across the beach to join Standish, dusting off his breeches at the knees. He picked his cloak up off the rock where he'd dropped it, for while it kept him warm, it much impeded his movements when he was about his work.

"Do we dine on venison and winter squash?" John joked as they made their way toward the Indian village.

"All things in their season, Alden, though I think he has a few geese for us. They've been overhead in droves these past few days."

"Anything aside from mussels will give me good content. I grow tired even of endless corn and beans, though I am grateful when we have them. Do you ever miss the food in England?"

Standish snorted. "I have been a soldier these twenty years, Goodman Alden, and lived in Holland more than England during the war against Spain. I don't imagine I long for English fare. So long as my belly is well sated, any fare will do."

Aspinet gave them warm welcome, warmer than John expected after a year of distance between Plymouth and Massasoit. He supposed that Governor Bradford set things right with the Nauset when he came in November to make the original trade. Hobbamock's English was much improved in the months since John last saw him speak with other Indians, although he was not yet as good as Squanto. John sat between Standish and Howland as they ate their meal, which did include gooseflesh and plentiful corn, boiled with nuts in the Indian fashion into a dish they called *nasaump*. Beside him, Standish and Hobbamock conversed in their own blended language. When they spoke to each other, they mixed English and the Indian tongue, such that no one else could understand them.

"Hobbamock says there are many strangers here," Standish whispered to John, "and they all look at us curiously."

John glanced around the room and did notice many eyes upon them, not all of which looked friendly. "Is there trouble?" he asked Standish.

"It seems some of them have come for Aspinet's judgment, and they will ask his advice on an important question after dinner."

After dinner, one Indian came up to them and began a rapid and animated conversation with Standish. Whenever Standish could not understand him, the man engaged Hobbamock to help them.

"He came from Paomet," Standish explained to John, "from the place where we first took the corn from Corn Hill on our expeditions around Cape Cod, before we landed at Plymouth. He remembers me from our last voyage to the Nauset"—Standish scowled—"because of the astonishing color of my hair." John sniggered. Standish glared at him, which made John chuckle aloud.

Standish grunted. "It appears he is the one to whom we promised we would make recompense for what we took, and he went back and sent the men who came to Plymouth, and with whom Governor Bradford negotiated our repayment."

Throughout the rest of that evening, the Paomet man stuck to Captain Standish like a sweaty shirt. John found it disconcerting, although the man himself was affable and courteous.

"He says he has six or seven gallons of corn at Paomet that he would give us," Standish told John and Howland. "He invites us to come and pick it up there. Do you think that we might go?"

John shrugged. "Do we have the goods to trade to him?"

"He doesn't require recompense—he says it is a gift to his friends." Standish raised his eyebrows. "I doubt the governor would be opposed to such a gift, do you?"

After a time, two men sitting by the fire took out a pipe and a bag of tobacco. Silence descended around the room, and all eyes turned toward them. Aspinet sat close by. They were all quiet for a matter of minutes. John was nervous. They left their weapons outside the village, per the peace treaty made with Massasoit. His muscles tensed, as though they might be expected to fight at any moment. He knew not how to fight with fists alone.

One of the men by the fire broke the silence. He gave a long speech, to which Hobbamock listened with great interest, eyes trained on the speaker. When he had finished, the man gestured around the room, inviting other men's opinions, Aspinet's in particular. Between Hobbamock's English and Standish's understanding, they pieced the story together for John this way:

Two men of different tribes were gambling with each other and had a falling out over their game. One of the men proceeded to kill the other in their argument. The killer was a *powah*, a man of high esteem among the Indians that they believed could call upon the Devil to help cure the wounded. The tribe of the murdered man, which was very strong, threatened to bring war against this killer's people if they did not put him to death.

As John learned when they treated peace with Massasoit, it was the Indians' custom that all sachems do justice by their own men. If a man should wrong another, his sachem should beat or kill him according to the degree of the crime he inflicted.

The question posed to Aspinet and the other men was this: should their sachem put the man to death who committed this crime, even though he was in such an esteemed position that they could not well spare him?

"What is your answer?" John asked Hobbamock, curious to see how the Indians viewed these matters.

Hobbamock shrugged. "I am stranger to them." But John could tell he was weighing the question in his mind. "Best to kill guilty man. Protect innocent tribe from war. One man dies, he deserve this. Best to save many innocent."

John could not help remembering Bradford's choice, which seemed to him much the same: kill one man, who tried to inflict war upon Massasoit, to protect the colony from making more Indian enemies? Or spare him, and threaten the peace they worked a year to build? He still felt Bradford's choice was the wrong one, though Bradford no doubt felt justified in it. Perhaps the fact that John was sitting in a Nauset village, with a shallop awaiting many hogsheads of corn and beans, did mean that Bradford was right, even though they had not spoken to Massasoit in ten months.

"We think much the same," Standish told Hobbamock with a hearty clap on the shoulder. "It is against our laws to kill the innocent, and we think it meet that guilty men should die."

Wednesday, 19 March 1623

In the morning, John finished the repairs on the shallop, outside in the bitter cold. The wind whipped at his exposed face, and lowering clouds presaged more snow. John hoped that they would get back to Plymouth before being caught in a storm. The work on the boat was completed, and the Nauset started loading their trade goods into it. Indian women brought the corn and beans with care and consideration, stowing the baskets in the boat. The Paomet man, whose name John did not learn at dinner the night before and had no way of asking, also came bounding down the beach with a basket of corn, spilling kernels and even dropping an ear in his haste to bring the corn to them.

Standish asked Hobbamock, "Is that not a woman's work, to bring corn? I have never seen an Indian man do it."

Hobbamock voiced this concern to the Paomet man, who shouted back with glee. Hobbamock sneered his distaste. "It women work. He never do before. Shows love to English."

After shoving his basket in the bottom of the shallop, pushing aside the tidy work of the women who came before him, the Indian man approached them, wiping his hands of the labor he'd just done.

"He want you go to Paomet. To get corn. He give more corn, if English go to Paomet."

Standish agreed, the plan having been half-concocted the previous evening. "We'll spend one more night with Aspinet, but I don't believe the governor would mind us dropping in at Paomet on our way back to Plymouth."

It was late in the afternoon when they finished, and though the short winter days were lengthening, night was soon coming upon them. They were not long returned to Aspinet's house before two imposing men entered who were unknown to them. One was built like Hobbamock, sturdy and broad-shouldered. On a string about his neck he wore a knife that was sharpened to a needle point. The other man was tall and spare, with a squared jaw and his hair bound back in a leather strap.

Upon seeing Captain Standish, head unadorned by helmet, red hair sticking up in tufts in all directions, the slender man grinned with apparent malice. Perhaps it was the baring of his teeth that made it seem so, or the flaring of his nostrils as he smiled. He approached Captain Standish and crouched in front of him, drawing out a long dagger. John recognized the dagger as one of English make. It was a recognizable weapon, as the handle was engraved in detail with the face of a woman. Goodman Weston carried one like it, carved into the head of a wolf. John glanced between the two strangers, wondering how they came by it. The stranger crouching in front of Standish spoke a long speech in his own tongue and waved the dagger in Standish's face. John could see Standish snarl, for whether or not he understood the Indian language, it was plain the man was threatening him.

"What does he say?" John asked Hobbamock.

Hobbamock, whose pride was tied up with the Englishmen, was also angry. "He insult English men. Say when he kill English and French before, they cry like child. Say much of himself, more than truth. Boasting." Hobbamock sneered. "He is not pniese, to say him great warrior. Not so great." He waved his hand as though shooing away a fly.

The insults were suspended for a moment as the stranger was distracted by Hobbamock's wave. Standish took the opportunity to knock the knife from his grasp and push him bodily to the ground. John tensed, unsure what he should do, but before the man or his friend could retaliate, Aspinet entered. Assessing the situation, he called for peace between them in his home. The two strangers went with Aspinet out of the house, the one stooping to pick up his dagger off the floor, throwing an incensed look at the English over his shoulder.

"Who were those villains?" Standish asked, spitting a wad of phlegm on the dirt floor.

"Wituwamat and Pecksuot," Hobbamock answered. "Massachusett. Pecksuot is pniese." He thumped his fist against his chest. "Warrior. Like me. Wituwamat villain." He struggled with the final word but was determined to pronounce it. Then he spat on the floor like Standish.

"I like it not," Howland quibbled. "Is it yet too late to leave today?"

"Leave? Let him think us cowards that would leave after pretty speeches?" Standish was riled. "We will not leave on their account, Goodman Howland. But perhaps we should get you each a knife, and sleep in shifts tonight, that we shall not be surprised by the miscreants in our sleep."

John found it difficult to sleep at all that night, and instead he turned over and over on his mat. The village was in eerie quiet, little whispers passing between the Indians, when they were wont to sing and laugh until late.

Thursday, 20 March 1623

As they prepared to leave the next day, the man from Paomet came up to them and again encouraged them to go with him and get more corn. John scrutinized the great store they carried already in the shallop, and felt the ache of tiredness. He did not sleep well the night before and little wished to travel farther instead of heading home.

"Oughtn't we just to go back to Plymouth?" He was eager to return, anxious to see his wife, despite how irritable and weary she was of late. The respite from her company jangled his nerves more; at least when he was with her, he could see her grouchy face and hear about her aches and other afflictions, and in so doing reassure himself that she was still living.

Standish looked toward the sky. "The wind will make our travel swift across the bay," he judged. "It should not take overlong to stop at Paomet."

The Paomet man was excited, pleased that they would go with him.

"At least one of the savages is happy for our company," John muttered to Howland.

"Aye, we were not well received by those men from Massachusett," Howland agreed.

"Nor by Aspinet afterward, when he found the captain standing over that insulting Wituwamat. He gave them much favor through all the night. I would almost rather we left as soon as you suggested it."

"I suppose Captain Standish is right, and we could not have shown them cowardice." Howland took the insult to heart, for though he was not a coward, he loved peace and hated to be part of any conflict.

They set out for Paomet, as promised, but Standish's judgment of winds did not account for the rough gusts blowing against them as they tried to sail northward. After a long time fighting with sail and oars, they were blown so far off course that Standish resolved to go to the Massachusett.

"I would urge against that plan, Captain," John cautioned. "If Wituwamat and Pecksuot represent the current feelings amongst the Massachusett, it's best we don't walk into their village empty-handed."

Standish acceded to John's request and, being unable to sail for Plymouth against a wind that dragged them south, and unwilling to go without the shallop, which was itself and for the corn it carried the very reason for their coming, they made camp on an empty stretch of shore, dragged the boat so far inland as they judged safe, and went behind the protection of the dunes to guard themselves a little from the wind.

The night was bitter cold, but after a day spent working hard against the wind, and without sleep the night before, John was overcome by dreams in moments. In his dreaming, endless savage eyeballs stared at him out of a crowd of empty faces. There were no friends among the eyes, which leered at him, coming ever closer. Soon he was surrounded, and he searched about him, trying to find the face of his opponent. His search was stopped when he felt a piercing pain in his belly. He looked down to find Wituwamat's dagger sticking out of him. The carved woman's face was drenched in blood. He closed his hand around her immobile features as he reached to pull the dagger out, but found he was not pulling it from himself, but from Priscilla. It was her enlarged, protruding belly in which the knife was standing, and as John drew it out, he cut her open and the babe inside spilled out of her in a flood of blood.

He woke, wet with sweat and shivering. His breaths came hard and fast. He heard the murmur of a voice speaking in the Indian tongue and took up the knife that Standish gave him. He crawled to his knees, wielding the weapon with an inexpert grip. He peered over at the fire, which burned low. The voice belonged to the Paomet man, who was talking with Standish. John dropped his arm, but he held the knife by his side as he came up close to the captain. When the Paomet man saw him draw close, he frowned, glancing at the knife in his hand.

"I'll relieve the watch, Standish."

"I was not intending to keep watch, out here, away from Wituwamat and Pecksuot, but found I could not sleep in this damned cold. Go back to sleep, Alden, if you're tired." Standish met his eyes and gauged his haggard expression. "But of course, feel free to keep us company if you cannot."

John sank down beside Standish, whereupon the Paomet man clicked his tongue in dissatisfaction and moved off among the dunes.

John glanced after him, elbow brushing Standish's arm as he leaned forward. "Did I interrupt your conversation?"

Standish chuckled. "It was not an incredibly productive one, despite my attempts to learn their talk. I am sure your company will be far more entertaining. He is unhappy we could not get to Paomet today, and I don't think we will try again tomorrow. We are closer to Plymouth now than Paomet, anyway."

"Does he mean to come with us?"

"What else? Leave him in the dunes, to walk back to Paomet or to Aspinet?" Standish shrugged. "If that is what he wishes, I will leave him, but I think he would like better to come with us to Plymouth."

They sat watching the fire dance on the bodies of Hobbamock and Howland, fast asleep. John could feel the warmth of Standish's body beside him, and the captain's closeness reassured him.

"How did you come to join *Mayflower*'s expedition?" John asked, curious after Standish's mention that he had long lived in Holland.

"Have I not told you, in the years we've known each other?"

"I have not asked," John admitted.

"It is a long tale," Standish said, though rousing himself up to tell it. John smiled. He had long known that his friend the captain liked conversations where he spoke the better part.

"Go on. I will not get back to sleep tonight." His knee knocked into Standish's as he settled into the sand for a lengthy chat.

"Well, let's see. I was recruited to go to Holland around 1603 by Sir Vere, who came to my family home seeking men to join England's fighting in the Eighty Years' War. I was born, you know, in..." And Standish told John of his story: his youth, his battle days, his settling down in Leiden and finding himself next door to English Separatists. He talked until the sky resembled a giant bass, dark at the spine with stripes in ever lighter shades, until just above the dunes lay a band of simple white.

Friday, 21 March 1623

They returned, at last, to Plymouth. As they came through the embracing pincers of Plymouth Bay, John saw their little town impaled round, saw the fortress standing high on the hill, saw smoke curling from the chimneys, and thought: *She's safe. She must be safe.* How could anything be amiss, when the town looked just as it ever did, the receding snow of spring still dotting the ground about in clumps? The wind blew them home and, though Gurnet's Nose did something to shield their little harbor, it still tousled John's hair and made him wary to don his capotain hat.

They unloaded the shallop. John strained himself to finish the chore, so he could go to see Priscilla. He wiped sweat from his brow, for though the day was cold, the work was hard. The barking of Goodman Browne's mastiff and Master Goodman's spaniel greeted them as they opened the eastern gate of the plantation, the two dogs running up to them and sniffing the Paomet man's feet with suspicion. The sentry, too, noted their coming and rang the bell to alert the town. Tilley came rushing down the street to meet Howland, but John saw Priscilla leaning against the door of their house, cradling her heavy stomach. He was flooded with relief. She was well indeed, somehow even larger than a week ago when he left her, and, it seemed, unwilling to descend the hill to say hello.

He loaded basket after basket in the storehouse. At last, Standish gave him the last of the items from their expedition.

John had shut and was laying a bar across the storeroom door when the sentry gave another clang of the alarm and opened the west gate to let a weary-looking Master Winslow enter. John hesitated, eager to spring toward his wife and greet her but compelled by Standish's gestures to accompany him to Winslow. He waved a finger at Standish as he ran away from him, promising to return.

"What cheer, wife?" he asked, trying to wrap his arms around her but unsure how to manage. She rolled her eyes and put one arm around his shoulder, embracing him, while her other hand massaged circles in her belly.

"The trade went well?" she asked, as he knelt in front of her stomach to lay his ear against her half-unbuttoned waistcoat. None of the suits from Birching Lane quite fit her in this shape, and she was not keen to alter one, being a week or two away, now, from changing shape again. He had listened to the babe's heartbeat on several occasions, and he listened for it now between the clamor of the sentry's bell and the rush of people gathering toward Winslow.

"Aye, well, not trade, but retrieval. Well enough. Where has Winslow been?"

"Massasoit took ill while you were gone, and a man came to tell us he was near to death. Winslow went to try to make peace with him before he died, and to meet some Dutch men who the messenger said were there with Massasoit."

He stared at her, bewildered, as second after second ticked by. His mind took each new piece of information, one by one, and jotted down a list of questions for which he was interested to learn answers.

"I don't know any more than that, dear husband, so go off and ask the man himself. I am certain, if he's returned, he will have much to tell both you and Captain Standish." She waved him off and breathed a shallow breath through pursed lips, turning back to go inside the house again. John hesitated for just a moment before running up the street to listen to Winslow's account.

Winslow looked bedraggled and road-weary. He spoke to Captain Standish as he stripped off his cloak and hat and ran his dirty fingers through his sweat-soaked hair.

"And so, I am relieved to find you back, you see." He blinked, opening his eyes wide and looking at the Paomet man, who still clung to Standish's elbow. Winslow blinked a couple of times at this man, and then at Standish. The Paomet man, for his part, glanced between them with unease written in his stance. Standish closed his eyes and rubbed his temples with his thumb and forefinger.

"We ought to speak to the governor," Winslow asserted, running the brim of his hat through his fingers in rapid circles.

"Aye. I'll just ask this man, now that we've no plans to go to Paomet, that he should just go back, and leave us for a time to talk things over."

After Standish declared in the Indian tongue that the Paomet man should leave—which the man took with an uncertain smile and a glance at Winslow—Winslow tottered down the hill toward Bradford's house. But Bradford was not home. Winslow sank onto a carpenter's bench outside of Bradford's door. John joined him.

"If he's out in the fields, he'll return soon," John said. "He'll no doubt want to see Standish. We just returned from the Nauset an hour ago ourselves."

The lines around Winslow's eyes relaxed with weary tenderness. "I'm relieved to see you back, too, Goodman Alden. When the Indians told us you and Standish went to the Massachusett, I was afraid for you."

Standish, freed at last from his tail, strode up to them. "Winslow, what do you mean by saying there's a conspiracy? Where have you been?"

John felt a sturdy hand descend on his shoulder. He looked up to find Bradford standing over him. "I should like to know the answer to that too, Master Winslow, if you would."

Bradford led them all inside his home, lighting the candle on the mantle in front of a large tin plate, to better reflect the glow. The light which came in through the oiled-paper window was gloomy. Standish shut the door behind them.

"Massasoit has told me there is a conspiracy of the Indians against us," Winslow began, and Standish interrupted, "Massasoit?"

"We got word that Massasoit was on his deathbed a few days after you left," Bradford explained. "Winslow went to visit him, after the Indian custom." He turned to Winslow and asked, "Is he dead?"

Winslow shook his head.

"Nay, nay, that is why he told us of it. He is much recovered, on the way to full health once more. Attributes it to the confection and the broth I gave him. I scraped off his tongue, which was quite thickly furred, and—"

"What of the conspiracy?" Standish demanded. John was just as impatient; medical cures could wait and imminent Indian attack could not.

"Ah, right. Yes, he told me that the Massachusett have gotten very vexed with the men at Wessagusset and mean to attack them in haste, but found they thought they could not proceed, lest we seek to avenge them." He smiled a little. "Avenge them—how theatrical, but then we could not very well let it stand, if they attacked, which was understood by the Massachusett. So they have been going around to other

321

tribes, asking them to aid them in their plot, that they might strike at Wessagusset while another group attacks Plymouth simultaneously. To evict the English from this land."

John thought for a moment that it was optimistic of the savages to believe that killing them and the men at Wessagusset would stop the tide of English, Spanish, French, and Dutchmen who were coming, year by year, to fish and trade and settle up and down the New World's coast. That would never be allowed. Such a wealth of resources and land would not be relinquished, not when the English had already settled their councils and their patents. King James would no sooner release this land into the hands of the Indians than he would let the French or Spanish overtake him. It was just a momentary thought, though, and John focused his attention on the impending massacre.

"Did he say what other tribes were involved in this?" John asked, with some dread. He suspected this was why Wituwamat and Pecksuot were visiting Aspinet.

"Well, they did ask Massasoit, of course, he being the closest to us, but he, despite not having spoken to us in so long, remained steadfast and refused them. This was a couple of days before I arrived, and he was quite ill already—many suspected him near death. But he says other tribes were enlisted, too: the Manomet, Succonet, Mattachiest, Isle of Capawack, Agoweywam, Nauset—"

"Nauset?" Standish asked. John felt faint with the recitation of so many names.

Winslow directed his clear pewter-gray eyes on Standish. "Aye, Captain, the Nauset, and the Paomet, too."

Winslow's gaze was eerie, for John had never seen him look so focused. Standish shuddered. Then, Winslow blinked a couple of times, and his dreamy quality returned.

"Massasoit says that Massachusett warriors, Wituwamat and Pecksuot, are two of the chief conspirators. They are, at least, the ones who came to him and asked him to join them, though he of course refused."

John's eyes shot to Standish, who snarled at the memory of Wituwamat.

"He suggests," Winslow continued, "that we cut them off, as you would the head of a snake. If we can kill the chief conspirators, the rest"—he wiggled his fingers in the air, farther and farther apart—"will fragment."

It was more disconcerting to John to be instructed to kill by the dreamy Winslow than by the clear-eyed one that came out for just a moment.

"We ought to do as he suggests," Standish leapt on the offensive.

"How do we know that what Massasoit says is true?" asked Bradford.

"We were nearly attacked while with the Nauset," Standish argued, "by the very villains Winslow names. It rings true to me, though I would to God it were not so."

"Does it not sound too familiar, too alike to the very plot that Squanto was accused of crafting?" Bradford asked. "To separate us, and then attack both groups at once, while keeping us unawares?"

"What does it signify if the plan is similar?" John asked. "The plan catches us with our breeches about our ankles, unprepared, and not yet eager for revenge. It is a better plan than attacking Wessagusset first, then waiting till we hear word of it."

"I do not like it." Bradford shook his head.

"Have you not said all this time that Massasoit is our ally? If you still wish to defend your act in saving Squanto, you cannot say that Massasoit is our enemy. What other reason has he to tell this convoluted lie?" John was exasperated.

"The yearly court date lies around the corner," Bradford said. "I would not go to war without the approval of the body of the company. That is the manner of governance we agreed on when we signed the compact. Our attack, if we must lead one, will wait two days more, will it not?"

Standish looked up toward the beams across the ceiling. "If we wait, and they attack the men at Wessagusset, it will be too late for us to recover their lives."

Bradford flinched, reminded that his choice to wait might leave Weston's men to die. *All the better*, thought John, *if they should be punished for dragging us into this untenable situation.*

"What's more, there will be many more of the conspirators armed against us, when they come here to fight." Standish rolled his head sideways to look at Bradford. "If you wish to delay, Governor, I'll arm the four entrances to the plantation all with sentries, and keep our four companies on shifts so we can be alerted in case of imminent threat."

"It will wait two days," Bradford whined, more agitated than confident in his decision.

Sunday, 23 March 1623

In the two days that followed, Plymouth received a visit from Wassapinewat, who was brother to Obtakiest, the sachem of the Massachusett. Wassapinewat confirmed Massasoit's story, adding that his brother Obtakiest had nothing to do with the conspiracy; it was some of his powahs and pnieses who took it upon themselves to seek revenge for all the wrongs done to them by Weston's men at Wessagusset.

This confirmation was difficult to take. Bradford looked overwrought with worry and anxiety.

John was not free of such anxiety himself. He spent those two days off and on imagining the outcomes of an Indian attack. He spent his hours at the fortress, checking over every inch for its stability. It was done, now: windows in place with bars to hold the wooden shutters closed; upper floor half-walled, with closing ports to put the cannons' noses through; a sturdy roof of timber beams enclosed in wooden planks. The door was dressed in rows of iron nails and could be both locked and barred from the inside. Nevertheless, John could see in his mind's eye the women and the children herded into the fortress for protection at the first sign of trouble. The enemy were skilled with bow and arrow. Plymouth's petty rank of scrawny men, though wielding the might of muskets, would be cut down by the tall, strong, proud young Indians as they descended in their multitudes. The savages' faces would be painted with black and red, their long black hair adorned with feathers and tails. Each wore the pelt of a leopard or some other horrific beast about his neck. John could well imagine some men of the congregation falling to their knees to pray to their absent God. The fortress door coming down, and a swarm of Indians pouring in, Wituwamat with his woman's-head knife at the fore. Priscilla's belly cut open and the baby torn from her as she crumpled, weeping. It was as he suspected all along. Plymouth would be a terrible place to die, without God watching over them. And without God's protection, there was no choice but to protect themselves.

"It is not right for us to strike at them first, without knowing that they will attack us," Bradford began, opening the floor of the yearly court date to debate.

"Surely, the double testimony of Massasoit's evidence and Wassapinewat's corroboration is enough to make you believe the threat to us is real?" Standish demanded.

"Although the Narragansett have oft threatened and insulted us, yet they have never come through and attacked us," Winslow commented.

This was true. Despite their invitation to war, arrows wrapped in snakeskin, sent more than a year ago to Plymouth, which was the cause of their building their impalement, and the many threats and jeers with which they taunted them over the summer, being the cause of their building their fortification, there had never been an attack or a single arrow aimed at them by the Narragansett.

"Perhaps it was a gift from God, to send them to pester us that we might be prepared for this new evil," Winslow offered.

John narrowed his eyes. Suggestions that were based on help from God were of less use than suggestions that they should unleash the plague the Indians believed they kept buried in the barrels in their storehouse. They could not rely on God here.

"Whether or not the Narragansett will attack us is a separate matter," Hopkins argued. "The Nauset have already attacked us once, and I own a coat full of holes that shows their aim with bows is true enough. They hate the English for the capture into slavery of their men, and even if we have proven we would not do the same, they may think it better to rid their shores of us before more men come like those who came before. If they are in this confederation with the Massachusett, it is best that we end this before they have the chance to attack us again."

"But we have made peace with the Massachusett, and with the Nauset," Elder Brewster of the Separatist church protested. "Why should they come after us when they have sworn to be subjects of King James?"

"Their quarrel is not with us, but with the men at Wessagusset, Brewster," Standish explained. "It is their good strategy that leads them to attack us, too, in fear of retribution."

"And Weston's men have well-earned this retaliation from the savages," John said. "Word has come to us from both the Indians and the Englishmen for months, and though they are on either side of the disagreement, both say that Weston's men have stolen corn and done other heinous things against them, whilst the English have threatened to treat the Indians with violence." He snorted. "Believe me, I would not like for us to kill our allies for the sake of such men as these, if I were not convinced that if we do not do so they will attack us here."

"So, what if we just call the men of Wessagusset here?" Bradford asked. "We have completed our fortress, and our impalement is sound; if we bring them back to Plymouth, we can defend them here against the danger of the savages."

"You expect we can protect them against the warriors of eight allied tribes of Indians?" Standish asked. "We are half starving, and from the word Governor Sanders sent, the men at Wessagusset are even weaker than we are here. We have not had resupply from the Virginia Company since they sent *Fortune*, so how long do you think it will be before we run out of match cords? We have not an infinite supply of cannonballs or musket shot and powder. And how long do you think the savages will wait patiently outside our gates, whilst we cower in here in fear? They have tools they can use to tear at our fortifications, and if enough of them come, our walls will not hold." Standish shook his head. "If we wait too long, there will be too many Indians for us to fight back. They are bound to overwhelm first Weston's men at Wessagusset and then us."

"Why would you protect the lives of these men who are determined to come and slaughter us?" Hopkins asked Bradford, his temper heated. "They will exterminate us, all of us, the way they did at Jamestown, without blinking. They will not regret their choice to come and butcher us, our women, and our children. Why do you argue that they are not our enemy *yet*?"

"Because it is not right to kill the innocent, and just a week ago Aspinet housed our men in his village and gave us corn. Would he have done that if he were plotting to kill us?"

"It is just the same as when Weston betrayed us, and you could not see his perfidy then, either," John addressed Bradford. "He smiled and told us pretty words, then backed out of our venture and sent another company of men to rival us. And now those men will be, as we were warned, the cause of our undoing unless we act swiftly and decisively. The Nauset have smiled at us and followed through on the promises they made to you three months ago. They did so to conceal their new plan of deceit and betrayal."

"Why do you think that man from Paomet was so eager to bring us to his plantation?" Standish asked. "No doubt they conceived the same plan as Squanto: to lure me away from the plantation and kill me where I was outnumbered, thus depriving Plymouth of its military captain. They would have killed me, Alden, and Howland, if we went with them, and then attacked the rest of you while you were undefended. I am grateful that God directed the wind to spare us from our visit to the Paomet, so that we could act on Massasoit's information."

"What's more, it is your fault that the Nauset and the Paomet turned against us." Hopkins added weight to the argument that lay heavier and heavier on Bradford's shoulders. "If you did not keep Squanto from Massasoit's punishment, then we would still have good relations with the Pokanoket, and Massasoit's influence in our favor would be stronger with the Nauset and the Paomet than the Massachusett's filthy words spread in their ears. As things stand, Massasoit would not even have warned us of this attack, had Winslow not gone to Pokanoket and saved his life. We would be slaughtered, without this warning, and you turn your back on this gift from God which you did nothing to deserve?"

"The Paomet would have been our allies from the start if we did not steal their corn at Cape Cod when we arrived," Bradford said, dredging up old arguments.

"And the Massachusett would be our allies still if Weston's men did not steal corn from them," said John, "but they have made many offenses against the Massachusett, and the Indians, rightly or not, seek death for their vengeance."

"We must stop the Nauset and the Paomet from attacking us here in Plymouth by going to Wessagusset and stopping the Massachusett leaders who have riled the other tribes against us," declared Captain Standish. "Even if we do go soon, we have no way of knowing when they mean to carry out this devious action. We cannot leave the settlement undefended, in case the Nauset come while we are away."

"Wait!" cried Bradford. "We are too frightened. We know that sometimes the Indians exaggerate, that they tell tales of their strengths and prowess in combat that are not true. When Squanto was captured and held prisoner by Corbitant last year, Hobbamock reported to us that he feared Squanto was already dead and that Massasoit was taken captive. We ended up injuring three of Corbitant's men when Squanto was not even harmed, and Massasoit's movements were of his own free will! What if this situation is just the same, but on a larger scale? What if they claim that they will kill all the English, to make themselves seem strong in the eyes of Massasoit and the other sachems? Although they are not in this fight, the Narragansett make a fine example. Though they have often threatened and insulted us, we have never come to violence! And when we first became friends with the Pokanoket, did Squanto not tell us that the Massachusett made many threats against us? But on our first visit to them, they greeted us in terror, and we made peace. If we react with haste here, we will end up killing innocents, whose crime was that they spoke too largely of their own ambitions. What defense have you to that?"

Everyone in the room was quiet. The sound of heavy breathing echoed.

"If we do not strike first, and this conspiracy is true, we will not know until all of Weston's men are dead and we have an army of Indians at our door," John said. He did not shout. He did not yell. He did not want to strain his voice anymore in trying to get Bradford to heed him. John was unwilling to wait for that moment to arrive, unwilling to wait for the savages to break down their walls and kill his wife and child. If Bradford did not agree, there were other men who would not wait the good word of the governor.

"I want not the lives of these conspirators upon my head, if they do not attack us first," confessed Howland.

"I will not weigh the cost of this decision upon the shoulders of the public conscience, when some men here have argued against it. Captain Standish and I will take all your arguments and decide between ourselves what is the best course of action." Bradford looked ragged, as though the verbal sparring dealt him physical blows. "As David said unto

God, 'Let us fall now into the hand of the Lord, for his mercies are great, and let me not fall into the hand of man.'"

Priscilla woke from a midday snooze to find John lying down beside her, stroking her hair, which lay unbound about her head. He saw her eyes blink open and smiled, taking her hand in his and kissing all the fingers, one by one. She smiled at him, still drowsy.

"Has your strength of fifty men yet saved us from damnation, my dear husband?"

"Not yet, my best beloved. Nor..." He hesitated, looking at her exposed belly. She could well imagine what he was thinking. "Nor do I know if I should go, if go we shall, to fight the Indians."

She frowned, still muzzy from sleep. "Why would you not go?"

He gestured toward her midriff, which was discolored, streaked with angry reddish-purple blemishes. Blue and greenish veins chased each around the inscrutable thing that her body had become.

"What use am I to you," John said, "if I go and leave you here alone when this babe comes?"

She raised an eyebrow. "What use are you to me if you stay and are thrust from the house by Mistress Hopkins and Mistress White while they attend the childbearing?"

He hesitated again. He was always trying to keep her safe, even from knowing what the threats against the colony were. It frustrated her, though in the end she heard all news from Tilley or from Mistress Hopkins.

This time, it seemed, he would tell all. "What if, while I am gone, the Nauset come and attack Plymouth? Who will defend you, if you are in childbearing when the Indians come?" He looked into her eyes, gripping her hand in his. "They mean to come, the Indians—they mean to come in force, and whilst the Massachusett kill all those at Wessagusset, the Nauset or the Paomet or any number of others of them may come here."

She shook her hand free of his and placed both her hands on either side of his head, stroking his bearded cheeks. She watched him close his eyes and felt him nuzzle against the palms of her hands.

"In that case," she told him, "I am sure that Captain Standish will take what men he needs to Wessagusset and will leave Plymouth well defended by the rest. Do you forget you are not the only man at Standish's disposal? There are many others in our settlement who wish to protect their families and their homes as much as you do."

"Then should I not stay—"

"You should go and be by Standish's side, if that is where he wants you. I am sure he will want you with him, John; he has come to rely on you very much. What's more"—she pushed herself into a sitting position—"though I may not look it to you now, I am well capable of delivering this child without you hovering overhead. Even if you were here, it would help nothing, as you would be distracted from the fighting by worrying over me, when I am strong enough to do this, at least, without you. Remember, husband, that you will be banished, now that we are in a settlement at last, even if this baby waits to come until your return from Wessagusset. Aren't you glad to be in civilization, where you can run far away from the woman delivering her child, without having to hide between hogsheads in the belly of *Mayflower*?" She poked his thigh, reminding him.

"If there is naught I can do," he said, steeling himself, "nothing I can do to help you in your childbearing, then I will do what I can to defend you from all else."

"And I shall ask God to watch over you and I both, so that we will meet again in safety, with our child."

John pressed his lips together. He still resisted doing things the Separatist way, and she felt he had been too distant from God for too long. He admitted feeling close to God when he was in church in England, but here his perceived distance always made him irritable and melancholy.

"Here," she said, wiggling her way to the edge of the bed. "Come with me."

He helped her up, and she put on a petticoat and drew her cloak around her shoulders. That would hide her state of undress for the time being. She led him out of the house and waddled up the hill toward the meeting house.

"You have put all your labor into building this fortress in the hope that it might afford me some protection." She waved at the cannons, at the palisade, at the reinforced door, and the sentry standing on the top floor with his musket. "You trust in your own hands—you trust what you have built will be strong and do what it was meant to do and keep me safe." She paused, huffing, then dragged him through the door into the open first-floor room. Some benches were inside, but no one from the yearly court day was still here. She sat on one of the benches and tugged his sleeve until he sat next to her.

"Now," she said, "you must see this building has another purpose. It was built as a fortress, but also as a meeting house. It is a place for men to meet with God." She closed her eyes, spread her arms, and opened the center of her body toward the heavens. The connection was indirect—the ceiling stood in the way. "You think that God cannot be reached here, John, but many men and women in our plantation have reached him. In all the time I've known you, it is *you* who has been unwilling to speak to *him*."

She took in a deep breath and felt the babe kick in her belly. She reached for his hand and laid it on the spot where the baby kicked. She was filled with joy as she looked into his eyes, but she was disappointed to meet terror in his gaze.

"Pray with me, John," she asked, as she asked him once before on a moonless night when she bore no hope of new life. Then, he had not prayed, but he sat beside her to keep her company in her deep desperation. Now, she could tell he still would not pray, but worry again and again about the things which were beyond his power to control.

She sighed and leaned her head against his shoulder, nuzzling into the soft wool of his doublet.

"I have faith in God, John, but also in you. As I told you before, I know that you will fight to protect me and our babe. And you must have faith, if not in God, at least in me, that I will, as I promised, fight the hand of death if he should come for me. And take heed, for once, when I tell you that all will be well."

Monday, 24 March 1623

Before Governor Bradford and Captain Standish came to a decision about what to do, or at least before they shared that decision with John Alden, a skeletal man held together by shredded clothes collapsed at Plymouth's door. It was Phineas Pratt, who carried nothing with him but a knapsack of the kind they used to gather groundnuts. Pratt was much diminished since John saw him last. Perhaps some of the men in Weston's company may have fared worse than Sanders told them, in the disorder caused by the men among them who would steal other men's corn. Pratt did not look like he had eaten anything solid in weeks.

At first, he kept muttering, "Wolves, wolves," and made to look behind him, as though he thought that wolves were following him. When they gave him some water and some corn, he regained some part of his senses.

"They mean to kill us all," he said at last, "when the snow is gone. When it is all melted, so they will not leave tracks in the snow, the Indians will come and kill all the English together in one day."

It was a third independent confirmation of the story they heard first from Massasoit and second from Wassapinewat. It was enough to make their decision. Standish resolved that the next day he should set out with eight men and go to Wessagusset.

In the meantime, Pratt was able to better tell them of the goings-on at Wessagusset, and of how the Indians were treated by the English, and how the English were treated by the Indians.

"At first, they were friendly and showed their love to us," Pratt said, after he regained much strength. "But then famine came upon us, and they saw our weakness. They began to insult us and tell us stories of how they'd killed French sailors and pillaged French ships. Pecksuot, who speaks some English, he said that they took away the Frenchmen's clothes and turned them into their servants, and that many cried, and none lived long. When they saw us in our weakness, they moved their houses closer to our palisade, for we quickly saw the need to impale our town around, as you did here."

John held his tongue. Why had Weston's men spent so much energy in impaling their town when they were near to dying of starvation? Would not their hands be better put to searching for groundnuts and shellfish?

"At length, the sachem came and accused us of stealing corn—which some of our men did, but we stocked and whipped them for it, and in front of the Indians no less. We had the worst offender bound by the wrists, and we showed him to them, but the sachem said it was not just dealing, that we should beat or kill him according to his offense." Pratt's lips were cracked and started to bleed as he continued his narrative. "It came to the point when we had no food left. We kept watch at night, and in one night I came upon three of our men, all dead from want of food. We let loose the man in bounds, for there was nothing left to steal, and within two days the Indians brought him back, saying they would show us the place he stole from them. We bound him again, not knowing what else to do. We grew weaker and weaker, and the Indians came more flagrantly among us, killing our hogs, striking any man who disagreed with them with knives, throwing dust in our faces." He squeezed his eyes tight shut and took a little gulp of water. "It may not seem like much, but every day they would do things to diminish us. To make us feel subservient. I was lying under my own blanket, all I had against the winter cold, and Pecksuot came and took it from me. My brother went out to collect groundnuts and stewed them in a pot, and they came up and took the food and ate it right in front of him. Neither he nor I has stolen corn from them, nor any other, and so we are too weak to fight against them. Some of the men sold the clothes off their backs for a bit of corn, and now they cannot brave the cold to go out and forage for anything more. Many do small tasks for the Indians, fetching them wood and water in exchange for a mere capful of corn. One has even gone to live among them, claiming to like it better than remaining in our settlement. None could blame him, for since Governor Sanders left for Monhegan, we even hanged the man who most often stole their corn, to give the savages some justice for their trouble. But our justice came too late for them, and they heeded it not, and still make servants out of us as they did the French."

John found himself hoping for a moment that the man they hanged was Andrew Weston, but he tried to put that uncharitable thought aside. They hoped to kill one guilty man to spare the rest, but their sacrifice, as Bradford's loss of Squanto, came too late.

"I learned seven or eight days ago that they planned to come upon us both at once. I asked that some man should go to Plymouth, should come here to warn you, but no man would go. So I told them I would go upon the morrow, at which one unfaithful man reported to the Indians. Pecksuot kept me under careful watch for the whole week. He said that, if I wished to go, he would send his boy Nahamit with me, but I knew if I did that, Nahamit would kill me in the woods. I pretended to go out to gather groundnuts and ran away to come to you. I could not get my musket nor a compass, so I just ran here and found my way along the woods. I wonder if they sent him after me, or if they left me to die, as Pecksuot said I would—die in the woods at the claws of bears or wolves. I am glad you already heard of their plot, for I am sure you would not believe me if I told you what I suspected: that they mean to kill us all, and soon."

John suspected it was the most Phineas Pratt had ever been allowed to speak in his life, and the man soon fainted again with the exhaustion of it. He remembered Pratt's timidity in their own conversations with him, his hesitance to speak unless asked a direct question. He was not such a man who would steal other men's corn, and it was more probable other men stole his corn from him.

It was the other men, like Weston, whose confidence in their own superiority frustrated John. Were it not for their incompetence and weakness, he would not now be forced to such lengths as the killing of the Indians who were once their allies. These English men, who boasted with such pride that they would not end up in perpetual want of corn, like Plymouth. They who scorned the women and children, and claimed a plantation of men alone would do far better. It was for the sake of these men that John must now go out and kill, or else wait and watch the Massachusett seek vengeance on his wife and child.

Chapter Twenty-One

The Massacheuseuks had formerly concluded to ruinate Master Weston's colony; and thought themselves, being about thirty or forty men, strong enough to execute the same. Yet they durst not attempt it, till such time as they had gathered more strength to themselves, to make their party good against us at Plymouth; concluding, that if we remained, though they had no other arguments to use against us, yet we would never leave the death of our countrymen unrevenged; and therefore their safety could not be without the overthrow of both plantations.

—Edward Winslow, *Good Newes
From New England*, 1624

Tuesday, 25 March 1623

John sniffed in the cold, damp drizzle that spattered them as they rowed through Massachusetts Bay. There were ten men in the shallop: Captain Standish, Hobbamock, and eight volunteers from Plymouth, of whom John was one. It was no surprise to John that Governor Bradford stayed at home, along with Winslow, Brewster, and his friend Howland. Instead he sat with Hopkins, whose grim expression boded ill for the fates of the Massachusett. John was surprised that Master Eaton elected to join the expedition.

"I like it not," the house carpenter admitted to John before they left, "but if we let them strike first, we'll have no defense. We are by far outnumbered here."

The bay wherein Wessagusset was situated was thick with small forested islands. Though they were in the shallop, the ground below the water was treacherous, and they took their time to navigate between the shoals and giant submerged rocks. At last, they came upon *Swan* sitting pretty at her anchor. They glided up beside the ship and called a "Halloo!" but there came no answer. The ship was floating dead, emptier than John had ever seen a vessel. He exchanged a wary look with Standish. Had the attack already come, and none of the men escaped? If that was so, had they struck at Plymouth as soon as the shallop with the captain departed? John hoped it was not so, but he could not stop the trickle of images from his nightmares appearing in his mind.

They brought the shallop to land near *Swan*, and John hopped into the frigid water to stick the shallop in ashore. They looked about them, uneasy at finding no signs at all of life. None of them had yet visited Weston's colony, and the land here was unfamiliar.

"How can we alert their attention, if they are ashore," asked Eaton, "without also alerting the Massachusett?"

"It doesn't matter if we alert the Massachusett, does it?" Hopkins asked. "We are here under the pretense of trade, to any Indians we see. They don't know their plot has been discovered, so they should not suspect us of any foul motives."

"Unless their plan has already taken effect," John muttered.

"If that's the case, Goodman Alden, it's already too late for us." Hopkins had no illusions about their safety, coming into the enemy's territory.

"Then we'll fire a musket shot and hope that it is Weston's men we find, and not the Massachusett armed against us." Captain Standish, whose snaphance musket did not require the lighting of a match cord, fired off a shot and reloaded.

They had brought their muskets. They carried their muskets with them even to church on Sundays. But under the guise of friendly trade, under the pretense that they did not know the Indians' secret, their match cords were not lit. In any case, John wasn't sure how long a match cord would stay lit in this gloomy weather, as drops of water landed on his hat and dripped off the brim onto his shoulders. Standish advised them not to draw any weapon against the Massachusett until the time to execute their plan came. The plan was undecided until they saw the state of things at Wessagusset. They knew not how many Indians were about, nor how many might be involved in the conspiracy.

They walked a little farther down the beach, and Standish fired off his musket again. Ahead of them, a pale face poked out from behind a tree. The man recognized them, for he stumbled out from his poor hiding place and lurched down the beach toward them. John recognized a filthy Joshua Pratt, bare-legged and coated in dried mud up to his knees. His shirt hung down outside his breeches, mud-spattered and grimy from carrying groundnuts and mussels.

"Praise God, you're here," he said at once. "Did Phineas manage to deliver his message to you at Plymouth?"

"Aye, we got his warning. If you know of the danger lurking, why do you leave your ship unguarded?" Standish demanded.

Pratt looked at him as though he were an idiot. "There is no food on *Swan*; the men have taken it."

"Why not use it as your defense, against the coming attack?"

Pratt's laugh was hollow, desperate, more like a miserable cough than a sound of mirth.

"The Indians live every day beside us, and we keep no arms against them. We have no defense against them, and many of our men choose their company, for they can at least provide them corn if men demean themselves enough to earn it. Here, come with me, I'll bring you to the plantation."

Pratt lurched forward, favoring one foot, though both his feet were bare. John scrunched up his toes inside his own boots, glad for such a small thing as having stockings to cover them. They followed Pratt up the beach, passing other men in bad condition, all missing one item of clothing or another. The men were crouched in the mud, digging for clams and mussels, seeming not to mind the pitter patter of the rain on their bare heads and arms. One body sitting in the mud did not move his hands for food nor turn his head to watch them pass. His eyes were glazed and moved no more. He had died where he sat, stuck in the mud, unable even to gather the strength to pull himself free.

Priscilla sat by Phineas Pratt's bedside, back at the familiar task of nursing the sick. She wanted to do something useful, when everyone else was acting to help the colony at this difficult time, but she could not bend over a garden plot or a washing tub, and the occasional spasms of pain in her abdomen made even mending difficult. So, she sat with Pratt, and gave him water, and talked with him of easier times, when he was alert enough for conversation.

"I should like to stand, and walk a little," Pratt told Priscilla. "I don't mean to trouble you, but could you stay nearby? I am afraid I might collapse again."

"As long as you don't move away before I can follow, Goodman Pratt. I am not the most able walker myself, these days."

She helped him out of bed, his arm thinner than a washing bat in her firm grip. Though they much complained of want at

Plymouth, she was glad that none of their company was yet reduced to such starvation as this. They made their way to the door of Master Winslow's house, where Pratt was being lodged. There was some anger in the company against the men at Wessagusset, and Bradford did not trust him to be placed in the common house, where some of the wilder men from *Fortune* still lived. The rain fell outside, but not enough to stop anyone from working. They took a few steps up the damp dirt road, not wet enough yet to be too muddy to keep balance. Their progress was slow, but Pratt was grateful to be out of bed and on his own two legs again.

"I hope things are going well at Wessagusset," he said. "I hope they are not there too late."

"They are not too late, or else we would be facing our attackers also," Priscilla told him as they reached the top of the hill outside the fortress.

He smiled a lopsided grin that Priscilla found most endearing. "That is a positive way to look upon the situation, Mistress Alden. I shall not lose hope, then, until the Indians are knocking down ou—" He was interrupted by the clang of the sentry's bell.

Governor Bradford, whose house was at the top of the hill near the fortress, rushed out and into the building to discover what the sentry saw.

"Perhaps I spoke too soon," Pratt worried.

"If it is an attack, we will be well protected," Priscilla reassured him. "But it may be best to get you back inside."

They turned to find a company of men with muskets marching past them, the second company of Captain Standish's militia. The men were on high alert for any signs of trouble. Priscilla and Pratt stood, transfixed, and watched the sentry command one man to open the western gate of the palisade. A lone Indian came in. At the sight of him, Pratt's face took on a mask of terror, and he wheezed, reaching out to take Priscilla's arm lest he should fall. She looked in alarm between him and the Indian.

Bradford, coming out of the meeting house, noticed Goodman Pratt in this condition. "Do you know him?" he asked Pratt, pointing toward the Indian.

"Nahamit. He is Nahamit. He has followed me from Wessagusset. He has come to see your weakness here and report it back to Pecksuot." Pratt gulped hard.

"Take that man and bring him into the fortress," the governor told the militiamen. "It seems it must for the first time be put to its intended purpose."

John followed Joshua Pratt, who led Standish, along with the rest of the men from Plymouth, to the Wessagusset impalement. They saw, as they approached, two of the Massachusett *wetus* erected very close outside the town. The Indian homes were domed structures, lined on the outside with sheets of bark. Two of the savages crouched outside their houses, and they bared their teeth in grins when they saw the party coming. One shouted a question, while the other laughed. Standish shouted something back and held up the sack of English beads and jewelry they brought. The man replied, lifting the corner of the beaver skin he wore around his shoulders. John tried to catch Standish's eye, but the captain looked ahead and followed Pratt into the settlement.

Wessagusset's palisade came up short when compared to that at Plymouth; John could tell it was erected in haste, and if it held itself together now, it wouldn't for much longer. They walked right through the open gate at the entrance to the town, with no man on guard, rendering the palisade useless. There were but three shabby wattle-and-daub buildings, one lacking half the thatch which should have covered the roof. The one they entered after Pratt was missing a door altogether.

Governor Sanders sat in a chair by the hearth. He was chewing on the nail of his thumb. Another man sat naked in the corner, shivering with just a blanket wrapped around his shoulders.

"I take it you've heard of the Indian conspiracy that Pratt came to Plymouth to warn us of," Standish said, getting right to the point.

Sanders jumped at the sight of them, Standish in his usual armor, the other men in plain clothes for the purpose of their deception. "Captain Standish! Why have you come here with such a company?" he asked, his eyes roving over the small group of men.

Hopkins grinned, showing his two missing teeth. "We've come to rescue you from your hour of need."

"It is by God's mercy that you've come to find us all alive, and not yet killed. But how do you mean to"— he faltered, embarrassed to say the word—"to rescue us, with such a small company of men?"

"We have brought with us more fighting men than I have seen amongst the whole of your company," Standish judged. "But we do not mean to wait and let the Indians attack us. Their intent is clear, and we have heard the ringleaders are Pecksuot and Wituwamat. We intend to cut them off before they have the chance to rally their warriors to come. Have you any other names that should be added to the list?"

Sanders drew in a heavy breath, leaning back in his chair. "Cut them off... well, I suppose if they should die, the others would lie quiet for a time. Some of our men have built their homes some distance away from here, and they say there are some amongst them who are as threatening as Pecksuot is here. But even if we did kill some of them, it would take a matter of days before the others were up in arms against us once again."

"That is why you should not stay a few more days," said John. "You and all your men, after we've done our work, should get on board *Swan* and leave this place."

"Governor Bradford has offered to receive you all at Plymouth, until you can find better," Master Eaton mentioned. "But if you should like some other course, we've brought some corn to help you on your way."

Sanders rubbed his face with his hand, exhausted. "Yes... yes, I suppose you're right, and we ought not to stay. But we will not impose on you again at Plymouth; at least I will not. The men up at Monhegan and Damariscove treated us very well, when I went there to trade, and I am sure a greater part of the men here would prefer to go that way in *Swan* and wait for further word from Master Weston."

"How many men have you remaining?" John asked. They had not seen anything like sixty men on their approach into the town.

"Perhaps fifty? About a third of the men have gone off up the coast, while I was gone." Sanders looked about the slipshod house, bemused. "I came back to find they'd hanged a man, to give the Indians content, and then scattered up and down the coast. Pratt warned me of an Indian conspiracy and kept saying we must get word to Plymouth, but that he could not go because Pecksuot watched him day and night."

"Call back all the men you can," Standish said, "and be prepared to depart once we've accomplished our task. We'll give your men corn when they arrive, so make sure they come. We'll wait to see what the villains do before we can make our plan to trap them."

"I'll send some messengers to fetch all those home who don't already live amongst the Indians." Sanders stood and headed toward the door. "But be cautious what you say," Sanders warned on his way out. "Pecksuot has learned a great deal of English since we've come here, and he uses it to taunt and insult all those around him."

The Plymouth men waited in the house, the naked man huddled in the corner, not moving from his place, his eyes darting between them.

"At least there is a fire," John told Eaton, "although the ceiling leaks and the workmanship is shoddy."

In fact, the rain started to come down harder, and in one place a steady stream of water came through the ceiling and fell into a large bucket. After some time, the bucket filled, and water started to slop over the sides onto the floor. Irritated, John picked it up and carried it outside the hole where a front door should have been. He tossed the water out into the muddy path that led between the houses. He'd just set the bucket down again when the two Indians from outside the pale walked into the house. One carried a couple of beaver pelts over to Standish and Hobbamock, who sat closest by the fire. The other marched over to the man huddled in the corner and snatched the blanket from his shoulders. The man fell forward, propelled by the strength of the Indian's pull on the blanket on which he was sitting. His nakedness was now exposed, and the Indian laughed, tossing the blanket on top of the now-empty bucket so that the rain from the ceiling poured down on top of it.

Standish smiled at the newcomers, but John could see the snarl tugging at his nose. Their game of deceit did not suit the captain. The Indians also played at deceit, coming among them and eyeing each man and his unloaded musket. Hobbamock negotiated the trade, and, as it was pretense, neither side much argued. The Indians dumped the pair of beaver pelts in Standish's lap, took the copper chains for which they'd traded them, and grimaced on their way out of the door.

"There'll be more, sooner or later," said the man in the corner, who took back his blanket from the water bucket and, wet though it now was, wrapped it around himself again. "They treat Wessagusset as if it were an Indian village and come and go however they please."

He was right. It was not long before another Indian came in, a strapping man. Hobbamock acknowledged this newcomer with greater courtesy, and John took it that he was a pniese. He did not bring goods to trade, but instead he surveyed them all with dignity, then bent to talk with Hobbamock.

John watched the water from the ceiling plop into the bucket, filling it once more to the brim. He took it and threw the water outside again.

When the stranger at last left, John went to sit by Hobbamock and Standish. "What was he about?"

"He say they know we come to kill them. He say they not afraid. He say begin, any time. They ready for you."

"When shall we begin?" asked Hopkins from his seat on Governor Sanders' bed. "It grows late already, though that may just be the rain growing worse by the moment. Do we mean to wait here all night, without even a door to keep the savages at bay?"

"I should like to get as many of the key men in a room with us as we can, before we do aught to alarm them," Standish said. "They have come to us already, so we have seen that they will come to us if we await them here. I think in either case we must stay here overnight, though. Perhaps we can take the one that has a door, to sleep in and keep watch."

Hopkins grumbled, but just then another pair of Indians came in, and the conversation ceased.

Throughout the evening more and more came, in small groups, never many at a time. They grew bolder as the night dragged on, and cast forth insulting speeches, as all could tell even without discerning it from Hobbamock and Standish's faces. John was tense, waiting every moment for one side or the other to start fighting, but Standish did not waver. He bore the insults, though his smile looked more and more like a grimace the longer he persisted. John tried not to think of Plymouth, where his wife would any day begin her labor, and may or may not even now be beset by the Nauset. John emptied the bucket in the corner twice more, but on his third trip out he threw the water without much attention. He saw it splash across the breechcloth of the pniese called Pecksuot. John backed up into the room, and Pecksuot and Wituwamat filled the doorway.

Priscilla sat in her chair by Goodman Pratt, who was sitting up in bed to talk to Governor Bradford. The weather outside darkened and the storm blew in. The house creaked uneasily around her as the wind picked up.

Winslow pushed open the door and slammed it behind him, peeling off his hat and hanging it with considered attention on a coat hook. Looking to the fire, he came close by it, smiling with pleasure at the warmth.

"What says he?" Bradford asked.

"Hmm? Well, I am less an expert in the language than the good captain is, but I fear he confirms the same tale that Goodman Pratt brought us."

Pratt looked relieved. Priscilla felt a cramp roll through her stomach, and she clenched her muscles. She felt the constant urge to urinate these days, and she hoped she had not judged the wait too long.

"Well, but he agrees with Wassapinewat and says that Obtakiest had no hand in it," Winslow continued.

Priscilla massaged her belly and shifted in her seat, but she felt a sudden pop and a dribble of wetness pooling between her thighs. She squeezed her eyes shut tight, a tad embarrassed, although it felt like a small trickle and not something to concern herself with.

"Does he not say more?" Bradford asked, disappointed. "It would be good to know when they plan to come."

"Well, as I said, I could not well understand him, though he did claim not to be a part of the conspiracy."

Priscilla sniffed. That was not the scent of urine, coming from between her thighs. Instead, it was a faint, sweet smell.

"He is as much a part of it as any other," Pratt argued with contempt. "He is Pecksuot's dog, and he would have killed me in the wood if he found me there."

"Ah, yes, he did name Pecksuot amongst the main conspirators."

"What more did he say of those villains?" asked Bradford.

"He said there were five who went around to the other villages to stir up trouble."

"Pecksuot has often told me of the Frenchmen that he took delight in killing," Pratt told them. "I imagine all the men who lead this rabble-rousing are eager to see violence against the English."

Priscilla hoped that John would keep himself safe, after she'd encouraged him to go off and fight these chief conspirators. Had she put her husband in the path of serious danger, telling him to join this fight with the Massachusett?

"Did he name any of the others? The men who most seek out violence against us?" Bradford asked.

"Yes; well, he named Pecksuot and Wituwamat—"

But Winslow was interrupted by a surprised cry of pain from Priscilla, who held her belly as a strong cramp overwhelmed her.

Pecksuot and Wituwamat strode into the room, Pecksuot's breechcloth dripping water onto the dirt floor. He glowered at John. John widened his eyes, trying to look innocent, and put the bucket back on the floor underneath the dripping patch of ceiling. He could not help but glance at Standish, but the captain showed no sign of moving on the Indians. A youth, perhaps eighteen or nineteen, followed Wituwamat into the room, holding his head aloft like a man who is far better than all the men around him.

Wituwamat stood right over Captain Standish and looked down on him. He must have sought revenge, John thought, after their last meeting, when Standish pinned Wituwamat to the floor. John's heart hammered against his chest. He wanted to ready his musket, but touched his knife instead and held himself back.

Wituwamat spoke to Hobbamock and waved his arm to encompass the room at large.

"He want I tell you what he say," Hobbamock told the Englishmen.

Hopkins lowered his hand to the hilt of his cutlass. John swallowed. Would this be the moment?

The sharpened point of the knife Pecksuot wore around his neck gleamed in the soft glow of firelight. He took the string and lifted it over his head, then reached into a pouch at his waist, where his breechcloth still dripped onto the floor.

He pulled out a whetstone and began to refine the point of his blade.

Sometimes, John thought, the savages said as much with silence as with words.

Wituwamat was not so coy. He took out his dagger again, the one with the woman engraved on the handle. He flipped the dagger, so he held the blade, and the carved portion was exposed. He smiled at Captain Standish.

"You remember?" Hobbamock translated as the lean Indian bent over the captain. "I show you her face before. She cannot see, she cannot hear, she cannot speak. But by and by, she must eat."

Wituwamat flipped the knife in the air and caught it in his other hand.

"He have other knife, man's face. He kill many English and Frenchmen with. By and by, he say, these two must marry."

Pecksuot, standing by the fire, still sharpening his knife with his whetstone, laughed. "Though you are such a great captain," he said in English, "you are such a little man."

Standish did look small, with Wituwamat standing over him, looking down on him, his dagger held at the level of Standish's face. John's throat constricted and he clenched his jaw.

Yet Standish did not act. He was vibrating with his fury, but he contained himself and grimaced in an attempt to smile at Wituwamat.

"I may not take up so much space as you do, Wituwamat," Standish said, attempting to join in the exchange, "but I have yet killed many men with my musket." He patted the musket resting beside him and let out a forced chuckle.

The youth, who walked with an arrogant stride behind the older men, responded to Standish's action. Hobbamock looked at Pecksuot, then at Standish, before translating.

"He say his brother, Wituwamat, cannot be killed by guns. He say, many try to kill Wituwamat, but no gun can do it."

John could well believe that Wituwamat antagonized enough men that many should want to kill him. It looked as though his brother followed in his footsteps, for he stalked about the room, and kicked dust over their shoes, and picked at their clothes, even poking Master Eaton in the cheek. Hopkins glanced at Standish.

"How long must we keep still—"

"Quiet, Hopkins," Standish commanded. "We are welcoming our Massachusett friends, so long as they desire our company."

Pecksuot, who spoke English very well, sniffed at them with his disdain. "Though I am no great sachem," he said, opening the pouch at his waist to put his whetstone back inside, "I am yet a man of great strength and great courage." He tapped Wituwamat on the shoulder and nodded toward the door, kicking Wituwamat's brother in the legs to ensure he followed. Pecksuot made a final gesture of contempt before he too went out through the open hole that had been a door, walking past Governor Sanders, just returned and standing as stiff as a musket barrel.

"I thought we waited their arrival to act," Hopkins said, while Pecksuot was still within hearing distance.

Standish shushed him, went to the door, and watched the Indians' retreating backs.

"If we strike too soon," he said in hushed tones to the gathered company, "then some of the main conspirators may get away. Sanders, have you found out the names of the other antagonists who are gathered with your men?"

"Aye, Captain," Sanders said. "They should return tomorrow."

"We'll wait for them to come, so that we can attack all at once. Meanwhile, tonight, is there a house that we can sleep in?" He held a finger up before Hopkins could interject. "With a door, if you please, Governor Sanders?"

They settled in the house the governor lent them and kept watch in shifts for the night, but John could not sleep. If God could not protect them here, they must protect themselves. That was what he thought, when he fought for them to come here and do the act that now would wait until morning. But with him here, who stood to protect his wife and child? John was doing all he could, but he felt too far away from Priscilla, when she no doubt needed his protection more than Standish did. He could not be here, protecting the colony from attack, and there, protecting her person, all at once.

Her voice rose in his mind: *You must have faith.* Faith in her strength, yes, but also faith that God was there in Plymouth and could watch over her. John rolled over on his side and glanced up to make sure Eaton was fast asleep next to him. Standish was on watch, staring hard at the closed door to their temporary dwelling. John bent his head and put his hands together. *O Lord in heaven,* he prayed, *if you are here—if you can hear our prayers—please protect her. Keep her safe.*

Priscilla groaned, the ache moving from the top of her belly to the bottom. She leaned against the empty window, oiled paper torn away, breathing the fresh scent of rain-spattered air. She was in her own house again, and the men who lived there, who were not on the expedition to Wessagusset, were scattered to other dwellings. Tilley stood beside her, flitting around the room, trying to find anything she could do to make Priscilla more comfortable. Mistress Hopkins and Mistress Winslow waited at the table, Mistress Winslow with mending in hand, telling Priscilla she was still in the early stages and there was little that they could do until the babe was ready. The iron kettle was filled with water and hung over the hearth, and each woman fetched some clean rags from their own homes, for birthing was a wet and messy affair.

The pain subsided in her belly but persisted in her lower back. She bent further, one hand on the windowsill, trying to relieve the ache in her back, but it did not work.

A loud noise clanged outside at the top of the hill, and Tilley looked up. "Have the Nauset come?" she asked in terror.

"'Tis the wind," Mistress Winslow reassured her, "banging things about at the fortress. I hope this storm lets up before morning."

Priscilla panted hard. If the Nauset dared to come into her house just then, she felt she could protect herself against them better than any man could, if she were not laid up with these sudden waves of aching pain.

"Have we any weapons in the house?" Tilley asked, still worrying about the imminent threat of Indians.

"Since we've barred the men from entry," Mistress Hopkins said, "if we have weapons, they will do more harm than good, since we do not know how to use them." Ever practical-minded, was Mistress Hopkins. She stood and came over to Priscilla, stroking her back and bending down to lift her smock. Priscilla felt fluid ooze between her legs as another wave of pain began and spasmed down the giant curve of her belly.

"They're not like to come, with the weather so bad as this," Mistress Winslow told Tilley, trying to be reassuring.

"Are they not more like to come? Goodman Pratt said they waited for the snow to clear, so they would not leave tracks. They will leave no sign in this weather and will surprise us all inside!"

"I don't imagine they like to be out in a storm any more than English men and women do," said Mistress Winslow.

"It would be to their advantage, if they came," Mistress Hopkins speculated, "seeing that we cannot keep our matches lit to fire our muskets in the rain."

Tilley gasped, and Priscilla moaned as another spasm hit her. The wind tore at the trees and the thatch of the roof. Whether the Nauset came or kept to their homes, she minded not, so long as she could soon have a babe in arms instead of one inside her belly.

Wednesday, 26 March 1623

John was awakened by a rough hand on his shoulder, unaware when he'd fallen asleep. He rubbed his eyes with his fingertips and blinked in the steely gray of a drizzling dawn. Standish was waking all the men, some determination having come to him while others slept.

"Instead of waiting for the men who are encamped elsewhere to come here," he told them, when they stirred from their blankets, "we should send half our party to them, and, when Wituwamat and Pecksuot come here, we will have half our men here to deal with them and send signal to the other half to cut off the Indians that those men name as conspirators."

The plan was well liked and, before they broke their fast, half the men of the Plymouth party marched away through the woods to the place Sanders named to them. John was left with Standish, Hopkins, Eaton, and Hobbamock.

John went out into the camp and found a place along the palisade against which to urinate. The steady flow had just begun when he was shoved from behind and crashed into the rough wood in front of him. He whipped around and saw the sullen face of Goodman Weston staring at him. He had deteriorated somewhat since John saw him off at Plymouth; never a bulky man, he was now bony, hollow-cheeked, and his hair hung about him in lank strands. Despite this, John could tell he did not fare as badly as the brothers Pratt, and he suspected Weston was among the thieves of corn from both his fellows and the Indians. What was more, John doubted Weston was stocked or whipped, because of his brother's influence among the company.

"Sanders says you all have come to *rescue* us," sneered Weston, "as though we sought out help from such as you."

"If you do not wish for our help, then you are free to face the savages alone," John told him, pulling up his breeches.

"You think you are so superior, now that the men here have fallen into disarray? You would take advantage of their weakness to try to make yourselves feel stronger than you are."

"You and your men have fallen short of your own expectations," John replied, disbelieving that a man could be so unaware of his own position.

Weston drew the wolf's-head knife that John had seen him bear before. "I expect that I could still best you, if you came upon me equitably, rather than interrupting a fine conversation with a fair maiden."

John's temper flared. "That maid is now the mother of my child," he told Weston, hoping his face would fall. But Weston was more of a brute than John credited.

"Are you certain?" he derided. "I can scarce remember even which maid she was, though there were so few available. Now, was yours the darling golden-haired bitch or the white one, with brown spots?" He referred to the dogs, the mastiff and the spaniel.

"You have even fewer women here, and look how you fall to want without them."

"Indeed, I want a maid to sit upon my lap and comfort me." Weston wiggled his eyebrows at John.

"You will get none willing, if you look like that, for they will at last see your outward appearance match your character."

Weston snarled and lunged at John, pointing his dagger as a sword, not accounting for the style of the weapon. John had no experience in close combat, and he dodged and kicked at Weston. He made contact near the knee and, already weakened, Weston tumbled on that side. John backed a few steps away, then turned and re-entered the house, where the other men were still waking. Weston was not the kind to brawl where he was outnumbered.

"What have you been busy doing, that you're breathing like that?" Hopkins asked him. "And your sleeve is cut—did one of the savages attack you?"

John shook his head. "Goodman Weston. I think he likes not that he in in a position to require our aid."

Hopkins snorted. "Aye, that sounds like him."

Though the gray light of morning now filtered ever brighter through the open window, Priscilla still lay abed in childbearing. It felt as though the rippling waves of pain had become a continuous, never-ceasing flow of aching muscles. She was so tired. She longed to sleep, but her body would not let her. Nor would Mistress Hopkins, who kept telling her that it was nearly over. It had been nearly over for a lifetime and a half, and all Priscilla wanted was to sleep. Tilley gripped her hand and brushed away the sweaty hair that stuck to Priscilla's face. She smiled and told Priscilla she would not leave her, and to have faith that God would lead her through.

She could not smile, struggled to breathe; she felt the burning of a ring of fire engulfing her where the babe was coming out.

"There's so much blood," said Tilley at Priscilla's side.

Priscilla turned to her and saw Tilley staring at where Mistress Hopkins was crouched between Priscilla's legs. She looked down again and saw a linen rag soaking in red blood. Her blood. She began to cry.

"At least you are not on board a ship, rolling in the fierce waves of a storm," Mistress Hopkins said.

"So much blood," Tilley said again, gripping her hand.

"It's time for you to move onto your hands and knees, if you can," Mistress Hopkins shouted at her, but she sounded very far away. Move? Move? She could not keep herself from breaking into pieces where she lay; how could she move? Priscilla's teeth were chattering, and through the rolling waves of pain she could not tell what was aching and what was shivering. How could she be shivering, when she felt as though her body were on fire? Burning, burning, between her legs where her child was being delivered. Was the child burning? Was this her repayment for Eve's sin in the Garden? Was this the pain of damnation, visited upon her in the land of the living? She had told John that death's hand came to all women lying in childbed, inviting them to join him rather than continue through their agony. She had heard from other mothers that it was true, but she had not felt the truth of it until this moment, when she wondered if she were dying and if, instead of God, it was the Devil who claimed her for his underworld.

While John and the others waited for the chief conspirators to appear, Hopkins killed a water bird to break their fast. John stared at it, impaled on a spit, dripping fat into their morning fire. John's mind ran back and back to Plymouth, wondering whether he would find his wife alive, or scalped by Indians, or killed by the child growing within her. When he returned to Plymouth, would he have a child? Would he have a little babe, an infant to raise in the New World? If he did, would his child still have a mother, yet living?

John's stomach was nervous with the knowledge of what was soon to come. He did not acquit himself well in the brief fight with Goodman Weston. The smell of roasting flesh on the spit made John want to retch.

They left the door open, that the Indians might find them there, and sure enough, Wituwamat and Pecksuot soon came. Wituwamat's brother followed after, and John watched him take a mussel right out of the hands of one of the wretched men outside. Perhaps his age could in part account for this youth's malice. A fourth man came inside with them, the one who, yesterday, took the blanket off a naked man and threw it into water.

Standish stood by the fire, where the water bird was roasting. "Come," he told them, "sit around the table, and we can eat together." His smile was more genuine than yesterday's.

They came forward and sat around the table as though they owned it. Standish's eyes flicked up to John's, who was closest by the door. His eyes flicked to the door, and back to John's, and Standish grinned.

John slammed the door and reached for the leather cord which bound the hair of Wituwamat. He pulled hard, toppling the chair in which Wituwamat sat. He drew the long knife which Standish gave him on their journey to the Nauset and slashed at Wituwamat's chest. The Indian wore no armor, no doublet, not even a shirt to spare his taut skin from the attack which John aimed at it. Blood welled up from the wound, but it was not deep enough, for the man reached down to his side to draw his own weapon. John thrust forward with his knife, driving the point into the man's chest below his collarbone. He encountered stiff resistance, something hard which stopped the blade from penetrating.

Panicked, John withdrew the blade and stabbed again, seeing a mess of flowing blood. He reminded himself that if he did not succeed now, he would be at this man's mercy, this man who claimed he killed many French and English men before, this man who yesterday thirsted for more English blood. If John did not succeed here, this man would incite more warriors to go after Priscilla and their child. This was all John could do to protect her from disaster. Terror flooded through him, and he stabbed once more into the chest of the man who lay defenseless under him. This time, at last, the resistance against his blade was weak. His knife tasted flesh, and, as Wituwamat promised, the knife ate hungrily. John's eyes were blurred and stung with sweat or tears or the wet rain which still leaked through the ceiling, but he plunged in his knife as far as he could and dragged it through Wituwamat.

The enemy yet lived, and his hand had reached his dagger, the woman's face carved in the hilt covered by his straining fingers. He seemed to lack the strength to lift it. John had no doubt that, had this fight been anticipated by his adversary, John would no longer draw breath. John withdrew his knife and slashed once more, this time earning a spray of blood from the arm he cut. Blood flooded in quick bursts, growing fainter as the blood from Wituwamat's chest pooled in the divot between his muscles. Wituwamat's hand lifted up, the dagger still held in it, and John scooted across the floor until his back made contact with the wall. But Wituwamat could not sit up, could not reach his arm any higher than his own body, sprawled across the ground.

John's face felt damp. He dragged a sleeve across his eyes to clear his vision, and his doublet came away spotted with red stains. He stared at the stains on the green wool for a moment, then looked back at his enemy upon the floor.

Hopkins, who dispatched the blanket thief without trouble, came into John's field of view and took Wituwamat by the hair. He drew his knife across the vile throat, and a small spray of blood came forward. Standish stood over the body of Pecksuot, whose needle-pointed knife stuck out of his chest. Pecksuot bore more wounds than any man should need to die. The pinprick point of his knife was insufficient to kill him with just one blow. Eaton had not dispatched his target, Wituwamat's brother, the mischievous youth. Instead, he held him down with arms behind his back, in such a fierce grip that he could not escape.

Hobbamock laughed, delighted with their victory, though he took no part in the fight. "He said guns would not kill Wituwamat, but you kill Wituwamat with knife." He looked over at Standish. "And Pecksuot called you a little man, but you are big enough to lay him to the ground." He cackled again, though he'd been unwilling to take any action that would impute this massacre to Massasoit.

John looked down at his own hands, drenched in the cooling blood of the conspirators. He looked at Wituwamat's body. The Indian had relinquished at last his dagger when Hopkins seized him, and it lay beside him in the dirt. Blood flowed out from beneath him and stained red the hair of the woman whose face was etched there. Though they won the battle, John knew that this scene would play as vividly in his nightmares as any of his dreams wherein the English were defeated. He looked at the knife still clenched in his own hand. He had, with this knife, killed a man. It was a necessary sin. *We must protect ourselves.*

Chapter Twenty-Two

Concerning ye killing of those poor Indeans, of
which we heard at first by reporte, and since by
more certaine relation, oh! how happy a thing had
it been, if you had converted some, before you had
killed any; besids, wher bloud is onc begune to be
shed, it is seldome stanched of a long time after.
You will say they deserved it. I grant it; but upon
what provocations and invitments by those
heathenish Christians?

—John Robinson, Separatist pastor, *Letter to
Governor Bradford*, 19 December 1623

Thursday, 27 March 1623

The next day was cloudy, though the worst of the storm blew
itself away. Rain continued misting through the air. The
shallop, laden with men, cut through the water on return to
Plymouth, which sat as ever in two neat rows of houses
aligned on either side of a broad main street, the town
impaled around with a fortress at the top of the hill.

The shallop rowed up close to the little hill by the water
where Plymouth's dead were buried and began to discharge
her cargo. Eight men who volunteered to go to Wessagusset;
six more, tattered and mud-spattered, whom these men
rescued from their own debasement; one Indian, who would
not dirty his hands for the sake of his English friends; and the
military captain, who bore aloft a gruesome gift for
Plymouth. As the men approached, the plantation's eastern
gate was opened, and a flood of relieved and joyful men and
women swarmed the returning victors. Husbands met wives,
fathers met sons, brother met brother, for both the Pratts
continued to live in Plymouth for many years thereafter.

Wituwamat's severed head was carried through the crowd up to the fortress, where it would meet Nahamit, still imprisoned. But those matters were not what concerned John and Priscilla, who saw each other through the gathering crowd, both weary, both blood-spattered.

Priscilla embraced her husband with one arm, the other curled around the swaddled bundle of their babe in arms. She was relieved to see him safe, though the dried and crusted blood adorning his doublet would be hell to launder.

John put his cheek against her cheek and kissed her, grateful to have wife and child both in front of him, where he could protect them. He greeted for the first time this cloth-wrapped infant, whose squalls at being woken from her slumber gave him great joy. This cry, this sign of life, heard for the first time made him smile, although in weeks to come he would bemoan the fact he ever had a daughter who would rouse him from his bed so often with her crying. He kissed again his wife's cheek, amazed at the incredible feat that she accomplished. While he took Wituwamat's life, she gave birth to Elizabeth.

The crowd that flooded the streets of Plymouth rejoiced at the remains of the life that John took. The severed head of Wituwamat was mounted on a spike up at the fortress: a warning. A warning not unlike the body of his teenage brother, which was hanged from a tree. A warning, if it entered any Indian hearts to commit treachery, that New Plymouth would not suffer any act of provocation. With that warning, the English town would live in peace for fifty years.

John leaned close to his wife and whispered in her ear, "All will be well." She shuddered, just a little, for the sake of the men who died to make it so.

Saturday, 12 April 1623

John sat on the beach, a large plank of wood held between his legs, as he stripped a narrow slice away from the main body of the plank. Halfway down the length, the piece cracked. He sighed and shook his head. He had grown more used to holding a hoe than holding cooper's tools, and though the old tools felt familiar in his hands, sometimes the sensation of plunging his knife into flesh came back to his fingers, and they shook. He set down the broken plank and his froe and stood to go to the side of the water and splash his face and neck. The water in the bay was frigid, the season still early. He scrubbed a fistful of saltwater through his hair, trying to calm himself before returning to his work. He did not yet wield a gun or blade better than a froe, although the memories still came to him. Memories of the hardness of Wituwamat's chest, the sudden spray of blood, the body of the youth strung up in a tree for all the Indians to see.

John splashed water on his face again, forcing the memories aside. He revisited them enough at night; he did not need them to plague him through his days as well. He stood, wiping his face dry in the crook of his elbow, and spied a shallop in the bay, making its way toward their harbor. He retrieved his musket from the place he was working and heard the sentry raise his alarm. It looked to be a single man rowing a small boat through the bay. Standish and a few of his active company, who were drilling in the street, opened the eastern gate of the plantation and stood, armed, on the beach: a very warm reception for whosoever this stranger was.

As he came closer, John could make out familiar bronze hair, though this was worn in a fuzzy cloud about the head, rather than in tame ringlets. The face it framed also felt familiar, although he was sure it was not one he recognized. Still, the newcomer shared the narrow eyes and, upon seeing his reception, the contemptuous smile of Andrew Weston. Yet, this man was a few years older, paunchier, and weathered. Still, John was not surprised when, at Bradford's coming through the gate, he greeted, "Master Weston!" with exuberance.

"I came all this way, to find my colony dissolved, Governor Bradford," Weston called, heaving himself out of the shallop. He wore a doublet that strained across his belly, the sleeves two inches shorter than his wrists. The breeches were no better, and John could see the hair of Weston's legs, visible above the stockings that ended at his knees.

"He is much altered," Standish said in surprise, at John's elbow. "There was an air of dignity when I saw him last, at the docks at Southampton."

John narrowed his eyes at the disarrayed man before him, trying to recall the docks at Southampton. It was almost three years since he boarded *Mayflower* there, but try as he might, he could remember no one who looked anything like this man. It was Weston in the flesh, the instigator of all their troubles. John imagined that he came to trouble them further.

"I was pillaged, you know, by Indians, up the coast at Piscataqua. They stripped me of everything down to my shirt, which I am fortunate enough to still have on under these borrowed garments. It is a tragic tale, Bradford, and I should very much like to share it with you. But first, do tell me what has happened to my men? For I am sure I came to find them, but a fishing vessel told me they've all removed to Monhegan!"

Bradford looked uncomfortable. "Perhaps it's best for us to talk more privately. Captain Standish? Would you be willing to relate your part of the tale?"

"Aye," Standish called, trotting up to Bradford and Master Weston. John watched them, withdrawing up the hill, and saw Standish draw Weston's attention to Wituwamat's head, mounted on its spike near their fortress.

He shook his head. *Weston.* Well, he would stay for a few days at most, before departing to join his men up north. It did not seem as though he'd brought with him any resupply, of course, and John doubted that he'd brought the salt pan that he'd promised to set up to recompense them for their hospitality. John set back about his work, knocking his froe into the plank of wood. Their own shallop, though not in dire need, was in want of patching, and John was the man most relied on to repair her.

It was not many hours later, when the sun was climbing close to the tree line, that Master Weston came back through the gate carrying one end of a heavy barrel. Bradford carried the other, and John watched, amused, as the ill-suited pair lugged the barrel into Weston's boat. *What has Bradford given away to Weston now, that we can ill afford to lose?* John wondered.

They fetched another barrel to load alongside the first in Weston's boat. When the boat was full, Weston pushed off from shore and got into the small craft himself, shouting at the last as he departed, "They're quite fine beaver pelts, indeed, Governor Bradford—I'm sure they'll keep me well provided for my journey back to Monhegan!"

John stood, knocking the block of wood from his lap.

"Beaver?" he asked. Bradford did not seem to hear him, so he marched over and repeated it into his ear: "You've given him our beaver?"

Bradford wore a pinched expression, as though he was much abused. "All the world has failed him, Goodman Alden; he was desperate for some help. He promised he would repay it, as soon as he is able. I knew it would cause a mutiny amongst our people if they heard of it, so I swore the man to secrecy before he departed. If you could also keep it secret, then..."

But John gestured toward the gate of the plantation, where Master Hopkins stood with an unamused expression, side by side with Howland, who was shocked at the governor's indiscretion.

"I think it is too late for secrecy this time, Governor."

Monday, 19 May 1623

The day was hot, and Priscilla sat back on her heels and wiped the sweat from her brow with her apron. Elizabeth lay in a cradle that John had made, at the end of the row of corn over which Priscilla was working. The first row of corn, which they planted three weeks prior, had started to grow seedlings of about six inches high. It was therefore time to plant the squash and beans in alternating rows between the corn, the way Squanto taught them. After many months of great want, their own crops would soon begin to grow again and, through their own labor, their wants could be addressed. The governor decided that, instead of a communal plot of corn at which every man should labor, each family was to be assigned their own parcel to grow what they could to feed themselves, and put aside a portion for the men in public offices and the fishermen who spent too much time on other business for the colony to grow their own corn.

John, who left their field to fetch some water, came back and greeted little Elizabeth in her cradle.

"The first child born in New Plymouth," Tilley exclaimed when Priscilla and John named their daughter, "and you've named her for me!"

John was still an astonished father. He was so concerned over her pregnancy that he'd not been prepared to greet the little girl who now slept peacefully (at last) beside them. Priscilla rubbed her belly, which still felt empty, even two months after her childbearing.

John picked up the water bucket and carried it closer to where Priscilla worked. She smiled at him and reached to take a spoonful of water to drink.

"You should rest," John said. "I can do this work myself."

Priscilla scowled. "Do you still lack faith in me, dear husband?"

He scratched the back of his head. "I wish to spare you what I can."

"There is no need to spare me from industry. The more we can set now, the more we reap at harvest time, and I have no more wish than you for us to spend another winter in great want."

He grinned at her determination and changed the subject. "I have just heard from Hopkins that Aspinet has died," he told her.

Priscilla frowned. There were several reports of their Indian neighbors' deaths in the past week alone.

"Is it the same story?" she asked. She saw him grimace and wondered what he thought of all this sad news.

"Aye. After the killings at Wessagusset, the Nauset also fled into the swamps and other remote places, like the Manomet and the Mattachiest. Most of the tribes who allied with the Massachusett have fled their homes and do not return even to plant their corn, or so Hobbamock tells us."

John hunched over the ground and started planting winter squash seeds with determination. He was nightly pulled from sleep by awful dreams, and she often woke to find him staring at his hands. He had not told her the details of the killings at

Wessagusset, but, looking upon the head of Wituwamat, she thought she understood.

"They fear our God is angry with them for joining in the plot against us," Priscilla said, rubbing his back between his shoulders. "If they had no cause to feel guilt, they would not flee."

"Every time they have tried to make peace with us, they have suffered some retribution. When they came to us with presents for the governor, hoping to resolve their treachery, as soon as they got close by Plymouth their boat was washed away, and all but one of them drowned. What kind of vengeance is that, by a righteous God?" John asked.

"So now you do believe that God is here, and is acting on our behalf against the Indians?"

He sighed. "I know not what to believe of the Separatists' manner anymore. They have confidence that God protects them, and, whether in famine or in plenty, believe that his hand guides them in every action. Whilst I have not the body of the King's church to guide me, I cannot tell without a priest what it is that God desires of me."

He rubbed a hand against his face, leaving a streak of dirt across his cheek. Priscilla reached up to him and wiped the dirt away, stroking his soft beard.

"You have done what you needed to protect me, and Elizabeth. You have succeeded in frightening our enemies, so that we need not go to war against them, and Plymouth has been made safe."

He took her hand and pressed a kiss into her palm, which itself was embedded with the soil of their field. She laughed and took a drink of water. The pair returned to planting crops on land which had been readied for them by a tribe whose men and women were now no more than bleached white bones too numerous to bury.

Epilogue

To this darkness, crying to God, the light came first
as by a soft general dawning of comfort for faith.
*"Sin is behoveable... but all shall be well, and all
shall be well, and all manner of things shall be
well."* Yet Julian, unable to take comfort to her
heart over that which was still so dark to her
intellect, stands... saying thus in her thoughts: *"Ah
good Lord, how might all be well, for the great
hurt that is come by sin to the creature?"*

—Julian of Norwich, *Revelations of Divine
Love*, written circa. 1373, published 1670

Friday, 1 August 1623

For eight weeks after they planted their crops, a drought
afflicted Plymouth. Their corn grew brown in the fields, and
it seemed that for the second season in a row they would have
a bad harvest. What was more, they heard word of two ships
that the Virginia Company sent to resupply them in February.
The ships were both pushed back by bad storms three times,
and there had been no sign of them for months. Believing that
God sought to deprive them of all future hopes, the settlers at
Plymouth set aside a solemn Day of Prayer and Humiliation,
that they might pray and seek mercy from the Lord in this,
their hour of greatest distress. This the Lord answered, for by
the afternoon of their day of humbling themselves before him,
the sky grew overcast, and for fourteen days together a soft
and gentle rain fell upon their crops. This did much surprise
Hobbamock, for the Indians' prayers for rain were more often
met with ferocious storms that leveled their crops to the

ground; and so they learned to practice caution in praying for changes in the weather.

During this time also, the two ships, which were thought lost or wrecked at sea, came to them, bearing many friends and relatives from Leiden. It had been three long years, and many whom the newcomers longed to see were long since buried in the little hill by the water. Nevertheless, their joy to God for bringing them together, and for bringing rain which would revive their harvest, needed to be sung in thanks to him for his glory, honor, and praise. So they set aside another solemn Day of Thanksgiving, to express their gratitude to God for all his mercy.

John sat in the meeting house beside Priscilla, who sat beside Tilley, who sat beside Goodman Howland. All the Separatists were engaged in fervent prayer, and John, who still did not trust Separatists enough to pray to God in their church, looked about at all the new faces of men and women who came to them on *Anne* and *Little James*.

"Elizabeth, you mustn't," Priscilla whispered to their crying child, pressing her against her bosom. "Shh, shh…"

Patience and Fear Brewster were seated with their parents, the two girls having stayed in Leiden while their father accompanied *Mayflower* as one of the congregation's elders. Two wives who had been left in Holland also joined their husbands, Master Fuller and Goodman Warren, who traveled first with *Mayflower*.

"What do you know of Mistress Southworth?" John asked Priscilla, looking over at the woman whom Governor Bradford embraced on her arrival with uncharacteristic enthusiasm.

Priscilla, in her fashion, made fast friends with several of the newly come women, who all fawned over Tilley and how much she'd grown since they'd last seen her.

"Well, she and Bradford have known each other for quite some time," Priscilla whispered, addressing John's real question. "She was amongst those who went from Scrooby to Leiden with her parents, so she has deep ties to the congregation. Southworth is her married name; she has two sons still in Holland, called Constant and Thomas. The family intended to come in *Speedwell*, but her husband fell ill before the voyage, and she stayed to tend his illness. He soon died. I imagine she's looking to remarry, so that her sons will have a settled place when they arrive."

John considered this. She still sat near to Bradford, who was looking toward the ceiling of the meeting house's lower floor, speaking his words of praise to God. It was true that if Mistress Southworth were married to the governor, her sons would have an easier time of things when they arrived in Plymouth.

"So many have left their children behind in Holland. Even Governor Bradford's son is still there, with his late wife's family." Priscilla bounced Elizabeth in her arms and nuzzled her nose against the baby's tiny face. "I should so hate to leave Elizabeth to be raised by others and cross the ocean alone."

John smiled and touched Elizabeth's cheek.

"Then we must raise our thanks to God, dear wife, that we are all together."

Author's note

While I did my best to stay true to history where possible, this is a work of fiction and some of the ideas presented herein are flawed, whether by choice, for the purposes of greater literary effect, or by accident, due to my inability to become an expert in every aspect of 17th century daily life.

To start, I am not a theologian and, though I researched the beliefs and practices of both the Church of England and the Separatists, some complex questions had no single answer, and many beliefs have changed throughout history. Even if we know that the Thirty-nine Articles were finalized in 1571, and the 1604 edition of the Book of Common Prayer was in use, it is difficult to say for any single man, especially in the common class, what his experience of religion may have been in 1620, particularly at a time when belief systems were changing so rapidly. Was your church's priest old or young? Where was he educated? Had he read the pamphlets distributed by religious dissenters, and been influenced by them, or was his fealty to tradition reminiscent of Catholicism? There were many paths to tread even within the world of Christianity.

While all that is true, it is unlikely that any priest at the time advised that prayer directly to God was unfathomable. After all, members of the Church of England recited the Lord's Prayer, which is directed to "Our Father." Though John's belief that God is unreachable is founded in practices of the medieval church, by the time of the reformation it has widely fallen out of favor. In this book, this belief is not meant as a literal interpretation of the Church of England's views at the time. It is meant more as a hyperbolic symbol of the hierarchy of the Church of England from which the Separatists are pulling away to have more intimate relationships with God. John's view that God had forsaken the New World was likely also not widely held, though it has some basis in other scriptural and religious events.

I have tried to stick as closely to the original historical record as possible, while taking license with characterization of historical people, places and events. If an event, such as Bradford's trade with the Massachusett and Nauset in October 1622, explicitly stated all of the people who were involved, and John or Priscilla was not among them, I did not place those characters at the scene. Other events, such as the massacre at Wessagusset, did not name all of the participants, and so I was able to describe those scenes in more detail from John's perspective. Any major liberties I have taken with history, I have tried to enumerate below. There are likely both more minor liberties and some mistakes based on insufficient knowledge, for which the author takes full responsibility.

The actions taken by the Native American characters included in the novel are based primarily on documents written by the English. My intention was, as may be seen by the epigraphs, to base as much of the book as possible off documentation that was written at the time. Unfortunately, there is not an extant historical record written by any of the Wampanoag or Massachusett who were then living. Despite this, my intention was to depict both English and Native American characters as individuals with their own motivations and sometimes complicated personalities. The English provided in their original documents a lot of reasons for the local people to be angry with Europeans, and I tried to incorporate that perspective although the book is told from the European point of view. I wanted to show that the relationship between the Plymouth settlers and their neighbors was not as straightforward nor friendly as modern Thanksgiving myths can make it seem. My goal was to broaden our perspective on this era in history and reexamine some of the flawed stories we perpetuate. However, I understand that the perspective I began with was very narrow, and it has only widened so much. There are many sides to this story and its effect on history, and I hope to continue learning.

Some of the more specific variances I made from the historical record:

One of the main reasons Plymouth could not do much trade with the local Native Americans in the summer of 1622 was want of any trade goods. They did not manage to acquire more English trade goods until *Discovery* visited the colony in September 1622. This was probably more of a factor in their lack of trade than was their argument with Massasoit. In fact, all Plymouth's Native allies but the Pokanoket seemed to be on good terms with them until winter/early spring of 1622-1623. It was at this time that the Massachusett, increasingly angry with the actions of the men at Wessagusset, reportedly invited the other tribes into a conspiracy. The Nauset were particularly inclined to hate the English, and likely easily swayed by a plan which would rid their shores of the English settlers altogether. The Massachusett garnered agreement from seven tribes, at least as Massasoit reported it to Winslow. It is uncertain whether they would have launched an attack in due course, or if Wituwamat and Pecksuot were just braggadocious young men who paid dearly for talking themselves up. In my own aside to history, even if they had succeeded, it likely would not have stopped—or even much slowed—the English from establishing settlements on their shores in greater and greater numbers. The Great Migration, especially of English Puritans, had already begun.

According to Winslow's narrative, Massasoit reported that the Nauset, Manomet, and Paomet were all involved in the conspiracy, as were the Succonet, Mattachiest, Agoweywam and Isle of Capawack, all joining the instigators who were Massachusett. Massasoit also told the Plymouth settlers that the Nauset, Paomet, Mattachiest, and Manomet leaders were 'kings under him,' and, though the leaders were sachems in their own right, Massasoit was the great sachem over all the Wampanoag. Massasoit means 'Great Sachem' and was as much a respectful title as a name, his other name being Ousamequin. The historical record does not name or give tribal affiliations for any of the seven confirmed deaths at the hands of the Europeans in the massacre at Wessagusset, except the Massachusetts, Wituwamat and Pecksuot. The leaders of the Nauset (Aspinet), Mattachiest (Iyannough) and Manomet (Canacum) are named among those who fled out of fear into swamps and other remote places, and died, following the massacre.

Manomet was the actual location where Captain Standish met Wituwamat. During that winter and spring, the Plymouth settlers (sometimes in concert with the Wessagusset men) traded at Manamoycke (the actual location of Squanto's death) and Nemasket, and with the Massachusetts, Nauset, and Manomet (the actual location of Hobbamock's conversation, originally with Bradford, about the justice of the death penalty). Corn was left behind with not only the Nauset, but also the Massachusett and at Manomet. The actual expedition to recover corn from the Nauset occurred in January 1623, at which time the sachem was very polite and friendly with Captain Standish. The English expedition to recover corn from the Massachusett was in February, where the people reportedly "pretended their wonted love." The scenes I have depicted here as at Nauset were more accurately the March expedition to retrieve corn from Manomet, and their sachem Canacum. I have merged these various trading expeditions for the sake of narrative simplicity. These place and tribe names are based on the understanding of the Plymouth settlers, as told through their writings. Anyone interested in learning more details should consult those sources (see recommended reading list).

During the time Standish is at Manomet (in the novel, Nauset), Hobbamock is with Winslow at Massasoit's. Presumably the captain himself (being the best linguist among them) translated Wituwamat's threatening speeches, but I wanted to include Hobbamock's views on the justice of the death penalty in the story, and this was the most appropriate place for it.

Giles Heale was the ship's surgeon, and while he was a witness to William Mullins' will, it is more likely that Samuel Fuller, one of the passengers, would've been tending to those 'tween decks, while Heale tended the sailors. Heale was a qualified barber-surgeon, while Fuller took on healing because of his position as a deacon in the Separatist church. For simplicity's sake, I merged these two roles in the narrative. There are other *Mayflower* passengers (Christopher Martin, John Billington & family, Isaac Allerton, and others) who I would've loved to include, and did, in earlier drafts. In the end, their roles also were combined with more central figures to try and keep control over an ever-expanding cast of characters. There are many more *Mayflower* stories, and the amount we know about the lives of the passengers is incredible.

The *Speedwell*'s story is true. Given sails larger than appropriate for her size, the ship may have been prone to leaking already, but the suspicion that her crew intentionally exaggerated the leaks to back out of their agreement to stay in America was confirmed. On the other hand, the suspicion that Weston arranged for *Mayflower* to land in New England is barely hinted at in the historical record, but the idea stuck fast in my mind. By all accounts, Weston was a reprobate, and in 1622 he was declared an outlaw from the Crown.

Plymouth probably did not hear of the Jamestown Massacre until the latter end of July or August, at which point they had already started building their fortress due to threats from the Narragansett. For the sake of narrative impact, I allowed them to receive the news somewhat sooner; the massacre took place in March, and during that summer they received not only *Sparrow, Charity* and *Swan,* but also other fishing ships, and *Charity* went back and forth to Virginia. The record does not state exactly when they heard the news from Jamestown, but lumps it in with the removal of Weston's men to Wessagusset, as "amidst these straits, and the desertion of those from whom they had hoped for supply," which could refer to any time after the arrival of *Sparrow.*

They also did discuss the proposal of the Wessagusset massacre at Plymouth's yearly court date, but it was decided that so weighty a decision should not rest on the shoulders of all their men, so the final decision was arrived at by the governor (Bradford), his assistant (Allerton) and the captain (Standish). At the time, the Julian calendar was in use. Dates shown differ from dates in the Gregorian calendar by ten days. They also started the new calendar year in March, which is why the election of offices, when not necessitated by death, and the yearly court date took place during that month.

'Master' and 'Mistress' are the polite forms of address for a well-respected man or woman, or a person of a higher social rank. 'Goodman' and 'Goodwife' (often shortened to 'Goody') were the forms for someone of a lower social rank. Husbands and wives would refer to each other politely, at least in public. 'Mistress' was used regardless of whether a woman was married or unmarried. The title 'Miss' was not in common use in the early 17th century, but I thought it might be confusing to have both Priscilla and her mother addressed as "Mistress Mullins." Children would probably have been called by their first names, but young people started to do the same work as men and women from an early age. It is unclear to me at what age one would stop addressing children with their Christian names and start using a more polite form of address. The age of marriage for women was generally 20, and Pricilla's age in 1620 is estimated at between 16 and 18 years. Also, the only use for the title "Captain" was military. Ship captains were only known as Master.

A froe is a wedged blade used primarily for splitting a block of wood into shingles or clapboards. Coopers used a special curved froe for making barrel staves. Aqua vitae translates to "water of life" and is a non-specific term used to refer to strong alcoholic drink, particularly brandy. A capotain is a tall-crowned, narrow-brimmed hat. A working man's capotain would often have been made of felt, though there are hats from Plymouth made of beaver. The "Pilgrims" would not have worn buckles on their hats or shoes; this idea was popularized in a later era of history, when interest in "the Pilgrims" exceeded the general population's knowledge of them. Similarly, black would have been worn on Sundays or for special occasions, if they could afford a suit of black clothes. It was very expensive to have black clothing, which is why people posing for portraits at the time (including Edward Winslow in 1651) wore their best black clothing. Everyday clothes would have come in a variety of colors. A coif was the main headwear worn by both men and women over several hundred years. By the 1620s, coifs were predominately worn by women, covered the hair and ears, and came in a variety of styles and patterns. For more information on period clothing, visit the author's website.

I employ the word 'savages' as it was used at the time, in reference more to where the Native Americans lived than what they were. The word did not carry the same weight of negative connotations that it has today. The original sources seem to use the terms "savages" and "Indians" interchangeably, and so I followed that usage in writing from the perspective of the English settlers. A wetu is a domed shelter covered with tree bark or mats of woven reeds. According to Edward Winslow in *Good Newes From New England*, "The office and duty of the *powah* is to be exercised principally in calling upon the devil, and curing diseases of the sick and wounded" (p. 59) and "The *pnieses* are men of great courage and wisdom, and to those also the devil appeareth more familiarly than to others, and, as we conceive, maketh covenant with them to preserve them from death by wounds with arrows, knives, hatches, &c. or at least both themselves and especially the people think themselves to be freed from the same" (p. 61). Also, "their *sachims* cannot be all called kings, but only some few of them, to whom the rest resort for protection, and pay homage unto them... Of this sort is Massassowat, our friend, and Conanacus, of Nanohigganset, our supposed enemy" (p. 62). As one may imagine, Winslow has more to say about all these terms and more in *Good Newes*.

Although this story is fictional, most of the events are based on true experiences as recorded by original sources. I began this journey wanting to tell people more about some of America's earliest immigrants, but I have learned there is a significant difference between immigrants and colonists. There is so much more to this story than I'd imagined. There are many more fascinating details of *Mayflower*'s journey and the settlement at Plymouth that, for one reason or another, were not included in the final draft. I encourage anyone who is interested in more information to see my list of recommended reading, and to seek out additional resources, whether in religion, in Native American culture or relations, in women's work, or in occupations, tools, medicine, and agriculture. I learned a great deal about all these subjects and more while writing, and the list of sources I consulted is too extensive to include here.

More information on a few specific books I quote or reference directly in the novel follows:

The text of Psalm 23 comes from the 1640 edition of *The Whole Booke of Psalmes faithfully translated into English Metre*, edited by Richard Mather, John Eliot and Thomas Welde (commonly known as The Bay Psalm Book), rather than from the 1612 Ainsworth *The Book of Psalmes: Englished in Prose and Metre*. This choice was made purely for clarity of understanding for the 21st century audience. The text of Psalm 100, sung in part by Priscilla in chapter three, is from Ainsworth.

The excerpts from *Of Plymouth Plantation* are taken from Caleb Johnson's 2006 edition, which includes many helpful annotations from a *Mayflower* scholar. Interested parties should also see Johnson's book *The Mayflower and Her Passengers,* and his website at www.mayflowerhistory.com.

The excerpts from *Mourt's Relation* and *Good Newes from New England* are both taken from the Applewood books editions, 1963 and 1996 respectively.

The two excerpts from *Revelations of Divine Love* were taken from an article by the Christian History Institute and from the Project Gutenberg edition.

The letter from John Robinson to Governor Bradford can be read in full at the Online Library of Liberty.

For full citations and other interesting reading, see the "Recommended Reading" list, or visit the author's website at www.amycmartin.com.

Recommended Reading

Ames, Azel. "The May-Flower and Her Log, July 15, 1620-May 6, 1621: Chiefly from Original Sources." Internet Archive. Boston: Houghton, Mifflin, January 1, 1970. https://archive.org/details/mayflowerherlogj00ames.

Bangs, Jeremy Dupertuis. *Strangers and Pilgrims, Travellers and Sojourners Leiden and the Foundations of Plymouth Plantation.* Plymouth, MA: General Society of Mayflower Descendants, 2013.

Bunker, Nick. *Making Haste from Babylon: The Mayflower Pilgrims and Their World: a New History.* London: Pimlico, 2011.

Cheney, Glenn Alan. *Thanksgiving: The Pilgrims' First Year in America.* Hanover, CT: New London Librarium, 2013.

Dempsey, John. *Good News from New England: and Other Writings on the Killings at Weymouth Colony.* Scituate, MA: Digital Scanning, 2001.

Fraser, Rebecca. *The Mayflower: The Families, the Voyage, and the Founding of America.* New York: St. Martins Griffin, 2019.

Graves, Dan. "Article #31: All Shall Be Well." Christian History Institute. Accessed April 25, 2020. https://christianhistoryinstitute.org/incontext/article/julian.

Heath, Dwight B. *A Journal of the Pilgrims at Plymouth: Mourt's Relation, a Relation or Journal of the English Plantation Settled at Plymouth in New England.* Bedford, MA: Applewood Books, 1963. [Note: the book contains a discussion of the original authorship of the text, but it is left uncredited. Dwight B. Heath wrote an introduction for this edition.]

Johnson, Caleb. MayflowerHistory.com. Accessed April 25, 2020. http://mayflowerhistory.com/.

Johnson, Caleb H. *The Mayflower and Her Passengers*. Philadelphia, PA: Xlibris, 2006.

Johnson, Caleb. *Of Plymouth Plantation: Along with the Full Text of the Pilgrims' Journals for Their First Year at Plymouth*. Philadelphia, PA: Xlibris, 2006.

Julian of Norwich. "Revelations of Divine Love." Project Gutenberg, September 2, 2016. http://www.gutenberg.org/files/52958/52958-h/52958-h.htm.

Longfellow, Henry Wadsworth. "The Courtship of Miles Standish." Maine Historical Society. Accessed April 25, 2020. https://www.hwlongfellow.org/poems_poem.php?pid=186.

Tribe, Massachusetts. "The Massacre at Wessagusset." *The Massachusett Tribe at Ponkapoag*, massachusetttribe.org/the-massacre-at-wessagusset.

McElroy, Dr. Sydnee, and Justin McElroy. *The Sawbones Book: The Horrifying, Hilarious Road to Modern Medicine*. Weldon Owen, 2018.

McElroy, Dr. Sydnee, and Justin McElroy, hosts. *Sawbones: A Marital Tour of Misguided Medicine*. http://www.maximumfun.org/sawbones/.

Philbrick, Nathaniel. *Mayflower: A Story of Courage, Community, and War*. Harper Perennial, 2007.

"Plimoth Plantation." Plimoth Plantation. Accessed April 25, 2020. http://www.plimoth.org/.

Pratt, Phineas. "A Declaration of the Affairs of the English People That First Inhabited New England." Pilgrim Hall Museum. Accessed April 25, 2020. https://www.pilgrimhall.org/pdf/Phineas_Pratt_Narrative.pdf.

Robinson, John. "Words of John Robinson." Online Library of Liberty. Accessed April 25, 2020. https://oll.libertyfund.org/titles/robinson-words-of-john-robinson-robinsons-farewell-address-to-the-pilgrims.

Robinson, John. "The Works of John Robinson, Pastor of the Pilgrim Fathers." Internet Archive. London: J. Snow, January 1, 1970. https://archive.org/details/worksofjohnrobin01robi/page/n3/mode/2up/search/parting advice.

Saints & Strangers. National Geographic, 2015.

Sloane, Eric. *A Museum of Early American Tools*. Dover Publications, Inc., 2002.

The Pilgrims. American Experience. PBS, 2015.

Winslow, Edward. *Good Newes From New England*. Bedford, MA: Applewood Books, 1996.

Recommended Museums

Plimoth Plantation (Plymouth, Massachusetts, United States)

Pilgrim Hall Museum (Plymouth, Massachusetts, United States)

General Society of Mayflower Descendants House (Plymouth, Massachusetts, United States)

Alden House Historic Site (Duxbury, Massachusetts, United States)

Rijksmuseum (Amsterdam, Netherlands)

Pieterskerk (Leiden, Netherlands)

Leiden American Pilgrim Museum (Leiden, Netherlands)

Dorking Museum and Heritage Center (Dorking, Surrey, England)

Acknowledgements

I'd first like to acknowledge the contributions made to this book by Caleb Johnson, in allowing me to use quotations from his edition of "Of Plymouth Plantation;" Applewood Books, for their permission to quote from "Mourt's Relation" and "Good Newes From New England;" and the Christian History Institute for allowing me to quote their extracts from "Revelations of Divine Love." For more information on any of these sources, please look on my recommended reading page.

I also greatly appreciate the firsthand research I was able to do at the Pilgrim Hall Museum and Plimoth Plantation in Plymouth, Massachusetts. John Kemp and the other staff at Plimoth Plantation took much time to talk to me, sometimes in character, sometimes out of it, which gave me so much inspiration. I was also lucky to visit the Leiden American Pilgrim Museum and the Pieterskerk in Leiden, Netherlands. Ward Hoskens, the curator at the Pieterskerk, gave me an incredible tour and spoke with me at length about the Separatists' lives in Leiden. The Dorking Museum and Heritage Center I have only been able to visit virtually, but I look forward to a visit in person when I can thank them for the information they provided on Priscilla's hometown.

My deepest appreciation goes to Angela Hoy and her team at BookLocker for getting this book into print and ready for the digital market.

My early readers helped me shape this novel, in particular Tiffany Delligatti who helped me in the novel's earliest beginnings, Lawrence Petery, who gave me feedback throughout the process on many drafts, Jasmine Rockow, who supported John's adventure through a rough patch, Jean Phillips, who eased the transition into the book's final form, and Craig Martin, who convinced me to let Priscilla speak for herself.

I'd like to thank Christine Duffy Zerillo, who gave me endless good advice on the publishing process. I would have created a far inferior project without Andrew Noakes at The History Quill and my editors there, Kahina Necaise, Naomi Munts, and Sarah Dronfield.

Much praise and many thanks to Jackson R. Phillips, who had much more vision for the book's cover than I did, and who clambered over rocks and waded through water with me to get the perfect images for it.

Finally, I'd like to thank my family, my mom Diane, my brother Chester, and my sister Sam, who gave me endless reassurance. I'd especially like to acknowledge my dad Steve, who has listened to me talk about this book for close to five years, and supported me and read my material from the early planning stages all the way through to the final draft. Thank you for keeping my spirits up throughout, for taking me both to Plymouth and to Leiden, and for laughing at me when I needed it.

About the Author

Amy C. Martin is a *Mayflower* descendant through her ancestors, John Alden and Priscilla Mullins. She has worked as a genealogist, helping others to find their family history, and currently works for the Antiquarian and Landmarks Society. Martin is an author of short fiction and has a deep passion for history. She is looking forward to writing more historical novels. She lives in Connecticut with her dog, Boots.

www.amycmartin.com

CPSIA information can be obtained
at www.ICGtesting.com
Printed in the USA
FSHW021111140820
72968FS